CLAUDIO C⸻

THE OLD SUITCASE

A JOURNEY IN THE PAST AND THE PRESENT
IN PIETRACUPA'S COMMUNITY

THE OLD SUITCASE
A journey in the past and the present in Pietracupa's community

This publication was presented
In *Estate Pietracupese* 2014

Copyright by the author Mr. Claudio Camillo

Translation by Mrs. Maria Beatrice Cesiano

Cover:
Emigrant by Annibale Di Sarro
Claudio Camillo of the studio P. Scarano – Trivento

Photograph:
Museum Pietracupa in the World, Peasant Museum
Family phoptograph

Printed: Litografica Iride srl – Via della Bufalotta n°224 – 00139 Rome -
First edition ended to print on July 2014,

Second edition on March 2015 by Youcanprint- Self Publishing
Via Roma, 73 – 73039 Tricase (Le)-Italy
www.youcanprint.it

English Version edited by Cheryl Durante, with much consideration and
sensitivity given to the "Voice of the Author"

ISBN | 978-88-91188-03-8

Youcanprint *Self-Publishing*
Via Roma, 73-73039 Tricase (LE) - Italy
www.youcanprint.it
info@youcanprint.it

In loving memory of my parents

To my family

To Pietracupa's community in Italy

and abroad

CONTENTS

This edition of the book is for the numerous English language readers and especially for the young people of foreign extraction, born and residing abroad. They will have the chance to deepen their understanding of the history of the first Italian immigrants, of the early 1900's, who have contributed with their work and commitment to the growth of receiving countries, and to let them understand how we were and how we are now in Italy. This is one aim of this book: encouraging tourists and our foreign origin people to visit this wonderful country, full of art and beautiful landscapes, and it will be also a way to build a bridge between different cultures and religions.

The Author

PREFACE

Mr. Claudio Camillo many years ago became interested in the human, social and political events of migrants. Executive of CIM (Confederation of Italians in the World) Mr. Camillo, as an experienced researcher, tried discovering the roots and the stories of our migrants in all the nations he visited.

At each World Congress of CIM the author managed to rebuild in his mind the reasons, the ambitions and the behaviors of those who decided to migrate.

They often migrate for need, sometimes they wanted to get away, some others wished to reunite with relatives who had already migrated.

Mr. Camillo had a completely different cultural and work background, as for years his job dealt with public transport. But he has always been interested in social problems, in needs of people, in the change of behavior of humbler people who wanted to better themselves by sorrowfully choosing to leave their places of origin for a still indefinable future.

The author tries understanding the state of mind, the passions and the drives of so many young people who abandoned their birthplace to go to countries they hardly had heard about, without knowing their geographical setting, habits or language.

A biblical exodus occurred in Italy at the beginning of the twentieth century; it was repeated in the '50s and again in the '60s, especially towards Europe.

Mr. Camillo is, above all, a man from Molise and he dedicates a great part of his book to the migration of the people from Molise.

For the first 50 years of 1900, their destinations were North and South America and part of Australia. People often say that there is another Molise in North America.

Particularly, one notices that, in comparison to three hundred thousand residents today in the region, there are at least six hundred thousand out of regional boundaries.

The first city of Molise is not Campobasso, but Montreal; and in Canada there are more people from Molise than those who have remained in Italy.

A large migration to which is dedicated an important part of the book, went to the United States of America, with particular consideration for Pietracupa's Town Hall.

The historical references contained in the book deal with the events that happened during the terrible years of famine and war.

Mr. Camillo shows all historical events with objectivity, gathering information and telling the events without the influence of his opinion. All that is told develops around a name, a community, a passion: Pietracupa. In fact, in the book, Camillo talks and tells above all of Pietracupa, a name in his heart, an indelible mark for himself and his family.

The writer of this preface is half from Pietracupa, the other half being of a community only some kilometres away.

When I was a boy and a teenager, I often would live at Pietracupa and the events of Mr. Camillo weave with my personal ones.

I must inform you that we are relatives, second cousins, and the events of Mr. Camillo are the same as my family. So I'll not talk about things that Camillo deals with in a detailed way.

I wish to remember only one person without neglecting the others, Uncle Angelico Camillo, father of Claudio. His refinement, his human qualities, his smile have deeply struck me and have taught me the meaning of affection.

I think that for all this too Claudio has undertaken the challenge of writing a book dedicated to Pietracupa and to his family. Its inhabitants are very grateful to him, I myself above all.

On. Angelo Sollazzo
President, Confederation of Italians in the World

INTRODUCTION

Last summer I had the idea of publishing a book about Pietracupa and its people when, tidying up the attic of my father's home in Street Vico I° St. Anna, I made out an old cardboard suitcase covered with dust which belonged to my father among the different various bits and pieces scattered on the floor.

As I was very curious, I took and opened it and found old letters, early poems, photographs, newspapers of the epoch and an old diary where I liked writing all that happened during my summer vacations spent at Pietracupa, a small village in Molise near Campobasso.

At the end of my studies and over the years, I have had neither time nor will to go on writing that diary, so I forgot about it, and my mother put it in the suitcase I found in the attic.

I began to read its '50s and '60s dated contents in an amused and affectionate way. When I finished reading it, my initial condescending air changed into one of great attention and due consideration about all that I had noted down.

The topics of the told stories reminded me of the conditions of life in many little villages in Southern Italy, and documented the reasons why our ancestors felt the need to leave their homes to migrate to great cities or abroad since the years before World War Two.

Each of them would leave with a **battered cardboard suitcase** full of doubts, dreams, hopes, in order to look for a life better than that they would live in the village, just as my grandfather, my father and many of Pietracupa's inhabitants of that period have done.

In the diary, through the lens of everyday life and the tales of its inhabitants, I've noted also the conditions of life of the peasants who remained to cultivate the soil, the social differences, the condition of women, festivals, feasts, peasant cooking, labour market, the games of children, the life and the problems of immigrants - memories and tales as a whole that have urged on my will to tell to the reader the stories of Pietracupa's community in the last seventy-five years.

All of that is referenced to the thread of the great historical events of the period, and how these events influenced the uses and the opportunities of life of members of the same community, who gradually migrated abroad and to the great Italian cities.

The stories of the book sort out the contents of my diary, my personal memories and the events told by many of Pietracupa's friends living in Italy and abroad.

I've wanted not only to recall our recent past, but also to spur the reader on to think about how we were, how we are now, and how to build the future questioning our past.

As a first draft, I've thought that some photographs displayed in the Museum "Pietracupa in the World", organized and looked after by lawyer Benedetto Di Iorio in Street Generale Durante, and in the Peasant Museum would be the natural visual completion of some of the topics dealt with in the book.

In the same way, I've thought it necessary to put in also a short monograph about the origins of Pietracupa, which the architect Franco Valente has discussed during Pietracupa's Summer 2013 in his essay "Pietracupa tells".

Mr. Di Iorio and Mr. Valente have agreed to my requests with great courtesy and participation, and for this reason I thank them. At the end, I add that, in writing the book I asked myself: *telling the past of a community of ancient traditions often means to transcend nostalgia or over sentimentality, or to hurt the feelings of the same community which wishes to show only positive things of its past, neglecting the negative ones.*

The answer I gave myself was: *I wanted to tell the reality of the life of Pietracupa's inhabitants in the last 75 years such as indiscriminately it has been lived by everyone, in whatever good or bad situation.*

The reality of a life, sometimes hard and sometimes happy, but one that has molded and made stronger the nature of us Italians, and Pietracupa's inhabitants in particular, and that permitted us to reach some unimaginable goals with our work and our determination. Keeping silent about stories belonging to the history of the community isn't useful to the clarity of our present and of our past.

 The past is not only nostalgia, the past is history: the history of men and women, the history of people who have laid the foundations for their country and for their children with their sacrifices.

On these foundations our children have to go on building their future, even if there are today's difficulties. They have to find the determination and the obstinacy and especially those values and feelings to make the negative things our fathers changed, whether they left with an old suitcase full of memories and dreams or remained to cultivate the soil.

For this reason I think it's important to keep the tree of our roots, the memory of our past.

The present questions the past in order to build the future.

For reasons of privacy, in retelling some events I've used imaginary names, putting them between inverted commas; and I've done the same thing by not writing nicknames of people of the village if not preauthorized by directly interested people or by their families.

In the '40s, for reasons of respect, the young people of Pietracupa would address the older by placing before the name "Aunt" or "Uncle" and I've done the same in citing the names of old Pietracupa's people. **The title given to the book, "The Old Suitcase",** refers directly to the casual find of the suitcase of my father. But it also refers to the many immigrants, and especially to the numerous migrants of Pietracupa to which is dedicated a chapter of the book dealing with their stories and life in the new countries of reception.

Most poems inserted in the paragraphs of the book were written when I compiled my diary; only some of them have been written subsequently.

I've wanted to add these poems among various events because poetry is the expression of the human soul and refines the story. Without poetry there are no feelings and no memories.

While I'm writing (in September 2013) to the eastern borders (Syria, Egypt,Libya) winds of war are blowing. The same winds of war that troubled the '40s, the years in which the events of this book began.

Pietracupa in the past with baronial castle

Pietracupa today

14

CHAPTER I
THE YEARS OF WAR (1940/45)

-*My Molisan Origins:*

My father's parents (**Ezechiele Camillo and Antonia Di Iorio**) were born at Pietracupa and married there. My father was born in 1908 and, on the birth certificate kept in the Church, the name of his mother has been completed with the nickname of the members of her family "**The Gallinella**" (**R' Gallinilli**). Progenitor of a branch of "Gallinella" was my **great Grandfather Vincenzo Di Iorio,** who entered into a second marriage with my **great Grandmother Angela Durante**. Together they generated three sons (Giuseppe, Umberto and Mattia) and four daughters (Antonia, Anita,Silvia and Concettina, who migrated to USA).

From the marriage of my grandparents were born seven children, three sons (Igino, Domenico and my father Angelico) and three daughters (Anna Maria, Elisa, and Adalgisa) and a fourth daughter, who died at the age of 8 months and who was buried in the cemetery of the village.

Igino and Domenico migrated to USA when they were very young and married with two Molisan girls, Aunt Mary Sardella from Pietracupa and Aunt Concettina Saulino from Civitanova.

Aunt Anna Maria and Aunt Elisa too married at Pietracupa, the first with Uncle Arturo Durante and the other with Uncle Vincenzo Porchetta. These men also migrated in the early twentieth century to the USA and later were joined by their wives. **My Grandfather**, during the years spent in Pietracupa, was a land surveyor; so he had more schooling than the average resident. In addition, being owner of some pieces of land, he took care of his fields and livestock to support his family. **My Grandmother** died at 44, due to suddenly contracting pneumonia after going to wash clothes in the river Biferno.

During these years, because of the lack of fresh water in the village, two or three times a month, women would go to wash clothes in the river. They used to leave at four in the morning, by horse or by donkey, escorted by a male relative. After a difficult trip of 20 kilometres, they would reach the river and would stay at least one night, sleeping under the trees,.

The brother of my Grandmother, **Uncle Umberto**, who on that occasion had gone to the river to escort his sister and the other women, told me the details of this tragedy.

When my Grandmother got back home, she was put in bed as she had a high temperature. She was treated by using leeches and, after three days, died. **My father**, after the death of his mother, decided to migrate to Rome when he was fourteen. He did his best in various jobs, until he was summoned by Castropignano's headquarters to do his military service in the First Regiment of Infantry.

When he finished his service, which was of about two years, he came back to Rome and had the chance and the ability to find a good job in the City Council Transport Company (ATAC). He met my mother who was born in Trastevere, married her, and from their union I and my brother were born.

My Grandfather, who survived his wife in the house of Pietracupa and having to look after a girl of ten years old, suddenly decided to join his other children in America, leaving for 8 years Aunt Adalgisa in a convent school, waiting until she ended her studies to call her to USA.

I never knew my Grandfather Ezechiele, who died in 1940 in Chicago. I have only two letters from him written to my father, one for his wedding and the other for my birth. However, in his desk in Pietracupa I found some technical reports about his work in the village.

The first time I went to USA **in September 1965**, I went to Milwaukee in Wisconsin to pay tribute to his memory at the family cemetary.

My father's brothers and sisters decided to leave the home of their birth and the pieces of land to my father, the only son who remained in Italy. Beyond economic value we have never thought to abandon it, because in that house and on that ground my Molisan family began its life, and from that land my origins come from.

All my American cousins, during the years, have come to Italy to visit the country of origin of their relatives. We have always welcomed them with great love and in receiving them we have found in them, though they were born and lived in the USA, something of Italy. I would even say something of Pietracupa. And this has been the emotion that makes you think about the meaning of life, to the deepness of the roots of every family, handed down from father to his son.

A particular personal memory that my Grandfather wanted to leave his family in Italy is **his golden pocket watch**, a symbol of an epoch, that we keep in the family with great love. I think it right to put in the book this information because it is indicative of so many other stories of similar families of Pietracupa's migrants and also because I'm proud of my origins coming from this little village of Molise.

I often meet, in my travels in Italy or abroad, some people who ask me from what Italian region I come, and I unmistakably answer: *my origins are those of a lucky man, because I am Roman and in my DNA I have the culture and the ability of Ancient Romans government; I'm Molisan and have the strength and the determination of the Samnites; and last, I am an acquired American and have the sense of democracy and justice of Americans.*

MOLISE

I plunge in the deep silence of your valleys,
green gems set among the sharp peaks of your majestic
and impressive mountains.

I follow your tracks marked by time and transhumance,
steep streets running down to the sea.
I feel with enchantment in the night
for the faint glimmers of your villages perched on hills,
lonely fireflies in the big Italian sky.

I watch the peaceful flow of your rivers
and slow gestures of your people with its
vernacular frank and sincere.

Molise, the land of the Samnites,
land of my ancestors,
land of strong and kind people,
I always come back to you
and find again my roots,
my childhood and that sense of peace and infinite
which appease my restless heart
in the whiteness of the snow and scents of spring.

Ezechiele Camillo

Antonia with Anna Maria, Elisa and Angelico

Igino and Domenico Camillo

Adelgise Camillo

Claudio and Ezechiele

20

Angelico and Clara

-WINDS OF WAR IN 1939/43

When I was six months of age, (in June 1939), my father and my mother decided it was time to take a trip to Pietracupa to introduce the newborn to the numerous relatives and friends. During those years, my family lived with my mother's parents (Grandpa Achille and Grandma Adele) **in Trastevere**, in Square Saint Cosimato 56.

My Baptism was celebrated in **Saint Mary in Trastevere**, the ancient Church where now there is the Community of Saint Egidio, a place visited during the centuries by many Popes and recently by Pope Francesco and by Statesmen like President George Bush and President Obama.

In that month of June 1939 winds of war blew in Europe. The Germany of Hitler had invaded Poland, starting the Second World War. But during that beginning of summer 1939, in Italy the situation was still not a serious one, and my parents could leave Rome with peace of mind to introduce their little son to their relatives and the **community of Pietracupa**.

I have no memory of that trip, being a newborn. My mother told me later the details of what happened. All our relatives welcomed us with great love as did many friends in our community, welcoming us and spontaneously bringing presents such as cookies, eggs, doilies, and so on.

My Aunt Angelina Di Iorio, cousin of my father, told me that, as our father's home was not yet conforming to required standards because of renovation, she had put up me for a day in her house. But she was afraid to take care of that little lively bundle as I was, so she remained awake all night long to look after me. Aunt Angelina died a short time ago, but beyond the family ties that linked us, she always had a great sensitivity towards her fellow man and a great love for family and her village; she was a real Pietracupa's person in the best sense of the word.

My second visit to Pietracupa took place **in June 1943** and the events I'll narrate of that period of my life are placed indelibly in my mind, both for their drama and for the memory of many dear people who are no longer with us.

On June 10th 1940, in his famous speech broadcast from the balcony of Piazza Venezia, the Duce, before a cheering crowd, told the nation Italy declared war on England and France, siding with Hitler.

During the first years of the war, the powerful Germanic Army had invaded and subdued many Northern European nations: Poland, Belgium, Holland, and including France which they forced to form a collaborationist government chaired by General Petain on June the 22, 1940.

When the United States came into the war, in January 1941, the destiny of the war drastically changed. The new American allies provided soldiers, war material, advanced technologies and logistics, ensuring that the enemies of the axis (Germany, Italy and Japan) moved back from their front line of attack, causing the death of many people.

On January 23rd 1943, the Italian – German Army, chaired by General Rommel, was defeated and had to retreat to Europe after bloody and epic battles in the African desert. At this point, the First Minister Winston Churchill told his allies the moment had come to strike the enemy in his weakest point, which for the British statesman, was Italy.

So **on July 10th 1943 the Allies landed at Sicily**, exactly a month after my family's arrival in Pietracupa. In 1943 my father would do his military service as a driver for a Colonel, Chief of military emplacement of Saint Palomba, a locality near Anzio, 25 Kilometres from Rome. He drove a sidecar, a kind of motorcycle with three wheels with a side place for a passenger to sit. Every time his Colonel went to Rome, my father took advantage of the minutes of free time to come and visit us in the house of Trastevere.

In February, in my family, **my brother Ezechiele** (who every one of us has always called by the diminutive and term of endearment "Lino") **was born**. So each occasion was a good one for my father to run home in order to have news about his newborn son.

The life of all Roman residents was very difficult at this time. People said that the cats that usually were lying under the sun in Colosseo and Foro Romano had all disappeared because Romans had eaten them, as there was no food.

Romans, ironically, have always joked about this topic; but the truth was not very far from the tales that were told along the streets and in the districts.

In order to buy some bread, people needed to have a ration book and they had to wait in endless queues before arriving at the final counter.

The black market was very prosperous for traders, but it was useful only for those who had money to buy food, without local police checking.

My father, when he realized that bad situation, with great foresight, convinced my mother it was time to go to Pietracupa with both children. He thought rightly that, in his small native village, one was less exposed to war's hardships and, in a small town it was easier to find a piece of bread. Then there was also our ancestor's land which, if plowed and sown adequately, could let some vegetables, potatoes, tomatoes grow.

The evening before the planned trip to Pietracupa (June 1943), in my building of Saint Cosimato Square, fascist authorities decided that some demonstration exercises had to be done in case of air attack. So, at the prearranged time, all owners had to go down to the cellars of the building to attend and to carry out the rules of the exercise. At 8 p. m., while everyone went down along the stairway, I was thinking that this was a game organized by adults to let children have fun.

So much so that I was telling myself that, *when Mr Marangoni meets me on the stairs he is usually surly with me but this evening he smiled at me.* I was so convinced the exercise was a game that, at the end of it, I was sorry the event had finished so soon.

The morning of the departure, my father, dressed in his uniform and driving the sidecar, came to take me to his barber in Street Garibaldi, near the present restaurant of VIP **"L'antica Pesa"** which, in that period, was an old Roman tavern.

The route between San Cosimato Square and Street Garibaldi was very short. But that day during those few minutes, it seemed to me that I had become the king of the world, because I was near my father and riding in a sidecar driven by him.

After saying good bye to our barber Ciccio, my father wanted to take the long way back home, passing before the great fountain of Saint Peter in Montorio. I often used to go and play there with my little boats. As we arrived on Gianicolo Hill, he let me stand on the balcony near the square to say good bye to Rome. That was the last time that, as a boy, I saw Rome in **its extraordinary beauty**. On July 19th of that very year a violent bombing hit Rome and there were many people killed.

Something had changed in the city, but more importantly, something had changed in the soul of its desperate people. The goodbye hug of my father was very moving; I remember he told me: *"now the little*

24

man of the house is you, take care of your brother and your mother and don't be naughty. I'll come back soon to you."

The train to Campobasso would leave everyday from Termini Station at midnight. It would go on to Cassino and then to Caianello. At Caianello the coach to Campobasso was detached from the train and was coupled to another train leaving for Campobasso. I think that this famous train is still in service.

Somehow, that evening we reached Termini Station, which was very crowded with soldiers, travelers and passersby, and we put our suitcase on the train. We had the chance to travel with **Guido and Angelo Porchetta of Pietracupa**, who kept us company all the way long.

After 8 hours by train, we arrived at the Station of Campobasso; we went up on the bus to Trivento and at last, after 4 more hours of riding through **Oratino, Torella and Fossalto**, we arrived at Pietracupa.

From this time on I have only hazy memories; I can't remember my first feelings about Pietracupa, which I was looking at for the first time as a boy because I was very tired.

Like in a dream, I remember that at the bus stop there was my Uncle Peppino/Castellino, and some other relatives to welcome us, and that we went to my father's house in Street Vico I° St. Anna, which was now remodeled. On the first night in Pietracupa, Maria of Aunt Bianchina, cousin of my father, came to sleep with us to keep us company.

We all slept in the big bed of the family, which had great wooden planks instead of springs as the bed base, and a mattress made of corn leaves (scarfuglia) instead of wool. It was surely prepared by relatives in a mad rush in that period of great economic difficulties.

My brother was put near my mother in a little wooden cradle we used to call "cundra" and at last we fell asleep.

-THE LONG FALL/WINTER OF 1943/44

Once they had settled themselves into the house on Street Vico I° St. Anna, our everyday life was spent according to the rhythms suggested by the needs of the moment and with the activities, customs and needs of all the inhabitants of Pietracupa. I must say that in difficult times, especially in small villages, people come together to try and help one another. In other words, a spirit of solidarity and collaboration permeates everyone.

I witnessed this spirit of solidarity during those days in a direct way; I would say in a physical one, even if I was just a boy. **In that summer of 1943**, Pietracupa had been repopulated by many of her children who had migrated to Rome, Naples and other cities of Italy. A great number of Pietracupa's migrants had the same idea as my father and had come back to their native home. Nevertheless, we have to think that many young men in the village had already left to go to the front to defend their country.

Once again, Pietracupa welcomed her children to her big rock to protect them, as she had done many other times in the past.

From a historical point of view, then, 1943 and 1944 were years full of events that deeply influenced the life of Italians and their political institutions and social economic future, as the following chronological events testify.

-EVENTS OF 1943

- On July 19th and 20th, the bombing of Rome and Naples by the Allies
- On July 25th, the end of fascism after the meeting of "Gran Consiglio"
- On September 3rd, the signature of the armistice with the Allies at Cassibile, and on
- September 8th the official broadcast announcement of the armistice by General Badoglio
- On September 13th, the declaration of war on Germany by Italy
- On July 10th, the landing of the Allies in Sicily, and on
- September 1st the landing in Calabria
- On September 9th, the landing of the Allies in Salerno
- On September 12th, the Liberation of Mussolini in Gran Sasso, by German people

A sneak pe

what's bein

Crime drama
NETFLIX

Fargo

Season: 1 Episodes: **10** Runs: **48–70min**

Why Women Kill's Allison
Tolman came to fame in
the first season of this
crime drama anthology
as compassionate and
humorous deputy Molly
Soverson investigating
a series of murders.
Seasons two and three
are also available.

Horror drama
NETFLIX

Brand

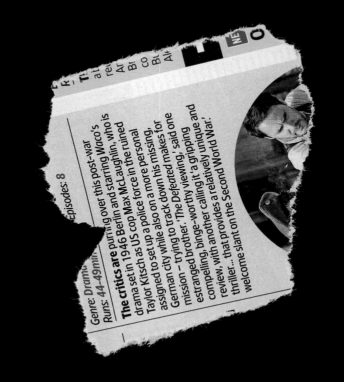

Genre: *Dram...*
Runs: *44-49mi...*
Episodes: **8**

The critics are purring over this post-war drama set in 1946 Berlin and starring Taylor Kitsch as US cop Max McLaughlin, who is assigned to set up a police force in the ruined German city while also on a more personal mission — trying to track down his missing, estranged brother. '*The Defeated* makes for gripping, binge-worthy viewing,' said one compelling, and review, with another calling it 'a relatively unique thriller... that provides a welcome slant on the Second World War.'

Waco's
T!
a t
re...
A...
B...
co...
B...
Al...

- On September 23rd, the constitution of the Republic of Salò and the Partisan fight in Northern Italy
- On October 1st the Allies came to Naples and later were sent to the front at Cassino to "push back" the German fortified line "Gustav" (Adriatic Sea, Ortona, Lanciano Castel di Sangro, Cassino, and Tirren Sea).

-EVENTS OF 1944

- On January 22nd, the landing of Allies at Anzio, to go around the line "Gustav" (Strangle Operation)
- On February 23rd, the massacre of Fosse Ardeatine in Rome
- On May 18th, the breaking through of the Gustav line and the withdrawal of Germans towards North (on Monte Lungo there was an Italian battalion of 5 thousand soldiers belligerents with the Allies)
- On June 4th, the Liberation of Rome by the Allies and the continuation of war along the "Gothic Line" in the Tuscan-Emilian Apennines (with the presence of partisan Italian Armies, aligned with the Allies)
- On June 6th, the landing of the Allies in Normandy (Overlord Operation).

All these events that happened in 1943/44 were very important for the inhabitants of Pietracupa, especially the **war raid** that hit directly the people of the small village.

Obviously, each family in Italy has had different events and reactions according to its own political beliefs and its economic and social conditions and according to the relatives who were engaged in the fronts of war. In this last case, one must note that Italian soldiers in Russia, in Greece, in Yugoslavia, in Africa, in Italy, reacted to the announcement of **the armistice of September 8th** and to the break up of the Army according to their conscience.

A clear example of all this is the event at Cefalù, in Greece, where Italian servicemen were killed by Germans because they had refused to collaborate with them.

For the same reason, many Italian servicemen were sent to the German concentration camps, like war prisoners.

With hindsight, historians have started a long analysis and discussion about all that happened in such a dramatic period. Each reader, through the lines of the events told in this chapter, may hypothesize an answer of his own to the questions that historians have posed and still do now. And may realize, above all, how the tragedies of the war hit first **poor people** who are not responsible for the war and, against their will, are obliged to pay the consequences.

When I watch in the epoch films of Istituto Luce (Cinecittà Studio C.)* those poor peasants escaping under the bombing of 1943/44 with their meager belongings in their arms, and ragged and barefoot children by their sides looking for cover, for a place to sleep, and when near Cassino poor old people, young people, even young girls being raped by Moroccan servicemen (goumiers) headed by French General Juin, I think and say to myself: *during that period I was there, just 100 Kms away from these tragedies; I've passed by Cassino in my goings and coming back; my father and many other Pietracupa's inhabitants have crossed these places by foot, by bicycle, by tanks; and, over my and their heads, bombs, bullets and war splinters and, above all, so much despair have passed and that is why, in this symbolic journey in the past, I wanted to tell about those terrible years of war spent in the village, during which Pietracupa's people were actors and witnesses to so many dramatic events.*

-VIA VICO I° SAINT ANNA AND ITS PEOPLE

At Pietracupa, all the residents of the same little street were very friendly and collaborative, as it happens at Siena where the inhabitants of the same district are linked all lifelong with a special bond of membership and solidarity.

It may seem silly when one thinks that Pietracupa had, and has nowadays, about 20 streets between two groups of houses, **Aia del Piano** and **Casalotto**, but this was the reality.

During the years of the war, the doors of the houses were always open and each inhabitant, knocking, could come in every house easily. Nothing was secret; everyone knew if the neighbor was either in the village or in the countryside, what would have been eaten that day, if he would have gone to the Town Hall, if she would have done the washing, if she would have lit the oven, if there was an ill person

---

* N. of T. Cinecittà Studio Company.

in the house, if the girlfriend and, above all, if the parents of his own girlfriend were present or not.

This was the way of life in that country environment; there was a kindly check of one neighbor towards the other and also a certain helpfulness to offer one's help in case of need.

I don't mean that all would go on smoothly and everyone was happy, because, as happens in all parts of the world, there were some arguments, sometimes a little bit lively. But neighbors indeed tried to solve problems amicably (unless there were private interests, in which case the thing was more difficult to manage).

In Via Vico I° Saint Anna, the people who lived at that time were special. My statement isn't a kindly way to remember my neighbors, but my judgment is justified by the events I'll tell you.

The families living in Street Vico I° Saint Anna were the following:

Beginning from the top, **on the right side** of the street there were: Aunt Caterina and Uncle Nicolino Durante, with their brother Uncle Peppino Settimio and his wife Aunt Nannina and their children (Settimio, Antonietta, Maria, Eva, Franca, and the future child Giancarlo).

Then there was Aunt Maria Incoronata, with children Peppina and Giovanni; then Uncle Federico Di Iorio and Aunt Rachele, with their two daughters Gina and Vittoria. And last there was my family and the family of Aunt Tonta, Grandmother of Vincenzo and Nicola Fusaro.

In the lower part of the little alley there was Aunt Assunta with her family, and at the end there was the family of Uncle Peppino Di Sarro, with his wife Aunt Letizia and their numerous children.

On the left of the alley there was the family of Uncle Umberto Di Iorio (brother of my Grandmother) with Aunt Teresa and Aunt Antonietta. After that there was the house of Uncle Pietro Santilli, with his family, and then the house of Felice Santilli, with Aunt Gemma, her mother Maria and their three daughters (Mariella, Angelina, and Edda) and the sister Pietrina.

Halfway down there was the family of Uncle Francesco Grande with Aunt Adelaide and her children Giovannina, Peppe, Baldina. Then there was the family of Uncle Nicola Di Sarro and Aunt Angela, with their children Domenico, Antonietta, Lidia and Amedeo.

At the end of the line of houses, there was that of Romolo Santilli, with Aunt Maria, their son Michele, Aunt Giovanna and the daughter Amerina.

At the end of the little street there was the stable of the family Guglielmi. Next to it was the building of the family of Professor Amedeo Tosti, descendant of the famous Professor Cardarelli, remembered at the epoch by a memorial stone put there by the Town Council; now it is the property of the family Di Riso.

In front of the Cathedral there was the village tobacconist, managed by Uncle Giovanni Di Sarro, with wife Aunt Peppinella and their numerous children and grandsons. Together with the family of Aunt Maria Di Sarro, who in later years settled in the house inhabited by the family of Aunt Assunta. Along the near slope there were the houses of Aunt Luigietta and Aunt Adelina.

About all these 50 inhabitants of Street Vico I° Saint Anna, during that summer and winter 1943/44 were the main interlocutors of my family and mine.

If I were a novelist, I would have many topics to be able to write the "Saga" of all these people. Some of them are still alive, some others migrated, and some have died. I could write the stories of their migration, the stories of their weddings, of their children and so on. But I'm not a novelist, and I'll write about **what happened during those days of war in the Alley** through the personal events of my family, which belonged to this community.

Via Vico I° St. Anna

30

-PIETRACUPA: TALES OF THE WAR

My mother, during those days of July 1943, waiting for my father to come back from the front, began to tidy up the house and to light the fire; she adapted to supply the water by the tub, drawing from the well of our cave, where she would do the laundry and then hang it out on the plants of briars in San Gregorio.

Our neighbors, especially **Aunt Adelaide and her daughters**, were always very thoughtful with us, also because **Uncle Francesco** was at the front. We often gathered in their house and would put a big dish of tomatoes and cucumbers (tortarelle) at the centre of the table, and we ate them with big slices of bread. Some other times my mother would prepare the sagne (pasta) with beans. I always remember the day when **Baldina,** watching her prepare the sheet of pasta dough told her: *zia Clara chelle sagne sò nere chinda n'tizzone.*"Aunt Clara, this pasta is dark like live coal". Still today we laugh about that funny remark, but eating pasta dough made of whole wheat flour was a big change from the usual.

My brother Lino, who was about six months old, was fed milk from the cow of Uncle Palmerino/ Belisario, brother of Aunt Adelaide. Every evening I had to go down to Casalotto with a container, to get the milk that was taken directly from the udders of the cow in my presence. Once I remember I slipped and fell down the stairs of the Church, but the milk didn't fall down. I came back home crying and told my mother I wouldn't go anymore to Uncle Palmerino.

But in that sunny July, my mother had to solve another much more serious problem. My brother Lino had become ill and needed to be seen by a doctor. The only available one was **Mr. Pompilio Cornacchione** who worked at **Fossalto**. We left from Pietracupa by foot at six in the morning, together with Mary, daughter of Aunt Bianchina. The trip was very tiring. Mother alternated with Mary to hold Lino in her arms, and I clung to her skirt dragged along across those fields downhill and uphill to arrive at Fossalto. Fortunately everything went well and little Lino recuperated.

A year later, **Mary died** from typhus that had infected many people of the village. God wanted to take such a beautiful and generous girl. My father, as he had promised, as soon as he obtained his first leave came to visit us at Pietracupa. It was August 15th. **Rome had been already bombed on July 19th** by the Allies and **on July 25th**, after the Great Fascist Meeting, Mussolini had been arrested.

When he gave us this news, my father also informed us about my Grandparents, who were safe and sound. But he unfortunately had to inform my mother that, during the bombing of the village of **Frascati**, where some members of her family lived, two Uncles of hers had died under the rubble, and the house where her brother lived had been completely destroyed.

My father had made that trip **by his bicycle** because, by then, all lines of Roma/Cassino had been bombed. In the following days, after his leave had expired, he went back to Rome to go to the front. But soon after the Armistice of September 8th and the breakup of the Italian Army, he behaved like the most other Italian soldiers "**all going home**". And the "home" with his family was in Pietracupa, so he went back there. In a film with Alberto Sordi, the director Monicelli tells bitterly and ironically about what happened to Italian soldiers after September 8th. The day he came back to Pietracupa, my father arrived at three in the morning. We heard loud knocking at the door and we became frightened. But my mother recognized at once his voice and opened the door and we hugged him with great joy.

In the following days, he told us of the hardships of that trip he took to join us in the village. He told us he had left Rome in a big mess and at Termini Station he had managed to catch the last train still in service, leaving for Sulmona.

When he arrived at Sulmona, which in the previous days had been bombed by the Allies, he set out for the village of Pescolanciano by foot, in the night, so as not to run into any German patrol. **At Pescolanciano**, he looked for the barber shop of **Uncle Peppino Barone** from Pietracupa (son of Francesca), to get him to point out a safe road to reach the village. Uncle Peppino welcomed him with great love, so that my father took advantage of being there and had his hair cut. During the cut, he fell asleep because he was so tired, and was awakened by the shrill voice of his fellow countryman, who proudly announced that he had given him a summer cut. In short, he had "scalped" him!

My father had with him an old "army haversack" where he kept some sugar, salt, and shaving soap - precious items and hard to find goods in those days of war. When he left Pescolanciano, he left a little of his shaving soap to Uncle Peppino for his professional needs.

Back with his family, my father became part of the community of the village, getting by doing all that the other people used to do to make ends meet and to survive, waiting for better times. So he took out all the farming tools of his family **to turn over the soil** and to plant some vegetables. At the same time he bought some cocks and some hens for eggs and a **little pig** to fatten up, to eat later with the products of her slaughtering.

I remember the commitment of my mother, who even though she came from an urban area, pulled up her sleeves and worked hard to breed the hens, to prepare the mash for the little pig, as well as to help my father in the fields. I still remember the tragedy of that little pig which didn't grow and was going to die; fortunately **Felice Santilli**, expert butcher, advised my father to call "**the pig doctor**" from a nearby village, a kind of special veterinarian able to cure the little pig. After his intervention, the little pig began to grow again and, in a few months she was slaughtered, right in front of our house, with the participation of the entire neighborhood.

We used all parts of the little pig, including the black pudding, the gelatin, the stuffed pig's trotter and "r'ciquori"*, which were put in the bread to give it, while cooking, an extra taste.

But our stable wasn't the only one to keep animals, hay, wood and some other things, for the needs of families. All the other stables of Street Vico I° Saint Anna were occupied less or more by hens, little pigs, donkeys, sheep, cows, horses according to the previous properties and the availability of their owners.

The life of the inhabitants of the Vico was a simple one. The men woke up in the morning and went out to go to the fields. The women in the morning were tidying up, preparing lunch, looking after animals, and as the bell rang midday (r'mesciurne), they set out with a container on their head to take something to eat to their husbands, sons, fathers who were busy working the soil.

The inhabitants of my alley had a farm (masseria) in the countryside which was a little house for the peasant activities, and often someone from the family remained to sleep over there in the days of threshing or particular tasks. Other times, if the family was numerous, its members alternated sleeping in that "masseria" according to their needs.

These farms of course had neither artificial light nor running water. I always remember **Giovanni, Peppina, Peppe, Baldina**, and over all **Giovannina** and the way their mothers reminded them to go to

---

* N. of T. R'ciquori are little pieces of pork fat.

33

the masseria: *a dà j alla massaria a tò le pummarole, che te sci scurdata? "you have to go to the farm to take tomatoes, don't you remember?"*.

Also, my mother, my brother and I often joined my father working at a little truck farm at "macchie" *. We considered the tomatoes and the potatoes obtained in that field like heaven's fruits. In order to reach the truck farm at the "macchie", we had to follow a long way and so we always stopped at Uncle Umberto and Uncle Alfredo, whose farms preceded our piece of land, near the road inspector's house.

The return from the fields would happen as if it was a holy ritual. At the ring of the church bell, everybody would leave the work to come back home from "the macchie"* from the "via nova"*, from "cantone"*, from "pinciara"* and from any other place in the neighborhood.

On the way, they would talk about the job, news from the front, events happening in the village, and maybe some gossip about Tom, Dick, or Harry.

At sunset, the streets of the village were animated by donkeys, mules, goats, sheep, as well as with the peasants coming back from fields. Then the pack saddles were removed from the animals, which were taken to the stables and fed. Mothers, daughters and grandmothers alternated to light the fire and prepare the supper with all that the family could offer.

During summer especially, women would spend time after supper outdoors, sitting in the fresh air, and would socialize talking about stories of the present or the past. People would recall stories of brigands, of witches, of "mamocci" (monsters), or of some other particular characters of past years.

The young girls, little by little, would stand apart and talk softly about their first falling in love or about the embellishment of some of their old and simple dresses. The children, after some little running along the road, would sleep in the arms of their Grandmothers or their mothers.

A beautiful feminine youth was present at Street Vico I° Saint Anna; the girls of the little street would gather in the open space in

---

* N.of T. via nova, macchie, cantone, and pinciara are names of pieces of land.

34

front of the house of Aunt Adelaide, and their smiles would mitigate that air filled with gloom by the war which shrouded the village.

Peppino, son of Aunt Adelaide, was often trying to pull the skirt of these girls for fun, being reproached by his mother and Giovannina. Among these very gentle girls, there was also **Maria, daughter of Uncle Peppino Durante**; she was 16 years old and was very beautiful. But mild Maria became ill of typhus and in a week she died. Now she lies in the cemetery of the village.

During winter, the gathering would take place in the houses in front of the fire that was always very scanty, so they drew close to one another to get warm.

The topics of dialogue were always the same, besides some funny story, to try to lessen the sad thoughts that passed through one's mind.

The time after supper for adult men would consist of going to the **numerous taverns of the village** and there they would spend the time playing long Italian card games (scopa and tresette) and when the owner of the tavern was involved, everyone would participate and liven up the evening.

Some drunken customer might also come, but the owner of the tavern, especially **Uncle Guerrino**, was always careful that the wine was adequately watered down, not only for economic reasons, but overall to protect the health and the quietness of customers.

Generally, during the years of the war, Pietracupa's people standard of life was as above described.

The news from the front was scarce, but they would often hear noises of war coming from the zone of Termoli and, in the sky over Pietracupa, would pass the airplanes of the Allies going to bomb Germans in the area of Cassino or along Trigno.

At about the end of October 1943, Pietracupa and the neighboring area was the target of war between the Germans withdrawing and the advancing Allies, who had landed at Termoli on October 3rd 1943.

Prof. Giovanni Artese, in his book "The war in Abruzzo and Molise", has given a very detailed description of all that happened October 22nd and 23rd 1943 along **the line of Trigno, called "Barbara-Stellung"** by **Germans**. There had been fierce fights between the two opponents, which caused the deaths of more than one thousand among the Allies and as many among Germans.

The fight along the river Trigno was kept active by Allied air attacks, by the fire of artillery and by antipersonnel and antitank mines of both opponents.

The blind fury of war in this area of Abruzzo/Molise hit also the innocent civilians and their villages. Among civilians there were about **400 who died:** in the villages of Vasto (30), Cupello (126), Lentella (2), Fresagrandinara (10), Dogliola (4), Tufillo (10), Furci (10), Palmoli,(1), Celenza(25), Carunchio (11), Castiglione (6), Agnone (2), Pescolanciano (2), Capracotta (14), Civitanova (2), Duronia (3), Torella (13), Pietracupa (1), Bagnoli (6), Trivento (2) Tavenna (5), Roccavivara (2), Montefalcone (4), Montemitro e San Felice (9), Acquavivara (11), Mafalda (10), Montenero di Bisaccia (20).

Later the front moved towards **the river Sangro**, where in December 1943 there were violent fights at Ortona. People fought house by house, to the point that the town of Abruzzo is remembered like the Italian Stalingrad.

I have a vivid memory of this war period involving Pietracupa's inhabitants, the village that gravitated around itself too in the area of "Barbara-Stellung" line.

It was a day at the end of October 1943 that we heard the sound of bombs hitting the village of Torella from the little wall of the Cathedral. Everyone arrived to watch what was going on and I remember the remark of Uncle Guerrino who said: *pe' la maiella, a Torella r'fanno escì r'fiumo "for the Maiella, they make the smoke go out at Torella".* Some days later **the smoke was made to go out at Pietracupa too,** when a feminine voice began to cry out along the village: *currete, currete, arrivano r'tedischi "run, run, Germans are coming".*

Many men, including my father and his old friend Felice, began to run towards San Gregorio to hide and to decide what to do.

The German army arrived at Pietracupa and settled just under Street Vico I° Saint Anna, in the house of Professor Amedeo Tosti Cardarelli, then an important member of the fascist regime. Germans didn't want to requisition the men of the village; they were escaping from the Allies and, while withdrawing, tried to slow down the advance of the Allies.

In the neighborhood of Pietracupa, Germans put a battery of guns on mount Bagnoli and a nest of machine guns at the road inspector's house, near the farm of Uncle Pietro.

At that moment, the village became the target of the Allies, so, we had enemies/former friends in the house and former enemies/friends out of it, managing to pursue the opponents.

The Germans staying in the village, began to enter the houses to requisition food and provisions for their support, and beasts of burden for the transportation of their weapons.

During these searches, two of them entered also my house after putting down their guns. They had their eyes on **a piece of pork fat** hanging from the ceiling; they took and split it in two using a military dagger. They took half for themselves and gave the other half to us. Another day my father, risking his personal safety, helped his friend Felice to hide his horse in a cave of our stable, adequately covered by branches.

Fortunately the Germans, in their next visit made to all the cellars of the village, didn't discover this concealment - thanks also to the participation of the horse that didn't neigh behind the branches.

Another story in which, in spite of himself, my father was an innocent protagonist, is that about a German soldier asking for **a mule** to transport army materials on Monte of Bagnoli. This soldier entered the tavern of Uncle Guerrino, at that time crowded with customers, and mimicked a mule, putting the index fingers of his hands up to his head. One of the customers in the cellar, misunderstood this gesture for horns, and laughed coarsely.

The soldier got angry for this and went out for reinforcements and was soon followed out by the coarse customer, who immediately disappeared. My father, unaware of the earlier event, later entered the cellar and sat in the place of the fugitive. So, when the soldier came back with other fellow soldiers, he was immediately told to go out and lead them to a stable where they could get a mule. My father, a little embarrassed and afraid to damage someone else's property, didn't know what to do. Fortunately **Uncle Annibale**, helped him find a mule that, once used, was given back to the owner.

The German soldiers walking along the streets of the village sometimes offered the children some candies; I've always thought they would see their own children left in their country when looking at us.

Those dark days of war were often colored by comic scenes, due to the antics of some fellow countryman, which made people feel happier.

The first comic scene I remember is that of **Aunt Letizia**, who every time she saw us escape to go to the refuge, would ask us: *a che ora commenza r'bombardamento?* *"At what time does the bombing begin?"*

Another scene was that of the barber of Pietracupa, **Domenico Carrelli**, called Uncle Cucciotto by everyone. His barber shop was situated in Street Vico I° Trento and all the male inhabitants of the village would go to his shop to have their hair cut or to have their beards shaved off.

In the Italian tradition, going to the barber is a moment of relaxation and socialization. The barber becomes a kind of friend and advisor, and Uncle Cucciotto and his barber shop were essential elements to create this familiar, calm atmosphere.

But in those days of war, as Uncle Cucciotto heard the noise of an airplane, he **would leave scissors, razor and customers** and, with a jump like a one hundred meters runner, he disappeared to look for a shelter.

Since airplanes would pass continuously over Pietracupa, it was not uncommon to see, during the day, men with their hair half cut walking down the streets.

But, the worst of that period of war was still to come. The Allies had settled at Torella and were preparing the attack on the German garrison of Pietracupa to weaken their resistance.

In this context, one afternoon, my father had gone to the countryside to work and my mother, having to supply the water in the lower cellar, told me to look after my brother who was asleep in his cradle. In about ten minutes, an allied airplane began to bomb Pietracupa.

My mother, who was coming back with the container in her hands, began to cry *"Claudio, Claudio, go to your brother"*; then she began to run to come to us.

While the grenades were hitting the village, I ran towards the cradle of my brother, hugged him and started to cry desperately. At the end of bombing only a heap of splinters remained in the street and on some doors of the houses. My mother said was saved because she was short; if she had been taller, she would have been hit by those splinters. In the following days the Allies bombed Pietracupa many times. When by day or by evening we would hear the noise of airplanes far away or of grenades arriving, there was a general stampede to go to shelter in the improvised refuges of the village.

During one of these bombings, the poor Nicola Sardella, on November 1st 1943, while going out of his house in the village, was hit by shrapnel, and was taken to the crypt of the Church used as a shelter. He died in the arms of his mother, in front of some of Pietracupa's people who had taken shelter in the crypt.

Another disastrous bombing was the one hitting the house of **Uncle Alfredo Camillo and wounding his sister Angelina.**

Pasquale Camillo, who at the time was the same age as me, told me the fact: "*as we heard the noise of bombs, my mother and I went down to the basement; the two sisters of my father didn't succeed in going down and remained on the upper floor.*

"*A bomb exploded over our house and Aunt Angelina was hit on a hip. In order to assist her, we were obliged to let her down through the window that looked out onto the back of the room in Street Aia del Piano, and we sheltered her in the near home of Uncle Nicolino Durante.*

"*At the end of bombing, my father went at once to Fossalto to look for drugs; two days later the Allies came in and carried the Aunt to Campobasso. Through a thousand difficulties, Father went many times to the town with the aim to help and take care of her. But among all that turmoil of soldiers, evacuees, wounded men, it was impossible to find her.*

"*Then he went directly to the head office of the Allied Headquarters where they told him that the Aunt maybe had been carried to a hospital in Puglia.*

"*From that day on, all the research done and carried on in the following years was unuseful. We never had any news of her after that.*"

On the war memorial of Pietracupa, together with other dead and missing soldiers of First and Second World Wars, the names of Nicola and Angelina have also been written.

Every year in the month of August, the village remembers all its dead with a civil and religious ceremony.

Another story of Pietracupa's people wounded during the attacks of the Allies is about Uncle Vincenzo. This happened in the shelter where all the inhabitants of Street Vico I° Saint Anna would go, the present stable of the family Patrizio Di Sarro.

That evening, it was very cold. A group of young men, of whom I only remember Michele Porchetta, lit a fire on the external square to get warm. My mother, her friend Maria, my father, his friend Romolo, and other people were sheltered in the stable, as was I and Michele, son of Romolo; my brother Lino, still unweaned baby, was sleeping in the feeding-trough.

Suddenly the square became a prime target for the Allies lying in wait near Torella. They started to bomb at low altitude.

The young men came back to the shelter in a hurry, but Uncle Vincenzo remained outside and was grazed in the lower abdomen by shrapnel. The wounded man was assisted and carried to Campobasso, where he was treated and later came back to Pietracupa.

My last chilling memory of the war is about me, and happened near **the wood of the Selva**. Germans had been leaving Pietracupa for a few days and my father, seeing the nice sunny day, thought to go to the woods to take the "ceppe"(tree stumps), taking me too for a walk in the open air.

We arrived at the Selva early in the morning; the forest was enchanting, drops of dew were still on the leaves and the scent of wood was lovely. We met Uncle Cesare, who informed us that an Allied airplane had been flying for a long time in the neighborhood, but it didn't give any problem.

However the situation was not as safe as we had imagined; the decoy airplane began to shoot at low altitude and at that point my father hid me in the hollow of a tree and said to me: *"don't move, I'm going a little lower down to shelter in an excavated zone; wait for me."*

I don't remember the time that passed before the airplane left the woods. I only remember I was trembling with fear.

As God wanted, nothing irreparable happened. My father came back to get me again and, together with Uncle Cesare, we returned to the village, happy for the danger escaped.

This is my last memory of the bombings at Pietracupa. After the escape of the Germans, bombing the village was not useful, because the enemy had gone away.

Uncle Umberto Di Iorio and Uncle Pasquale Camillo, who spoke English, offered to contact the Allies along the lines of the neighborhood Torella/Fossalto to stop the war activities against civilians.

The next day **the Allies entered the village**. From Murillo we saw them come towards Pietracupa; they were walking in single file, with their rifles in their hands and their helmets on their heads.

This scene of war has been reenacted many times by war documentaries of the '50s.

That very morning, near the "Briscinia" (prison) the Allied Headquarters named a new Mayor, **Mr. Nicola Portone,** and a new town policeman, Uncle Antonio Di Iorio. But a few days later **Uncle Peppino Castellino**, who remained in office for many years, up to his retirement, was restored in his lawful role of town policeman. The Allies remained in the village for about a month and organized their performance according to the tested logistics which permitted them to win in **the landing at Normandy (on June 6th 1944)**, where also an American Italian cousin of mine, son of Uncle Dominic, **Nick Camillo**, participated and was wounded in that fight.

Pietracupa's winter of 1944 was a particularly snowy one. I remember that my father one evening in February, coming back home from the tavern of Uncle Guerrino, said: *"the sky is clear; tomorrow it will be a nice day."* The following day, my mother, opening the door to take the fodder to the animals in the stable, was knocked down by a heap of snow a meter and half high.

I have never forgotten two things of that day: the view of snowy fields with Mount Saint Angelo covered by snow and the mobilization of all the inhabitants of the village, who were busy clearing snow from the roofs to restore the functioning of the village.

Shovelling the snow

The solidarity of Pietracupa's inhabitants shown in those difficult days of war was deeply meaningful, and a great lesson for my training of life, letting me understand that we are not alone and that we have to help each other.

The front of the war, by then, had moved to the north, towards the line Gustav, and my father who had a license to drive trucks, presented himself at the Allied Headquarters at Campobasso to be employed by a firm of Molise to carry provisions and war materials to the soldiers involved in the first line.

On May 18th the line Gustav was "broken". Escaping Germans withdrew towards Rome and, **on June 4th,** they abandoned Rome

42

and moved back along **the Gotic Line** on Tuscany / Emilian Appennines.

This year (2014), in the Square of Benedictine Abbey, the 70th anniversary of the Battle of Cassino was remembered in the presence of Italian authorities and of English Prince Harry, grandson of Queen Elizabeth, who placed a wreath in the military cemetery near the same Abbey.

In Rome, at the Museum of Vittoriano, the Mayor of Rome organized an exposition to celebrate 4th of June 1944, and the end of all the events of those terrible days, on the occasion of the 70th Anniversary. Similar events took place in June 2014 to remember those killed at **the landing at Normandy.** All the presidents of the world (Putin, Obama, Merkel, Hollande, etc), including our President Napolitano, were present on Normandy beaches, that saw many young soldiers die.

Last year I visited the area of the Allied landing and the cemetery of American soldiers. The silence which was in the air in that open space of the cemetery suspended on a ridge rising straight from the sea, the movement of waves breaking on the beach, and the thousands of white crosses on the graves gave me a sense of peace but, at the same time, of anguish in remembering those dramatic events that I myself and many of Pietracupa's people witnessed in another time of the Second World War.

-THE LIBERATION OF ROME AND THE EVENTS OF 1945

On June 4th 1944, Rome was liberated at last. The Allies entered the eternal city and the Romans, after months of tragedies and hardship, welcomed them with great joy.

The Allied Head Quarters that settled in Barberini Square remained in the city for some years.

The Second World War in Europe ended on May 8th 1945, with the occupation of the Chancellery of Berlin by Russian soldiers and the death of Hitler, who committed suicide in the underground bunker of the same Chancellery.

In the war zone of the Pacific Ocean, on August 6th and 9th 1945, American President Truman let two atomic bombs explode over Hiroshima and Nagasaki, which forced Japanese Emperor Hirohito to sign the surrender of Japan on August 15, 1945, communicated on September 1st 1945.

In the documentaries of the epoch, the shots of the liberation of Rome are preserved. We can see both American General Clark in his Jeep in front of Saint Peter's Basilica, and Pope Pius XII blessing the Roman people who rushed up in great numbers, celebrating after the terrible days of the Saint Lorenzo bombing. On that occasion the Supreme Pontiff rushed up to Verano Square with his white habit spotted by the blood of wounded people. A statue of Pius XII, erected in front of the old Church of Saint Lorenzo, commemorates this event.

The postwar for Italians and Romans was a difficult period: the black market, prostitution for food, the problems of home and of work characterized these years of transition to normality and well being. Many of our cinema directors of Italian Neorealism - Rossellini, De Sica, Castellani and others - dealt with those topics in epoch films like Sciuscià, Roma Città Aperta, Ladri di Biciclette, Era Notte a Roma, Sotto il Sole di Roma, Napoli Milionaria.

The writer, Curzio Malaparte, in his novel "La Pelle", described the tragic side of the postwar. But somehow or another, one thing was certain: People were feeling around them a light atmosphere of freedom after twenty years of fascist dictatorship.

With the announcement of the liberation of Rome, many of Pietracupa's evacuees who had resided in Rome returned to the city and began again the jobs they had abandoned on September 8th 1943. The first to leave were my father, Uncle Peppino Durante with son Settimio, Uncle Menicuccio Di Iorio, and another I don't remember. They left by foot in June 1944, as the public transport buses hadn't been restored yet. Later my father told me the ups and downs of his last trip from Pietracupa to Rome by foot.

When they arrived at Ceppagna, the last village of Molise, by then exhausted from the journey, they stopped to rest near a farm. In front of them there was the Mountain of Nunziata Lunga, which splits Molise from Lazio. During this stop, Uncle Menicuccio caught sight of a hen's nest full of eggs and, because of his hunger, he took an egg and put it in his pocket indifferently. After leaving the farm and having eaten the eggs, they began the climb of Nunziata Lunga, whose name describes it well.

At the time the present tunnel that joins Lazio at Molise didn't exist, and it wasn't child's play covering the Nunziata Lunga. Moreover, during June 1944, the road was covered by military tanks and by Jeeps with American soldiers who, after the Conquest of Montecassino, would go to Rome liberated.

Uncle Peppino Settimio, the elder of the group, at a certain point stopped one of those Jeeps passing by, saying in Pietracupa's dialect: *accideteme, ma purtateme alla casa, nun ce la faccio chiu* ("kill me, but take me home, I can't stand it anymore"). Uncle Peppino Settimio was taken to Rome, just near his home, in the quarter of Saint Giovanni.

The other travelers, including my father, arrived some days later, sleeping in emergency shelters and in the open air. Rome, during that June of 1944, was invaded by Allied military coming from Anzio and from the front at Cassino. My father presented at once to ATAC, the City Council Transport Company, where he worked before September 8th, to begin his job again.

By then "the night was going to pass" as De Filippo acted in his already cited comedy, "Napoli Milionaria". The life in the city began to resume its rhythm of normalcy, waiting for the end of war.

On June 5th, the king of Italy abdicated in favor of Prince Umberto; General Badoglio resigned as Chief of Government, and the First Government, supported by the antifascist army chaired by Ivanoe Bonomi, was formed.

The ATAC (the company for which I worked too from 1964 to 2004) in that period went through a lot of trouble to give the city of Rome that push to normalcy, starting the public transportation necessary for the mobility of the citizens.

But in June 1944 there were still the after effects of repressed hate towards the chief of the former fascist regime. An example of this atmosphere of hate is tangible in the episode of the killing of the director of Prison Regina Coeli, Donato Carretta. Mr. Carretta, who was called to testify in the trial versus ex Police Commissioner, Mr. Caruso, in the crowded courtroom of Piazza Cavour, had been accused by a woman of being a collaborator with the Germans.

The crowd become fierce, took Mr. Carretta, threw him into the Tevere, and then some boatmen ended the job by drowning him with the oars of the boat.

Years later, people verified that Mr. Carretta had never been a collaborator with the Germans. On the contrary, he had favored the release of many partisans imprisoned in Regina Coeli.

Appearing well fed and well dressed in those days in Rome was very dangerous because anyone could be accused of having been a collaborator with the past regime and with Germans. My father, who appeared ruddy thanks to the pizza of "gandigna" (flour of corn) he had eaten at Pietracupa, knew that.

We cannot forget that during June 1944 along the Gotic line, not only the war against Germans, but also the civil war against the enlisted fascists of the Republic of Salò, was taking place. This civil war between Germans and fascists against partisans produced very emotional bloody events from both sides.

Events that aren't yet historically settled and which are subjects of analysis and debate even recently happened after the publishing of the book by P. Pansa "Il sangue dei vinti" ("The blood of defeated people") too.

In October 1944, my father at last let our family know it was time to leave Pietracupa and go back to Rome. We left Pietracupa by a bus of the firm S.A.T.A.M. (Saliola Augusto Molisan Car Transport) leaving from Salcito and arriving at Rome in the district of San Giovanni.

Leaving Pietracupa, I was leaving the 14 months spent among my Molisan relatives and the people of the native village of my father. I was leaving tragedies and fears; but I was bringing with me something that never abandoned me - my belonging to this small village of Molise. And every year I have always gone back to Pietracupa, my father's home, to breathe in that atmosphere binding me to my childhood memories.

The trip from Pietracupa to Rome on that day in October was a classic one on an improvised bus, passing through all the small Molisan villages on its way. The travelers were people who were going back to Rome and commuters who were carrying foodstuffs, hens, eggs, flour, or wheat from one village to another to sell them.

Foodstuffs, at the time, were controlled by hard customs laws, so travelers would get checked by Carabinieri (Police).

Anyway the peasants needed to sell goods to live and, for this reason, the roof of the bus, accessible by an external small stepladder, was a warehouse of sacks, hens, chickens and pork products. That day, my mother was also carrying a little sack of flour along with our suitcases, in case we needed it at some future time.

When we arrived at Venafro, the bus was stopped by Carabinieri for a check that had to be done in another place. I can't describe to you

46

the travelers' despair. At that point my mother went out of the bus with my brother in her arms and began to talk to Carabinieri with her Roman accent, saying that they shouldn't give poor people the trouble because of a few pieces of bread. She was so convincing that the bus was authorized to leave.

A few kilometers from Venafro, the climb of Nunziata Lunga began. It was the first time I was traveling that road. Halfway up we met an uncovered truck carrying a man whose head was bleeding. They told us that the wounded man had fallen down from the same truck where he was riding. At the end of the climb and at the beginning of the slope towards San Pietro Infine, from the bus's window an apocalyptic scene appeared in front of me: San Pietro Infine was a pile of debris and no houses were there. Going on downhill towards Cassino, this catastrophic vision was a fixed constant, worsened by the presence of destroyed and unusable guns and tanks, left in the uncultivated fields near Via Casilina.

When we arrived at Cassino, the town was nonexistent; there was only the debris of houses, churches, and war surplus scattered everywhere. It seemed like a ghost town.

Raising our eyes, we saw that Monte Cassino Abbey, cradle of Medieval History and monasticism where Kings like Carlo Magno and popes had stopped, was a pile of rubble under which priceless cultural valued works of art were lying destroyed.

All this was due to the madness of war, to human madness, and above all to the lack of culture and sensitivity of the men in power who had to decide the destiny of a population.

The documents analyzed after the war showed that, in Monte Cassino Abbey, there weren't Germans barricaded to defend the emplacement, and the debris produced after the Allied bombing of the Abbey created the fertile ground to let Germans take up new emplacements of defense. That is why the Army was stopped for about 5 months, with relative losses of human lives from one side and the other.

After leaving Cassino we stopped in a small restaurant in the countryside. Then always along Street Casilina, we crossed Frosinone, Ferentino, and at last we arrived at Rome. Upon arrival at Terminale of S.A.T.A.M. the bus was placed in an old garage/courtyard in open air, equipped in a simple way near Street Sannio.

Both at the departure of buses and at their arrival, the courtyard was full of Molisans, who were there to wait for the bus to receive or send packages and boxes, or to assist and say goodbye to travelers leaving or arriving from Molise.

The courtyard and the bus have been the historical point of union between Pietracupa and Rome for a long time.

During the early years, people who lived in the area would rent a little wheel barrow to carry the suitcases of arriving or departing travelers. It was a kind of Turkish or African bazaar, where people would meet and speak.

That very day of 1944, my father came to pick us up and we returned to my maternal grandparents' home after about two years of absence. At home, all my mother's brothers and sisters with my little cousins were waiting for us. The hug between Uncle Armando of Frascati and my mother was moving. Uncle Armando had lost his house in the bombing of Frascati. As I said above, my heart is half Roman and half Molisan. That evening, the half Roman part of it was beating rapidly.

Seeing again San Cosimato Square, the small fountain in the opposite market, the old bakery Bagagli, the restaurant of old Mr. Corsetti, a friend of my grandfather, the gate of the Roman College, brought back my old memories. But, in my bed that night, the other half of my heart also beat quickly. I missed a little of that small loggia in Street Vico I° Saint Anna. I missed my Pietracupa neighbors and friends.

In 1946, my father rented a house in Street dei Sabelli 82 and from Trastevere (characteristic district of Rome) we moved to the San Lorenzo district. I remember moving day. My father had asked his company for a streetcar to carry the furniture. We carried our furniture by this engine from Avenue Trastevere to Street Tiburtina on the old bus line.

Our building in San Lorenzo was intact, but the building next door was not there anymore. It had been bombed on July 19, 1943. Its debris, showing the holes from bombs, was still visible in Street dei Sabelli, that has now become an elegant street for the students of the nearby University "La Sapienza". We lived in the new house for ten years. In the Church of Immacolata, I was confirmed and received my First Communion, and attended the nearby Catholic school up to secondary school.

During those years, our Roman house was a place of welcome for many of our Pietracupa's friends and relatives. I may objectively affirm that my father was a generous man and the door of his house was always open to welcome and put up people from his native village. I'll tell you about some episodes of these pleasant and humane relationships that characterized the honest affection of my family to Pietracupa and its people.

The end of the Second World War was announced on May 8, 1945. In Italy, after the capture and the execution by firing squad of Mussolini at Giulino di Mezzegra on April 28, 1945, and the unconditional surrender of the German Army in Italy, signed on April 29, 1945, Mr. Ferruccio Parri, on June 19th, formed the new government, including all the representatives of antifascist parties. Parri's Government fell on November 24, 1945 because of the opposition by Christian Democrats (CD) and Liberals. The task to form a new government was given to Congressman Alcide De Gasperi of the Christian Democratic Party, who on December 10, 1945, dissolved his resolution presenting his first Ministry, including the representatives of all antifascist parties. Substantial economic assistance was granted by English and American Allies through the UNRRA, which is a particular agency of United Nations, to promote a quick recovery of the Italian people.

-THE CONSEQUENCES OF WORLD WAR II

Deaths among soldiers and civilians resulting from the Second World War on the different European Fronts are estimated at 50 million people, not including the injured and maimed. Suffice it to think that in the battle of Cassino in January 1944 and in the battle of Anzio on January 22nd 1944, because of the bad weather conditions and the strategic uncertainties of American General Lucas, the opposing belligerents were forced into a war which claimed thousands and thousands of victims.

The numerous military cemeteries of Nettuno, Anzio, Pomezia, Cassino, Venafro, and so on are the proof of how many young lives were destroyed on Italian ground and how many stories were weaved during the War. There is the story of Angelita from Anzio, a five old girl found dead in a trench, or the one of the father of Pink Floyd's drummer, whose grave was found only in 2013, after years of searching.

Whole cities were bombed and destroyed, with great destruction also to our artistic and cultural heritage. For the first time, new types of war bombs were experimented with - like the atomic bombs launched over Hiroshima and Nagasaki that resulted in about 100,000 deaths and with lethal consequences for the survivors hit by radiation.

The racial hatred provoked by Nazi ideology towards Jews, gypsies, the disabled, and political opponents produced massacres and barbarities, as Mathausen and Auschwitz/Bierkenau concentration camps demonstrate, with more than two million deaths.

Two years ago I went to Poland and visited the Warsaw Ghetto and Auschwitz/Bierkenau concentration camp with the famous sentence on the entry gate "Work makes us free". I saw the arrival station of trains, the barracks of prisoners destined to die, the chambers of torture, the barbed wire under 8,000 volt tension on which many desperate men committed suicide, the gas chamber with the chimney spewing outside the acrid smell of burnt corpses. All these things have awakened in me some feelings I cannot express in writing.

I prayed for these dead people in front of the image of the Black Madonna by Jasna Gora, near Czestochowa, far from Auschwitz some hundred kilometres. In the interior of the Basilica I observed also a fresco of the Battle of Cassino with the representation of the Madonna protecting Polish soldiers, headed by General Anderson, during the final attack on the Monastery on May 18th 1944. The dead also lie in the small cemetery near the Monastery.

Another black page on crimes of Nazi barbarity was written in Rome during the German occupation in March 1944 and is about the massacre of Fosse Ardeatine.

The German Headquarters, after the Partisan attack on Rome in Street Rasella on March 24th 1944, during which 33 German soldiers had been killed, in reprisal shot 335 people to obey the order of Hitler himself.

Commander Erich Priebke executed the order, putting on the list of conscripts five persons more than the 330 indicated by the order of Hitler. Priebke was processed and given a life sentence; but because of his age, was given house arrest in Rome. He died on October 11, 2013 when he was 100 years old and, because of strong polemics about the funeral and on the destination of his corpse, he was buried on October 27, 2013 in a cemetery in an Italian Military prison, the location of which is still kept secret.

I have a direct and very moving memory of Fosse Ardeatine. The Roman people at the end of the War, when the place of massacre had been discovered, rushed over there to pray for the dead.

My parents took me to the cave of Pozzolan, where the corpses of innocent victims lay. I remember that the cave was in its original state and the simple coffins of bare wood, simply organized, were deposited at random on the floor, with only the names of the dead people inside. During that visit in the cave, there were a lot of their relatives crying desperately, together with numerous Roman visitors.

Now that site has become a mausoleum, and every year Italians commemorate these poor victims, together with National authorities.

The Second World War that at first saw the two great world powers, Russia and USA, allied, soon after the signing of Armistice, saw their relationship become based on conflict. This triggered that distrust of one another which characterized the years after the war, designated by historians as "years of Cold War". This ideological war started by the two nations strongly influenced the post war period, with serious repercussions for all the countries of the world aligned with one or the other Power.

During this period there were moments of dramatic tension, during which was feared the outbreak of a Third World War. In Italy, this opposition had very strong implications between the two parties that represented the ideologies of the two hegemonic powers, namely the Christian Democrats and the Italian Communist Party. The heated debates in Parliament, street demonstrations, strikes, violent clashes with the police, the rugged dialectical opened by party newspapers, characterized for more than forty years the scenario of the young Italian Republic, until the fall of the Berlin Wall that took place on November 10, 1989.

However, Italy, in the difficult moments of her history, has been shown to have in herself the strength and democratic structure to unravel its internal conflicts. Political parties today still retain in their Statutes the founding principles of the ideologies of the past - but, included as part of a globalized world context and in a European reality that finds it hard to reach the effective unity of the Member States of the Community itself.

The dream of the founding fathers of European Economic Community (EEC), like De Gasperi, Adenauer, Schuman, has not found its full realization yet.

The Second World War, although it brought tragedy and death, helped to create a new spirit of survival, participation, and, especially, great solidarity among us Italians and specifically among Pietracupa's people.

At home, my mother always confessed to me that the best time of her life was spent in Pietracupa during the war because she had her family close to her and the warmth and solidarity of the people of Pietracupa.

CHAPTER II

THE YEARS OF RECONSTRUCTION (1946/1950)

The Events in Italy and in the World

The years from 1946 to 1950 were crucial to the normalization of Italy and Italians, both in the world context and in the European one, after twenty years of Fascism and a world war that had seen us defeated. The main events that characterized this historic Italian period can be summarized as follows:

1946 - King Vittorio Emanuele II abdicated in favor of his son Umberto II. On June 2nd and 3rd both the constitutional referendum and the elections to appoint the members of the Constituent Assembly were organized. In the referendum, the majority of the Italian people voted for the Republic, so on June 13th, King Umberto II, left in exile for residence at the Portuguese Cascay. On June 28th Enrico De Nicola was elected President, Provisional Head of the Italian State. On July 13th Alcide De Gasperi formed his second government by including in it both the socialists and the communists.

Sports activities began to function again, with the dispute of the Tour of Italy, when there was the victory of Gino Bartali over the emerging Fausto Coppi. In the football league, the Torino won the first championship after the war.

After the dark years of the war, people wished again to dance, to hear the music of the great American bands (Glenn Miller, Tommy Dorsey and so on) and the songs of their singers (Frank Sinatra, Bing Crosby).

The plots of films produced in the USA, such as Gilda and Gone with the Wind, let Italians dream; and big stars like Rita Hayworth, Ava Gardner, Ingrid Bergman, Gary Cooper, Tyrone Power, Clark Gable enchanted audiences all over the world, including Italy.

Domestic trade took place through the black market as well as the small alley or country economy; payments were made by the old coin or by Am-Lire issued by the Allies waiting for the stabilization of the economy.

1947 - In January, the Head of Government in office, Mr. De Gasperi, traveled to the USA to apply for a loan of $100 million in exchange for the consolidation of the democratic regime in Italy. He managed to get it. On February 2nd, however, he launched his third coalition government, still including members of the Socialist and Communist Parties in it. At this point, in a period of intense Cold War between the Soviet and the Western bloc, both the Catholic Church and American President Truman forced De Gasperi to resign and form a new team government, excluding communists and socialists.

Therefore on May 31st, a new government, composed of Democrats and some personalities such as Sforza, Merzagora and Einaudi was formed, in tune with what the USA desired.

1948 - The new Italian Constitution (January 1st) took effect and Enrico De Nicola was elected first President of the Italian Republic. On April 2nd, the USA Congress approved the Marshall Plan, by delivering $5 million to the Italian State. On April 18th and 19th general elections were called. The Christian Democrats won with 48.5% of voters and the Popular Democratic Front (PDF, made up of Communists and Socialists together) only had 31% of voters. So De Gasperi, at the end of May, launched its fifth government, always with the 'exclusion of communists and socialists'. On July 14th, the secretary of the Italian Communist Party (PCI), Mr. Togliatti, was injured in Rome in an attack committed by graduate student Antonio Pallante. The CGIL (Trade Union) immediately proclaimed a general strike of workers, and Italy was shaken for many days by violent protests and local uprisings harshly put down by the police. The death toll of this uprising was 21 dead and one hundred injured.

On the same day of the attack, Gino Bartali snatched the yellow jersey of Bobet and later won the Tour de France, always coming first in Paris. This victory, according to many historians, was one of the reasons that the rebels discontinued the protests that would have taken them to a civil war. Another reason for moderation was the responsible attitude that the Communist leader Mr. Togliatti showed immediately after the attack. Soon after the attack he sent a radio message to the nation asking the militants of his party to desist from any revolutionary acts and to return to the ranks of constitutional normality.

1949 - De Gasperi Government applied for admission of Italy to NATO, a Western Bloc countries' Defense organization. After heated debates in parliament, popular demonstrations and protest strikes by the leftists, Parliament approved the request of Italy to join the other nations belonging to NATO on March 19th. A measure of great social importance, carried out by the De Gasperi government in February, was the launch of the National Institute for Workers

54

Houses (INA-House), necessary to address the housing problem in Italy.

On July 13th, the Holy See, in the heated opposition between the political right and left parties, issued an excommunication decree against all communist militants and all those who read the Communist press or voted for the listings of PCI. This measure may give the idea of burning conflict between opposing political groups and the harshness of the dialogue between the militants of either party.

The problem of agricultural workers, always dominated by the great landowners, exploded in the month of October at Melissa in Calabria, where the police opened fire on farmers who were occupying vacant lands, killing three laborers. So took place the struggle for possession of large estates, undertaken by farm laborers forced to a life of hardship and misery, which led to the death of 62 people and 300 wounded in 1949-50.

The events in the world were characterized by the division of the two Germanys; they came together again only after the fall of the Berlin Wall in December 1989. Other events of the year which had great historical importance were the division of Jerusalem between Transjordan and Jerusalem, resolved by the UN, and the proclamation of the Republic of China, which took place in October.

In the field of sports, the year was marred by the terrible tragedy of the great Torino. On May 4th, the football team was returning from a trip to Portugal when the plane crashed into the hill of Superga. The Turin, then, with his team won his 5th championship. In cycling, Fausto Coppi performed the great feat of winning in the same year the Tour of Italy and the Tour de France.

The return of freedom of speech and thought opened new areas of work in the world of journalism and publishing, both for party newspapers, dailies, and for escapist newspapers. Gossip such as the love story between director Roberto Rossellini and actress Ingrid Bergman, or marriage between Prince Ali Khan and actress Rita Hayworth, interested the public. Gradually the outside world was presented with the true image of an Italy rich in art, culture and scenic beauty, and open to welcome famous artists like the great Louis Armstrong, unequalled American jazz trumpeter who came to Italy in October with his band for a concert.

1950 - Pope Pius XII opened the Holy Year, which brought to Italy millions of pilgrims from around the world. On January 12th, the De

Gasperi government resigned and on the 27th of January, a new government was launched, always with Communists and Socialists in opposition. In February, US Senator McCarthy accused 200 officials of the Department of State of being activists of the Communist Party, opening the season of "McCarthyism", the famous witch hunt that involved many stars of the cinema also.

On May 11th, after long protests quelled by the police, agricultural workers, laborers and Italian employees won for the first time in a country of the Western bloc, the national contract of the farm workers. On June 25th the Korean War began when the US military, commanded by General MacArthur in defense of South Korea, was attacked by North Korea, a country of the China / Soviet bloc .On August 10th the law establishing the Fund for the South, Board for Construction of major public works for the development of the southern Italian regions was enacted.

All these historical events of the years from 1946 to 1950 deeply affected the lives of Italians, especially the people of the small villages of southern Italy including Pietracupa.

Through the stories of life lived in the capital of Italy and the events experienced in the small village of Molise, the reader can get an idea of how these events were implemented and what impact they have had on the habits and citizens' level of life.

-THE POSTWAR PERIOD IN ROME AND THE HOLY YEAR

The level of comfort or discomfort of Roman citizens after the war could be taken as a benchmark for all other Italians living in the north, the south, and the center of our peninsula. In Rome, all locations of the Constitutional Bodies of our State - from the Quirinale Palace (seat of the king and then the President of the Republic), the Palazzo Madama (seat of the Senate), the Montecitorio Palace (seat of Parliament), as well as ministries and all offices of political parties and Trade Unions - were placed. So any political ferment, every famous person arriving or departing, every decision of the executive power, had a direct and immediate impact on Roman citizens.

Analyzing how people lived in Rome after the war was like analyzing the state of comfort or discomfort of the Italian people. Certainly the bibliography of those years' events is very rich and comprehensive.

But I want to add some minimal aspects to the official voice of the historians, more personal, about the life of individual citizens, telling some anecdotes I lived in the city, my memories of that time, my expectations, my relationships with others and, especially, my relationship with Pietracupa and its people.

These are the memories of a boy who began to attend primary school and was about to be formed as a teenager, as a young man, and then as a man. My memories of those years so full of changes and political tensions are many.

The first thing that comes to my mind is the restoration of public transport service. Watching again, now, a few films of the Week Incom, you can capture the spirit and characteristics of the life of Romans at that time, clinging to the running boards of the bus or tram, or riding in search of unlicensed pickup trucks, replacement of the crowded public transport, all worried to get to their jobs on time. It was easy, getting onto the trolley, to hear some argument about the classic "dead hand" that some distracted traveler would forget to remove from the back of the nice Roman girls. But there was no fear of today's rapists.

A typical character of those years was the "ciccarolo", the famous collector of cigarette butts who recovered tobacco from cigarette butts in order to sell it on the black market. The symbol of commerce and sales of those years was Piazza Vittorio; it was considered the square of miracles, like an Arab souk. There was everything, old sewing machines, second-hand tires, coffee makers, spare parts of all kinds, recycled clothing, various bicycles stolen or not. Those who went to Piazza Vittorio never remained disappointed. Even Porta Portese was a place dedicated to such trades. In a scene from the film "Bicycle Thieves", which at the time I saw playing live in Monte Sacro, the lively and a bit 'equivocal' atmosphere in these squares is described.

Black market was the soul of commerce. I remember that in via della Scala in Trastevere, there was every day a long line of men and women, even the elderly, who were selling smuggled cigarettes, shoes, soap and food. Nowadays in the street there are always illegal vendors, but with the presence of migrants from Africa and India.

The streets of Rome were full of American military Jeeps, and soldiers roamed the city, not only to look at its cultural beauties, but above all they were looking for girls willing to entertain them. Often, because of starvation, many girls were ready to accompany them.

They had only to guard against the American military police patrolling the streets.

The soldiers wanted to have fun, to listen to swing music, to dance the boogie woogie. So the first dancehalls were born in the city, where it was possible to listen to the hit songs of famous American composers, such as the song "Angelina".

In 1945, after five years of silence, it was possible to resume postal communications with Italian relatives in the USA. The first exchange of letters between my father and his brothers and sisters was very moving, especially since the news was positive. But with great regret we were informed that my cousin Nick Camillo, enlisted in the USA Army, had been wounded in an act of war in Europe and had returned to the USA. My first encounter with Nick occurred about twenty years later in Chicago, where he was born. But I will talk about him and the other American cousins later. However, another American soldier, also our relative, came to visit us in Rome: it was Alfredo Di Iorio, son of Uncle Angelico, born in America and a relative of Dad.

Alfredo didn't speak Italian at all; but in the bar below our house there was a young lady who spoke English well, and so it was possible to start a dialogue through a third party. His stay in Rome was very short. The American command sent him immediately to Paris where he met a sweet French girl, married her, and returned with his wife to Wisconsin. After the war, Alfredo and his wife came for the third time to visit us for Holy Year; we spent a wonderful holiday week with them.

I did not see Alfredo again, although I went to America another 12 times in my life. But when I see pictures of those days I feel deeply moved remembering those times and that Rome that is no longer.

The postwar was also a time when we had the opportunity to experience the great generosity of our relatives who were in the United States. In fact, all those who had relatives in the United States received parcels from their relatives, sensitive to the humanitarian campaign that the US promoted in the states, in favor of Italy. In those years, my family received many parcels containing gifts sent to me and to my brother. Each arrival of the "American Pack" was a source of pleasant surprises because, in it, we found sweets, toys, clothes and even generic drugs we didn't know.

In this regard, I remember the first time I wore jeans found in the package. My classmates made fun of me for my new clothing. Now I say that I was a forerunner of the Italian jeans, which is currently the most worn garment around the world. Another memory is the medicine Vicks VapoRub that they sent us and which we used to make "gargling" with the hot water. Now the Vicks VapoRub is a generic medicine that you buy normally at the pharmacy. Other times, we found in the package envelopes containing powders whose use was difficult to understand, also because the knowledge of English was not of common use. And so as not to do like a family of our knowledge which had mistaken the ashes of a deceased person for a food broth, we would always expect a translator to understand the components of powders.

Even the Catholic Church in those years played an important role in helping, influencing and leading the Italian people towards normalization, although from the viewpoint of its Catholic aims. As I wrote earlier, I attended primary and part of secondary school at the Catholic Institute of Blessed Leonardo Murialdo in Via of the Etruscans in San Lorenzo. Every morning at the Institute, all pupils of primary classes were taken to the church of the Immaculate to hear Mass before they went into the classroom for lessons.

At recess, announced by a loud bell, pupils of all the classes were accompanied to a large courtyard and this recreation area for about half an hour became a place for games, discussions about football, bartering of figurines, and then the complete silence came down again. In the late afternoon, it was still possible to go back to the religious building to spend some time in a gymnasium used for games of all kinds, or to the large open-air courtyard, always accompanied by some religious or an adult to optimize the free time of the young.

Next to the courtyard there was a cinema where every Thursday and Sunday you could see some movie. The films that were screened were generally adventure or war or sentimental ones, all strictly permitted by the Vicariate.

In the seventies, that hall was sold or leased to private individuals who use it for the screening of avant-garde films, both prohibited and not prohibited kinds, and is called Cinema Tibur. Every time I go to the Cinema Tibur, my memories take me back to those years after the war, during which my interest in the art of film was born. And thinking that, just next to the entrance of the place, is located the large entrance door of my elementary school, I think about my mother who accompanied me, my classmates, my life path.

The Parish community of the Institute had formed a small theater company that presented on stage comedies for teens. In this company starred a dear school friend, Vinicio Raimondi, who as an adult practiced the profession of "magician". Vinicius was nationally known and appreciated.

On December 8th, the feast of the Immaculate Conception, a grand procession was organized in honor of the Madonna; it ran through all the streets of the district, also in memory of the victims of the bombing of the Allies of July 9th 1943.

But the pride of all San Lorenzini, lovers of football, was the team's ball of SPES, which trained and played in the sports complex in Via dei Sabelli, owned by the Knights of Columbus. President of the team was Fr. Libero Raganella, native of San Lorenzo, the figure of a parish priest before his time, who for many years characterized the sporting environment with the expressions as an old Roman and man of Church.

In those years, the parish would organize summer camps for all the kids in the district. One year I myself was a guest of the colony too in Bolsena; I had a lot of fun between the hills and the lake full of mysteries and ancient stories of the Queen Amalasunta.

The days of celebration in Rome were always the same, and you spent them with the whole family. The walks along the Roman streets were the liveliest, and the least expensive, activities in those years of hardship.

We lived in S. Lorenzo, and the afternoon walk to the center of the town was a ritual and a relaxing custom for all of us in the family. We reached Via Marsala, where renovations of the Termini Station were ongoing; we went to Piazza Esedra, and we stopped on the edges of the Fountain of the Naiads to listen to the music that an Italian orchestra performed outside of Bar Esedra.

Then we reached the ice cream shop Fassi in Piazza Vittorio and ate the house specialty, the famous "Caterinetta", still produced and exported abroad, or tasted the famous Bar Algida's cremino, an all-Italian novelty.

At the end we went to the park in Piazza Vittorio, where an orchestra would play in the Greek Bar and singers of all kinds were performing.

You could hear the typical Italian festive and musical mood in those days in every street. Player pianos invaded the city on two wheels with the little man who asked you for money, giving you a ticket with your horoscope. Orchestras with mandolins and puti pù (a typical Neapolitan instrument) arrived even from Naples, would sing in every alley Neapolitan songs like "Simmo e' Napule paisà".

When we came back, we passed the legendary Cinema / Theatre Ambra Iovinelli, a place of successful popular curtain raisers, where the viewer could first watch the film on the bill, followed by the live performances of comedians, dancers and singers. The Cinema/Theatre Ambra Iovinelli was the training ground for the success of many famous Italian artists, such as Toto, Sordi, the brothers De Rege, the brothers Maggio and famous singers such as Claudio Villa and Antonio Basurto.

The Easter Monday, the First of May, and April 25th were special days when all the gardens and lawns of Rome were invaded by citizens who with snacks, lunches, accordions and guitars passed lightheartedly these days outdoors.

Sometimes we went to small *fraschette* (taverns) where it was customary to follow the custom of "*fagottaro*" ("food in the shopping bag"), that is to say, taking something to eat from home and paying only for drinks.

My family, in those days, would go to Uncle Armando of Frascati, and it was nice to go to the Villa Aldobrandini, that only on feast days was open to the public.

The resumption of sports activity also helped to calm the minds of Italians starting them towards a normal life. The beginning of the football league, the national team matches, the exploits of the great Torino, of Valentino Mazzola, of Bagicalupo, the challenges and the derbies of the teams of the heart, the victories of the great cycling champions like Coppi, Bartali, Magni, were events that re-united Italians and made them understand they belong to a people rich in inventiveness and courage.

The RAI (Italian Radio) had an important role with the resumption of regular radio broadcasts. Not everyone could afford the purchase of a unit. But, by going to the neighbor who owned one or to the neighborhood bar, it was possible to listen to the news, music programs and especially the football games broadcast by Nicolò Carosio. The marketing of the radio allowed each family to adopt this appliance, useful for information and for cultural development, as well as an entertainment tool. The melodic songs of the time, sung by Claudio Villa, Luciano Taioli, Clara Iaione, orchestras of Pippo Barzizza, Armando Fragna, Gorni Kramer, and those beautiful songs like *Old Rome, Ancient Village, Luna Rossa, Nannarella*, would spread along the streets and cast out sad thoughts.

The world of cinema in those years also spurred an important development: district cinemas began to open their doors to project films from the American circuit that the former regime had forbidden. The comedy of Charlie Chaplin and Laurel and Hardy, musicals of Ginger Rogers and Fred Astaire, films of the great Hollywood stars such as "Gone with the Wind", "Blood and Arena", "Duel in the Sun", convinced Italians to attend the theaters. They made them dream in the dark, feeding their "American Dream", which I will speak of in one of the later chapters.

Even Italian cinema played an important role during this period. The directors of neorealism developed a following around the world and films like Sciuscià, Roma Città Aperta, Ladri di Biciclette, captivated crowds of spectators, receiving awards and recognitions everywhere. Italians liked not only movies by famous artists with dramatic content, but also brilliant films and comedies whose performers such as Totò, Macario, Dapporto, the De Filippo brothers were the main popularizers of that kind of irony which is all Italian. In the years following, actors and directors that brought success to the "Italian comedy" include Sordi, Gassman, Vitti, Giannini, Tognazzi, Risi and Monicelli.

The variety, especially in curtain raiser theaters like the Ambra Iovinelli or the Cinema Palazzo or Cinema Volturno or Cinema Alambra, were places of entertainment for all the Romans who wanted to delight in the flicker of the lively soubrette and the jokes of the comedian on duty.

For the better-off, the Teatro Sistina, managed by the famous pair of authors Garinei and Giovannini, was the temple of Italian variety show, producing big shows on the bill that saw the participation of famous artists such as Anna Magnani, Wanda Osiris, Delia Scala, Carlo Dapporto, Erminio Macario, Renato Rascel, and Marcello Mastroianni in the role of Rodolfo Valentino.

Even the publishing industry implemented its business mainly with books and magazines of Popular Entertainment such as Grand Hotel, Gioia and so on that were sold like hot cakes among the girls who wanted to dream of fantastic and golden worlds, in a still difficult post war period, but that heralded a better future. The boys were delighted by reading children's comics such as the Intrepid, Tex Willer, the Masked Man and Mandrake. For the little ones there were the stories of Goofy, Pluto and Donald Duck by the renowned Walt Disney productions. Particular attention was paid to the Company Panini picture cards of athletes, actors, animals and flowers that all the kids were buying in sealed envelopes and glued into the albums of the collection, sharing with each other any duplicates found in the envelopes.

My grandchildren, Alexander and Julia, now buy the baseball cards, Batman, Peppa Pig, which reflects the insights and imagination of the Italian postwar epoch.

A special note should be paid to the edition of the first trade fair of Rome. This exhibition was organized for the first time in the gardens of Villa Borghese. My father took me to visit it, and I remember that I was interested to see in the various stands many technical and commercial innovations that showed the desire, and especially the ability, of the Italian people to operate and produce qualitatively and quantitatively, both for the domestic market and especially for the international market.

-THE HOLY YEAR

The five-year period from 1945 to 1950 ended with two events of great historical and religious interest: the proclamation of the Holy Year and the proclamation of the dogma of the Assumption. Pope Pius XII, who ruled the Church during the entire period of the war, wanted to give prominence to these two events, letting a message of peace and religion pass on all human beings affected by the appalling tragedy of the war.

The city of Rome had returned to be the point of reference of every human being in search of spirituality and certainty for the future, not only Catholics but also people of other religious beliefs. The chronicles of the epoch report that four million pilgrims visited the Eternal City, of which a million and half came from foreign countries. The tourism boom due to this arrival of foreigners in Italy, brought not only an influx of foreign money to the State and its citizens, but Italians realized that tourism could become a great job opportunity too. The beautiful scenery, art, cities, Italian beaches and mountains visited in the occasion of the Holy Year, attracted tourists who made propaganda back in their own countries of origin so that Italy could become a meeting place for all international travelers.

But even in this atmosphere of reflection and religiosity of the Holy Year, the specter of war was always lurking around the corner. The ideological conflict of the dominant superpower in the world was the reason for the outbreak of the Korean War in June of 1950. The North Korean communists, helped by Russia and China, passed the boundary of the 38th parallel, forcing US President Truman to intervene in defense of the South Koreans. People feared the outbreak of a third world war. That did not happen, but the risks were great, and the war in Korea, with its ups and downs, ended with the armistice of July 27th 1953 signed in Panmunjon.

Many young Americans flocked to defend the freedom of the people of South Korea and many children of Pietracupa's immigrants in America participated in this war in Asia.

The mood of the Italians during this international crisis was not the best. Italy was slowly recovering from the wounds of World War II. In 1950, the living conditions of average Italians was certainly not thriving: in one house out of four there was no running water; six out of ten homes lacked toilets; two out of three families were without gas, a bathroom, radio; six out of ten families were devoid of cars and / or motorcycles; average income was less than 50,000 pounds per month. So the news that came from Southeast Asia was received with great concern, both because of fear of a new world war, and also because the USA was our usual ally.

-THE FIRST REPUBLIC: THE REFERENDUM, ELECTIONS, POLITICAL EVENTS

The Roman events of the '50s, described in the previous section, are only a corollary of all the political and economic events that shaped this five-year period of Italian history. The dramatic changes that laid the foundation of our Republic, especially the economic and social policy measures, took Italy briefly towards a position of real well-being, so that in the '60s people were talking of an economic miracle.

But in order to understand better how we got such a miracle in a short time, it is necessary to retrace the historical journey that also led us to reach top positions on the world stage.

The first difficulties that the reconstituted political parties had to overcome after the fall of fascism were of a constitutional kind. It was necessary to hold a referendum to decide whether the people of

Italy had to still be Monarchist or Republican. Simultaneously, it was necessary to make members of the Constituent Assembly deputies to draft the text of the new Constitution- elect.

The national historical parties such as the Christian Democrats, socialists, communists, liberals, and republicans opted for an Italy headed by a President of the Republic, while the royalists and the nostalgic fascists opted for an Italy headed by the King.

June 2, 1946 was an historic day for Italy, both because of the result obtained, and also because of the fact that, for the first time, women were allowed to express their vote democratically, beginning the way to equal rights with males. The results of the referendum of 1946, amid controversy over alleged election fraud, produced the following results: 54.26% of voters expressed a favorable opinion for the Republic and 45.72% of voters expressed a favorable opinion for the Monarchy. So King Umberto II accepted the verdict and left Italy for exile in Portugal, in observance of the Constitution of Italy.

The results of the election for the members of the Constituent Assembly, decreed the following political preferences of Italians among the various contending parties: Christian Democrats (DC) 35.2% of the voters; the Italian Socialist Party (PSI) 20.7% of the voters; the Italian Communist Party (PCI) 19% of voters; other minor parties (Republicans, Liberals, monarchists, and so on) obtained much smaller proportions.

By this time, the recurring theme of Italian politics, at first after broad agreements between the Christian Democrats and the Left parties, was the strong opposition of the two main political blocs: the American government and the Catholic Church financially supported the CD, and Russia supported the Left.

The Christian Democrats in all voting policies since 1946, have always received the relative majority, so that they have always governed, either with single color teams or with the support of smaller parties of the Center, and twice with extreme Right parties. The alliance with the Communists in the following years, took away the privilege of being the first party to represent the Italian Left to the Socialists; this power passed to the Communist Party.

About the subject of Referendum, I would like to dedicate a personal note to the atmosphere that was present in 1946 in Rome and, especially, to the activism of the Romans' participation in party headquarters and presence at the rallies of their leaders.

My father, although a Catholic, was a militant socialist and believed in the ideas of freedom, social justice and equality among men, held in the principles of socialism. He used to tell me that Christ was a socialist. Moreover, even today, many of the European nations are governed by coalitions belonging to the international socialist, including the current Democratic Party (PD). There was the anomaly in Italy, perhaps to blame the political choices and the behavior of the leaders of the past.

With these political views, my father attended the section of the Socialist Party of San Lorenzo. Sometimes he let me listen to the speeches that leaders would hold in the district, in the Piazza dei Sanniti. At the end of May 1946, in this square, I saw on stage and listened to the three historic leaders of the time, De Gasperi, Togliatti and Nenni. All three were united to convince the Italians to vote for the Republic. Subsequently, in 1948, all three came back to the square, but each on his own, in favor of his party preference.

June 2, 1946 is an historically important day and Italians, in memory of the important constitutional changes, each year on June 2nd celebrate the birth of the Italian Republic. I still remember those days of June 1946. I remember that, during the days preceding the date of the vote, there had been a bustle of friends, relatives, residents of the building, all ready to give advice and tips on who to vote for. The streets were animated by the last speeches of the election campaign and the building facades on the streets were covered with posters glorifying one symbol or another.

My family went to vote in a polling station installed at a school in Viale del Re. There was a long line and I was getting tired; but then, close to my mother, I started to count the trams passing by on the avenue and I cut myself off from that turmoil of people, military and political activists. In comparison to that atmosphere of great activism and participation by all the people, the current election campaigns, followed only by "those in the know", make me think that something has changed over the years. The voter is a little baffled, and participates less in the political debate. I add only that to cast one's vote in the general, municipal, European elections is a way to keep alive the freedom and democracy of the people, and it is good that this right is exercised.

In July of 1948, the country was rocked by a major news item, which threatened to ignite a civil war in Italy. It was the attack on the Secretary of the Communist Party, Mr. Palmiro Togliatti. The memory of that day is still vivid in my mind. My father had enrolled me as a member of the Navy Cologne of Ostia, managed by his company, and every morning a bus ATAC would pick up members. After a day at the beach, in the evening it returned to the stop, starting in via Tiburtina. Generally it was my mother who came to pick me up.

But that day of July 14th, I found my father waiting for me at the bus stop. In a worried tone he told me to go hastily with him. On the way from Via Tiburtina to Via dei Sabelli, there was an unusual silence, and all the people I met were walking briskly to reach their homes. Entering the building in Via Sabelli, I heard the voice of Mr. Nanni, an old communist Bolshevik, screaming in the stairs and telling all present to take to the streets in revolt against the "regime" of the government in office.

As I wrote earlier, that day all worked out for the best, even if in Italy there were many dead and some police stations besieged by the rebels. In those situations I thought that the excesses were detrimental to the people. In this regard, the bloody showdown between red partisans and Republicans, which occurred at the end of the war, shows that hatred ignites hatred.

COMRADES

I met you with my father
in the former headquarters of San Lorenzo,
in the sultry evenings of '40s.

I heard your speech, I have shared
your expectations, your desire to believe
in and fight for a more fair world.

I walked with you in the middle
of your red flags, in the squares of Rome,
among the scents of May that blossomed.

I understand your silence,
in the dark maze of mines in Tuscany.
I ate with you in humble country homes,
listening to your stories of misery and hopes.

I struggled, sung, dreamed united with you,
in a thousand battles of the '60s.

And now, comrades, my friends, where are you?
Where is your faith, your desire to fight,
to rush to the defense of the oppressed?

I want to hear your voice again,
socialism is not a cold expression,
but a set of hearts, voices, strong men who believe in its ideals.

-PIETRACUPA'S COMMUNITY IN ROME

History is full of episodes that highlight the close relationship that has characterized and contrasted, over the centuries, the events between the ancient inhabitants of the land of Molise and the inhabitants of Rome. Just think about the episode "Forche Caudine" and the many Roman remains still present in many places of Molise such as Isernia, Boiano, Sepino, Pietrabbondante, Trivento and so on to realize the above statement.

This relationship has never been interrupted, so the city of Rome was the first and natural destination of each Molise inhabitant who was trying to find fortune outside his region of origin. Coming back to the present day and in particular to the years preceding the Second World War, in the Eternal City there was a fair number of Pietracupa's people who worked and resided permanently in Rome with their whole family. Others, instead, were working in Rome, but were waiting to find a final location to move their families to in the city. Others were in town to work temporarily in order to earn the money needed to implement their property and return to life in the village.

This flow of emigration, which began in the late nineteenth and early twentieth century, experienced a growing trend, and the climax was reached in the '50s, '60s and '70s, years during which most of Pietracupa's inhabitants moved permanently to Rome. The reasons for emigration elsewhere, and particularly to Rome, were primarily economic and social ones. In the next chapter on migration, the topic will be addressed in more details.

The first of Pietracupa's inhabitants to come to Rome found job opportunities, especially, as laborers at the many stables in the capital, or as locksmiths, or at construction companies and railways, or in the craft sector as helpers to tailors, barbers, shoemakers, and so on.

The labor market of that time demanded laborers who were able to train and clean horses, mules, donkeys and their wagons and carriages, since the whole transport sector of citizens, things or people was run by private companies such as Fattori / Montani, Salviati , Paolucci, who offered chances of jobs at low wages.

In old photos you can see the famous tram pulled by horses, carriages for tourists, and wagons with barrels for the transport of wine and oil that ensured the mobility of goods and people. So that the worker who was familiar with animal care, like peasants from Molise and Abruzzo, was preferred to be employed by the companies that had the "business" of city transport. Equipped stables were located in some strategic areas of the city, such as St. Peter, St. John, Trastevere, Via Flaminia. In these districts gravitated workers of the sector, who often were allowed to sleep in rooms obtained from the same stables.

The advent of motor vehicles and the allocation to municipalities for the management of local public transport (taxis and municipal firms), allowed many of the old Pietracupa's people, former grooms, in possession of drivers licenses to be the first recipients of the licenses for the service of taxis offered for sale by the Town Council. And then they had the opportunity to become part of the family of so-called *tassinari* (taxi drivers).

This is the reason why many of the operators of Roman taxis are Molisani or come from families of Molise. It must be noted, however, that many preferred to continue to work on Roman tourist carriages, often immortalized in the photos of tourists all over the world.

Uncle John Del Monaco and Michelel Sardella, were two famous conductors of Roman carriages also interviewed by several newspapers of international circulation. I have a friendly and affectionate personal memory of both of them. Every time I had the chance to see them at the Pincio or Piazza Venezia, they always used to greet me with a joke in Pietracupa's slang, by which they wanted to remind me of our common origins of Molise.

Modern civilization is trying to get rid of the carriages, an image of a world considered outdated and cruel to animals, especially on the part of the Association of Animal Rights activists who protested openly against the mayors of cities that offer tourists that kind of service. In New York, Mayor Bloomberg decided to remove carriages and coachmen from Central Park, and the same thing is happening in Rome.

Personally I do not agree with these decisions, and I hope that Mayor Marino of Rome and the new mayor of New York, the Italian-American Bill De Blasio, will make sure to find a solution that protects the integrity of the animals and the pursuit of romantic Roman and New York carriages. Both are a symbol of a bygone era, but tourists from all over the world wish to find them during their holidays in Rome or New York.

Another area to which the grooms were recycled after the advent of the motor vehicles, was the field of housing and maintenance of private cars, the so-called "garages". Since the '50s and' 60s, with the accelerated implementation of the production and sale of cars, perceived by citizens as an indispensable asset, there was also the development of the motorized maintenance industry. So the old grooms from Abruzzo and Molise changed the old stables and converted them into modern garages.

Touring around Rome, you can easily meet managers of garages from Abruzzo and Molise, especially in districts of Trieste, Salario, St. Giovanni, San Pietro. I haven't done statistical research to quantify the phenomenon among the members of Pietracupa's community. I can only say that many children and grandchildren of those who first started these activities, are currently employed in the same industry. Pietracupa's community in charge of taxis and management is very numerous and respected by all other colleagues. Particular mention should be made about the first of Pietracupa's people who emigrated to Rome. And on the way, I might point out some people I got to know who were the precursors and councilors of their countrymen who later joined them in the city: Uncle Peppino and Uncle Emilio Porchetta, Uncle Peppino Durante, Uncle Romolo Porchetta, Celestino Camillo, Uncle Felice Meddione, Uncle Masella, Uncle Alfredo Santilli, Uncle Dionisio Delmonaco, Vincenzo Di Sarro, and many others.

Pietracupa's coach drivers in Rome

Pietracupa's coach driver in the period of elections

Camillo and Porchetta family with the taxi

Pietracupa's taxi drivers on vacation

-PIETRACUPA: THE RETURN OF VETERANS, THE REFERENDUM, ELECTIONS

Once the dark years of the war ended, the life of Pietracupa's inhabitants began to resume its normal course. All men that had been called to war started to return home: those who came from the Italian front, those from the Russian front, and those from German concentration camps in which 650,000 military dissenters had been held.

Each of them came back with his own story, with his own sufferings, but with the joy of having escaped death and being able to embrace their loved ones again.

Each arrival was immediately announced to local people with the classic "door-to-door", and it was a joy to meet the friend or relative who you could finally hug again after years of separation.

At that time I was six / seven years of age, so it was the first time I met some people that I had never seen before. They soon become family, as well as countrymen and close friends.

Among these I remember Celestino and Patrizio Di Sarro, Uncle Aldo Ferri, Giggetto Grande, Uncle Francesco Grande, Uncle Mario Di Iorio, Uncle Michele Vanga and many other of Pietracupa's people.

In particular, the return of **Uncle Francesco Grande** was greeted with a big party for all of us of Vico I ° S. Anna, and I have a pleasant memory of it.Uncle Francesco, after the celebration dinner held for his return, **took the violin** and started to play songs of popular music.

I am a lover of classical music and, every time I go to a violin concert, I remember that picture of Uncle Francesco with his instrument, and all of us there to listen to him in that stony and steep Pietracupa's alley on a warm summer evening.

Uncle Francesco, on that occasion, took in the alley again that atmosphere of calm after the storm by Leopardi (great Italian Poet). Every veteran, once back in the village, resumed full activities interrupted at the moment of leaving for the front.

75

-The referendum, elections

In the referendum year, Pietracupa had a population of about one thousand five hundred inhabitants. Public facilities were the city hall, the municipal school, the two Catholic churches, a post office, the town florist, a tobacconist, five cellars with access available only to adult men. Workers employed in public / religious facilities were five (town clerk, municipal guard, forest guard, warden, municipal messenger, janitor, sacristan, midwife, with the municipal guard covering three roles by himself). To these employees you have to add a local doctor, **Dr. Corrado Fraraccio,** born in S. Pietro in Valle, who lived with his family in the house owned by the family Di Risio.

I have not been able to find data relating to the results of the referendum and the elections for the Constituent Assembly of 1946 in the town of Pietracupa. So I have no knowledge of political inclinations of citizenship in that year and following ones.

I can only say that the village participated with great interest in the constitutional and political events of 1946, as well as the years to follow.

One thing is certain: by their nature, Pietracupa's people are and were fierce connoisseurs of politics. Even today, in the square facing Bar La Morgia, you can attend interesting political debates.

In the year 1946, my father took some days off to come to the village to raise awareness among his neighbors and ask them to vote for the Republic and for socialist candidates during the referendum held in June. I missed this particular concerning my father, but a dear old friend from Pietracupa reminded me by saying: *I always remember your father when in 1946 he came to Pietracupa to talk about socialism, of human equality and social justice; his words opened new spaces and new ideas of life to me who was a young boy and had never heard of socialism in the years of the fascist regime.*

Also, in the subsequent voting policies of April 1948, I remember the activism of many Pietracupa inhabitants who would sponsor one party or another.

These people would go around the village, painting on the walls the tricolor flame of Italian MSI, formed in December 1946 by some veterans of the Republic of Salo. Nevertheless, in the rest of Italy, the air of freedom and democracy blew, even if on some occasions there were incidents of political intolerance.

A particular importance must be given to the municipal elections which were held in the village to elect the mayor. On these occasions,

76

local frictions sometimes prevailed on the moderation of political debate and, considering the fierce character of Pietracupa's people, over the years the municipal elections have had the characteristics of real battles that ignited the minds of the contenders in the field, causing sometimes the loss of some old friends.

War memorial

78

-THE MAYORS OF PIETRACUPA FROM 1918 TO 2013

In the main hall of the current offices of the City of Pietracupa is shown a picture with all the names of the Podesta and Auditors who have been elected and followed each other from 1918 to 2013, as listed below. The municipal seat of these mayors initially was located in Via Pozzo Nuovo, but was later moved to Via San Rocco, and is currently located at the multi-building in Via del Casaleno, which also includes the doctor's office, an area pharmaceutical office, and the headquarters of the post office.

Belisario Del Monaco	1918 - 1920	Mario Durante	1960 - 1964
Cosmo Durante	1920 - 1925	Antonio Durante	1964 - 1970
Silvio Cirese	1925 - 1927	Antonio Durante	1970 - 1975
Silvio Cirese	1927 - 1937	Angelo Gallo	1975 - 1980
Antonio Carnevale	1937 - 1942	Mario Durante	1980 - 1985
Nicola Portone	1943 - 1944	Felice Risio	1985 - 1990
Nicola Portone	1944 - 1945	Nicola Porchetta	1990 - 1995
Domenico Saliola	1945 - 1951	Mario Durante	1995 - 1999
Pasqualino Saliola	1951 - 1953	Felice Risio	1999 - 2004
Guerrino Carnevale	1953 - 1956	Felice Risio	2004 - 2009
Michelino Delmonaco	1956 - 1960	Camillo Santilli	2009 - 2015

I personally met many of these fifteen mayors / podestà of Pietracupa and I enjoyed respectful friendships with the oldest because many of them were the same age of my father.

With the youngest, as it happens in small villages, relationships with the mayor are direct and familiar, although sometimes this can cause a difference of opinion between the mayor, as a representative and defender of the general interests of the community, and the individual citizen.

But this is a common constant in all parts of the world, and the ability of a mayor is in his skill to interpret the basic needs of citizens and strive to resolve them in the general interest of the community.

In this book, while **abstaining from making political and management judgments** on the work of the mandate entrusted to them over the years, I wanted to highlight **the human aspects** that have resulted from the relationships and contacts I had with them as a citizen belonging to Pietracupa's community.

I met **Uncle Belisario Del Monaco** in the '40s. Often he would come to visit his daughter Adelaide in Via Vico I ° S. Anna. He was an old man of fine physique, very kind and affectionate. His son Palmerino was a close friend of my father and, as I have already mentioned, at that time I would go to their house at Casalotto to get milk for my brother. When Uncle Belisario went to his daughter's house, he was surrounded by all his grandchildren who affectionately cuddled their elderly grandfather. He died on October 29, 1945, at age 85.

The teacher Silvio Cirese, was a very authoritarian and charismatic figure both in his ways and in his behavior because he was a primary school teacher for several generations of Pietracupa's people. Behind his austere bearing, you could see a lively figure of an old affectionate man towards his last two small grandchildren, Felice and Vittorio.

I remember an anecdote that took place between him, already old, and Uncle Antony Di Iorio, his night assistant, who slept in a house nearby his. The agreement between the two was that the teacher Cirese would call his assistant in case of need with a kind of cowbell. One night, the teacher wanted to test whether the system was working, so he triggered the cowbell. The result was that Uncle Antony, in his underwear, immediately rushed out at the first peal finding, as a prize for his quick response, a bottle of wine.

Uncle Antonio Carnevale had the house in Via degli Orti. During the '40s and '50s he had just opened a tailor shop in Via Vico I ° S. Anna, where there is now the tobacconist of Osvaldo La Guardia.

Uncle Antonio trained many of Pietracupa's young tailors. But his shop was also a meeting place for friends and clients who would create a nice atmosphere of entertainment. He was very tall, somewhat austere and wiry, like the American President Abraham Lincoln. I remember his wife and little daughter Pasqualina living in the family house (later bought by the owners of the oven FLO. CAR.) just in front of my father's former cellar.

In the '50s / '60s both of them emigrated to Canada and returned to sell some property damaged by an earthquake. His brother, for a few years managed the post office, then relocated to Casalotto. Another brother, father of Mario and Franco, was headmaster at a secondary school in Rome.

The teacher, Nicola Portone, taught for many years in the town of Pietracupa. I have no personal memories of him, but my father

80

was his pupil in primary school and told me about him in a very positive way, both because of his educational quality and for his humanity towards pupils and in general with regard to Pietracupa's population.

 He was the first Mayor of Pietracupa to mark the transition from the institutional figure of Podesta, during the Fascist era, to that of Mayor in the Fascist era. I was told by some people that, during the German occupation in Pietracupa, some telephone lines installed in the village were the subject of an alleged anti-German attack by some villagers. The commander of the garrison wanted to issue the order of "retaliation" in respect to the population. But the resolute and qualified intervention of Teacher Portone stopped the Commander from issuing that order.

The citizens and the City of Pietracupa, at his death, resolved to name a town square in his name, in memory of his merits, that of a mayor and a teacher as well.

 Uncle Domenico Saliola was a close friend of my father. Everyone in town called him the "Old Mayor". He was a witty man and could always advise you on any problem of a practical nature. Uncle Domenico, a widower, emigrated to America and remarried there with a Pietracupa woman. He spent his last years of life in the village and now rests in the cemetery.

I met **Pasqualino Saliola**, son of Uncle Domenico, rooting for him and for the legendary Pietracupa football club. He married in 1953 and moved to America. In 1965, on my first trip to the USA, I visited him and we both recalled the times spent in the village. Pasqualino, now retired, was a very active young man and qualified in his professional career as a surveyor for American companies.

 Uncle Guerrino Carnevale, was one of the most representative and productive men after the war. He managed for many years the "tavern" in Via Trento, the main meeting place in the village where they played cards, ate roasted fava beans and, between one glass of wine and another, properly diluted with water, the patrons were spending their free time.

 He was a skilled communicator and a reference point for advice and help of various kinds. He had a family of four daughters and two sons. But I will have to talk about Uncle Guerrino and his family again in a following chapter because he and my father were close and sincere friends. He remains a very charismatic character, both in Pietracupa and in America, where he later emigrated.

The master Michelino Delmonaco, was the brother of parish priest Don Manfredo, and teacher at Pietracupa's school in via San Rocco, located just near their homes. All his old pupils remember the teacher Michelino with great respect and gratitude. In the summer of 1950, I was a student of teacher Delmonaco for a month. I consider him a very friendly and able teacher.

The brothers Mario and Antonio Durante were part of my friends "extralocal students" group, whom I will discuss later. Their cousin Elena was also part of the group. She was a sweet and affectionate girl who died at a young age, with the great regret of us, all her friends. From 1960-1985 Mario and Antonio were elected 5 times as mayors of Pietracupa - for a total of **25 years of management** in this municipality.

Mario was also elected Councilor for Molise Province and President of the Mountain Community. He had a law degree and a propensity for regional political activities, which for many years was in the hands of the DC. Pietracupa was the seat of his hard core fans, and people say many of his friends there were helped to find the longed-for positions in some public institutions of Molise. Obviously, he could not please all the aspiring candidates, so someone had to be excluded. The disappointment and resentment of some has persisted for a long time.

The arrival of Mario and Antonio in the village was always accompanied by a large retinue of friends and admirers who were competing to be noticed by them. But this was not just a habit of those years; even now the retinue with politicians and the demands for jobs are always in vogue.

My relationship with Mario and Antonio was always one of great respect and great cordiality. Mario died some years ago and he rests in the cemetery of the village.

Angelo Gallo died very young because of a car accident that happened near the Motel Roberto (now Villa d'Evoli), on the road to Campobasso. His death left heartbroken not only his family, but also the many friends who respected and loved him. One of Angelo's brothers worked in the same company where I worked in Rome, and Angelo always sent his greetings. He was a very polite person. I always remember, when Fr. Orlando gave me the news of his death, I felt sincere sorrow.

Felice Di Risio lived, and still lives, in the family residence in Via Vico I ° S. Anna, just in front of my house. His parents were close friends of my family. I always remember Felice's dogs and his love for hunting. He had a very creative mind. Often we would meet in Rome in his first year of University at the Faculty of Law. I remember one day in early summer we went to the sea, but Felice had forgotten his swimming trunks; he went swimming half naked because of the great heat. Another chance encounter I had with him was in Milan during a National Congress. He was with his wife Adriana and, with great fluency and youthful behavior, they rode their two bikes to get around Milan. He is still a great admirer of the singer Adriano Celentano and mimics very well his gestures and voice. He is a very determined person. Felice has always told me that he loves his home region and his native region, and that he has never wanted to leave them; in these places he finds the serenity and the pleasure of living that big cities do not offer him. His choice is also very appreciated by his wife Adriana.

Nicola Porchetta is an old friend from my younger years. I met him during football games in the famous football field Casarino. His and my families have always respected each other, as it should be in a community of people that you have known for years. Nicola is a surveyor, lives in Campobasso and was also a trainer of the team of that city, when the Campobasso football team played in "Series B" of the Italian League.

His sister Felicia lives in Rome; but at Pietracupa she lives right near my house, so when Nicola comes to visit his sister, it is nice to have a chat about how life is going. The nice thing about this small village is the perpetuation of traditions and respect between families, so my kids are always in contact with Alfredo, son of Felicia, armed with a strong friendship initiated as children.

Camillo Santilli is the "last but not least" of this series of the mayors of Pietracupa, being the mayor currently in office. His house is right in front of mine, in General Durante and, during the summer, the daily meetings with Camillo, his gracious wife and his family, are nice occasions to exchange opinions on many current topics. This proximity to our home, unfortunately for him, forces the current mayor to withstand my complaints on some disruption of the moment. But, it is also gratified by my praise for the initiatives of his good management.

A private memory of the friendly relationship that existed between my father and his father's family is confirmed by the following anecdote: Uncle Michelino and Aunt Ida, Camillo's parents, ran a renowned pastry shop in Boiano. My father, every time we returned to the village,diverted to Boiano - not only to greet his old friend from Pietracupa, but also to give us children a taste of the sweets, always on display in their pastry shop.

From the list of Pietracupa's Mayors I have not commented on the figure of **Cosmo Durante** because, honestly, I have no knowledge of his management and I have no immediate memories. I can only say that, having been Pietracupa's Mayor / Podesta in the period from 1920 until 1925, undoubtedly he managed the City in very difficult years. These are characterized by the transition from an authoritarian regime to a democratic one (October 24, 1922 march on Rome). So I assume that he had optimal management capabilities to safeguard the interests of Pietracupa's citizens.

I conclude by stating, for the record, that in 2009 **Giovanni Guglielmi** was elected Mayor and, after a period of management of **the Prefectural Commissioner,** the current mayor in office was elected.

At the end of this topic, I can affirm that the Pietracupa of the '40s, even if present in a nostalgic way in the memories of those who lived in the village, had poor roads, sanitation was absent, and insufficient cultural activities. But that Pietracupa no longer exists. Now it is a pleasant village that is visited by tourists and this is attributed not only to the community, but also to the commitment of all these mayors who have contributed over the years to achieve this goal, often with few resources available and facing the difficulties that occurred during the years of their management.

Pietracupa is a little gem that must be maintained. The culture, beautiful scenery and historical treasures and other resources must taken advantage of. Proceeds could be invested in new jobs with the influx of tourists and vacationers.

On this subject, I can't fail to mention the destruction of the "Road Inspector's House" on the via nova, which left the nearby "well" as a mere relic in the middle of an intersection regulated by neglected traffic signs. I don't know which administration ordered the demolition of the roadhouse, but it was a wrong decision.

That little roadhouse was the last image of Pietracupa that our emigrants set in their minds before leaving the village. It was the site of hugs, tears, hopes for their return, even when we left with the cart and horse. It was also the natural shelter for the peasants to rest when returning from the fields.

When, at the time of the road works, I found out that the roadhouse was to be demolished, I went to Campobasso Local Authority-Arts and Entertainment department to try to stop the destruction. But it was too late.

Similarly, the well on the via nova was the meeting point of our grandmothers who drew water for drinking. It was a symbol of the village even during threshing, made within walking distance. It is now reduced to a ridiculous ruin.

I do not think it would take huge investments to give that site a decent accommodation. These things should not happen again. We must be careful to ensure that all the artistic and cultural heritage of Pietracupa is safeguarded and preserved.

Westfield Mayor's bureau - Town twinned with Pietracupa

Road Inspector's house on via nova

Well on via nova

-THE POSTWAR IN PIETRACUPA: THE FAMILY AND COUNTRY LIFE

Pietracupa's families came, for the majority, from a patriarchal and peasant tradition. The family was made up by the head of the family; all components (both male and female) followed his orders. The goals were the maintenance and management of the house and the farm, the maintenance and managing of agricultural property or rented plots, the care of livestock, the processing and sale of crops and livestock, the needs of individual family members (clothing, cigarettes, leisure, etc.) and, not least, the institution of the dowry for the daughters.

The family number was always large and ranged between 3 and 10. The reason why this birth rate was so high is both for environmental reasons (long winters, lack of social structures and diversion), as well as for the logical reasons related to the need of manpower for the land, that the fascist regime preached and implemented with subsidies to large families.

In the absence of advanced technology, farmers were the main element that could support the national economy with high agricultural yields at low cost, especially in small southern villages. The level of education was low; there was a latent illiteracy because the majority of the boys had to go to work in the countryside or tend the sheep. Hunger was great, especially in large families. But it was possible to feed themselves with simple foods such as bread, corn flour pizza (*pizza gandigne*), *sagne*, eggs, milk, cheese, *caciova* (egg and cheese meatballs), salad and cucumbers (*tortarelle*).

 The meat of veal was unknown, pork or lamb or sheep were rare commodities. Brawn / headcheese, sausages and lamb chops were bartered or sold to third parties in commercial activities; the little left over was eaten on special occasions such as threshing, plowing, harvesting, and so on. Only during the festivities of Christmas and Easter was it possible to eat meat and some sweets (*fiadone, pastiera*, etc.). The same happened for the festivities of **St. Anne (July 26th) and St. Anthony and St. Gregory (September 11th)**.

Marriages between young people followed a rigid procedural protocol. Generally the affections would be present since the school years. A practical example is the ritual of palm that the young man offered to his favorite on the Sunday before Easter. This kind gesture

87

alerted the family and the girl to the sympathies of the young man. So intense activity of the two families, committed to address the seriousness of the youth and the economic conditions and prospects of life that he could offer to the girl, would begin.

Judgment was required from all members of the family, including relatives and close friends. It is obvious that, if the young lover qualified or lived in, or was about to leave for America, or had sufficient material possessions in his family, the chance to win the hand of the girl was greater. The final consensus formally was expressed by the girl. But if her father did not agree, it was difficult for the marriage to occur.

Another important aspect that characterized the lives of residents in the village was linked to the social differences between the various members of Pietracupa's families. Obviously, as in all areas of the south, within Pietracupa's one thousand five hundred inhabitants, social differences were very obvious and known by everybody.

The hierarchical levels that distinguished these differences were essentially three: the first level belonged to the elders of the village (army officers, senior civil servants, professors, teachers, judges and canons); to the second level belonged the upper middle classes (merchants, landowners, artisans and so on); to the third level belonged the farmers who worked their own and others land and were mostly semi-illiterate.

Those belonging to the first level were always revered by the nickname of "Don". Those belonging to the second level were revered the same, but without "Don", for the chance to lend money or offer job opportunities to those of the third level, which were the poorest and the most numerous.

However there was a certain even positive chain of interrelationships between these three social levels of people belonging to the same village. After all, regional roots were the basis that united them.

We have to note that, even in this twenty-first century there are castes as then. But the phenomenon is more nuanced in the context of a more culturally aware society and in a globalized and economically more advanced world.

If we take for comparison the story of black **citizens in the United States,** migrants from African countries of today, it is clear that, unfortunately, differences still exist, although from a different point of view.

The modest peasant houses consisted of a few rooms. So in large families living spaces were insufficient to ensure privacy. The houses were built with stone walls, sloping roofs and wooden beams covered with tiles. They generally held between one / two bedrooms for all members of the household (ranging from 4 to 15 people), a kitchen with a fireplace with the inevitable cauldron (*r 'quittrille*) to allow for the preparation of food for family and herds, a shelf for the resting of the water basin (*tina*), and the oven to bake bread. The decorations which complemented the ornament of the house were perfectly similar to those on display in **Pietracupa's peasant museum**.

The mattress was of wool in more affluent families or of leaves of maize or straw in the poorest households. Annexed to the house there were stables or cellars for the shelter of animals and for the storage of grain, tools and everything else necessary for agricultural activities, which were the main resources for the sustenance of the family. The luckiest farmers had available even modest accommodation buildings in the village, with an adjoining yard, used for animal shelter and for every kind of work. Often, these houses were permanently inhabited by families of "*parzenauli*" who worked the land for the rightful owner, according to the customs in force at that time. **Other peasants** worked the lands of others with a lease. And then there were seasonal or daily workers, required only as needed, who, especially in the summer, emigrated to nearby Puglia as seasonal workers, sleeping outdoors or in makeshift shelters.

The lack of running or spring water was a huge handicap for the inhabitants. Generally this lack of water was provided for by artificial wells made inside the houses or by putting *tina* (copper basin) under the channels of drainage of the roof on rainy days.

Drinking or cooking water was supplied by **five public wells of spring water**, but they were far away from the village. These wells were: San Pietro pit, fountain Mastro Liberto pit, pit Serra Graffia, and pit Fontraselva. The latter was the closest to the village and was most often used by the women, who came with the classic "*tina*" resting on the "*spara*" (the round cloths wrapped on the head) and the bucket with rope, to draw water.

Even the well on the via nova was used for its proximity to the village. But the potability of its water was questionable. There was, then, the Well to the canton, whose water was drinkable; but this well was privately owned by Uncle Pietro Santilli. Uncle Pietro, on request, granted people access to his well. But if someone took the water without his permission, he forced him to throw the water back into the well.

The water wells near the village had also a social and meeting function for adult women. Without considering fatigue, it was a relaxing time because they could interact with other women waiting their turn. Even for young girls it was a moment to relax, with the addition of a few moments of pleasure when some young suitor, with mock casualty, met his favorite girl on the way back and exchanged some youthful chatter full of implied proposals about engagement and marriage. The following poem, recalls meetings at Pietracupa's wells, and is a tribute to those delicate girls, now grandmothers, that went to draw water and inspired those lines.

Women at the well

Washing of the face and hands was done in the "service bath" existing in every house, consisting of an iron structure with a basin resting in the circle of support; on the bottom shelf was a pitcher for water, and in the side soap dish was placed a soap piece (such as Marseille) which was used for laundry, often homemade.

I have a special memory of the bath to which my mother, in the summer months, subjected my brother and me to as kids, in our well "fonte di sorice" in open country. She used to fill the tubs with water from the well, let it warm in the sun, and began to wash us throwing buckets of water over our heads.

90

The bath was always followed by a hearty breakfast and prolonged exposure to the sun. Those baths inside the tubs of "Fonte Sorge", with all the greenery around and the pleasure of genuine food, are a fond part of my childhood memories.

Toilets were totally absent both in country houses and in countryside farms, due to the lack of water and municipal sewers into homes. Therefore stables and outdoor places were stations for the needs for both men and women. However, in the case of sick at home or the very elderly or in extreme weather conditions, each family had a chamber pot (urinal) for pressing needs.

In the village there was a tacit agreement between the men where to go for their outdoor needs. The places, as far as I remember, were behind the church of San Gregorio, in the Morgia inside the cave above the church, near the bell tower, along the ditch Aia del Piano, near the grove of Canton and then, when in the countryside, anywhere it was possible. Even the boys and girls of primary school, were organized, "motu proprio", to go during the break hour in a backyard near the school, with another boy or a girl to act as guardian.

Many times, this caused embarrassing situations, especially with the use of the chamber pot. In one case, some careless person threw the waste out of the window, without paying attention to the unsuspecting passerby, who was swamped by the contents of that container. I remember a lady, that one morning had been drenched by the chamber pot of an alleged senior guilty, hurriedly walking down the street screaming, *r 'pissed de r' vicchi, piuzza* ("*urine of old people smells bad!*"). Another time one careless man, going home a bit tipsy at a late hour, mistook the boot of his sleeping wife for a chamber pot and filled it with his urine. Awake in the morning, the cries of his wife could be heard a mile away.

In Rome in the '40s, towering along the streets were the famous urinals, which were later removed. But it had been the custom of some to urinate on the corners of the streets or on the facades of building and that no longer happens.

The alternating of seasons marked the daily work of the farmers, according to the cycles of nature (plowing, harvesting, grape harvest etc.).

The use of money was considered rare and, in most cases, there was barter; e.g., a sack of wheat, eggs, corn, cheese in exchange for labor, exchange of products and also in the case of debts to compensate.

91

When bartering, people had to be precise. I remember seeing a lively discussion of a lady who said to another: *"yesterday I gave you a big egg, and now you're returning to me a small egg; you can't, you've got to give me two small eggs"*.

As mentioned previously, the liveliest moments of the day in the village were the morning and the evening, when the stony, rough and dirty streets became animated with farmers on their way to and from the fields, the animals which were taken to graze, or pigs and chickens that scratched the streets. The alleys were filled with people speaking of the activities of the day, of their family problems; sometimes disputes flared up, especially due to problems of proximity.

The techniques of rural work were **archaic**. Plowing fields, seeding, harvesting, threshing, processing of corn, grapes and other fruits of the earth were performed with the use of human strength and the use of animals and simple tools appropriate to a primordial working system.

The grain, then, was transported with the so called "cars" (donkeys, mules and horses) to the mills of Torella, Castropignano or Bagnoli, also chosen because the second manager of the mill turned a blind eye to the legal limit of grain that was ground up ("storage grain").

The state of the weather in the different seasons was another factor that influenced the abundance or the shortage of products from the earth. **This country world**, even in the midst of so much hard work, so many difficulties and so much poverty, had its own even ethical charm. The day of wheat harvest, which was carried out in the courtyard, was an important day. The patriarch of the family organized the work by calling to work all the members of his home and friends, generally neighbors or relatives.

Sheaves of grain were threshed in the farmyard and the women of the family, at home or on the farm, would prepare a hearty meal for the participants; e.g., sagne, sauce, sausage, caciova, fresh bread and wine. The wine never failed to quench the workers' thirst, as it was placed in a flask and stored in a clay pot hanging from a rope so it was always fresh.

In the evening, when the bags of grain were set aside, a light of joy gleamed in the eyes of all the participants. I was a guest / spectator at some of these activities of threshing, and I got a feeling of deep inner joy. I remember an old uncle who, at the end of the work, looking at his bags of wheat, turned his eyes to heaven and thanked the Lord for giving him an abundant harvest for that year too.

The atmosphere of those afternoons in the countryside, the intensity of the colors of nature, the red sky at sunset, the gestures and voices of farmers have made me understand why many famous painters or poets have praised in verse or on their palettes **the beauty of that world.** And especially why many farmers never wanted to leave their homes and their land, despite living in the midst of many difficulties.

The **processing of corn** (*scarfugliare*) was another manual activity aimed at obtaining the final product, corn flour, which was widely used for household nutrition and even for animals. For economic reasons, the "scarfugliatura" was done in the evening after dinner by candlelight and all the relatives and friends of the country would help. They then, in turn, invited one another to perform in later times, the same operation on their own *"granoni"*. But the **"scarfugliatura" evening** was enjoyable. Participants sat in a circle or scattered around and began to sing or tell funny stories of the past.

It was also the occasion for some boyfriend (or some pretender boyfriend) to stay close to his "promised" and search through the opaque lights of candles, to touch or hold hands with his "girlfriend". I was told of a young man who, during the scarfugliatura, following an accidental shutdown of the candles, took advantage of the favorable moment to try to hold hands with his girlfriend, who was sitting between him and her mother. But the mother was faster than the youth, and swapped places with her daughter - and so was the recipient of the gentle caress of the future son in law! The unsuspecting youth, when the light of the candles was restored, noticed the exchange and, red with shame, vanished like lightening. It took a few weeks to clarify the problem and let peace return to the boyfriend and his loved one.

Corn leaves

Peasant community in'40s

These stories seem trivial, but they are full of important rules of life and morality in force then. **The grape harvest** was the last seasonal effort before the cold winter. The harvest is a symbol of abundance for the farmer. In Pietracupa it was performed using archaic but effective and genuine systems; the final act was completed by pressing the grapes barefoot in vats and the wine was then deposited in the barrels.

Sharing the taste of the new wine with all the friends and participants in the harvest was an indispensable act for every peasant, as a good omen to celebrate the event. And in every street in Pietracupa it was possible to breathe in the musty smell of the grape. The rite of the harvest, dear to God Bacchus and chanted by the ancient Romans, is still celebrated by Pietracupa's community in October, with the so-called "Grape Festival", though agricultural lands intended for vineyards are only marginal compared to the past.

Peasant life in '50s – The goatskin of new wine

Peasant life – grazing

Girl of south

SOUTHERN GIRL

I watch you in the distance with the basin
of water on your head, girl of South,
delicate flower, born between stone houses
and rocky roads grading downstream.

Advance solemnly, softly, immersed
in your thoughts full of youthful dreams and expectations.

I would like to stop you, talk to you, offer you a flower,
but the sun is at sunset
and my shyness is great.

You walk beside me silent and proud,
Smile at me and disappear into the horizon
of incipient evening.

Good luck, girl of the South, in this harsh and barren land,
among these rude and strong people,
you can see that ray of moon
lighting your way to a world of love.

Peasant life of 50s – Tomato sauce in the sun and "ceppe" to make the fires

Peasant life – Transport by oxen

Peasant life – The food in the "square wooden basket"

Peasant life – Working in the fields

98

Peasant life – The threshing in S. Gregorio

-THE ARTISANS OF PIETRACUPA

The working activities of the inhabitants of Pietracupa were not only directed to the care of the fields and the products of the land. There were a fair number of artisans who performed professional activities, necessary to provide all the services needed for the life of the community itself; e.g., the barber, the shoemaker, the mason, the "pinciaro", the blacksmith, the butcher, the pastry-cook, the tailor, etc. The people who were doing the crafts were very well prepared; professions were handed down from father to son, as well as among relatives and friends.

Every young person in the village aspired to go to one of these masters to learn a trade, with the prospect of performing some day the same activity either at home or elsewhere. Between the 1940s and early 1950s, there were a large number of artisans who worked continuously in the village, before the advent of the great exodus of the '50s, '60s and part of the '70s. The exodus, in some ways, helped many of these workers, facilitated by their profession, to find job opportunities in host countries.

For the record, I must add that many of these artisans were not unanimous in giving all good opinions about some of their old masters; not because of their skills, but for the relationship of subordination they wanted to impose on their students, using them in other activities not relevant to the job they had to teach them. On this last point I just want to add that the disagreements are to be evaluated in relation to the uses, the customs of the period and the lack of appropriate legislation on apprenticeship.

The professions and the artisans in the village, in the early '50s, according to my memories of that time, were distributed as follows:

Barbers: Uncle Domenico Carrelli, Uncle Alessandro di Fonzo, Palmerino Delmonaco, Ninetto Baron;

Shoemakers: Pietrangelo Di Iorio with his assistant Giuseppe Santilli, Pasquale Lombardi, Giovanni Rompicone, Uncle Arturo Vanga, Uncle Umberto Festa, Nicola Santoro, Uncle Corradino Delmonaco; Oreste Carnevale, Vincenzo Ciavarro;

Tailors: Antonio Carnevale, Uncle Mario Di Iorio, Uncle Giovanni Cacchione, Renato Di Sarro, Giovanni Di Sarro, Domenico Festa, Giuseppe Grande, Uncle Giuseppe Di Iorio and Vincenzo Di Iorio, Michele Saliola, Giuseppe Barone, Giovanni Saliola, Gennaro Delmonaco;

100

Joiners: Remo and Patrizio Di Sarro, Uncle Domenico Di Sarro, Pietro and Nicola Saliola, Giuseppe Santilli, Renato Guglielmi, Antonio Ciavari, Giuseppe Di Iorio;

Blacksmiths: Angelotto Festa, Uncle Angelo Porchetta;

Butchers: Felice and Romolo Santilli, Uncle Nicola Di Sarro, Americo Santilli, Pasquale Camillo;

Workers at the kiln: (**Pinciari**) Uncle Giuseppe Grande and children, Uncle Francesco Grande;

Pastry cooks: Filippo Cacchione, Vincenzo Cacchione Jr. , Filiberto and Giovanni Delmonaco;

Masons: Uncle Antonio Cacchione, Graziano Brunetti, Uncle Giuseppe Di Sarro, Domenico Di Iorio;

Restaurateurs: Uncle Guerrino Carnevale, Uncle Peppino Patrizio, Uncle Vincent Cacchione, Uncle Antonio Guglielmi, Uncle Alessandro Di Fonzo, Americo Santilli;

Miller: Pasquale "Marcellina".

In the summers I spent in Pietracupa I had the pleasure of spending some of my time with many of these artisans. They were and are special people, **very skilled in their craft**. I can say that they were an irreplaceable resource for the needs of the community.

Often during the summer, after finishing my commitments for daily study, I would go to their shops. It was always interesting to observe and get news on their work. I decided also to include in the book the human aspects and character of some of these people who, in a certain sense, with their activity, characterized the life of the inhabitants of Pietracupa in the postwar years.

Uncle Domenico Carrelli, called "**Cucciotto**" was my first barber in Pietracupa. He can be considered a real institution for the village during those years.Going to Uncle Cucciotto was like going to a great hairdresser and meeting a variety of people who, with their colorful stories, gave the place a touch of liveliness. Uncle Cucciotto emigrated with his family to the USA and never came back to Italy.

Palmerino Delmonaco had only a short period of employment in Pietracupa; then he went to Milan and later he was established in Rome, where he opened a large barbershop in Via Urbana, in the heart of the city, which is currently run by his sons. Sometimes I went to his shop, where a photo of Pietracupa would tower. Among the customers of his shop there are many important people in the field of culture and politics.

Uncle Alessandro Di Fonzo was the owner of a barbershop in Via Garibaldi, inside which he had installed, together with all the tools of the trade, a chair / armchair brought with him to Italy from the USA, where he had stayed and worked for many years. A funny anecdote of the importance that this chair had in Pietracupa's collective imagination, was that of a patron from the country speaking to a somewhat bearded elderly old lady; she said to her: *Zia Rosa, và da z' lessandro che te mette n'coppa la seggia pelitrona ("Aunt Rosa, go to Uncle Alessandro that puts you on the armchair".).*

Uncle Alexander also worked with the parish priest for the Sunday services, singing religious songs; his modulated voice and his facial expressions were a show during religious services. In adulthood, I made Uncle Alexander forgive all the times that, as a child, I would throw from the top of the square of Orti, some small stone onto the roof of his shop in order to listen to his verbal reactions according to his singing tone.

Ninetto Barone was the last barber of the village. He carried out this activity until the year 2000, after which he stopped working. Pietracupa hasn't had any barbers since then. We hope that the new hair salon, recently opened, can meet the needs of men too.

Ninetto is a man of high morals and educated, who never refused to come to my father's house to cut his hair and beard when my father became old. His manner was always one of great kindness and respect toward others.

Uncle Pietrangelo Di Iorio owned a shop for the production of new shoes and the repair of old shoes. His shop was always well stocked with leather uppers and all that was necessary for the production of leather shoes. Uncle Pietrangelo had a robust physical structure, black hair styled as Rudolph Valentino, and he was always very helpful. Over the workshop, he had a house where he lived with his wife and two daughters Luisa and Rosaria. The first daughter later married his collaborator **Giuseppe Santilli,** who moved to Rome and started working at the municipal company AMA. Peppino, in his spare time, never

Cobblers

Butcher

Butcher Pasquale

Carpenter

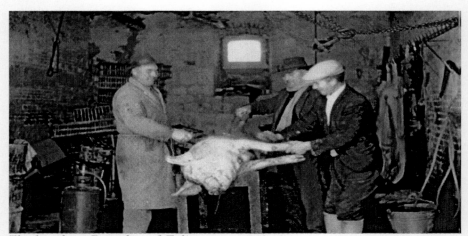

The butchers Romolo and Felice

disdained to exercise what he learned from his father- in-law, because, as a craftsman, he too was very much in demand by his customers.

Rosaria was a teacher in the schools of Molise. I knew her because of an old friendship begun in the days of my childhood in Pietracupa with **Nicola Santoro**.

Our plots of land, located at le "macchie", were adjacent to those of Nicola's family; so every time I went to the countryside, on the way we would meet and talk about this and that. In those times, the land was an unassailable good, and was also a resource that every owner had to defend, so those who adversely affected or crossed, in one way or another, the property of others without permission, caused quarrels and disputes. With the Santoro family there have never been any problems in this regard.

I met Nicola many years later, when he had moved to Rome to work as a shoemaker for a private firm. I remember that one evening, on the occasion of Vincenzo Di Iorio's return from the USA, we met to celebrate near Via Veneto the return of this relative of mine and his childhood friend.

We entered a nightclub and we danced with some fascinating entertainers of the local, but this dance and the resulting drink of champagne cost a lot. A few weeks later, I met again Nicola and reminded him the beautiful evening we spent at the night club. I have never forgotten his answer in Pietracupa's slang: *Bloody hell! We spent ten thousand pounds! For a week I did not have lunch in order to recover the money spent and to be able to pay for the room to my landlady.*

The barber Uncle Alessandro

Carpenter

Building Works

Nicola married a girl from Campania and had many children and emigrated to the USA. He lives with his family in Los Angeles, working on his own producing shoes for his sophisticated Californian customers.

I visited Los Angeles in 1988. It is a city in which the characters of cinema and entertainment live in their enormous villas. People tell me that Nicola, thanks to his ability, is the supplier of shoes to many of these American stars.

Pasquale Lombardi would carry out his work in the shop in Via Generale Durante and, as he had been a player on the soccer team of Pietracupa, his shop was always full of friends and admirers who amiably entertained with Pasquale, not only to get their shoes repaired but also to talk about football and the challenges with neighboring villages. For me, Pasquale was a great friend, always available and ready to joke. His premature death greatly saddened me.

Along with his Uncle Antonio Carnevale, other tailors of the old generation and the new masters were: **Uncle Peppino Di Iorio** who had his workshop in Via Roma and was a relative of my father as well as the son of **Uncle Achillone**, brother of my paternal grandmother. My meetings with Uncle Peppino were always very affectionate and respectful. It is the same love and respect that I share with his **son Mario** when we meet and exchange some funny jokes about the Gallinella family. From the professional point of view uncle Peppino is another member of those legendary Pietracupa tailors who trained and started many young people of the village in this profession.

In the field of fashion tailoring, Italy is in the vanguard with respect to many other nations. Designers such as Valentino, Versace, Litrico and so on are all from the South of Italy, and their initial activities started from experiences in small towns in Calabria, Sicily and Molise. As in a dream I remember, in those years, in the village was appointed an **Adduocchio or Adducchio**, from Pietracupa, who ran a great tailoring firm in Milan that counted among its clients artists such as Bramieri and others.

Uncle Giovanni Cacchione owned the shop in Via Trento. His place was always full of "apprentice tailors" such as Vincenzo Di Iorio, Domenico Festa and others who emigrated abroad. Uncle Giovanni then moved to Rome, always doing the job of a tailor in the populous district of San Giovanni.

His eldest son Ottavio, married Lina, the daughter of Uncle Guerrino Carnevale, and moved to America. On my first trip to the USA in 1965, I visited fleetingly the pastry shop they had opened in Westfield and I spent an hour of pleasant conversation with them, remembering the days of our youth in Pietracupa.

Renato Di Sarro is to be considered among the tailors of the new generation. Renato attended a cutting school in the city of Turin; after obtaining the certificate, he worked at Armani International Group as a tailor. Then he returned to his native region and opened a shop in Via S. Anna.

Renato now resides with his family in Campobasso; but during the summer or on weekends, it's easy to meet him in the streets of Pietracupa. I often stop to talk with him and the joy that shines from his eyes when he extols the beauty of Molise has convinced me that Renato is in love with the Molise Region and, especially, with this village, in which he wanted to stay despite having had tempting working offers out of the Region.

Patrizio Di Sarro and his brother Remo Di Sarro employed good furniture makers in their workshop in Street Trento. They made quality furniture crafted not only for Pietracupa's families, but also for many families from neighboring villages aware of their professional skills. Both built, in the 50's, and gave me as a present, a beautiful wood "chariot" with 4 wheels (like modern wagon).

Remo was then married to Concetta Cacchione and from their union was born Letizia, currently employed in Pietracupa's municipality. My grandfather Ezechiele and Uncle Giuseppe, father of Remo and Patrizio, were close friends. Later on, my father and my own family too have maintained cordial relations with Uncle Giuseppe, Aunt Letizia, their children and their descendants.

Last fall, Mark, last son of Patrick and Rosinella, happily married Giorgia, a very nice and pleasant Roman girl. At the ceremony, officiated by the parish priest of Pietracupa, were my daughter, her husband and many of their young friends from Pietracupa, all belonging to the group of local babies born in the 1970s. Now they are a cohesive group of young forty-somethings and I consider the future of our country, together with other younger children living in the village, to be in good hands.

In my house at Pietracupa I have installed a wall bench made for me by Patrick, who died a few years later. Every time I sit on it, I remember a great friend and a great craftsman like Patrizio.

Remo and Concetta, in recent years managed the bar "La Morgia" situated just below my house in Via Generale Durante, so I often visited with them. A funny anecdote about the memory of Remo happened one summer evening when Remo, inspired by the music, started playing outdoors old Italian songs with his "euphonium", receiving a thunderous and sincere applause from all the numerous people present.

I have a special memory of **Uncle Angelotto Festa**, the "blacksmith" (*ferraro*) of the village. He was a very tall and powerfully structured man; he worked hard in his shop in Via Garibaldi and the front square was always full of pack animals waiting their turn for the replacement of worn horseshoes.

In my eyes Uncle Angelotto appeared as a modern Vulcan God that drove his bellows to stoke the fire and then heat up, pound, and shape the iron on his great anvil. He was a very kind person and during a break from his job, if I passed by, he always asked news about my studies and my family. Once he also gave me a horseshoe as a lucky charm.

Uncle Angelo Porchetta was another important blacksmith of the village. His wife, Aunt Carolina, in the early postwar years worked with my father to cultivate the property of my family. Aunt Carolina was an active person, hardworking, highly moral and honest. Whenever I think of the rural world and the values that this country world would inspire, I remember her.

In the period of the great exodus from Pietracupa Aunt Carolina followed her daughter Carmelina's footsteps, leaving that rural world which for many years had been her reason of life.

Uncle Joseph Grande and his sons were the "pinciari" (tile makers) par excellence, known for their professionalism throughout the area of the High Molise. Uncle Giuseppe's family consisted of two daughters and five sons.

The furnace processing "pinci" (typical tiles for roofing) was located in the south of the village. Uncle Joseph was a man of small stature, but sported a large mustache that gave his figure the air of a gentleman of an old epoch. The only son who followed, for a certain period of time, his footsteps was Uncle Francesco, who had set up a new "Pinciara" in the north of the village, near the three crosses.

Many roofs of houses in Pietracupa and Molise house are still covered by the "pinci" of that epoch, difficult to find on the market

109

today. Uncle Francesco then emigrated to America, but returned to Pietracupa to spend his days of retirement.

The Pinciara, now owned by an heir of the Grande family, is still intact and could be used as a museum exhibit in a hypothetical tour through Molise, including Pietracupa too, because of its history and its beauty. My thinking may be utopian, but it costs nothing to fantasize.

Uncle Felice and Romolo Santilli, were both the classic demonstration of the truth of the maxim saying "unity is strength". For many years they worked together in slaughtering, both as traders and as producers, as well as distributors and retailers of the finished product. In a certain sense, they were the forerunners of a handicraft processing chain that rationalized the use of the resources that the Molise market put at their disposal in the area of sheep, pigs and poultry.

Slaughter and meat processing were the final acts for the subsequent sale of the finished product in the village and in the region, or even in the city of Rome, through a network of local dealers and customers formed by many families of Pietracupa's and Molise. The uniqueness and excellence of their products, such as hams, sausages, brawn, abuoldri and so on, assured them to be able to count on selected and certain customers. For their business, they used local labor, and all members of their families were committed to contribute to the business activity. I always remember the effort that Aunt Mary, Uncle Romulus's wife, put into preparing the famous abuoldri made from the intestines of sheep, a new product of Molise cuisine.

Michele Santilli, son of Uncle Romolo, is a dear childhood friend with whom I spent many days of my early youth. Michele lived and still lives just opposite my house in Via Vico I ° S. Anna. We were born almost in the same year, so it was natural to meet and play together in the steep square in front our homes. Thanks to Michele I got to know the beauty and the difficulty of Pietracupa's country world. Michele's days were marked by precise jobs, like the water supply to the sources of the village, long runs to check on the cattle at the farm, business meetings with local people. In short, a nice program for a boy of high hopes. In his commitments he was also helped by a young worker from **Schiavi d'Abruzzo named Mario**. Mario was part of a family of eleven children and, as it happened in those days, even if you weren't of age you had to go to work for people who needed hands for agriculture. Fortunately for him, in Uncle

Romolo's house, he was treated with respect, as if he was an additional child.

I haven't seen Mario anymore. I remember him in an affectionate way. When I saw him working I said to myself *"poor boy - so young he had to abandon his father's house because of need, without enjoying the direct affection of his mother, his brothers, of his world as a child"*.

I am very lucky compared to him and in my mind there were thoughts of great solidarity for that young friend of mine, from whom the necessities of life had taken a valuable asset, his family.

In following years, I was informed that Mario, as an adult, moved to Rome, married and now is running a garage owned by him for storage of private cars.

Michele married my cousin Antonietta Di Iorio; they had two nice children and grandchildren, including Dario, the great champion of the national basketball youth team.

After marriage Michele spent time working in Libya, then returned to Rome and was employed at ATAC, the company where I worked too for about forty years. About Michele, who now I often meet in Pietracupa, I have a nice memory of the time at ATAC, when I met him on the tram, impeccable in his ticket inspector uniform. When he asked me in a professional tone, *"Please sir let me see your ticket,"* I showed him the card service and then, with big smiles, we fraternally embraced, to the amazement of other travelers.

My father's family, together with Uncle Felice and Uncle Romolo's, were tied by friendship and respect. Uncle Felice is my godfather in the confirmation, and Uncle Romolo served as godfather for my brother Lino's confirmation. So we also were linked for a relationship of "godfathering" which, in southern Italian society has great ethical significance.

Uncle Nicola Di Sarro lived opposite my house in Via Vico I ° S. Anna; Aunt Angela, children Domenico, Antonietta, Amedeo and Lidia were his family. Uncle Nicola was a man of noble bearing and had his butcher shop right below our kitchen. I remember sheepskins that he would lay in the sun to let them dry, and the sign reading "Butcher" over the door of his shop. Aunt Angela was a nice old woman who, especially in the summer, was busy making the tomato sauce which then used to lie in the sun on long wooden tables. On this occasion, the aunt was particularly careful to remove flies and hens in the alley, with a nice cry "Shah there, wake there."

In the summer evenings, in the small square in front of the house, Lidia met all the women and the youths of the alley to have nice talks under the soft lights of the dim lamps in the street.

Amedeo was the bandmaster of Pietracupa's band. Everyone speaks about him, including me, as a nice person of great feeling and great deliberation. I always remember that, as a young man, he was delighted to play his clarinet and he was very clever indeed. Amedeo married Angelina Porchetta at Pietracupa. My father, who had been invited to the ceremony, told me it was a lavish event.

Amedeo later moved to Rome, opening a butcher shop in the Appio district. Later he also embarked on another activity in the field of urban mobility: running a taxi. He died as an old man and, honestly, I felt great sorrow at the passing of a friend, with whom over the years I had spent many pleasant and serene days.

Uncle Filippo Cacchione was Pietracupa's symbolic pastry chef. His inimitable "sponge fingers" were famous even outside the Molise perimeter. He had modern equipment at his home in Via Garibaldi, near the three crosses. In times of increased activity at his pastry shop, it was easy to see Uncle Filippo with a white hat on his head and wearing an apron, busy kneading flour, milk, sugar and other secret ingredients so as to produce both the famous sponge fingers and other delicacies coming from his oven.

I consider Uncle Filippo an active and intelligent man who knew how to seize the fleeting moment to carry out new projects useful for him and for the community. During Pietracupa's exodus, he also opened a travel agency that issued tickets and travel documents necessary to navigate to the countries of South and North America. I remember that, outside his door, were displayed some posters with the image of the great ocean liners of the time: Saturnia, Vulcania, Raphael, and so on.

A funny anecdote about Uncle Philip is about his love for the theater. One summer of the '50s, two actors, husband and wife, came to Pietracupa to act in a comedy of the Italian repertoire. In the absence of a room or a public space, the show was held in a Casalotto house that was bustling with people. With great amazement of the people present, to the cast of the comedy also belonged Uncle Philip, who starred with great skill.

This quality is part of his background as a man accustomed to communicating with others and able to assess situations, to solve problems in case of difficulty.

Uncle Antonio Cacchione was both a discreet and quiet person, and a hard worker with extensive experience in the construction industry. His wife Cesira was a very active and energetic woman. His two children were Concetta and Vincenzo, the first managed the family bar in Trento; the second however, was studying in Campobasso to graduate as a surveyor but during the summer he would help to manage the bar.

We were great friends with Vincenzo. Then, after marrying Gilda, he moved to the United States and had great success in the construction field. Vincenzo died, not a long time ago, at a fairly young age.When I walk in front of his house near the three crosses, I remember his smile and his gentle manners, as well as our youthful antics.

For some time Uncle Antonio was commissioned to restructure the municipal cemetery along with his assistant **Graziano Brunetti**. The cemetery was in a state of great neglect and, after the war, the town council thought to entrust the renovation of the facade and interior to a skilled person. Uncle Antonio's style was that of a professional who understood the importance of local architecture and could intervene to build or repair buildings, while respecting the aesthetics of the past.

Graziano was a character symbol of Pietracupa; almost all the inhabitants of the village have called him to perform some maintenance building. Personally I remember him when, deep in thought, behind the Aia del Piano he would be looking at the view that mother nature gave him every day. A funny anecdote of his use as a builder of the cemetery is related to the joke that he often used to say: *I own a small book where I wrote all the names of the next customer / inhabitants of the cemetery.* It was a nice way to be ironic and chase away the sadness.

Uncle Umberto Festa married Aunt Olga, cousin of my father. Talking to them has always been a pleasant thing; they both had a frank and sincere vernacular, and Aunt Olga colored her speeches on the family as a seamstress can do on a hem of silk. Both moved to the Marche, in the city of San Benedetto del Tronto, where Uncle has carried on his business in the field of footwear. Aunt Olga, at the ripe old age of 90-plus years, lives with her daughter Lina, who I met a few times during her fleeting visits made to see Pietracupa relatives. Recently, I got to talk with her by phone, on the occasion of Anita's visit in Italy.

Lina and her husband Dario have a beautiful family, enlivened by the presence of their daughter, employed in tourism activities. The brother of Uncle Umberto, Domenico, is a dear friend from my summers spent in the '50s in San Gregorio, along with Uncle **Giuseppe Di Iorio**. Domenico is a high-class person. He now lives in Westfield with his family and spends his days quietly retired after years of hard work in the field of men's tailoring.

I must say that the city of Westfield has been lucky enough to accommodate many of our artisans, trained at Pietracupa in the postwar years. From Dino Di Iorio up to Giuseppe Grande, from Peppe Porchetta up to Nicola Fusaro, Giovanni Di Sarro, the Brothers Giovanni and Gelsolmino Di Sarro, and the brothers Guglielmi from Milwaukee, and to all graduates and technicians belonging to Pietracupa's community, including the latest arrivals of the new generation.

Giuseppe Di Iorio is of my own age. In Pietracupa's 1950s summers, he was always busy with family activities. But he always would find time to engage with me in reckless races down the slope of the crosses, in our wooden wagons, which were the envy of our peers. Peppino is a skilled carpenter and, when he moved to Rome, the Italian State thought well enough of him to take him in its staff at a prestigious Ministry. During the summers, we don't race anymore with our wagons, but we do take long walks together, during which we talk about everything, about our families, politics and about the difficulties that young people nowadays have finding jobs.

The brothers **Pietro and Nicola Saliola** made history of Pietracupa's craftsmen in joinery work. I do not need to weave the praise to demonstrate their skills, their professionalism and their devotion to family and work. My father was very attached to them and to Uncle Cesare and their mother, whom he was bound with by kinship ties. Personally, I can add that the artisans of the '50s were able to show that the crafts in Italy wrote an important page in the production and economic fabric of the nation. The era of industrialization, however, needed and needs craftsmen who, with their inventiveness and their creative ability, could try and manage to occupy that market niche that distinguishes the industrial product from the handmade one.

In 1993, I had the opportunity to be invited by a member of the Soldini family to visit their shoe factory in the town of Anghiari, near

114

Arezzo. The shoes of Soldini family are sold around the world and their factories are at the forefront of the technology sector.

During the visit, Dr. Soldini led me to a small department where some workers were busy experimenting and producing garments of excellence. The coordinator of this group was the Soldini father, who, dressed in a white coat and a dress similar to the artisans of my village, was among those to guide, advise, and implement cutting-edge products, just as our Italian and Pietracupa's artisans did and still do.

The luck of Soldini shoe factories began with that old craftsman who, from a small bench cobbler, came to create an industry that competes in global markets.

-PIETRACUPA'S SURNAMES, NAMES AND NICKNAMES

At Pietracupa, like in many other villages in the south of Italy, it is very easy to trace any person residing in the village. You have only to say the the surname, and especially **the nickname of the person**, to have immediately every inhabitant in the village ready to provide the right information to find his house. Pietracupa's family names have ancient origins and the most recurrent ones are included in a number varying between 8 and 10 units: Camillo, Durante, Sardella, Del Monaco, Cacchione, Saliola, Di Iorio, Porchetta, Santilli, Carosone, Santoro, Portone, Cirese, Guglielmi, Meale, Vanga, Brunetti, Ciavarro, Ciavari, Delmonaco,and so on. Not all families that have the same surname are related to each other, but they come from strains of different people who settled in the village over the years.

A special feature of Pietracupa's community is to give the first-born male or female the name of his paternal grandparents. The reason for this tradition is the peasant family organizational system of the period, where the patriarch had a key role. So every patriarch, both for reasons of respect and for hereditary reasons, demanded that his first heir was baptized with the name of the father if he was a boy or of the mother if she was a girl.

This situation leads to the conclusion that, if the patriarch had a family of ten males, his name was reproduced in as many grandchildren; that is why, in Pietracupa's municipality birth register, there are numerous people who have been baptized and recorded **all with the same name and surname of their grandfather**.

In the century in which we live, parents tend to baptize their child with names chosen according to the tastes and to the characters in vogue at the time. It is symptomatic that, in the years when **the footballer Maradona** was playing on the team of Naples, many of the future children from Campania were baptized with the name of Diego.

In past centuries, there was a strong tradition of religious devotion to the patron saints of their own villages or to saints celebrated for their recognized miracles.This tradition was respected at Pietracupa too. So the names given to Pietracupa's boys and girls were Antonio, Gregorio, Anna (patron saints of the village) as well as Maria, Assunta, Concetta, Rosa, Giovanni, Angelo, Pasquale, Gennaro, Rocco, Giuseppe, Luigi, Donato, Domenico, Carmine, Vincenzo - all important saints in the history of Catholicism.

Other names like Quintino, Ottavio, Romolo, Felice, Filippo, Manfredo, Giulio, Palmerino, Rodolfo, Dario and so on were given in ancient times and handed down in following years, for the above reasons.

In this framework of perpetuation and repetition of names, an important way to distinguish one person or family from the other is **a nickname,** which was coined *ad personam* according to the case or to the anecdotes of an individual's life. Generally nicknames were given in the midst of time and the people of the village **handed them down** from father to son.

Nicknames are a very interesting tradition that many scholars have debated in recent years. But many present descendants categorically refuse to be called by their ancestors' nickname; others are indifferent, others are even proud of it. But anyway, many of Pietracupa's people continue to identify various persons by their household nickname. Some years ago, in a shop in Pietracupa, I was a spectator of a heated discussion between an angry woman in respect to another person who had pointed out her husband by the family nickname. The first woman told all the accolades and cultural merits of her husband to make it clear to the other that there was no need to call him by that nickname.

I myself believed that some surnames of village families were those with which they are cited regularly; instead, I found that these are nicknames given to their ancestors. In the future, where I have doubts, I will make sure whether it is their real last name or only a nickname.

Some of Pietracupa's nicknames were coined because of physical defects of the recipients, which I think is something distasteful. Other nicknames were given for various reasons that I think are funnier and most representative of the irony and the spirit of observation of Pietracupa's people. In fact, this last category can be divided into three specific sub-classes: **first**, nicknames given to persons receiving praise, often copied from famous public figures; **second**, nicknames given to the work performed by the recipient himself; **third**, nicknames created as a result of eccentric attitudes of life, for the way of behaving, the way of expressing some dialect phrase, by the individual recipient. About this last group, Pietracupa's people imagination was really great.

To understand how some nicknames of Pietracupa's people came about, I'll tell you the following anecdotes that relatives of the named persons, or the people themselves, have very kindly revealed to me and allowed me to write it in this book.

I will start with the nickname "**Gallinella**" (**little hen**), which was given to **the family Di Iorio. Aunt Domenica Berardo**, my family's historical memory, told me the origin of this nickname.

She told me that an ancestor of mine had fathered eleven children, and during the winter, as it happened in all the houses of the village, the various members of the family sat around the fireplace to warm up. The occasional friends who came to their house were surprised by this brood of young and old, crouching near the fire, in the same way as do **the hens and their chicks** when they rest at night in the coop. This episode gave rise to the nickname "**Gallinella**".

A branch of the Gallinella family was the one which my grandmother Antonia belonged to. Her parents, **Vincenzo Di Iorio and Angela Durante** had given birth to seven children and the eldest son **Giuseppe / Emilio**, municipal guard in the town of Pietracupa, was given the nickname of "**Castellino**". This nickname was given to him because he had been a guest for a few weeks of family friends in the town of Castellino on the Biferno. On his return to the village, he had begun to praise the beauty and fresh air of this village of Molise. So his fellow villagers, tired of his stories and a little envious of his trip, nicknamed him "Castellino".

The cute nickname, "**Peparulo**" was given in the '50s to **a municipal secretary of Pietracupa** who had a large nose full of veins and reddish tones. This feature inspired other employees to consider his prominence similar to that of a large pepper, and from this was born the above nickname.The nickname fit very well to his character, because the secretary was from another village of Molise, at which he was a frequent guest for lunch with Pietracupa's friends. Being a connoisseur and lover of vintage wines, after lunch his nose was particularly colorful, perfectly resembling a large red pepper.

The nickname "Truc-Pol" given to **Michele Di Iorio** was coined on the same day of his birth, during the war years. Some villagers of Pietracupa finished the usual courtesy visit that they would pay to the family. Leaving the newborn's home, they noticed an American Jeep parked in the street by soldiers present in the village. On the front of the Jeep, there was written the English words "**Truck-Pool**". Because the engine cover had the same shape of plump baby Michele, as memory of the event and also as a good omen for the thriving infant, they decided to call him, "Truc-Pol", converting to Italian that American writing seen on the hood of the car.

His father Alberto, however, was nicknamed the "**Maccaronaro**". The origin of that nickname is linked to the fact that Michele's father was a producer of pasta and used a kneading machine of advanced technology which allowed him to implement the production of this product, which was of primary importance for feeding the people.

Even the nickname "**Sogghiesi**", which Uncle Vincenzo Ciavarro was called, comes from the profession that he himself exercised in the village, **the shoemaker**. In Rome, in the old days, shoemakers were named, "pecioni" or "sole", with reference to the products they used in their work. At Pietracupa, one of the tools that was used to sew the shoes was named "Sogghia" and Uncle Vincenzo, being a skilled craftsman for working shoes, was nicknamed the above term. He was born in the year 1908, the same year of my father's birth, so they were tied by deep bonds of friendship, cultivated since the time of their primary schooling. He passed away after a busy work life, always spent in the village.

Giuseppe Saliola told me the anecdote for which his father was nicknamed "**Baron**". The story comes from the fact that the father had two families of relatives who took care of him, so the young boy was fondled and protected by both of these families. In a time of economic hardship, his position was that of one lucky person, the same way as the nobles of the past who were awarded with the title of Baron.

Last summer, while driving on the Salita Grappa, I ran into **Gino Santilli** a dear friend since the days of my childhood, with **his**

brother Giovanni. I always believed the last name of his family was "**Pelone**" because, in the village when occasionally people spoke about them, they always added that word, which may be a normal Italian surname, to the name of the individual. Fortunately, on that occasion I clarified the misunderstanding with him, apologizing for the mistake. Gino was very kind and wanted to tell me about the incident which resulted in that nickname.

He told me that one of his young ancestors had gone to San Pietro Source by horse to draw water, pour it in barrels and then carry it home for the needs of the family. Once finished and having to water the horse in one of the two pools overlooking the water spouts (a larger and a smaller one), he addressed one of his older kin, asking him in Pietracupa's dialect: *Should I water the horse in the big pool (r 'Pelone) or in the small one (r' Pelillo)?*. The other answered him, "*Water him in the large pool (r 'Pelone)*.

San Pietro Source was always crowded with people waiting to draw water and "Pelillo" and "Pelone" were considered by those present pleasant expressions. So, from that day on, they favored the young guy with the nickname "Pelone ".

But this casual meeting with Gino was also an opportunity to talk about Pietracupa, its history and its people. In particular, he told me a very touching episode concerning his grandfather **Giovanni Santilli**. He told me that, in the period of World War I, during which many adults had left for the front, his grandfather began to teach the village children the alphabet, necessary for them to learn to read and write. This gesture of the grandfather Gino was indicative of the solidarity and willingness to help one's fellow humans.

Culture is freedom in all its meanings, and this episode indicates the beginning of a road that each individual must travel to get to understand the meaning of "freedom".

Gino stressed that his grandfather used to say *Favor the culture because it is priceless, it allows you to relate with the King and the servant of the King*. These are wise words for a man who lived in a time of hardship. They are words sown and germinated also within his family, and which Gino and Giovanni themselves have transposed and implemented in their life path.

Palmerino Delmonaco told me about the origin of the nickname "**Polish**", which he is usually identified with in the village. In past years, between the beginning of World War II and the postwar, all Pietracupa's young people, in their moments of free time, went to

Casarino field to play football or bowls or other games like that, which consisted of a big iron plate with a hole in the middle, that players had to launch over a fixed pole to score the point. Palmerino was very skilled at this last game and, whenever he centered the pole, he celebrated by shouting, *"plate, plate"*. The other players, repeatedly defeated and resenting his cry of victory, translated this cry to the only word phonetically resembling the nickname "Polish".

A cheerful and musical nickname is **"Fifino"**, given to an ancestor of **Antonio Delmonaco** who last summer told me the story that gave rise to this nickname. Antonio told me that his ancestor used to go to village parties, bringing with him his guitar to entertain the customers. As standard practice, before starting to play the requested songs, he would proceed to tune up his musical instrument, causing it to vibrate with delicate sounds similar to **"flin, flin"**. His fellow citizens, to pay homage to his talent, nicknamed him "Fifino" in memory of his syncopated "flin, flin" – and also probably as a memory of the beautiful and simple good times at Pietracupa party evenings.

My neighbor **Nicola Fusaro**, who had emigrated a long time before to the United States, during a holiday spent at Pietracupa, told me the story that gave rise to the nickname **"ceca la negghia"**.

At Pietracupa, in the years before World War II, every citizen offered a day of free labor to the community, to carry out activities of general utility like shoveling snow, cleaning the streets, repairing crumbling embankments and so on.

An ancestor of Nicola, despite having previously agreed to the mayor's appointment for his presence in the Town Hall, couldn't appear on the day and time established. He told the furious mayor of the time that the reason he couldn't appear at the Town Hall was that it was foggy and he couldn't see because of it. Obviously the justification was known by all the villagers, and it was because of that Nicola's ancestor was nicknamed "ceca la negghia". I really do not know if it translates literally to "the fog blinded me", or as I believe, "there was the fog."

In Pietracupa's relaxing summer evenings, people often talk about politics, and it is easy that tempers can heat up. **Giuseppe Delmonaco** was once a supporter of Ugo La Malfa, whom he often quoted for his Republican political thinking, which, during the 1960s through the 1980s, was very fashionable. This youthful, ideological position, which he professed with civil and correct manners, was

120

sufficient to ensure that his countrymen dubbed him, "**La Malfa**" (who, by the way, was also one of the founding fathers of our Republic).

 Giovanni and Gelsomino Di Sarro, last summer told me an anecdote from which was born the nickname "**Bottiglione**" given to their father in the years of his youth. In the tradition of Molise, food products from farm work had a great economic importance for every family. Everyone tended to keep those with the highest nutritional value, such as the brawn / headcheese, ham, cheese, olive oil and wine, to use them on important occasions and as a bargaining chip with other useful products for their daily living. It was normal practice to store the wine from the last harvest in the cellar in wooden barrels or large glass bottles. We need to say, however, that it was also customary for young Pietracupa boys to "outwit" their parents by going to eat in secret some brawn or drink a few glasses of wine directly from the winery.

 The father of Giovanni and Gelsomino was not free from these local customs, so sometimes he resorted to the delights of the God Bacchus, going to his cellar to drink a bit of wine kept in bottles of large capacity.

This youth's "unscheduled raids" were discovered by his parents, who called him strictly and told him not to act that way in the future. The news was propagated among the villagers, who immediately gave the youth the nickname "Bottiglione", in memory of those wine pranks with the bottles.

 I personally met the father of Giovanni and Gelsolmino, Uncle Amedeo. He was a serious and responsible person who carried on his family successfully. So the anecdote is told only to illustrate the general nostalgic aspects of that peasant society so far away from our time.

Andrea Guglielmi in the month of March, told me the origin of the nickname "**Melone**", currently pointed out with all the members of his family. The reason is very old, even though I thought it was the real surname of the family. Andrea told me that one of his ancestors had a beautiful vineyard bordering another equally gorgeous one. In those days, two contiguous vineyards had to be separated by a "not farmed" zone. The ancestor of Andrea, devoted to agriculture and lover of assets that providence gave to the peasants, considered it unseemly that such a large piece of land remained uncultivated. Therefore, in the free zone of his property, he proceeded to sow melons. Pietracupa's people appreciated this gesture, meaningful of the love that every farmer should have for his land. From that day on, Andrea's progenitor was nicknamed "Melone", in memory of his unconventional behavior in favor of God's goods.

Domenico Saliola, whom I met last year at Pietracupa, told me about the origin of the nickname "**Brigadiere**". He told me that, as a boy, he had managed to get a little hat of the military kind, with a visor, given to him as a present. Proud of his headgear, he would tour the village happy to let people see this novelty that set him apart from all other boys of his age. **His contemporaries**, in turn, were attracted by the new look of Domenico. But, having glimpsed in this cute hat the figure of a police sergeant, from that very day for all Pietracupa's people, Domenico became "r 'Brigadiere".

In seeking the origins of Pietracupa's nicknames, someone told me that the Molise village Tourist Office has established a register of the nicknames of all local families to certify their historical significance related to the reasons of their origin.

The anecdotes of these few Pietracupa nicknames reported here indicate a cross-section of uses and habits that outline with great evidence the lives of our ancestors.

Losing their meaning, unless it is offensive, is like losing a bit of the history of the progenitors themselves, and so it is like losing a bit of the history of our community.

Fr. Manfredo Delmonaco

-PIETRACUPA'S PARISH PRIEST, FR.MANFREDO DELMONACO

In small Italian municipalities it is usual to say that the most important people of the local community are the Mayor, the Doctor, the Marshal of the Carabinieri, and the parish priest - as well as already pointed out in previous chapters, any elders at national or regional level born or originating in the municipality itself.

Fr. Manfredo Delmonaco was for many years Pietracupa's parish priest, and he was very familiar with the environment and the residents of this small town where he was born in the year 1908.

Some residents, the same age as the parish priest, told me about the festivities and joy with which they welcomed the young parish priest, the day of his ordination in the Cathedral of Pietracupa

Fr. Manfredo was a pastor reserved from extraordinary manifestations and seemingly distant from small personal quarrels. But he was still a religious figure who comforted his faithful in the difficult years of the war and after the war.

We must consider that the Catholic Church, since the 1960s, was a catalyst to important changes in its way of attending to the changes of modern society. The content resulting from the work of the Second Vatican Council, called by Pope John XXIII and concluded by Pope Paul VI, faced and innovated some aspects of Catholic organization, orienting them to the spiritual needs of modern people. For instance, the mass was no longer only celebrated in Latin; it could be celebrated in the vernacular of the region. Therefore the difficulties faced by parish priests, especially in small villages reluctant to change, weren't easy to overcome.

In the '50s, I had the opportunity to get to know Fr. Manfredo because, during summer vacations, I used to go to him to keep alive my knowledge of Latin, which was then in fashion. On these occasions, I had the chance to witness **his preparation and his personal knowledge**.

I have a special memory of those days. Military conflict in Korea between the USA and North Korea had just started. Fr. Manfredo always listened to radio reports of the ongoing conflict and, as a man of the Church, he was truly saddened.

One of the features that his parishioners affectionately complained about concerning the behavior of their staid priest, was that he was very "concise" in carrying out his religious functions.They claimed, affectionately, that between the bell's sound for the start of the Mass and the blessing, there was a very short time.

I can say that everyone has his own style in conducting public or religious functions. The important thing to observe is that Fr. Manfredo was always present for the spiritual and human resources needed by the young people and towards his parishioners in general. Fr. Manfredo spent the last years of life with his brother's family and grandchildren in a town near Naples.

Last summer Lucio Delmonaco, when talking to me about his uncle Fr. Manfredo, described a **very human** figure. So I perceived a very different image from that of the austere and serious priest described by some citizens. On the contrary, from some family anecdotes told by **Lucio**, I understood that Fr. Manfredo was an open minded and jovial person in his relationships with his family, and that his way of appearing outside was part of the important religious ministry he had the role to play in the community.

PRIMARY SCHOOL AND TEACHERS

In small mountain towns, especially in southern Italy, **the primary school** played a very important role for learning the rudiments of education necessary to be able to read and write. But attending primary school was something more. It was also a way for children to socialize with each other under the guidance of teachers, which through a trail outside the usual family patterns, would prepare the student to face the future.

We note that, in the years between World War I and World War II, **the percentage of illiteracy was very high** in Italy. The phenomenon was due to the fact that children from their early age were needed in the fields to provide help to their rural families, so there were few children who could finish the five-year cycle of primary schools.

The lucky ones who could attend school could be counted on the fingers of one hand and came mostly from wealthier families in the villages.

The teaching staff engaged in primary school consisted of masters born in Pietracupa and were therefore aware of the conditions and each family origin of their students. From the statements made by many elders of the epoch as well as friends of my same age, I received unique common judgments about them, especially for some discriminatory behavior they had with pupils.

This was due to the fact that people living in the same village could easily get involved in quarrels and family events that could compromise the serenity and the impartial judgment of some teachers.

Primary school

Primary school

School during the '30s

Primary school during the '50s

Primary school and families

Primary school during the '60s

An anecdote, told me by a grandmother was particularly impressed in my mind. The episode concerns a teacher who, during a lesson in class teased about the poverty of a child, who answered the insult by throwing at the teacher a blunt object. In the next school survey following the episode, all the students were unanimous in defending their classmate who had been punished severely by his master.

Apart from these aspects of local character, all teachers' commitment and the results of their work are considered **worthy and highly educational**.

In previous chapters, I talked about some of them and also their civil commitment, as podestà or mayor of the Town Hall, from Nicola Portone and Silvio Cirese, up to Michelino Del Monaco.

But we must also remember the teachers Ricciuti, Anna Cirese, Giovanni Di Risio, and all other teachers and mistresses from Pietracupa (and other villages) who took their places over the years at the school in Via S. Rocco and later in the school of via of Casaleno.

We must not forget the contribution of Fr. Manfredo Delmonaco in the field of religious education, and the commitment of many of Pietracupa's young graduates such as Belisario, Romano, Gregorio and so on, who, as part of the state connected with the television program "The Bucket List", by the teacher Manzi, organized a classroom to teach reading and writing to a number of elderly and illiterate of the village, with excellent results.

Because of Pietracupa families' exodus which took place in the '50s / '60s / '70s, the school population was greatly reduced and, therefore, the few pupils of school age in the village were enrolled in the school boards of neighboring villages. So Pietracupa's schools ended their cycle of operation on site. But what is left of all these pupils who, over the years, have studied at village primary school desks ?

The values of life captured on those desks, the memories and love that blossomed in the classroom, that left tangible signs over the years, both for friendships found and for the consolidated affections, for the memories and nostalgia of what could be but has not been, are remaining from an age in which the first hints of youth would germinate.

I remember the blush that appeared on the cheeks of a Pietracupa's old woman, now a grandmother, when I reminded her of the episode of the palm that one of her school mates had given her.

All Pietracupa's people whom I spoke with about school unanimously expressed a positive opinion on their public education experience.

From my father, who had as a primary school teacher **Nicola Portone**, to **Aunt Gemma Santilli**, who passed away last year at the age of 100, who every time I lingered to talk to her, recited perfectly and precisely the poems learned with the teacher Portone.

Many years ago, at a symposium organized in Rome by the Family Molise Association, I managed to talk to some teachers of primary

128

school, who, in recent times, had also taught in Pietracupa's primary school. Knowing my origins, they spoke about their experience on site in Pietracupa. All were unequivocal in stating that Pietracupa's children distinguished themselves from their contemporaries in the region, both for their alertness and intelligence, and also for being, despite their ages, little philosophers.

I do not know what to say except that, everywhere they have gone, Pietracupa's children have always been respected for their commitment and seriousness.

Recently Pietracupa's Town Hall adhered to a fun event to celebrate the fiftieth anniversary of '40s / '50s pupils; they were fun events where childhood memories were the backdrop to the speeches of the "young" seniors of my time.

-PIETRACUPA: FEAST DAYS, POPULAR BELIEFS, LEISURE, THE BAND, THE FOOTBALL TEAM

Feasts

Every great and small town, every village has its own patron saints that are celebrated every year on the day of their anniversary, which is set by the Catholic Church.

As I said previously, Pietracupa has three patron saints, **St. Anne**, who was and is celebrated on July 26th. **Saint Anthony Abate and Saint Gregorio Magno** who initially were celebrated on September 10th and 11th and, since the '70s, are celebrated on August 19th and 20th.

The celebrations for the patron saints are not only of deep religious significance but also a good omen and protection for the whole community; the Saints can intercede with God to protect the community itself and every individual member from diseases, epidemics, earthquakes, weather disasters, famines, and so on. No need to bother the history of the Saints or read books on traditions related to religious feasts to understand the importance that every believer gives to these events in honor of the patron saints. In New York, a multiethnic and multireligious city, in the district of Little Italy, every year in September they celebrate **the Feast of San Gennaro**, established by Italian immigrants from Naples since the 19th century.

Pietracupa's people have always been linked to festivities' traditions. Take note that in such cases not only the residents who live in the village, but all Pietracupa's descendents in Italy or abroad, schedule their vacations to be present at these events.

The event is also an opportunity to greet relatives, old friends from the past, and to relive the atmosphere and the scents of the village, and that devotion to the patron saints, prayed to and venerated since the early years of childhood.

Certainly after the war, the resident community in the village was more numerous than today, so the organization and management of events was more oriented to local community needs and tastes according to the customs, traditions and above all the resources of the time. The organization of the feast followed for years the same procedural rules: a committee, chaired by the Parish Priest, after hearing the opinion of the residents, used to compile the program of events. Then they proceeded to raise the money to pay the costs by going from house to house to collect it.

Especially in the '50s, the opportunity was good to ask families to welcome into their homes the members of the bands for lunch.

During the village's feast, **the band** was always a component of primary importance for the success of the events. Its job was to accompany the Saints in procession and, especially, to hold the evening concert in the square, as the final and most long-awaited event by the citizenship and outsiders arriving in the village.

In the postwar years, these feasts had a special meaning. After the dark days of the war, people returned to everyday life and even the feasts resumed new importance in a more serene and joyful atmosphere, even if the conditions of life were still quite difficult. I pleasantly remember those simple festivities in Pietracupa.

From early in the morning in Piazza Nicola Portone, the stalls of vendors with various trinkets and sweets would settle in. Among these retailers there was always someone who was often in Pietracupa loudly touting his wares: "*combs, little combs, shoe laces, chromatine* ". Another character always present at the feasts was "**Zi Mirro**", with its primordial equipment to package, on-site, an ice cream cone of only cream and chocolate. The stall of "Zi Mirro" was the most crowded by the children of the village for whom, at that time, tasting ice cream was a rarity they could only afford during the celebrations of the patron saints, when parents and uncles or grandparents were more generous in offering some money to their children and grandchildren.

Another character who was there as usual was "**ci frisco**", with a nice sales pitch that by his voice and facial expression tried to imitate musical instruments and various birds, followed by the good-natured smiles and the participation of Pietracupa's people, who often invited him to lunch in their homes .

These festivities were also an opportunity for the young girls of the village **to wear a new dress,** home sewn or bought in a store or from some stall hawkers. **For men**, the arrival of the feasts was an opportunity to wear **their only dress clothes for important occasions**, completed by the inevitable wide-brimmed **hat,** which was often the brunt of jokes by strangers, who called them "*hats of sola*" (*of poor quality stuff*).

The arrival of the band was the busiest time of the day. Members of the Committee welcomed the bus with the players and immediately asked the band leader to begin to walk the streets of the village to play songs of popular music as the announcement of the beginning of feasts.

This initiative was aimed not only to create a joyful atmosphere; it was also an opportunity to remind and encourage the laggards to pay alms for the Saints of the village, to be delivered on the spot to the members of the committee, who followed the piper with the ever-present "beggings" notebook. **After the mass**, all participants came outside the church to compose the procession in honor of the saints that were carried on the shoulders of village young people.

Pietracupa during the '30s – S. Anna Feast waiting for the "shoot"

Procession during the '40s

Procession during the '50s

This was the most representative moment of devotion by the population to their patron saints. The procession was formed according to a strict protocol: women in front in two columns, then the parish priest and mayor in the middle, followed by the Saints, the band and, last, the men of the village.

All components of the procession used to first go over a stretch of road praying or listening to the religious hymns; mid-term, in Piazza Nicola Portone, the long column was stopped on the way to allow people to pay homage to the Saints with a series of fireworks prepared on the overlooking hill. The long line of people, musicians and Saints would begin again the path going towards Via Kennedy and, after passing through the narrow streets of Casalotto, would return to church.

I must say that the visual effect of these processions was very nice. Lights, colors, songs, atmosphere, men, women, musicians and statues of saints were composed in a light, almost sacred way. I always remember an elderly man (and usual blasphemer of St. Anthony) who, during one of these festivities, seeing pass the statue of the saint, with tears in his eyes turned to him, saying, "*St. Anthony, I have always behaved badly with you; you must forgive me because I love you.*"

Celebrating the patron saint was not only the procession and meeting with friends. It was also an opportunity to make an out of the ordinary meal with a menu based on sagne with sausage gravy, roast lamb, roasted potatoes, vintage wine, homemade pastries. All these goods from God were present on all tables.

That is why, **in the memories of the young or boys** during those years, those celebrations took on a special meaning which is difficult to understand. But I believe it is found in the expectation of being able to eat in abundance all together and to be able to enjoy that special day where, even to the poorest, providence shone a glimmer of light.

The most long-awaited event of the festival was **the evening concert** that was held alternately one evening in the square of "Briscinia" and the following evening in front of the bar of Uncle Alessandro Di Fonzo to satisfy all residents.

The people of Pietracupa have always been passionate listeners of **the opera** by the great Italian masters such as Verdi, Puccini, Rossini, Bellini, Leoncavallo and so on, as well as of Neapolitan songs. Therefore, in those years, the choice of a prestigious band was a necessary condition to satisfy all the inhabitants of the village. The ensembles of the city of Casalanguida or Gambatesa and also the City of Lecce were the most popular. Some of these bands were hired by the Committee of the festivities to perform in the village.

My interest for the opera was born on those occasions. I remember some sprightly seniors listening to the first handset, or the group of clarinets in concert, expressing their judgments with great competence. We boys, with high hopes, were so involved in the band concert, that the next day we imitated the musicians with reed flutes, wooden square boxes and pestles of wood, pot lids, caught sneaking into the home kitchen to imitate the original band. Our musical expressions were always met by the smiles of the people and by the cries of our mothers, who feared the breakup of their tools of the kitchen used as musical instruments.

The concert in the night always finished with a floral tribute to **the conductor**, delivered by one of the prettiest girl in the village.

The final applause was the culmination of the feast days, during which I supposed that a curious angel, sitting on top of Morgia, was present to listen to the music and the whispers and the applause of that simple people that Pietracupa that night was offering him.

Other occasions where it was possible to celebrate, and especially eat better than usual, were the Christmas and Easter holidays.

Holy Christmas, apart from the aspects related to the Christmas feast, in the '70s was enjoying a new importance in the village with the tradition of '**Ndocce**, which are torches made of branches and brooms that are set on fire the night of December 24th. The pagan meaning of "Ndocce" is linked to the winter solstice and to the victory of light over darkness, as is clearly explained on the internet municipal website. But the Catholic ceremony in recent years, simply celebrates the birth of the baby Jesus.

During the ceremony, the crypt and the torches along the steps of the church make Pietracupa seem like the city of Galilee, where the Madonna gave birth to the Savior. The national press has just appointed **Pietracupa "the Bethlehem of Molise"**.

The Easter period, instead, was an opportunity for the women of the house to demonstrate their skill, and all pledged to make the cakes typical of Molise, like *fiadone, the strufoli, pastiera, the cioffe, and scarpelle.*

Roast lamb and fried potatoes in a pan covered by the embers of the fire, were the highlight of the Easter menu. It included handmade sagne seasoned with meat sauce, a roast, potatoes and bread. The wonderful and fragrant bread of Molise, fruit of the earth, and of the labors of the peasants who kneaded and baked it in the oven at home, smelled and indeed spoke the language of nature, when it was touched, cut and eaten. The famous heel of bread dipped in the remaining sauce in the dish was a treat of the diners that could not be refused, against all etiquette imposed in the book by Monsignor Della Casa.

But besides the occurrences of a religious nature, Pietracupa's people celebrated and still celebrate other instances of a civil nature, especially those which have roots in the ancient traditions, such as **Carnival and the Grape Festival**. It should be noted that **Pietracupa's Carnival** did not follow the usual events related to the parade of floats, as was the case in most Italian towns and villages. But the people of Pietracupa used to celebrate this event with a folk representation called "**The process to Carnival**", which took place along the streets of the village.

 The plot of the representation traveling along the narrow streets and squares was as follows: the Carnival, played by a puppet, was tried and sentenced to death; after the judgment he was mocked by a character dressed in white ("the death") and by a host of screaming devils, with pitchforks, dressed in black and with their heads covered by sacks, and was led up to the balcony of the Mother Church. From this place, by means of a metal cable suspended in the air, the puppet was brought down in the square below to be finally burned, amid the cries and the joy of the citizens. Pietracupa's Carnival, a tradition that has its roots in the ancient Saturnalia of the Roman epoch and in purification and propitiation agrarian rites, represents the evils that affect humanity. With this ritual of condemnation and murder of the puppet, who personified evil, the community intended to purify and exorcise the evil forces so that they stay away from the village. Reaching the goal of the death of the offender, it would begin a phase that was voiced with demonstrations of joy and jubilation, accompanied by toasts of hot wine and tasty snacks, which would take again all participants to more concrete gastronomic pleasures linked to the Carnival. Last February I was a spectator of this event sponsored by the City of Pietracupa that intended to restore it. I must say that I appreciated very much the young peoples' improvised acting in the show and the script pertaining to its crucial moments.

The 'Ndoccia

Popular beliefs

The previous story on Carnival leads me to speak of ancient popular legends still present in the imagination of the inhabitants of Pietracupa, legends that derive especially from the history and customs of medieval Europe, dotted with ancient folk beliefs suspended between the pagan and the religious.

The story of the **"R 'Mazzamurill"**, reported in the tourist poster published by the Town Hall of Pietracupa, is an example of how a legend built by the imagination of the people of the village arises and spreads over time.

"R'Mazzamurill" would impersonate a sinister goblin wandering near the bell tower of Morgia, a place full of caves and a cliff dangerous for passersby. The story highlights the fact that every careless child who was captured by the monster became food to eat for this hungry character, who then completed his work of dying his hat with the blood of his young victims.

This grim legend allowed mothers to frighten their children in order to keep them away from Morgia's dangerous cliffs.

The legend continued up to the '60s. But, with the emancipation and especially with the emigration of the inhabitants, it lost its modernity. So in 1996 the Mayor and the City Council, wanting to keep alive the memory of this legend, adopted as **City Council mascot** this demon, who in the past had stirred the dreams of children.

Another legend associated with medieval beliefs is the alleged presence in the village of ghosts, evil witches, people seized by the devil, and so on. Believing that **"evil witches"** can live incognito next to us, is a very widespread suggestion among the Italian population, so that various authors and historians have covered the subject with essays and treatises.

The Catholic Church itself during its two thousand year history addressed directly this issue. The proof is the martyrdom of **Saint Joan of Arc**, burned at the stake as a witch and the numerous witch trials opened by the Tribunal of the Holy Inquisition. I do not intend to get into specifics of the topic, but I just want to point out that these beliefs still exist and, on this subject, I want to tell my personal story, experienced in Pietracupa.

As a boy, when I was with other people of my age taking a certain route through the village, all these friends told me to run and make the sign of the cross because, according to them and their parents, in that route lived **witches**.

My curiosity and also my fear increased when, in the evening, adults who gathered in the alley to get some fresh air, sometimes discussed this topic, coloring it with anecdotes and fairytale details, accusing these alleged witches of turning into black cats and entering Pietracupa's homes at night, for evil purposes. These speeches were often integrated with fantastic stories of persons running into the activities of these evil hags.

Obviously the stories I listened to in silence frightened me a lot, and, in my walks in the village I was careful not to pass near the houses where people thought there were witches.

Only as an adult did I get to consider the matter in a different light from the past, ascertaining that the alleged witches of that alley were simple and friendly people, with peasant habits and also respectful of the laws of the Lord.

The same topic regarding the **"evil eye"** and **"exorcism"** is a paranormal aspect that still invests the imagination and the way of life of many people and triggers debates by men of science and religion.

On the subject of the **evil eye**, I want to tell another anecdote of which I was the main actor during a dinner at the home of a dear friend who knew how to read tarot cards and predict the future to her interlocutors. At that dinner, in an ironic and skeptical way, I wanted her to read the cards for me too.

My friend began the ritual of reading tarot, employing the special cards. She made me choose some cards in the deck and read them carefully. In the end she revealed to me some details of my near future that really later in part actually did come true.

That evening, the unexpected magician and friend, wanted also to ascertain if some unknown enemy had given me the evil eye. She started her esoteric ritual, putting oil in a dish filled with water and, after moving these ingredients with a finger, deduced from the position of the oil in the water that some evil person had given me the evil eye. She put a hand on my head, whispered some formulas with incomprehensible words and finally told me that she had removed the curse of the evil eye.

I have not had a way to meet that sorceress friend again, and I haven't had other experiences in the field of the esoteric. But I wanted to tell this personal anecdote to say that, at Pietracupa, the belief in the evil eye was very widespread among the inhabitants of the village.

During an exposition of many years ago, in the Municipality of Casalciprano, people were talking about some magicians and clairvoyants of the Molise Region, and **the Wizard of Pietracupa (R 'Magaro)** was mentioned, with his **ritual of the "greve",** a bag that was donated by wizards to their customers as an object that would drive away bad events. From my point of view, these magicians, in those years, were the positive subjects influencing the psyche of simple and easily influenced people, in a peasant society where loneliness, the inexperience of the individual, and the failure of social services were the primary causes of existential distress of many weak people. Obviously, to learn from the media scams of alleged healers of our time, I criticize charlatan magicians and profiteers of gullible or sick persons.

I got to know personally Pietracupa's "magaro". He always told me that he had a great relationship of friendship with my grandfather's family and my memory, though faded over time, is respect for the personality of the individual, beyond his activity.

I remember many customers who were standing with their horses in front of his house, waiting to be received. Certainly he had some merits as a sociologist and counselor.

Another topic that I wanted to include in this chapter is that concerning **Cola Martello**, a Molisan robber who was killed at Pietracupa. Brigandage developed in the south immediately after the unification of Italy. The phenomenon in those years started from the demands of the peasants, unhappy and hungry because of the bureaucravy of the Savoy monarchy.

Already the first symptoms of this discomfort had been shown during Garibaldi's period with the massacre of **Bronte peasants**, killed on the orders of **Nino Bixio.** In later years these ferments stirred up even more the population of Molise, as the writer **Carlo Iovine** in his novel **"Lady Ava"** describes with great reality.

From this historical point of view, folktale Cola Martello can be placed, which shows how **a true story can become legend** and popular belief, handed down from father to son.

It is said that Cola Martello, before being killed, left for a while to **a family of Pietracupa a** bag containing the proceeds of his robberies. After the killing, his wife, aware of the fact, went to these custodians to get back the bag with its contents, but her request had a negative response.

Since that very day, Pietracupa's inhabitants (neighbors of the robber's handbag custodial family) would say that every night an **owl** (*checchevaia*) would rest on the roof of their home, hooting all night, as if it were Cola Martello coming to claim the return of the bag belonging to his family.

Between belief and reality, we can add the topic of **gypsies** and their reputation for being kidnappers. This belief was cause for alarm among the people of Pietracupa as the village was often the destination for the passing of gypsies' caravans, which would stand by the little road inspector's house on the via nova.

The arrival of the caravan was announced with the usual door-to-door system throughout the village, and all the people remained vigilant until the caravan itself would go out to other destinations.

I still remember the shaking of all the inhabitants of the alley who remained vigilant, still, and silent as the gypsies passed, and to their demands for food or money, particularly mothers who were holding their children tight to their skirts. If some farmer was the owner of a farm in the countryside, he immediately would run to his property to make sure no gypsy had taken it over.

It is said that "**Uncle Vito**", a robust and brawny farmer, having seen Gypsies enter his land, unceremoniously chased the unwary invaders out and soundly beat them. It is rumored, too, that the gypsies gave their word of mouth to others and in the following years were very careful not to approach the property of Uncle Vito.

-*Leisure*

But beyond civil and traditional peasant festivities, all the other days how did Pietracupa's residents spend their free time?

Pietracupa's inhabitants, in those years, could not take advantage of cinemas and theaters, which were almost non-existent in the Molise region. There was no TV, the reading rooms and municipal gyms did not yet exist, the party headquarters was absent. Those who owned radios or cars, or subscribers to the national newspapers could be counted on the fingers of one hand. So men spent their free time mainly in the so-called "**cellars** ".

In the interior of the wineries, wine, beer and fizzy drinks were mingled with chickpeas, roasted beans, and candy, the only edible elements in those days. The winery was the main place for socializing

141

and meeting of the country men. There you could talk about everything, the family, the daily work, the immigrants, and it was the place from where the news of various kinds was drawn and propagated - from gossip about some guy or about that woman or that girl, up to the important local and national news.

In the period of the local and national elections, then, the winery became the place for debates and heated discussions about the candidates and parties. The presence of women was virtually banned; only boys could enter to alert their fathers that dinner was ready, or that their presence was required at home. These requests were often a cause of severe rebukes from the parent, who in this way would highlight his independence and his charisma **as father, as well as master** of his spare time to the other customers.

Card games were the main entertainment of the customers of the cellar, and the scopa, the tresette and the briscola reigned supreme on the various tables. The appointment of the master and the sub was the final act and the most important of the game, as it decided the allocation and distribution of the drinks as stakes. Considering the hot and stubborn temper of Pietracupa's people, both during the game and the assignment of the drinks, there were discussions and reproaches which often flowed in quick-handed gestures and some coarse words igniting tempers and, unfortunately, interrupting old friendships that were hard then to recompose.

I remember during one game, **two friends**, who in every day life would respect each other as brothers, because of an improvident behavior in the distribution of the drink by one of the two, began to resent each other, also entering into issues concerning their privacy, so the verbal dispute ended in slaps. Other times, some customer with a personality milder than the others **was made to drink too much**, so that all those present could enjoy his utterances as a drunk.

In a certain sense, the cellar was a kind of **"pirate tavern"**, a place where people could breathe in that noisy and smoky atmosphere, masterfully described by many ancient and modern writers who outlined figures of customers and environment details of great scenic significance .

In museums around the world, Flemish school paintings are displayed and Caravaggio also painted figures of customers of taverns.

These paintings remind me of Pietracupa's cellar goers who filled the air with their joy, with their dialect, with their way of being, with their humanity, those very narrow **square meters of space** heated by a poor charcoal brazier, within which they spent their simple and proletarian free time, allowing them to remove from their minds the difficulties and problems of that rural world.

In the '50s at Pietracupa, there were six "cellars" scattered in the center of the village: the winery run by **Uncle Guerrino Carnevale**, the one run by **Americo Santilli**, the winery run by **Uncle Alessandro Di Fonzo**, the winery run by **Uncle Vincenzo Cacchione**, the winery run by Uncle **Peppino Patrizio, and** finally the cellar of the cooperative run by Uncle **Antonio Guglielmi**.

Every customer would choose at will his favorite local, according to proximity to their homes, pleasantry of the manager and the customers of the same manager, and also according to the quality of the wine sold. The cellars also ran the **game of "bowls"**, a typical Italian game, where the members of the two teams challenged each other to a race to achieve the highest score in the game, needed to win the final.

The discussions between the players in the race were the same way as the card games. The only difference was that the contest took place, not in a flat and confined area, but in an open area on the bumpy roads of the village of the time.

In this way, the difficulties for the players were greater, and insults for a wrong toss were frequent.

During the game the verbal advice in Pietracupa's slang given to other players of the team, such as "*hit bowl and little bowl*", "*blooms the little bowl*", "*for the score*" echoed loudly in the playing of the contenders, featuring every match with vivid demonstrations of the game.

In case it had not been established in advance that the stakes had to be shared equally among the players, you had to proceed to a final shot of bowls to determine who should be the "master" and who the "under" for the management of the stakes. This was the most delicate moment of the whole game, when among the contenders the same discussions stirred up and created the fortuitous enmities described in the previous topic on the card games.

-The band

As I highlighted previously, Pietracupa's people had a great interest in music, not only as listeners but also as direct musical instrument players. So, over the years, it was natural that a small **band** was formed by many young people of the village, who would often meet during their free time to rehearse opera arias or popular music to play on the occasion of some party or some special event.

The members of **the band** had learned the basic concepts of music from relatives or older people of the village who, before the war, had taken music courses taught by graduate masters who had come from outside.

Also, this musical activity of the recreational kind was a smart way to socialize and to spend free time to cultivate a hobby of particular cultural value.

I must say that, immediately after the war, more times, Pietracupa's band had performed in the square and had great success among the inhabitants of the village. It is also important to remember many of its components, coordinated by **Amedeo Di Sarro**, who for many years was the leader and the coordinator of this Pietracupa's City legendary band: **Rodolfo, Giovanni, Uncle Arturo, Uncle Francesco**, Riziero Grande and his brother Donato, Sandrino Porchetta, and so on.

Band members were often invited to some private event or some celebration in the alley, and it was always a special night for the people of the village who had so few meeting opportunities and good cheer.

Obviously, the band does not exist anymore.The tradition has gone off with Pietracupa's exodus to other shores.

But it is not uncommon, during the summer, listening to some old nostalgic people taking up again with other friends the old musical instrument of the past, to play the opening phrases of the Carnival of Venice, Piemontesina or Molisana that the master Eldo Di Lazzaro, of Trivento adoption, wrote in honor of the region which gave him hospitality.

144

Pietracupa's band

Sandrino, who left us this year, had still remained to represent Pietracupa's band memory. He, at August parties, joined the band on duty to honor the memory of the old village band.

Pasquale Camillo, this summer, showed me the old original drum that accompanied those players who were full of joy with the desire to entertain and have fun.

I conclude the topic, recalling a funny anecdote about Pietracupa's band. In the postwar years, the whole band was invited to perform in August in the district of Frosolone called "**Cerasito**". It was a good opportunity not only to play on tour outside, but also to enjoy a special and hearty lunch offered by hospitable inhabitants of the township.

At this musical tour, "Pietracupa's Portuguese" often joined in; pretending to be musicians, they would accompany the band and enjoy the hearty meal put at their disposal. One summer in the '50s, **Uncle Domenico Di Iorio**, who during the concert in the morning pretended to play a clarinet, joined the group on tour, awaiting lunchtime.

A resident of the district, at the end of the lunch, turned to him to ask him to sing a song. Then Uncle Menicuccio had to pretend to be too full from the hearty meal eaten and pretended a providential illness that allowed him to overcome the difficulty of the situation,

145

and especially to justify his false absence from the final evening concert.

-The football team

Football, over the years, has been and still is the most practiced sport by the Italians, both in large cities and in the most remote areas of the north or the south of the peninsula. After all, football is basically a popular and cheap game; you have only to get a ball, a square, four stones to indicate the doors of the game, and any rich or poor youth can immediately gather two opposing teams to give the classic four kicks to the ball.

Many of the great international football champions were born on the outskirts of the small provinces: just think about Angelillo, Sivori and Maschio, dubbed by the press "angels with the dirty faces", not to mention Pelé, Garrincia, Maradona, Eusebio and our Italian champions, Piola, Bacigalupo, Loich, Menti, Sentimenti IV, Amadei and so on.

Italy in the years before World War II, won **the cup "Rimet"** twice (1934 and 1938), and twice again won **the World Cup** of Nations in 1982 and 2006.

Therefore every Italian heart beats for its professional and amateur football team that is established at national, city, village, neighborhood, school, company, bar friends level and so forth.

This means that the most beautiful game in the world has been and is an integral part of leisure and fun life of every Italian, both as a direct player and as a spectator and supporter, not to mention as avid gambler and Sisal coupons player. In this popular context, Pietracupa, in the '50s and '60s, had one big flat area where all the kids gathered to play football. This was **the famous field "R 'Casarino"**, located in Via del Casaleno.

Today's **Casarino** is just a faint memory of how it was in those years; the restructuring made over the course of time transformed the primitive area into a multifunctional sports field, with changing rooms, showers and infirmary where you can play tennis, volleyball, football.

At that time it was little more than a bumpy field, where pigs from the nearby stables also scratched. But the good will and passion of young people of that time, with the meager resources available, had adapted it to a football field. Challenges between Casalotto and Aia del Piano enlivened Pietracupa's summer Sundays.

If, as often happened during the match, the inner tube of **the only ball** deflated, there was a hasty rush to put on a "patch" and inflate again the air chamber, with an emergency hand pump. It could happen that, after many interventions the tube couldn't be repaired. Then children resorted to the classic **ball made of rags and tatters**, necessary to finish the match.

Play among youth was not only a pleasure, but also a way to discuss, socialize and exchange, during the game, some not always so sweet words. But the most precious jewel of Pietracupa's football was the so-called "local national" who represented Pietracupa in football challenges with neighboring villages like Fossalto, Salcito, Torella, S. Angelo, Civitavecchia, Duronia, S. Biase and, in the years of splendor, and who even with titled Boiano entered into an interregional championship.

In the absence of telephone lines, football matches with these villages, were agreed to spontaneously among young people, who met at a trade show or agricultural land border. On match day, players and supporters, early in the morning, walked through the fields to reach the opponents' village.

As in every self-respecting challenge, when there was something wrong, often verbal confrontations flared up between players and fans of opposing factions. But, after the game ended, all went back to usual with a general drink at the bar of the host town. The hardest moment was the return to the village by foot, where players and fans crossed the fields by the shortest route, singing or cursing for the eventual outcome, taking refreshment with fruit, fresh chickpeas or cucumbers picked up in the fields they crossed.

The people of the village, seeming disinterested in these events, were immediately informed about the outcome of the game by the "door to door system". All, without distinction, up to the nice grannies always dressed in black, rejoiced or wept, thus showing their attachment and affection for their favorite team.

I have a clear memory of **the first football game** played after the war. Men, women, young, old and children were crowded on the cliff overlooking the field Casarino or appeared on the "*murillo*" to follow the phases of the game. In the game, the **San Biase** won by **14 to 0**. The final applause of the spectators and the smile of **Vincenzo Cacchione Jr.**, the legendary former goalkeeper of the team who all sweaty in a football uniform was embraced by his supporters. It is this image of the epoch I have of those days when **Pietracupa's people could smile again** and rejoice in a newfound air of peace.

Vincenzo later emigrated with his family to America, where he died a few years ago. But every time he returned to the village on vacation, we would remember the exciting matches of Pietracupa football in the '50s.

Not only Vincenzo, but all of Pietracupa's **"best youth"** of those years and the following years belonged to the football team of the village from Riziero, Rodolfo, Pasqualino, Belisario, Antonio, Gregorio, Giosué, Peppino, Michele, until the years of great exodus and even later with the arrival of village natives on vacation.

But the game of the heart, the one that always remained alive in the imagination of the older generation, is the match that **Pietracupa played away against the Boiano on September 23, 1950.** The old Pietracupa people often tell their grandchildren the story of that game, and compare it to the global challenge Italy-Germany 4-3 in 1970.

The match with Boiano had a thorough technical preparation, with the inclusion **of Guido Porchetta and Rulli**, young promises of Molise who lived in and played in Rome in the 1st Regional Division formations as the Albatrastevere.

The whole village had organized with trucks and private cars, to follow the awaited challenge at Boiano. The emotions of that Sunday of September were unforgettable. I was present, but the article by the reporter of the newspaper Tempo, sent to me by **Cosmo and Lucio Del Monaco brothers**, is still more accurate than my memories.

The formation in the field was as follows: **Lombardi, Rompicone, Di Iorio, Saliola I, Del Monaco, Cacchione, Bruni, Rulli, Porchetta, Santilli, Saliola II.**

The first goal of the match was scored by Rulli, at the 12th of the first half, with a masterful blow from outside the area, the ball bagged the top corner. With 20 minutes of the 1st period, the locals achieved a draw with a network to four feet from the door, with the helpless goalkeeper Lombardi, who had managed to touch the ball but not to divert it.

The Boiano scored another goal 38 minutes into the 1st half. **In the second half**, Pietracupa reached a draw after 10 minutes with a very beautiful action devised by the trio of point and finalized by the striker **Porchetta.**

Reaching a draw, Pietracupa's yellow / black team started to do spectacular game actions and Rulli, at the 28th minute, scored a goal that was unjustly canceled by the referee, and again at 32 minutes the same colluded and inept Boiano referee denied a clear penalty to Pietracupa for a knockdown in the area of Porchetta. The obvious bad faith of the referee was demonstrated again when time expired, he granted to Boiano a free kick that went directly into the goal, scored a goal. It was a goal that should have been canceled, according to the International Football Regulament. To no avail, all of the players protested. The only appreciable thing about that meeting was the technical evaluations of **the chronicler of Tempo,** who recognized the bad judgement of the referee and the supremacy on the field of Pietracupa. **Pasquale Lombardi**, the most bitter about that unjust result, was for many years the soul of the team and was called the Bacigalupo of Pietracupa because of his goal saving interventions.

Pasquale was a shoemaker, but if the team needed to repair the air chamber of the ball, he was always ready to get busy for it. He was the first to show up at practice and was of an immense kindness and generosity towards fellow team members and to all his countrymen. Since 1974, partly as a result of the restructuring of the field Casarino, during Pietracupa's summers were held **soccer tournaments, volleyball, tennis** that saw the participation of the **"new generation"** of the twentieth and twenty-first century, in a sort of relay between different generations, where the torch was passed from father to son to the grandchildren, and I hope so for millennia.

Following the football tradition of the past, today Pietracupa's youth have decided to register their team in the regional football tournament, by including also Pietracupa's natives, in a pact of communion among people born and descending from the same village who meet, esteem and help each other, dispelling the old saying that goes: "you are Pietracupa or Roman people only if you are born and live in Pietracupa or Rome."

Pietracupa's soccer team is the one of all who love this little town of Molise.The team, with many young people who alternate replace on the field, is very valid, and keeps alive not only the blazon of the team, but nourishes the spirit of vitality and looks for future perspectives of youth residing in the village, eager to remain living in the place where they were born and to overcome the difficulties of the moment in the same way as they are doing in the ongoing tournament, taking first prize.

They **are to be praised** because of this spirit of rebirth and love for Pietracupa.

1948 – Pietracupa 14 – S. Biase 0

Early after war – The first football game

Pietracupa's national team during the '50s

CHAPTER III

THE YEARS OF ECONOMIC DEVELOPMENT (1951/59)

-The Events in Italy and in the World:
The world events of the decade 1951/1960 consisted of ideological and political confrontation between the two great powers, the USSR and the United States of America.
The so-called "**cold war**" between the two countries is the fixed constant of the time which influenced the behavior of all other nations aligned with one or the other superpower.
It was an encounter /confrontation involving various strategic areas of the planet. It started with **the space sector** with the supremacy of the Russians with the launch of two satellites Sputnik and Laika in 1957. This was almost immediately imitated by the USA, which during 1958 and 1959, launched into space Lunik and Explorer space stations. During these years of the arms race, the United States in 1951 fired the H bomb and in 1954 launched the atomic submarine Nautilus.
Many political figures of the past are gone from the world stage, e.g., Stalin who died in 1953, **Winston Churchill** who abandoned the policy in 1955, and **Peron** who fled from Argentina after a military coup.
Other characters entered the political arena, e.g., General **Dwight Eisenhower,** elected President of the USA in 1952, **Khruschev**, signatory of the Warsaw Pact who succeeded Stalin in 1955, and **Fidel Castro,** elected supreme leader in Cuba after the revolution of 1959.
In 1953, Elizabeth II was crowned Queen of England; in 1958, after the death of Pius XII, **Pope John XXIII** rose to the papacy.
Winds of War blew in 1956 in Egypt, with the conflict between the Israelis and Egyptians for the Suez Canal, and also in Vietnam, with the French forced to abandon Indochina.
In the year 1956, Russian tanks entered **Budapest** and smothered the revolt of the Hungarian people. News of peace arrived from Korea in 1953, where the armistice was signed between the warring parties in the field.
In the late '50s, there was a turning point of detente between Russia and the United States. Khruschev, in 1956, during **the XX**

Congress of the Communist Party, denounced the crimes committed by Stalin, and in May 1959 he visited the United States. In October of the same year, Khruschev went to China, beginning the ideological clash between the two major nations of the communist party.

In such a complex international scenario, in **Italian history** there were significant events that affected the future of our nation: **in 1951** the Treaty establishing the European Coal and Steel Community (CECA) was signed; in 1954, the city of Trieste was given back to Italy, after a long period of allied administration; in 1955 Italy was admitted to the UN; and, in 1957 she signed the agreement for the organization of the European Common Market.

Interior political, economic and social policies were very articulate and complex: in 1953, the year of the political election, **Alcide De Gasperi** was voted out by his party and left the world of politics; he died the following year at his home in Trentino. The mandate to form the new government was entrusted to **Congressman Pella** and later, in February 1954, he was succeeded by **Mr. Mario Scelba** with an executive committee comprised of Social Democrats and Liberals.

In 1953, **Congressman Gronchi**, part of the left wing of the party, became President of the Republic. In 1954, **Congressman Amintore Fanfani** became Secretary of the Christian Democrats. The governments of the '50s took turns at the Palazzo Chigi with single colors or centrist formations, always headed by a member of the Christian Democrats. After the general election of 1958, **Congressman Fanfani** resigned from the secretariat of the party. In 1959 **Congressman Aldo Moro** took over; he was of the so-called current "Dorotei", which in later years, opened the door to the formation of **center-left governments** involving proponents of the Italian Socialist Party (PSI).

The '50s were years of **economic development**. Italians, after a long period of fascist autarchy, entered the free European market. They behaved with greater insight and energy than the others.

Small business owners starting with a single truck set up large transport companies; craftsmen who built chairs and tables invented mass production; those who made stoves built **appliances, such as Ignis**, a great appliances firm.

Large firms like Fiat and large groups as Piaggio or Innocenti changed. They increased production by marketing new models like the 1100, Vespa or Lambretta, and the legendary cars Fiat 500 and Fiat 600. This accompanied the dreams of Italians finally free to move about in a country where the natural, scenic and cultural beauty could be admired by everyone.

The small companies also benefitted from the general economic situation by offering supplementary work or satellite activities to large companies.

Many companies operating in traditional sectors (jewels, leather and footwear, canning, clothing) took advantage of the favorable economic situation, also in view of the fact that it was possible to find a flexible and low paid workforce in the market. **The governments of the time** contributed with support and guidance operations (1951 tax reform and 1954 Minister Vanoni development plan), to bring order into State accounts.

In the late '50s, the problems still to be solved were **the agrarian question** and **the development of the south, still** not solved today.

These last two unresolved issues, in the '50s, caused the depopulation of the small farming villages, with the great exodus of farmers in search of better living conditions, to other nations or to the big industrial cities of central / northern Italy. People abandoned their country even though they were aware they would have to face huge problems related to logistics and integration in the places of their destination.

Also **RAI, Italian state television,** had an important role in the social and cultural development of Italians. It began to broadcast on January 3rd 1954, and allowed all Italian citizens to improve their language, to investigate historical and cultural issues, and to spend moments of serene entertainment too, with escapist programs such as "*Rischiatutto*" and "*Musichiere*". The **Italian San Remo song festival** started on January 29th, 1951 with the winning song "Thanks for the Flowers" sung by Nilla Pizzi, allowed not only the opportunity to make known abroad our songs and our singers, but it also started the mass phenomenon towards world music and its performers that, after sixty years, still persists.

In the international music scene, singers such as Elvis Presley and Paul Anka introduced rock and roll and new musical songs like "It's Now or Never" and "Diana".

Finally, in the **sports world,** there was a phenomenal recovery. Italians were attracted to the sporting exploits of Coppi, Bartali,

Magni, De Filippis, Baldini, Nencini, in cycling; by football challenges between Milan, Inter, Juventus and Fiorentina and, especially, by our national football team which turned the hearts of the fans on winter Sundays, sitting in front of the radio or the television, to hear the news of the legendary Nicolò Carosio and Nando Martellini.

In 1952 in Helsinki and in 1956 in Melbourne, were opened **the Olympic Games,** where all our athletes performed well and made themselves appreciated.

In the field of boxing, Duilio Loi and Mario D'Agata won the world championship in their respective categories, imitating the Italian-American from Abruzzo, **Rocky Marciano**, world champion in the heavyweight category.

In **the world of motor sports,** the exploits of Ascari, who died tragically in '56, and Taruffi brought honor to the Ferrari team.In motorcycling, world champion Liberati and even Ribot's Dolmello / Olgiata excelled in the Europa races.

Even in **the film world,** the great directors of Italian neorealism, as De Sica, Rossellini; Italian Comedy, as Monicelli, Risi; or the dramas as Antonioni, Fellini, who directed films of high artistic value, backed by a group of actors and actresses of great talent and personality such as Gina Lollobrigida, applauded by the American public in *"Pane Amore e Fantasia* ", Giulietta Masina or as Anna Magnani, first Italian actress who won an Academy Award in 1956 with the film "The Rose Tatoo" or as Marcello Mastroianni and Sophia Loren.

All this creative and dynamic fervor of the Italian people highlighted the resilience and commitment of people attentive to changes in society, in order to progress in their own development.

But the '50s were marred by two sorrowful events. The first was **the flood of Polesine** in 1951, with 200 deaths and extensive damage to Italian cultural heritage, for which the whole nation brought relief to flood victims.

I remember, in Rome, the commitment of Bersaglieri (members of the rifle regiment of the Italian Army) who, in the courtyards were playing the tune "We are Rich and Poor," to ask people to give clothes, provisions, biscuits and so on for flood victims.

The second was **the sinking of the ship Andrea Doria**, the pride of the Italian navy, launched in 1953. It sank in 1956 near the port of New York, leaving 10 dead and 100 wounded.

Pietracupa in the '50s, Family, The bus, Daily life, Development, Students,The status of women,Marriage

In the '50s, Pietracupa's families had begun to lead again the normal everyday life in the same manner and with the same pace of work that had characterized their recent past in the fascist epoch.
But something was changing in their minds and in their spirit. First of all, the experience of war, coming in contact with fellow soldiers from other regions and having traveled across the Italy and foreign countries and, especially, the new-found freedom to leave Italy without incurring the constraints of an authoritarian regime, were very important.
To all this there are also the political events of the young Italian Republic: **Italy's adherence to CECA**, which opened job opportunities in European countries that had signed the agreement; the resumption of relations with family members living abroad; industrialization in major Italian cities; and, especially, the **low profitability of agricultural work**.
All these were reasons why many young people began to emigrate, realizing that the nation was abandoning the agricultural sector, and turned their interest to **manufacturing. In 1951**, the residents of the town of Pietracupa numbered about **1,300 inhabitants. In 2014 the residents counted in a census amounted to 223 people** equally divided between male and female, mostly elderly, and about twenty-five young people between 18 and 23 years of age.
These data all indicate that the percentage of residents in the municipality was reduced by 87% between 1951 and 2014 and that 88% of current residents are over 60 years old. It is to be noted that, during the winter months, many older people go to their children living elsewhere, and then the people actually present amount to only about **99**, more or less the make-up of a **medium size building in Rome**. Depopulation started slowly since the '50s, but at the beginning of that decade the village was still full of people who lived and worked on site. From that decade, I resume the thread of memories to tell **how life was in the village**.
Every summer I returned to Pietracupa with my mother and my brother to spend the summer vacation; my father joined us in September at the Patron Saints feast.
During these years, as I have already had occasion to say, traveling Roma / Pietracupa was managed by **the company SATAM** of the

Saliola family from Salcito. They performed the service with a vintage bus which for many years was the legendary "umbilical cord" linking Pietracupa to Rome.

 Giggino, the unforgettable driver of the bus, was not only the bus driver, but also tutor, assistant, Jack of all trades for all Pietracupa's residents in Rome and in Pietracupa, who always needed to interface with him for so many reasons. The coach and its driver were sort of carrier pigeons taking every day news, parcels, food, and letters from one end of the two opposite sites to the other.

The trip, with a brief stopover at Cassino, lasted about **seven hours.** At the time, the actual tunnel that now links San Pietro Infine to Venafro was not yet built so the bus had to climb the Monte della Nunziata Lunga over a rocky road overlooking a ravine. So the twists and turns on the switchbacks weakened the resistance of travelers, often taken to retching.

But for me, travelling on that bus was synonymous with **vacation time**. Clean air, meetings with my relatives, with my friends from childhood, waiting to see the wheat fields again, to spend the cool summer evenings outdoors, to listen to the singing of the crickets and see the stars in the night, to savor the quiet during the sunny afternoons, listening to band concerts during the holidays, to observe the polite smiles of my Pietracupa's female contemporaries who, in the peasant culture of the epoch, were apparently icy, almost unapproachable - all things that the city couldn't offer and that coming back to Pietracupa I would find again.

For this reason, after the bus passed the Fossalto Road Inspector's house, I was taken by a certain euphoria and enthusiasm I cannot describe.

Even the arrival of the bus in the village was something special. In those years the owners of cars in the province of Campobasso were very few and on the rough provincial "Garibaldi" the only regular vehicles traveling the way from Pietracupa, Salcito, or Trivento were the bus to Rome, the bus to Campobasso (conducted by the famous **"Scatolone"**), and the bus of **the company Scarano** to Naples, The rest was silence. For this, the arrival of the bus and especially the bus Rome / Salcito was the main event of the day. It lent some novelty to Pietracupa's everyday routine in a period which, as I wrote earlier, there weren't telephones, television, cinema or social places, and newspapers and radios belonged only to few lucky persons.

The end point was near the above mentioned "**road inspector's house**", consisting of two covered rooms, one reserved for road maintenance men and the other was a waiting room for travelers.

In this place, every day precisely at two, a knot of people **waiting for the bus** would form to greet the villagers coming and also to help them carry luggage from the road house to the houses in the village. If incoming travelers were many, the line of people on the move looked like a colorful procession, at the end of which, especially the boys, would receive some candy or chocolate from newcomers.

Recently I was moved by the story of a dear Pietracupa friend who reminded me of those early '50s arrivals, telling me that my mother always gave him a chocolate, and for him it was a rarity because it was virtually non-existent in the village.

This time for me was the holiday and, especially, my free time I would spend with the other boys of the village, my contemporaries.

We used to play at bottonella, saltacavallo, nizza. Our meeting points were the "Briscinia", the Murillo, the Casarino, **San Gregorio** and **the Croce**, in Piazza Nicola Portone. Now that area is called the "**Villetta**", but at the time it was called "**the Croce**" because of the large cross that soared on one side of the square. We kids would sit on its base to talk, bicker or run in its surroundings. **All those guys**, my contemporaries, are by now grandparents like me, and all made their way of life as they dreamed.

But now, I would still like to remember them in a sort of circle, **the circle of these 75 years** in which we have always met in the same square, embellished over time, but always the same in our memories: Michele Santilli, Giovanni Santilli, Antonio Di Iorio, Gervasio Porchetta, Romano Ferri, Benedetto Di Iorio, Pasquale Camillo, Giuseppe Santilli, Giuseppe Camillo, Vincenzo Cacchione, Antonio Camillo, Giovanni Saliola, Nicola Fusaro, Giuseppe Grande, Gino Brunetti.

Some funny anecdotes bind me to many of them, like the night I **made a surprise serenade** for an unknown girl from San Biase together with Pasquale Camillo and Romano Ferri; the serenade ended with the braying of a donkey led by a farmer; or "night raids" to tempting **fields of fruit** owned by some relative of ours, who with Romano and Benedetto sometimes I visited silently; and, still, the strumming on the guitar, with **Cenzino Cacchione**, to mimic Peppino di Capri, Celentano or Carosone, then artists unknown to the public.

157

But before us **there was another generation of young people** who characterized the life of the village in those years, and those young people were the first to emigrate elsewhere: Riziero Grande, Rodolfo, Pasqualino Saliola, Antonio Del Monaco, Gennaro Delmonaco, Palmerino Delmonaco, Pierino Di Iorio, Cenzino Cacchione, Michele Porchetta, Sandrino Porchetta, Oreste Carnevale, Domenico Festa, Giuseppe Di Iorio. They were beautiful youth who made themselves appreciated.

One of my special memories of those years is the wonderful and loving relationship that has bound my family with that of **Uncle Giuseppe Di Iorio**. Uncle Giuseppe was my father's cousin and lived at Pietracupa near the "briscinia", with his wife, mother-in-law, and two daughters Linda and Antonietta. He was not only a good looking man, but also a true gentleman in his manner and bearing, always friendly and helpful to all the people of the village.

He knew music, was an experienced hunter of game, and loved the good things in life, and above all his family who would follow with great attention, as it was in the style of "Gallinella". In the '50s, realizing the difficulties of life in the village, he thought to seek his fortune **in Milan** and was one of the first Pietracupa's inhabitant to emigrate to that city.

He was later joined by **Oreste Carnevale, Domenico Festa** and **Nicola Saliola** and by all Pietracupa's people passing through Milan, as they used to do in those days, where the friend would call for or house other friends.

Uncle Giuseppe was a tailor and had started his business with great success in Milan, later calling to join him his daughter Linda. The vicissitudes of life led him to Milwaukee in **the United States** to Aunt Anna Maria and Uncle Arturo, then to New York, where he was joined by his family. But an incurable disease hit him and he returned to Pietracupa in 1965.

Uncle Giuseppe, like all Pietracupa's people, loved his country very much. Every year in August, he would return to his home, and the days I spent with him and his family were some of the most beautiful of my boyhood memories.

Every time I go **under St. Gregory oaks**, I remember **vacationers' and residents' usual afternoon siesta**s under the oak trees.

Uncle Giuseppe illuminated the scene with his speeches and his tales of life in Milan, and his hunting, in which my brother and I often participated.

A special event during the holidays was represented by the usual invitation that Uncle Peppino / Castellino, elder of the family, addressed to his grandchildren - to go spend **a day outdoors at the** *vella* (place where there were many farms), at his farmhouse in the countryside.

Aunt Domenica cheered the company with her special dishes of peasant gastronomy and then, under the trees of the grove in front of the house, we would talk of many past and present things.

They were magical moments, where everyone would feel the charm of the atmospheres of past times, now gone. This was Uncle Peppino: **a modern man, but with an ancient heart**. Pietracupa of the '50s was an effervescent and politically very busy village.

I read some excerpts of local news on "Momento Sera", signed M.D.M., which reported in 1952, **"in the village, having passed the election for Mayor, and it's time to leave behind gossip, evil feeding the breeze of slander or worse"**. In another article, the correspondent complained about why some people were allowed to let pigs and hens roam the streets with impunity, which smeared alleys, while others were fined for throwing a few buckets of clean water on the ground for washing it. The square of the Dead Soldiers of Hungary (dedicated by the Pietracupa Town Hall to Hungarian dead of the 1956 Russian invasion) indicates a clear policy of the City Council at the time, beyond the human factor and the right to freedom of every people, which nationally was also the reason for the detachment of Socialists from the Communists.

Rome. Meeting among cousins. Uncle Giuseppe, Aunt Angelina, Angelico, Clara and Lino

Uncle Giuseppe
Linda and Lina

Uncle Giuseppe Di Iorio,

Uncle Giuseppe, Vincenzo, Bianca and Mary in the USA

Visit in Milan

-Development

The '50s, for Italy, were years of social and **economic development.** Pietracupa benefitted from the new climate of economic and infrastructure recovery that the government brought forward to give the nation a modern face with the goal of a superior role in the European and World political scene.

Bodies created by the State, such as **the INA Casa (National Institute for Workers Houses) and the Cassa per il Mezzogiorno**, were intended to support organizationally and economically society's rebuilding, and the large infrastructure sectors needed for rehabilitation of the urban fabric that had been destroyed by war, and create roads necessary to give Italy a new face.

In this climate of rebirth and national activism, the most significant event in the lives of Pietracupa's people was the construction of **the Molise aqueduct**.

Mr. Lucio Del Monaco sent me a newspaper article about this event in 1954, when Congressman Sedati, Undersecretary for Public Works, attended the ceremony of the inauguration of the aqueduct at Pietracupa, also attended by the Mayor, the parish priest, the authorities of the Province and, of course, all village people .

In front of a newsstand of a modern style, after welcoming authorities, read by schoolboy Giuseppe Vanga, son of Michele, the water began to flow among the shouts of joy and applause of those present. All were moved because of this monumental work **carrying water into the village** after long years of waiting. The celebration ended with the manifestation of twenty pretty young girls of the village, in costume of Molise, who started a dance and a folk song praising the clear water of the fountain that would replace the muddy, putrid water of artificial wells.

After this first step, there were jobs for connecting the south of the village to the 74 highway and, last but not least, the highway Garibaldi, the main artery road for the connection with Campobasso, **was restored and paved** throughout its length.

Also, Morgia was the subject of stabilization and safety work. This fervor of reconstruction at the national level, produced the desire to invest and to start new businesses. New business throughout Italy, and especially in the southern regions, had always been reluctant to follow market novelties, unless in the relevant field of agriculture.

Pietracupa, in this new climate of awakening, **did its part**. First of all they opened a **new mill** along the road to San Gregorio; it was run by Uncle Pasquale and Uncle Giuseppe. **New shops** selling basic items, managed by Carnevale and Cacchione family, were opened; **the biscuit firm** of Mr. Cacchione, with its famous sponge fingers, began to produce again; **the trade in sheep meat**, pork, poultry and dairy products gained pace with the brothers Felice and Romolo Santilli, spreading out also to the capital; **trade transport** started slowly to appear on the local scene with an old truck run by Uncle Guerrino and Uncle Domenico Di Iorio.

A group of local investors (Santilli, Durante, Iannacone) launched a **service of mechanized threshing** in the summer months, with the technical assistance of **Uncle Luigi Grande**; workers specializing in knitting and embroidery made a niche for themselves; **local restaurants**, run by Uncle Guerrino and Uncle Patrizio, welcomed the new road workers in Pietracupa; **the construction and hydraulic industries** had a remarkable development, especially with the advent of running water.

So Pietracupa gave a positive response to the opportunities that **the market offered**, even if limited to a few people, with initiatives which still stimulated the induced market, with positive effects on the labor market.

The agricultural sector, which was the main source of 90% of Pietracupa's inhabitants, in 1950, was gratified by new farming machinery that Italian industry put on the domestic market with government incentives.

So the archaic systems of work were complemented by new equipment which, on one hand eased peasants' fatigue, but on the other hand created problems of manpower exuberance and lack of laborers' training.

So began **the crisis of the agricultural system**, to the point that farmers left the land to turn their attention to other sectors in the emerging industrial or mining societies, marking the start of the **sunset of that farm society** tied to the economy of small divided estates, considered marginal on the chessboard of the industrialized countries.

All these were the reasons for the great exodus of Pietracupa's people that started in recent years. But **in the early '50s, something new** affected village activities. I will focus on this air of renewal which I breathed on returning to the village in the summers of the '50s.

The mill was one of the compulsory stops for my morning walks. Uncle Giuseppe or Uncle Pasquale, between the sacks of flour, showed me all the mechanical apparatus that moved the engine. I would leave the room completely covered by flour, but still the mill was very popular with internal and external customers.

The legendary truck of Uncle Domenico was the only local motorized means to transport wood and sacks of grain, and even to go to the novenas and the Feasts. On these occasions, the Uncle would insert a series of tables in the body of the truck and the vehicle was ready for departure, giving the green light to travelers who, running, hogged the best seats, often after heated discussions.

1954. The inauguration of Molisan aqueduct

Molisan aqueduct

Molisan aqueduct

Pietracupa during the '50s – Brave men on the rock

With **the mechanization of agriculture**, donkey and horse threshers disappeared. The mechanical means did stop at village strategic points (Pozzo Nuovo, Cantone, San Gregorio, Baraccone, Vella, Piana and so on) and to these places, peasants carried sheaves to be threshed.

The scenes of life observed during the hours of threshing were a feature of the rural world in apparent recovery; sheaves, sacks of grain, farmers, mules, donkeys, threshing technicians, were the dynamic scenario of those areas of work, the symbol of an apparently alive rural society that soon would be gone.

But in those moments there was the essence and energy of people that gathered the result of years of hard work, and a light shone in their eyes especially when **their hands touched the grains of wheat** that came from the hatch of the thresher.

The village was in the process of transformation, running water had opened up new job opportunities that **Gaetano**, a former Salcito blacksmith, had been able to grasp, and for years he was Pietracupa's official plumber.

Even communications between remote people were improved with the installation of a telephone line. I want to dedicate a special memory of **the first public telephone** installed in Pietracupa in a cabin of Uncle Vincenzo senior cellar in ViaTrento. With that single active phone line, it was an adventure getting in touch with a friend living in Rome.

From Pietracupa you had to call the operator of Campobasso who would put you in contact with the operator of Rome. If the line was free he immediately called you and you could speak with the person you want. If the line was occupied, **you had to start over**.

So, especially in the summer, the phone booth was a kind of living room and parlor of public phone users and convivial waiting.

It was a romantic world that I remember for its simplicity. Compared to today, when we are all running out of breath, when everyone, including children, has a cell phone in hand, by day, at night, on the street, on the bus, in a pizzeria, the bathroom, and so on.

-*Students*

With the arrival of summer, all the lucky students residing at Pietracupa, who attended high school in the city, would come back to the village to spend their deserved vacation with the family.

In the same way as all other students living in the city, they were happy to spend the holidays in the native country of their parents, out of the city heat and in a serene environment.

The Italian school of the '50s was still an elite school, very expensive and very selective, as society was also elitist in those times.

Every father would dream for his children of a better future than his own and, especially in the south of Italy, the achievement of the longed for piece of paper by a son or a daughter was a matter of commitment and of great pride for the whole family, even if achieved with many economic sacrifices.

I remember the warm and joyous celebration that **Uncle Domenico Saliola** organized on the occasion of **his son Pasqualino's** surveying diploma; the whole village was present.

A similar party was held for Antonio, son of Uncle Eduardo, for Domenico Carnevale, for Belisario Delmonaco, for Paolino Delmonaco, for Paolo Tullo, for Romano Ferri, for Benedetto Di Iorio. The village was proud of its children and rejoiced with them.

There wasn't a real relational gap between local and outside students. They respected each other, but it goes without saying that the first often were busy with their family activities and had little free time. So the outside group was more compact and had a better chance of staying together.

This "outside group", of which I was a member even with my brother Lino, included Aurora , Amelia and Elvira Del Monaco sisters and their brother Lucio coming from Naples; Mario and Franco Carnevale coming from Rome; Teodoro Salvatore and their brothers and sisters coming from Villa di Briano in Campania; Giovanni Santilli and his brother Giuseppe coming from Rome; Michele Guglielmi, his sister Franca and his wife Lidia coming from Florence; and, occasionally, there were even more friends of passage as Augusto, the brother-in-law of Dr. Mascione, the doctor of the village.

Our close friendships started in those years. We might only meet during the summer. But those days we spent together were days of joy, jokes, outdoor picnics, of shy, virtuous and innocent sympathies in the bucolic scenery that Pietracupa offered us, such as the oaks of San Gregorio, the grove of Canton, the via nova and the lawn near the river Biferno for trips outside the village.

I could tell thousands of stories about that time, as opposition by the families to the love story of Lucio and Vittoria, or the first trousers worn by Amelia with the astonished *ma che sci n'ommo*? - "are you maybe a man?" pronounced by an old woman of the village. Or the strict check of the pleasant **Aunt Elvira Durante** - always attentive to her nieces as she followed nearby - arousing their affectionate hilarity. But the thought that some of these dear friends have died when they were still young doesn't permit me to write anymore, and I prefer to keep in my heart the memory of **their smiles**, of their joy

167

of life, of their sweetness, of the friendship they gave me with great affection.

But one thing I still want to add on the subject is that all these friends have one thing in common with me: **the love for this little town in the Molise region** that has always been in their hearts. Everyone, with husbands, wives and children in tow, during the summer, has always returned to their homes in the village. And **Franco Salvatore**, in a particular way, considered it pleasant settling in Pietracupa. Many have written books, articles in newspapers, and have always worked at local events to express in a tangible and collaborative way their feeling for the village of their parents.

-The status of women

In the preceding paragraphs I have spoken of the rural world and the father's role, the undisputed patriarch of the family, sole repository of all the important decisions concerning the house and the members of the family. He held this role with great authority and severity, in a particular manner regarding the women of his house, which he considered the weak point of the system. This is not to say that all men would beat and abuse women. But the dominant culture in those years was a **macho culture**, where all charges and decisions **belonged to the breadwinner**.

The woman was an adjuvant element of the farm system, who helped the family with activities relating to the care of the home, of her husband and children, and work in the fields. In my mind I have always alive the image of the return from the fields of Pietracupa's farmers with the man on the back of the donkey or horse and woman walking with bundles of wood or quartaro (square wooden basket) on the head with their children in tow.

The girl of marriageable age, as I said, was not entirely free to choose her life partner, but had to submit to the approval of his father who decided about the man she was to marry.

Choosing which was often linked to economic convenience of the family or complacent intervention or mediation by relatives, friends and various advisers. The girl had to have a mild behavior, marry very young, and, especially, get to the marriage chaste. Every engagement that ended without a marriage was a premonitory element for the girl to remain a spinster.

Another typical aspect of the time, the subject of stories and novels by many famous writers, was the sexual abuse that **the landowner, the noble or powerful man on duty** would have the opportunity to inflict on young unskilled and illiterate girls, who served in their homes or on their farms. Often, these girls, after being abused, became pregnant and procreated children not recognized, who remained their sole responsibility, without any help from the mature guilty party.

I do not want to disturb King Vittorio Emanuele II and his relationship with the beautiful peasant "Rosina" or "Gradisca" of the film "La Dolce Vita", but this was the picture of the overall situation in an Italy in the developing world, which saw in the following years **the struggle carried on by women**, who were able to assert the principle of equality between men and women and to enact laws on stalking and killing woman.

But there remains a long way to go, as the chilling news events of our day still show.

I decided to bring some stories of women to highlight and document the thoughts, opinions, and difficulties of the '30s - '50s Pietracupa women.

Aunt Lisetta was a beautiful, dynamic, joyful, educated girl. Both parents were primary school teachers and affluent, so life smiled on her and she was full of expectations for a bright future next to a man whom she would marry only for love.

Her meeting with Uncle Domenico met these expectations. So, as was the custom of that time, she asked her father for permission to marry the young man she loved.

The father, an austere and narrow minded man, denied his consent to the marriage, believing that his daughter could aspire to a better marriage, and told her to stop any contact with Uncle Domenico or otherwise he would disinherit her and chase her away from home. Aunt Lisetta was the first Pietracupa brave woman who chose love and, without thinking about it twice, took her suitcase, left her parental home, albeit with great sorrow, and married Domenico. Her life was prosperous, peaceful and blessed by the birth of Gervasio and Franco, my dear childhood friends.

"Franceschina" lived in Pietracupa and was in love with a young man in the village who reciprocated her love with great affection and tenderness. One day, this young man asked to formalize **their secret engagement** and wanted to go to her father to ask for her hand.

"Franceschina" told me of this meeting, explaining to me that, because of her shyness, she eavesdropped behind the door adjacent to the reception room. When her father called her to ask her assent, she exclaimed she consented and ran away with redness and tears on her cheeks.

As it happens in all the countries of the south, the news had gone around the houses and there were interwoven opinions about this engagement, whispers, and above **all, the cries of an aunt** rushing into the house of her father saying that this young man was not reliable.

In fact the aunt advised to marry another man, who had emigrated from northern Italy and who could offer his daughter a more comfortable life. Unfortunately the words of her aunt had their effect and "Franceschina" was forced to celebrate the marriage with the young immigrant. But, after the ceremony, she wanted to spend a period of rest and reflection with her family, and also to be able to learn the personality and feelings of her bridegroom.

This was enough to make her understand that the young man was not made for her and at this point she asked for help from her father who, realizing his error, helped his daughter get an annulment of the marriage at the Sacra Rota. Franceschina then emigrated to the United States to some relatives. She never married and she dedicated her whole life to work, to her family and to her niece and nephews who filled her loneliness.

At the end of her story, the face of "Franceschina" was sweet and thoughtful; in her expression there was all the regret of a young love ended for trivial reasons, and of a youth unlived, except for those few moments that one day she had pronounced for the first time, before her father and her first love.

"**Graziella**" was a beautiful, gentle, mild-mannered and polite girl. Many boys were in love with her, but in her heart she loved"Giorgio" a youth of the village with whom since the days of the school she would exchange affectionate notes. The parents did not consent to this love between the two of them and did everything to split up them. "George" left for other shores and "Graziella", left alone, apathetically accepted the marriage proposal of a wealthy young man in the village. "Graziella" always suffered much because of that abandonment, and that young boy who once sent her love notes always remained in her heart. Her smile was no longer what it had been and gradually even her brilliance and her heart dulled behind that unrealized dream.

"**Giustina**" was a self-possessed, young, affectionate girl, who was temporarily working in Pietracupa's Town Hall, a few kilometers away from her village. "**Giannino**" was a young Pietracupa student belonging to a wealthy family of the village, and his heart was immediately struck by the ways and the smile of the girl. So he started a sweet relationship with her, made up of looks, love notes, delicate gifts and romantic walks out of the village. At Pietracupa nothing has ever escaped the watchful eyes of the people, who immediately informed the family of the young man, who stepped in to tell "Giustina" and "Giannino" to terminate their idyll. But they did not, because you cannot put a stop to love. Then the two elder sisters of "Giannino" put on the brakes: they took the unfortunate girl in secret, beat her angrily, and warned that this was only the beginning if the affair didn't immediately end.

Unfortunately, this love story was over. "Giannino" is now a happy grandfather and has a beautiful family. But, when this summer I reminded him of this episode, an expression of nostalgia and sweet regret appeared on his face for that past of sweet romance, but also practical girls.

I have known **Maria** for a very long time. In addition to meeting in the summer, we exchange greetings on the occasion of Christmas, when I used to phone her husband Romano.

Last summer, in one of the moments of calm, under the big tree in front of the bar, she told me a story of her life I really did not know.

It is the story of a positive and concrete, and at the same time romantic and gentle, woman in love with her husband since their schooldays. Maria was born in Africa and, with the fall of colonialism, her family moved back to Italy.

She attended the last year of primary school at Pietracupa, birthplace of her father and at school **her affection for Romano blossomed**. Then she left for Milan, where her father ran a taxi. But Maria and Romano always remained in touch through a lot of letters. Maria wanted to work with her relatives in the United States and left for Westfield, the American Pietracupa.

The distance slowed the flow of letters between the two, and also her sister informed her that her lover had some casual behavior in the village and advised Maria to find another man. But it was not true! Romano was aware about the behavior of his girlfriend in Westfield. Knowing that a villager was courting his girlfriend, he wrote to him to leave her alone.

Maria was not enthusiastic about American life and style and for this reason she returned to Italy and spent her first week at Pietracupa. Her relations with Romano had broken off. But one evening strolling in Via Trento she met him and she **told me**: "*I was under the arm of my friend Rina when I saw Romano from a distance coming towards us. I had a sinking heart and, clinging to Rina, I said to myself this is the man of my life.*"

It is a delicate story, imbued with the scent of old times. Romano and Maria are now happily married and live in Milan; they have a beautiful daughter, Sabrina, who is an appreciated teacher.

172

Concetta and Remo wedding

Antonietta and Michele wedding

Michele and Cecilia wedding

Parents in bride's home

Antonietta and Michele wedding – coming out of bride's home

-Marriage

The reader of these stories will wonder whether *there was any opportunity for fun for young Pietracupa women*. The fun moments happened especially **at weddings or feasts in the village**, where there always was an accordion player who encouraged young people to dance the salterello, the waltz or tango - of course watched over by their mothers or relatives who sat in a circle in the room, and every non-linear behavior was the subject of comments and feedback from those present.

Only at the end of the '50s, **Uncle Michelino Santilli** and **Aunt Ida** offered a room along the Via Garibaldi, where, on Sundays, young men and women who were passing by could listen to an old gramophone. There were a few pieces of music of the epoch, such as Media Luz or Jealousy or Cumparsita, and it was possible to dance a few waltzes or some tangos.

Uncle Michelino was an organizer and a formidable communicator, and I think that many marriages materialized in those meetings organized by him.

The wedding parties in the village had to follow a well-defined ceremony that included the display of the dowry and gifts received, that every friend and relative had to view in the bride's house as a wish for abundance and good fortune.

In the nineteenth century, a formal act was even drafted in which the movable and immovable property that the bride would bring, like a kit, were reported in the marriage document.

The church ceremony was very characteristic, the procession of relatives started from the bride's house and went to church followed by a swarm of kids racing to collect the sweets that were thrown in the air as good luck messages.

The lunch had to be plentiful and tasty. If for various reasons, the newlyweds left for their honeymoon, the festivities dragged on for another week in their home.

The last question that the reader, amazed at such simplicity and purity, will ask Pietracupa's people will be this: *but has any licentious talk attracted the curiosity of citizens?*

Is it possible that anything forbidden would never happen at Pietracupa? For privacy reasons, and, above all for good taste, I will not tell risqué stories; I do not know.

The baritone of a famous opera sings **"slander is a breeze"**. Certainly some breeze has expired on this subject, on some door of the house or farm entered in error by some distracted man or some scuffle between women in defense of spousal identity. But all this is part of another story, linked to all human beings' lives, with funny or dramatic stories which are the same in all countries of the world. There have been and will still be rumors and legends, but they are not subject of this book. Anyway, from the '40s up to the present day, the village has been graced by the presence of a **beautiful feminine innocence** which, with their sweetness and love, let inside the community a new modern air, in different situations of the epoch.

I pause to name a few girls belonging to the period of my youth like Tonina La Guardia, Erminia Guglielmi, Linda Di Iorio and her sister Antonietta, Anna and Antonietta of Uncle Dante, Ubaldina and her cousins from Rome, the nieces of Aunt Luigiotta, the nieces of Uncle Giovanni Di Sarro, Anna Di Iorio, Emy Saliola, Maria Di Iorio daughter of Uncle Pietro, Maria Di Iorio daughter of Uncle Alberto, Antonietta Delmonaco now all happy grandmothers or aunts.

Today's forty-somethings, in the same way as their mothers, return to the village with their children, and so it will continue for years to come. This '70s group, consists of my daughter Claudia, my niece Elizabeth, Stefania Camillo, Mariangela Saliola, Roberta Di Iorio, Cinzia and Esther Camillo, Carla Porchetta, Virginia Ciavarro, Sabrina Ferro, Alessia and Francesca, nieces of Uncle Corradino, Manuela Di Sarro, Alessia Iocca, Sandra Piras, Chiara niece of Uncle Augusto, and so on.

-Pietrcupa's anecdotes and characters of the '50s

On January 3, 1954 the RAI, Italian Radio and Television, began broadcasting its first television programs, triggering one of the most important revolutions in the social and economic life of Italians.

It fostered the cultural evolution of a basically rural and poor people who, through the medium of television have had the opportunity to gain more knowledge about what once was the heritage of only a few people, redrawing the map of information and knowledge of the public.

At the same time, it offered **opportunities for recreation and entertainment**, especially in small Italian villages, to the myriad of people belonging to the rural world who could find only rare moments of fun if not in bars or by relatives.

The cost of a television was between 160 thousand and a half million pounds for the most advanced equipment. The average annual income per capita was around two hundred and fifty pounds, and the number of unemployed at that time was about two million. From these data, it is easy to understand that Pietracupa's community considered it appropriate to install **a TV in a rented common room,** and various citizens supporting the initiative divided up the spending.

The first television room was located at Casalotto near the site of the old Town Hall. It was later moved to the Aia del Piano in Via Garibaldi. The television was a very important tool for the evolution of Pietracupa's people of the older generation, especially in the 1960s, with the program "Non é mai troppo tardi", led by teacher Manzi, that allowed many elderly and illiterate people to be able to learn reading and writing. But these two places used for watching TV programs were, at the same time, holders of anecdotes and habits that characterized the evenings that Pietracupa's people spent in those rooms.

I still remember the brisk pace of "**Uncle Clemente**" who every night, strutted his way into the room, and, when I met him in the street all elated, he said: *I'm going to see the dancers so I can restore myself"* (*m'ricrio*). Inside the room, when the grandmothers, dressed in their usual black skirts, saw the dancers appearing on the monitor in tutus, would whisper among themselves, "what a scandal; those are whores". Often, many sympathetic and elderly spectators dozed off, filling the room with their gentle snoring that was immediately ended by **Uncle Antonino Di Iorio** who was delegated to keep order in the room.

Various perfumes, whispers, and sometimes heated verbal fights during political debates were typical scenes of those years in **the television room** at Pietracupa.

To all this we must add the kind note of ever present young, shy and romantic suitors, who were glad to sit by the girls of their heart, being ecstatic to observe them instead of watching the dancers on the TV.

It is not an easy task speaking of characters that marked a period of time or a historical period in the life of a country, a city, a nation.

Referring, then, to Pietracupa's microworld of the '50s, I can only say that all **the inhabitants of the village were the main characters** who featured the history of the village, with their attitudes, their work, their character strengths and weaknesses, their individual and family stories, even if starting from these years, the village changed its face.

The rural world dissolved. The best youth of the village began to leave for other destinations and their stories are intertwined with others, different from the daily affairs of the small native village.

Of that past, today only the elderly's memories and grandparents' stories told to their grandchildren remain in the village or around the world. This perpetuates in their imagination that dear, simple and romantic rural world, totally different from today. With this premise, I deem it important to indicate **some public figures** who characterized the village in the '50s, just to clearly trace those years and that country world now totally transformed.

A character I remember with particular affection is "**Uncle Matteo**." I would meet him every morning in front of the church of San Gregorio. He was a full of verve and a brilliant old person. "Uncle Matteo" was remembered by the community in the village to have held a commemorative speech on the occasion of some leading local's funeral.

His speech began with the quote: *"chains are unleashed as bombed rubble"* and ended with: *"women weep in front of this dead corpse."* I was not present at that ceremony, so I'm not able to say how things really happened. I can only admire the spirit of participation and involvement of "**Uncle Matteo**." He was not political, nor a man of high education. But, hats off to his sharp mind and the courage to

178

express his ideas - even if, in the heat of his oratory, he ran into some error.

A particularly dear character, not only because he was the brother of my grandmother, but because he was a smart, clever and at the same time a very sensitive, very ironic, and very generous man of great class, was Uncle **Giuseppe/ Emilio Di Iorio**, nicknamed **Castellino**.

The life story of Uncle Giuseppe is the story of many of Pietracupa's men. He left at age 17, as an emigrant, to go to work in Brazil so he could earn enough money for the dowries of his four sisters (Antonia, Concetta, Silvia and Anita), as was the custom of the village at that time.

The foreign firm with which he had found work, was a multinational entrusted by the government to build a large thoroughfare necessary to connect to each other many provinces of the large Brazilian territory.

Therefore, workers from all over the world were sent to construction sites set up **in the heart of the Amazon forest,** far from population centers, housed in shacks without any health and hygiene comfort. Some years ago I went through the Amazon rainforest as a tourist and I must say that life is impossible because of the heat, the mosquitoes, and the hidden dangers of the forest. Thinking about those poor workers, and especially about **the poor young man of 17**, it was natural to say to myself that they were really **cannon fodder.**

Uncle contracted a very high fever one day and was transported to a kind of quarantine hospital prepared in the remains of the barracks yard, awaiting the arrival of the doctor who only once a week would visit the sick.

During the medical examination, the Uncle told the doctor: *"I have in my pocket the salary for the month; if you heal me it is yours; if I die it is always yours."*

Fortunately everything went well and so, once healed, he could return to his Pietracupa. But four sisters to marry off was a large number in relation to the dowry that he had to give to each of them. So, since it was necessary to defend the good name of the family Di Iorio, Uncle again took up **his cardboard suitcase** and emigrated again, going to **the United States this time**.

He remained in the US a couple of years, initially working as a laborer in a company constructing railway lines. Being an intelligent

179

and communicative person, he was quickly noticed by the Site Manager, who entrusted him with a lead role of manager in a team of all Italians, thus removing him from strenuous manual labor.

Uncle Peppino achieved his purpose, returned to Pietracupa, started **on the front of World War I fighting on the Piave**, married Aunt Domenica Berardo (Aunt Menguccia), and was village municipal guard for many years.

In the style of "Gallinella" family, to which he belonged, Uncle liked the finer things of life, such as good food (he was a great gourmand), the beauty of nature, including in these beauties also the charm and female smile, but he was mostly **a very generous person**.

Domenico Meale, last summer, told me the following anecdote about Uncle Peppino's generosity: *"I had to leave immediately for the city of Verona, as I was called by the Italian employment center to go to work in Germany. Therefore, I had immediate need of money to buy a train ticket, essential to reach that center. As I hadn't any cash in the house, I immediately turned to a loan by "Aunt Immacolata", affluent and wealthy woman of the village, without children, with the commitment that I would give the money back immediately in the days to follow.*

"Aunt Immacolata" answered my request: 'Domenico start to walk at once to Verona, because the road is very long and I do not know if you'll have time to get there by tomorrow'.

In despair, I turned to my uncle Peppino Castellino, who immediately told his wife to give me the money required and said I could repay it when I wanted, whenever I returned to the village. He hugged me, wishing me good luck."

Speaking about Uncle Peppino, a myriad of personal memories come to my mind. I always see him there at his farm at the *vella* or in the evening around the fire at his country house or during his invitations to dinner with my whole family, where he inquired about the trend of my studies.

Even his visits in our home in Rome, during Easter, were pleasant, with the unforgettable evenings at the cinema / theater Iovinelli, where he wanted to go to watch, after the film of the day, the "naked females" of the variety show.

But in addition to these corollary stories, he was a man who had sound principles. And, not having children, he was proud that his numerous nieces and nephews had the respect of others and success in life.

To demonstrate the affection he had for me, at the achievement of my high school diploma, he gave me a watch which I keep among the most precious things in my life.

Uncle Peppino was also a fine, ironic and good-natured observer of **others' vices**.

I remember two very funny stories tales about Uncle Peppino. The first tale concerns his tailor, who always sewed his clothes in a large size (like a big sack), and would tell an angry Uncle Peppino, *"Be quiet! I am a good international tailor"*. The second tale concerns his young female doctor in Pietracupa. When, during his first examination, she said to him: *"Uncle Peppino, please let down your pants"*, Uncle Peppino answered, "indecent request!" and left her office, coming out to the street.

As the last story in this series, it is a hilarious episode, that of his tenant who assigned to his uncle the primary choice of wheat sheaves to split, saying: *z 'Pepì, I pick and you choose. (uncle Pepì I pick and you choose).*

Uncle Peppino in the morning would choose the sheaves composed in the farmyard; but at night his tenant broke them up for him according to his own advantage.

He died lucid and serene, making the sign of the cross.

Uncle Eduardo Camillo was Pietracupa's municipal guard who succeeded Uncle Peppino. He was very intelligent, dynamic, with high communication skills to citizens, even though he had a strong character and loyalty to the duties imposed by his public role. His mother, Aunt Rose, was a strong woman and had this only son. In years of great economic difficulties she worked in the fields with great alacrity to ensure him a decent life. **His wife, Aunt Fortunata**, went along and collaborated with her husband, with the tenacity and strength of Molise women, to complete the project to let **her son Antonio** study and achieve a high school diploma, necessary to start a business as a clerk far from the hard life of a farmer. Antonio repaid the parents for these sacrifices after graduating.

Unfortunately Antonio died recently of an incurable disease. When a childhood friend dies so suddenly, you remain crushed, stunned and saddened. My years of childhood and early youth spent at Pietracupa are tied to **Antonio,** with the first advice on technical drawing, merry laughter, the stories of his youthful loves, his period as military lieutenant, his work at the National Electricity Board

(ENEL). And also his marriage to Rosaria, the birth of Cynthia and Esther, the birth of his grandchildren and, especially, that meeting in the village again, with the same youthful spirit and the same desire to think about the future with optimism. The last time I saw him was in Naples. Already ill, he said, *"Claudio, I do not want to die, I still have many things to do"*. Fate has been cruel. But as was said in the church during his funeral, ***Antonio has not left us,*** *he is still with us, he follows us, speaks to us. You have only to know how to listen to him.*

Uncle Pietro Di Iorio has been for years Pietracupa's mailman, a serious, discreet man, dedicated to his family and, like every southern Italian, he made sacrifices so that his children Mary, Benedict and Gino took the right way to a peaceful and successful life with goals fully achieved.

One of my personal memories of Uncle Pietro relates to his way of calling us from the street to hand over the letters, always polite and precise. I would wait a week to hear his voice out on the threshold of my house, to receive comics like Tex Willer, comics that my father sent me via mail from Rome. The telegraph and postal service, in the '50s, were the only means to communicate with other countries or cities.

Uncle Corradino Delmonaco was a gentle and kind person, always ready to greet and ask information about my family and the progress of my studies. For many years he was the employee of parish priest, Fr. Manfredo, and functions sung in church were always accompanied by his voice and the sound of the old organ which sounded from a suspended stage located above the entrance door of the Church itself. A special memory I have of him, is his desperate cry during the procession dedicated to San Gregorio, on the occasion of a theft and the launch into a well of his statue by strangers. This episode demonstrates his great piety and his respect for the patron saints of the village.

Uncle Arturo Vanga was an employee of Pietracupa 's municipality, a lively and always active man, having the joy and energy to run a very large family. Uncle Arturo was the official auctioneer of the village, charged for communicating in all ways public or private notices, for the citizens and residents of the village. This task was done, from immemorial time, in a very typical way.

The auctioneer, with a trumpet, blew the signal of his presence in the street. Then in precise Pietracupa dialect and in a ringing voice, he conveyed the message which he had the task of transmitting to the people.

The first years of our presence at Pietracupa, **my mother did not know Pietracupa's dialect,** so Uncle Arturo, always with much warmth and kindness, repeated in Italian everything he had previously said in dialect. During his institutional role, he always found time to speak with each person in the alley with news and stories that ranged in all directions, and the pleasantry and the brilliance of this Uncle, in those atypical times, have always remained fixed in my mind.

Uncle Arthur was also the assistant pastor of Fr. Manfredo, responsible for the control and the maintenance of religious rooms, including the tower and belfry complex. At the time, the bells were rung by hand with **the classic ropes**, which he enlivened with great skill according to the functions in place, producing sound chimes that spread throughout the valley.

In the '70s, the role of auctioneer and collaborator of the local parish priest, Fr.Orlando, was entrusted to **Bassano.** He had a mild impairment in his leg; but, in spite of this, he always carried out with commendable commitment the tasks entrusted to him. I remember his climbing up the ladder of the bell tower to go to ring the bells, always on time, always accurate, even with his physical difficulty.

Dr. Corrado Fraraccio was, in the '50s, Pietracupa's local authority doctor. He was born in the neighboring village of San Pietro in Valle and had married a kind and cultured woman from Campania, coming from the United States; from their union were born three children. His house was just in front of my father's, in the dwelling currently owned by the Di Risio family.

The arrival of a doctor was a great asset for the needs of Pietracupa's inhabitants, forced, before his arrival, to travel to Fossalto for a doctor's care.

Dr. Fraraccio was a person who immediately earned the respect of all Pietracupa's people with his professionalism, his availability and his friendly and kind manner. My family was very close to Dr. Fraraccio's family and, when they came to Rome, they were always guests in our home. Mrs. Fraraccio was very fond of Rome's artistic beauty, so **I would often take her to visit museums**, which helped me increase my middle class school knowledge.

I think that it was in those years that my interest in the art world was born and that led me over the years to visit the most important Italian and foreign museums.

During our stay at Pietracupa, we were often guests at lunch in their home and, with their first two children close in age to me, I spent some leisure time there during those quiet and sunny summers.

During the '60s, Dr. Fraraccio decided it was time to leave Italy and look for other job opportunities in the United States, enticed in this project by the many Pietracupa residents in Westfield. His wife advised against it, as she knew the difficulties that they would find in the USA.

I did not see Dr. Fraraccio any more, nor members of his family. Only in 1965, during my first trip to the USA, we exchanged phone greetings. I knew of him by **Diamante Delmonaco and his wife, cousin of Corrado**, residents in America.

I must add that in the following years there were other local authority doctors in the village such as **Dr. Mascione, Dr. Pirolli, and Dr. Di Girolamo** fondly called "**Barbitto**" for his witty goatee. This last doctor, without neglecting the others, resembled Dr. Fraraccio for pleasantry and helpfulness shown to Pietracupa's people. When he was hit by a stroke, in the Roman clinic where he was admitted for rehabilitation, there was always a succession of friends and Pietracupa / Fossalto people who went to visit their prestigious doctor.

Uncle Guerrino Carnevale, already mentioned in previous chapters, was an important figure both in the village and at Westfield, Pietracupa's twin community.

The members of his family, consisting of his wife Aunt Maria, four daughters (Clorinda, Teresa, Lina and Antonietta) and two sons (Domenico and Vittorio) have always worked in unison with Uncle Guerrino at all times of his life, both in Italy and in the United States.

His commitment as Mayor, as manager of a "tavern" in Pietracupa, a club in Westfield, and all his business activities undertaken during the years of reconstruction in Italy and later in the United States, outline **the personality of an active and intelligent man.** He knew how to interpret the changes of modern society, facing and managing them in a positive way for himself and his family.

But in this cast of characters one cannot fail to mention Uncle Peppino Patrizio, Uncle Filippo Cacchione, Uncle Palmerino

Belisario, Uncle Micheluccio Durante, Uncle Annibale Di Sarro and his son Gregorio, Uncle Pasquale Camillo, Uncle Augusto Delmonaco, Uncle Nicola Guglielmi and Uncle Antonio Guglielmi, and many other memorable figures who characterized the life of the village in those difficult years after the war as well as during the economic recovery of our country.

Finally, I cannot fail to appoint three important elderly, living in the village: **Antonio Santilli**, **Uncle Michele Vanga** and **Uncle Mario Di Iorio**, true custodians of the memories of the '50s.

Last summer I got to talk to them, getting useful information to write this book. I was especially touched by the story of Uncle Mario Di Iorio, which I write in its entirety below.

"In the '40s during the war, I had been sent to fight on the Croatian front. After the fall of Mussolini that took place on September 8, I left the front and, with makeshift means, I tried to go back to Pietracupa. I embarked on a long journey along the entire peninsula by train, on foot, in the company of other fellow soldiers, and I finally returned to my house in the village.

"About Croatia I have only the memory of the sea that I saw there for the first time in my life, and that I have had no occasion to see it again in the years to follow.

"After my return to the village, I always continued to work in the fields, paid for my work as a seasonal worker in Puglia. In that region the work was hard because you slept outdoors and ate bad food.

Dr. Fraraccio and wife with Angelico

Uncle Guerrino and young peasants

Uncle Eduardo and young peasants

Uncle Peppino Di Iorio/Castellino

Antonio Santilli

187

"I never thought to abandon my country forever. I have always worked and never took vacation days to go to other places. I made all this sacrifice to help the members of my family."

In this story of Uncle Mario there is the essence of the feelings and the duty to the family that inspired each responsible person, in those heroic years of our country, hard years where hunger was so great.

And it's Antonio Santilli who told me an episode of the big appetite that gripped the stomachs of some workers: *"One day, I, Mario Di Iorio and Peppino Di Iorio had been called by the contractor of the provincial way, to work in the area of "Barracone" near Pietracupa. For refreshments at lunch, we decided to buy 75 eggs from a farmer (25 each). Unfortunately, the next day I did not go on the job. The day after that, sure to eat my 25 boiled eggs during lunchtime, I asked my friends to hand me my share of the eggs remaining with them.*

"Between the playful and the serious, my friends told me that the day before, because of my absence, their hunger had grown, so they decided that 25 eggs were not sufficient, and that it took about 38 to quench their hunger. Therefore, they divided my share of eggs, which had not been used because of my absence at the building site."

Uncle Augusto Porchetta was a very respected and appreciated man of ability and willingness to help his fellow citizens. As a young man they called him "mischievous" for his character of an original and brilliant man.

In 1990, during the renovation of my house in via General Durante, I had to resort to him to free my attic of a litter of field mice. Uncle came in the house with a series of old metal traps and, within a week, he cleared the attic of the unwanted intruders. The memory I have of that mouse hunt is the mocking expression of Uncle Augusto.

He, at each mouse caught, would take it by the tail, saying, "Come honey of the house, now I'll soon sort you out". This episode made me always think of the Pied Piper leading the rats away from the city.

General Durante would spend with his wife, a week's holiday in the village, right in the house located in the street that, later, was dedicatd to his memory, as an illustrious citizen who had worked hard to help the people of the village. I did not have many opportunities to talk to him, because he had an austere and militaristic attitude.

Romano Ferri, by the way, told me the following anecdote that confirms this opinion of mine: *"When I was in town, I agreed with him that every day at 1300, I would have on his table a bottle of water*

from St. Peter's source, with melted inside of it a packet of Idrolitina.
(a substance that makes water fizz).
"One day, for various reasons, I handed him the bottle 10 minutes
later than the time appointed. So the enraged General made me stand
at attention, and by a formal rebuke he told me that the unfortunate
incident was not to happen again.
In Rome, in the district Trionfale / Balduina, there is also a street
named after General Durante.

-The Great Exodus, Pietracupa's community in Rome

Since the late '50s and during the decade of the' 60s, **the great
exodus of Pietracupa's people** to the big cities of the Italian
center and north (Rome, Milan, Turin, Ferrara) began, to the
European nations (Germany, Belgium, the Netherlands and
Switzerland) and to the American continents (USA, Argentina,
Venezuela). The reasons for this exodus were mentioned in previous
chapters and will be detailed in the following one.
 The only certain fact is that the village began to lose its population
and a demographic recovery due to births never started, nor did it
increase in population from neighboring countries.
Therefore, little by little, the village went to depopulate together
with its crafts and agricultural activities. The only citizens
remaining on site were all employed at pay-fixed public institutions
(Municipality, Province, Post, The National Road Board (A.N.A.S),
State Property), or were retired from the agricultural sector. Only
during the summer months did Pietracupa repopulate with the
presence of her children who had emigrated elsewhere, returning
during the festivities to meet again their relatives staying in the
village.
My memories of the great exodus of the '50s / '60s / '70s are about
Pietracupa's people first departures to the United States. I
remember my mother saying to me, *I'm glad that the brothers
Carrelli have been able to obtain a visa for the United States. Working
at the Town Hall, they found the right way to get it.* Being able to
obtain a passport for the United States was an event, an especially
difficult enterprise.
 I remember the hardships of Vincenzo Di Iorio who, accompanied by
his Uncle Saverio, suffered for a long time to go from Pietracupa to

Rome, close to USA Embassy, in order to be able to emigrate to that nation.

A funny anecdote related to those days is the memory of Pietracupa's young bachelors, who were going to emigrate to America, which was observed with great interest by village girls and their families.

Going to America was synonymous with a trip to well being, **to the new frontier**.

Pietracupa's community in Rome

In the 1950s and 1960s, a substantial number of Pietracupa's people abandoned their country to migrate to the Eternal City in search of work and a better prospect for life for themselves and for their families. The exodus began slowly, following the example of their neighbors or relatives who had left previously to start working and then call the rest of their family to join them.

Therefore, in Rome, in a few years **a vibrant and large community of Pietracupa's people** was established. They were very active and very cohesive. The early days of their settlement were hard for all.

The biggest problem was that of housing, because of the lack of accommodations and, especially, the high price of rents that forced many families to adapt to live temporarily in makeshift homes, some without running water, located in the peripheral areas of the city (Mandrione, Centocelle, Quadraro, Cinecittà, Acquedotto Felice, Borghetto of Station Prenestina, Uva of Rome), often sharing housing with other relatives or village friends.

No need to resort to the news of the era or film Settimana Incom, to realize that these were the conditions of a city and a nation that were coming from the wounds of war, difficulties that all Italians overcame in the following years, with great effort and positive results of growth and livability in comfortable homes.

In the city of Rome, Pietracupa's people never lost their identity as a community of Molise with the desire to meet and help each other. The above mentioned bus Roma / Pietracupa of SATAM was the point of contact with the village, and the neighboring small restaurants of **"Giovanni Salcito"** and that of **"Signorine"**, both near Piazza Re di Roma, were the natural meeting places for all Pietracupa's people for a game of cards or to chat, as it had been in the village.

190

Uncle Felice Tornariello / Meddione Shoemaking, a short walk from Piazza of Re di Roma, was another of the landmarks where every Pietracupa inhabitant could go to learn the news about the village and its people, who had scattered everywhere. Uncle Felice was a massive and strong-willed man, hard worker, and he had the good fortune to run the shop in a strategic place, so every countryman arriving or departing, stood in his shop, leaving the latest news of the village. Uncle Felice, as a good communicator, amalgamated and would tell it to other people, eager to hear it.

Even the tailor shop run by **Uncle Peppino / Settimio Durante**, in the Via Appia, was a place dedicated to the rest of the friendly Pietracupa's people searching for help or for a chat with his son Settimio or with Antonietta, Eva and Franca, Uncle's pretty daughters.

We met with **Franca**, who is married to my cousin **Pasquale Saliola** and lives in Hollywood, Florida. Often we telephone, recalling the times spent at Pietracupa and her pleasant suitor of the period who brought her the palm, and we smile fondly about our youthful memories.

In these years, my family had very close relationship with all of Pietracupa's community, and particularly with the families of Uncle **Romolo Porchetta** (Biancone), **Uncle Filippo Santilli** and with old friends **Felice and Romolo Santilli**, who often came to Rome to sell Molise food products.

We spent many Christmases and Sundays together, going with their taxi to some little Roman taverns. With my childhood friends **Michele, Giovanni** who recently died, **Giuseppe, Romolo, Maria, Giovanna,** those childhood and youthful memories that, although time dilutes with its unstoppable flow, are still an indelible part of our being Pietracupa's people and our roots.

I would have many stories to tell about these years. Especially the funny episode of the visit of **Aunt Menguccia to her godmother**, who opened the door with a rolling pin in hand, telling her *Cummà, stingh'a a fà a cannellate cù Maria,* (*"dear, I'm coming to blows with Maria"*) her Pietracupa roommate.

Or the episode of *te torce r' male (you are getting angry)* of Uncle Federico Di Iorio to his roommate who, secretly, often used to flavor a piece of bread putting it in his own sauce while cooking in the common kitchen.

And as a last "gem", the story of **Giacomello. He was** Pietracupa's extroverted character who often appeared cocky in Uncle Felice Meddione's shoemaking shop, with an overcoat that rivaled the finest Roman dandy.

These are stories that tell about the difficulties of a bygone era, stories now distant and erased by time.

Giuseppe Brunetti – Migrant in Venezuela

CHAPTER IV

THE EMIGRATION

- *Molise ,land of migration*

I thought about the title of this section reading two interesting articles on the internet. The first written by **F. Pizzi**, nephew of Fossalto's parish priest , on behalf of the Italian Clerical Conference (CEI) and the second written by **Dr. Giampiero Castellotti,** president of "Forche Caudine" Association. Both articles concern **emigration in Molise.**
I've obtained a lot of useful information from them, to summarize in terms of historical, statistical and social emigration of millions of Italians who, since 1870, conducted the first great exodus to the countries of South America, the United States, Canada and Australia. Again in the 1950s there was another great exodus, this time to the north of Europe and Rome and the great northern industrial cities.
The migratory phenomenon in Italy, accentuated in Molise and Basilicata, began at the dawn of the 19th century at the time of Murat (1815) and of the Bourbons.
From 1876 to 1900, about 110 thousand people officially departed from Abruzzo and Molise, and in the period from 1901 to 1915 almost half a million people left, for a total of over **600,000 emigrants over 40 years**. We have to note that, currently, over **one million people from Molise are scattered throughout the world** (1/3 in Italy), compared to 300,000 residents still in the Region. Out of five million immigrants with an Italian passport, 130,000 are from Molise.
The first flow of emigrants from Molise was directed to the countries of South America (Argentina, Brazil, Venezuela) countries that, after the liberation of slaves, had need for a workforce and therefore were interested in implementing a policy of welcoming immigrants. These travels were favored because of the low cost of a ticket, which was cheaper than a railroad ticket to a European country. On the outward journey a ship would carry cargo; on the way back it was carrying emigrants who were leaving to escape poverty and the inadequacies of local resources.

But they departed also, **with the idea of returning home** following a pattern of social betterment aimed at reinvesting savings and remitting money back into their own country, initiating that **"migration chain"** in respect to their friends and relatives, which characterized the phenomenon of Italian emigration.

In the years from 1905 to 1925, over 55,000 people returned to Molise. On their return, they stimulated, with tales of their own experiences abroad, the departure of other compatriots.

In 1871 the Province of Campobasso had one of the lowest rates of emigration, with 134 expatriates, of whom 90 went to the Americas. In 1872 Molise expatriates numbered 809 people, of which 609 had moved to Buenos Aires, 91 to Montevideo (Paraguay), 85 to Brazil and 24 to European countries. Of all these emigrants, 492 were farm laborers, 228 unemployed, 15 artisans, 7 industrial, three landowners, and a priest. The vast majority were illiterate, so figures of scribes and translators made their appearance, to allow the migrants to maintain ties with their families in Italy.

The first emigrants were adapted to become farmers, blacksmiths, masons, peddlers, grain merchants. But, gradually, by engaging in the work, many of them became traders, entrepreneurs, shipping and bankers.

The members of this first generation of immigrants have always maintained close ties with their country of origin, materializing their affection with offerings for festivities, remittances of money back to their families, donations and so on. I agree with Dr Castellotti when, in his article he says: *For many immigrants, however, the place of origin is understood as an idea, an ideal, an essence that often does not take account of the changes of time and which constantly is the result of an excessively ostentatious pride. The community, however, continues to be a well-defined, moral, social, cohesive, rich in values universe, tarnished but still vital; dialect, gastronomy, oral traditions, but above all, devotion to work, to family, to duty. Even today, many marriages take place between people with similar geographical origin.*

A great country that welcomed many of the emigrants of the first wave is **the United States.** Between the years 1892 and 1924 more than 22 million Europeans emigrated to that country; of these, about four million were Italian. The first cities to which Italian emigrants were concentrated were New York, Chicago, Philadelphia, Cleveland, Pittsburg, Princeton. An intense film of a few years ago

194

titled "**Lamerica**", by director Gianni Amelio, represented the odyssey of the first Italian immigrants who left for America, leaving their wives, like **white widows**, forced to live years and years away from their husbands. In the film sequences, the drama of the journey and arrival at the port of New York, the suffering of stops and **quarantines at Ellis Island,** called the island of tears, in front of the Statue of Liberty, was reenacted. Often travelers who didn't pass the visits threw themselves in the cold waters of the sea.

But **living conditions in the new land** weren't any less dramatic than the departure and arrival. Our countrymen encountered enormous difficulties due to lack of knowledge of the language and the difficult integration into the tumultuous American society. This was the great contribution, in terms of sacrifice and commitment, given by them to the great nation. Do not forget the sociological difficulties encountered by our first countrymen contemptuously called "**Black dago**". And remember the dramatic and unjust lynching of nine Italians in the year 1891 in the city of New Orleans, in addition to the drama of four miners who died in Monongah mine in Virginia.

It's important to remember, however, the commitment and the personality of Italian individual s such as: the writer **Arturo Giovannitti from Ripabottoni (CB)**, the poet of the workers, the first union trader in the USA who fought for the rights of Italian immigrants; **Saint Francesca Cabrini**, the patron saint of migrants; **Francesco Meucci**, inventor of the telephone, before Bell. And also the tragedy of the killing of **Sacco and Vanzetti** in 1927 in Boston, only recently pardoned, and all the famous people of Italian descent in the USA, like the great tenor **Caruso**, the New York City Mayor **Fiorello La Guardia**, the actor **Rudolph Valentino.**

We remember also so many humble and silent workers who built roads, railways, bridges, and contributed to the development of a large and democratic country, which is the United States of America. This brief historical summary is to ward off even the usual stereotype of **the Italian Mafia**, which many detractors, envious of the genius and the seriousness of the majority of Italians in the world, seek to soil the image, with the dark side of events common in all nations, even if they are events to fight. On this subject, I can't fail to mention news as recently as 1990 concerning a great manager of American building, **John Segalla**, who was refused membership in a prestigious golf club in Connecticut because his last name was of Italian origin. **John Segalla**, as a good Italian native, built his own golf club, which has become **more prestigious than the previous one.**

That news surprised me, thinking that the highest concentration of Italians and Italian origin people reside in New Jersey and Connecticut (20%) and that, in total, the percentage of Italians living in the USA, is 5-6% of all residents.

We should add for completeness that, in Italy, there was also emigration for political reasons. Not only in the period of Murat and the Bourbons, but also in the immediate period following the unification of Italy, the one of brigandage developed for social and land claims. We also cannot forget those of the fascist epoch, when dissidents emigrated mainly to France and England.

The second major migratory flow started in the early 1950s and lasted until the late '70s. As far as overseas countries, there was the flow to Venezuela and Canada. But, mostly during this time, emigration was aimed at the Northern European countries such as Germany, Belgium, England, Switzerland, The Netherlands. During Italy's economic boom, a domestic emigration to the big industrial cities of northern Italy also started.

Italian workers who emigrated to European nations left their native countries thinking to return as soon as possible to their homes. But, with the advent of the second and third generations, households established in foreign lands have settled permanently in their receiving nations.

The reasons that pushed Molise people to emigrate in the '50s to new destinations far from their region, are to be found in the **retracted and not very dynamic condition of Molise society**.

Its inhabitants were attracted by the model of national development based on strong referrals and urban consumerism that were totally different from the way of life and social organization that could offer them the old fashioned rural society which, also because of a lack of political support for agriculture, led its workers to other prospects in life.

Currently the emigration phenomenon is characterized by a silent migration, freed from the dramatic mass departures and arrivals of the 19th and 20th centuries.

The cause of this phenomenon of silent emigration may be charged to **the stereotype of today's emigrant**, represented by a person with mid-level or university education, cultural knowledge, with experiences of travel and an evolved life, who moves in the context of a globalized economy, looking for new job prospects.

To all this must be added the decline of those values linked to the rural world, replaced by the principles of a society expressed by **liquid human values** where everything goes and flows rapidly, within extended families, where the institution of the family, understood as a pivot bearing system of life in the rural world, has waned.

The role of head of the family has faded slowly and every individual, especially among young people, has thought to plan his life away from his country in order to follow a dream and a hope for new values and new realities of life that can fill the large existential and economic emptiness that often afflicts them. At the end of this chapter, I consider it important to mention something about the phenomenon of immigration in Italy. This topic is often linked both to the repatriation of Italian immigrants, and to the massive influx of immigrants from Eastern Europe and third world countries - topics that are often the subjects of news and debates between politicians, men of culture and men of religion.

I think it is superfluous to begin this discussion on immigration, illustrating all the problems related to clandestine arrivals in Italy of poor human beings who arrive exhausted on dilapidated boats, in search of work, freedom and more humane living conditions. The matter is now the subject of the news and debates in the media and the political world known to everyone. Let me just tell you a little personal anecdote and the reflections that it stimulate in me.

On summer Sundays I go often to **Trivento market in Molise** and look very carefully at the many stalls run by Chinese, Moroccan, Indian vendors, who are sometimes accompanied by their Italian wives. Looking at all this, I realize that Italian society is changing, and I see you have to live with the new migration reality of the modern world and consider newcomers as an **added resource**.

For this you need to find the right balance to govern living together peacefully and without prejudice and discrimination, as it was also stated in the third Regional Conference of Molise in the World, June 7-10, 2003. It refers to the difficulties encountered by emigrants from Molise in the years of the great migration and called for fair treatment for newcomers.

Currently in the Molise region there are about 5,000 immigrants, approximately 0.2% of all those present in Italy. They are mostly from Romania, Albania, Ukraine, Poland, Tunisia and Morocco. They perform manual labor in construction, agriculture, trade and in hotel activities.

Women, in the majority, are employed as caregivers in Molise families. Many of them migrated to Italy to find new job opportunities, with the prospect of a possible reunion with their families that remained at home. During my Pietracupa stays, I saw some of these Romanians taking care lovingly of many elderly people, with great commitment and affection, in the same way as the farming families of the last century took care of their elderly at home. I have known in the village many Romanians and Poles, engaged in building, hydraulic and electric activities, all well-liked and gratified by the friendship and respect of Pietracupa's population. Often I have seen a veil of nostalgia for their country and for their families from their discussions, neither more nor less than used to happen to our Pietracupa emigrants in the last century.

We have to realize that we are engaged in the European Community and we are moving toward a multi-ethnic society.

-Stories of Pietracupa's emigrantes

Pietracupa's immigration flow followed the same routes described in the previous paragraph. The reasons for leaving are the same as those that caused Molise people in the years of World War II and during the '50s and '70s to migrate to foreign lands or to industrial Italian cities.

I haven't managed to find the data of local departures in order to have a statistical outline of their influence in a regional context, but these data aren't important for the goal of this book.

The most important things are human and social aspects linked to these great facts of our fellow countrymen who formed important families all over the **United States** (Chicago, New York, Schenectady, Westfield, Florida, Connecticut, California, Arizona) and in **Europe** (Germany, Belgium, England, The Netherlands) and **in Italy** (Rome, Milan, Turin, Ferrara). There is a minority of Pietracupa emigrants in Argentina, Venezuela, Australia, France and England.

This generic information on the movements of Pietracupa's emigrants in the world, as I said previously, is not enough to describe in detail the anxieties and difficulties which our countrymen faced before, during and after their travel **That's why I wanted to give voice to their tales,** from which one can understand all drives and drama that accompanied their travel to fit in the reality of new host countries. From the tales I've heard and collected in this section of the book, you get a fairly clear picture of what I said earlier. With objective sincerity, I can say that they have been not only pioneers, but overall brave, even if not heroes, and have contributed to the development of the nations in which they settled, with their hard work, adaptability, reliability and above all of humanity.

United States of America.
1)   **Uncle Arturo Durante and Aunt Anna Maria Camillo.**
Uncle Arturo, who emigrated to the USA in the early 1900s, came back to Pietracupa (1920) to marry Aunt Anna Maria, my father's sister. After the marriage, he immediately left for Chicago to start all bureaucratic acts necessary for the emigration of his new wife from Italy to the United States of America. **The aunt** embarked from the port of Naples and she had to make the long outward journey alone, without the company of any acquaintance.

199

I want to emphasize that, in the rural society of those times, every young girl had to behave in a sober way determined by strict rules and conventions of the time. The experience of a young lady from a peasant society was contained in the microworld of her country, and only a few times in her life would she even have the opportunity to travel with her family to the provincial capital city, which was Campobasso for Pietracupa's people. Therefore it is easy to imagine the anguish and fear that gripped the aunt in addressing the long journey.

Aunt Anna Maria, coming from a rural although well off family, told me the drama of her departure: the night before being accompanied to the port of Naples she never slept, she felt within herself a great sorrow at having to leave her home, her family, her people, her childhood and memories of her youth.

The ferryboat to New York during the '50s

Pietracupa's community in Milwaukee

Porchetta/Camillo family – Milwaukee

Tony Camillo family - Chicago

Pietracupa's community in Milwaukee

Dr. Michele Santilli family   Anita Fasanelli – Stamford

But she experienced the most dramatic events during the journey on the ship and **on her arrival in New York** while staying in port.

The Aunt, polite but reserved, being pregnant for three months, suffered from seasickness from the rolling of the ship. In addition to physical discomfort, she was forced to travel on an ocean liner full of immigrants from all over the south of Italy, a bit noisy and extroverted, and she had to adapt to those conditions of travel with no privacy. On arrival in New York, she had to stop at **Ellis Island** for the ritual quarantine that took place in the huge and gloomy corridors and wards of the building used for health care visits and customs controls. English was the spoken language and those poor emigrants did not understand orders and questions put to them. These stops were truly hellish because of the confusion, noise, lack of privacy and the uncertainties related to the severity of the officials responsible for carrying out the check-up rituals.

As God wanted, Aunt surpassed even the rock of Ellis Island and was immediately able to embrace Uncle Arturo, who was waiting in the offices at the pier, to start with him her new life in America.

After the birth of Antonietta (Toni), Felice (Phil), and Luisa, the family moved to Milwaukee and Uncle, a skilled tailor, was able to start his business **of craft tailoring**, also hiring personnel to help him meet the numerous requests received from the customers of

Italian and American origin. He was especially proud of making religious garments for the Archbishop of Milwaukee.

Unfortunately, a severe sorrow struck Uncle Arthur's family: Luisa's sudden death at the age of just twenty years old. The misfortune was overcome with great resignation and with great faith; the family had and has deep Christian roots. My personal memories with the Aunt were always marked by great respect and affection.

During my school and adult age, we used to exchange extensive correspondence, between me and her that I still keep with great affection. She would write in perfect Italian and her letters were pages of wisdom, gentleness and deep Christian spirituality.

My father was the last and only brother who remained in Italy. The other two brothers and three sisters lived in the USA. So, in the difficult years after the war, they would always send parcels containing the most varied items from clothing, to food, including sweets and the famous American candies for which my brother and I were greedy.

Aunt Anna Maria and Uncle Arturo always had strong ties with Pietracupa's community. In the '50s / '60s, they did their utmost to help some of their compatriots emigrate to the USA, giving American authorities the appropriate guarantees of sponsorship and welcoming them into their home until they could become established in their host country.

Uncle Arturo, Aunt Anna Maria, Louise and Phil now lie in the Milwaukee cemetery; but the dear cousin Toni is gratified **by the love of her niece Cheryl, daughter of Phil**, and **his grandchildren Dawn Maria (Dee Dee) and Damon Arthur**.

I and my brother Lino went to Florida in January 2012, to Fort Myers, to celebrate **the ninetieth birthday of Toni**. It was an unforgettable ceremony, not only for the rite of the Mass celebrated in a characteristic Hispanic style church, but also for the nice lunch held in a typical Italian restaurant, with dishes of our Italian cuisine, which characterized the event in a superlative way. **Beautiful flowers** came from all over the United States, the presence of friends and relatives of Pietracupa's community (Giovanni Di Sarro and his wife, Alberto and Vittorio Guglielmi with their wives, Gloria Di Iorio with her husband, Anita Fasanelli) enhanced those moments of celebration. In my greeting speech, turning to Toni, for a moment I was moved, thinking that a little of Pietracupa, and then also a bit of our history which has its roots in the small village were there with us and permeated that **atmosphere of the American coast**, heated by a sunny January.

2) Uncle Vincenzo Porchetta and Aunt Elisa Camillo

Uncle Vincent lived with his family in Milwaukee, a short distance from Uncle Arturo's house. After the marriage with Aunt Elisa, celebrated at Pietracupa, their union was blessed by the birth of six children, two boys (Angelo and Gregorio) and four females (Giovanna, Antonietta, Evelina and Mary). Giovanna, Antonietta and Gregorio are no longer with us; but the whole Porchetta family who lives in America, was blessed by many grandchildren and great-grandchildren who have established themselves in their country of birth and continue the tradition of Porchetta / Camillo in the USA. Many of them came to visit Italy and, just last summer, **the son of Mary**, **Tommy**, was in Pietracupa with his family to enjoy the festivities of the patron saints. This year Keith Porchetta and his wife Karen came to visit us in Rome.

I reserve a special mention of my cousin Angelo, of whom I will tell later about some memories of our meetings. Angelo has made a very important career as a manager in the field of film industries. Likeable were the stories of his early childhood and his difficulties facing the different realities of these two worlds, especially because at home we all talked Pietracupa's slang.

3) Aunt Adalgisa Camillo and Uncle Norbert Grund
Aunt Adalgisa (Adele) left us recently (03/29/2014) at the age of 95 years. She was the last aunt who remained alive among the brothers and sisters of my father. Writing this chapter, I feel quite touched because my aunt was aware that I was writing this book and was anxious to receive a copy. Fate has been unfavorable and I will send to my dear cousin Joanne and her family the promised copy.
The life story of Aunt Adele is very moving, at least for the period of her childhood and her early youth spent in Italy. As I have said previously, the aunt, born on May 4th, 1916, became an orphan at 8 when my grandfather (her father) enrolled her in a convent school in Rome, where she studied until she left for the United States in 1934.

After joining her father, brothers and sisters residing in Chicago, she immediately found a good opportunity to work in a multinational company, thanks to her studies in Italy. During one of her **vacations to California**, Aunt met her partner in life, Uncle Norbert, married him, had Joanne, and spent all her years in the sunny city of **San Mateo**, a pretty village 30 km from the beautiful Californian city of **San Francisco.**

Domenico Camillo family - Chicago   **Camillo family in Chicago**

Arturo Durante family   **Phil and Cheryl Durante**

I once asked Aunt Adele *"why have you never wanted to make a trip to Italy to visit your native village and Rome, your adopted city?"* With a veil of sadness she replied: *"Well Claudio, Italy, which I love, brings to my mind many sad memories. I became an orphan when I was a little girl and losing one's mother at that age is a very hard thing to overcome. I always remember the long ladder near the family home of Pietracupa along Vico I ° Sant'Anna. I would sit on the steps and remain for hours crying and thinking.*
"In the college of nuns in Rome, where I was a student for many years, life was marked by rigid regulation and even there I had to climb a long, steep staircase to reach the bedroom. My father had emigrated to America, and only my brother Angelico, who was a bit older than me and sometimes Uncle Peppino / Castellino from Pietracupa, came to visit me. The rest was obedience, solitude and silence. In California, in addition to the mild climate, similar to what you have in Italy, I found my ultimate reason for living."

Aunt Adele had the joy of seeing grow two beautiful grandchildren, **Brian and Karen,** who finished their university studies with great profit, receiving many academic certificates - especially Brian, who is currently a researcher at the University of San Diego.

Joanne came with her husband Tom and children to visit us in Italy two years ago. She wanted to visit the convent where her mother had studied, and Pietracupa's family home with long ladder.She took photos of her mother's childhood places , to show them to her on returning to California.

Beautiful or sad as they are, **memories are always part of ourselves**, are images of the path that every human being takes in his life and therefore they always remain as tangible memories inside our hearts.

 Now that she has left us, I keep the memory of her beautiful smile, her kindness, her great personality and her wonderful Italian expressing, speaking a perfect Italian. Unforgettable, also was the hospitality offered to me and my family in the summer of 1986, when we had a great week of vacation in California, in her house in San Mateo.

4) Uncle Domenico Camillo and Aunt Concettina Saulino

Uncle had already emigrated to the USA for several years and returned to Pietracupa in the '20s to spend a few weeks of vacation, with the hope of meeting in the village some young girl **to marry** and take back to the USA. The days passed but he could not find any girl of his choice willing to accept his offer of marriage.

One morning, tired of lounging in the village, he decided to go along with his Uncle Peppino / Castellino to the nearby town of **Civitanova** to attend the festivities in honor of the patron saint. Fate wanted that uncle, while wandering the narrow streets of the village, to notice a young girl who, with a tub in hand, was on her way to a nearby fountain to draw water. Uncle remained dazzled by the ways and the beauty of that girl and immediately instructed Uncle Peppino / Castellino to question some of his acquaintances in the village to get more detailed information. The conclusion of this beautiful story of the past was that **Uncle married,** within a few days, **the beautiful girl he met at that time**. Her name was **Concettina** and, after a brief honeymoon in Rome and Venice, he brought her to Chicago with him. From this union, Nick and Tony, my dear cousins, were born. Both have always lived in Chicago and worked at the City Hall of this great American city.
Nick, in his youth, was a famous baseball player; then, during World War II, he was called into the army to go fight in Europe. He returned to his homeland after being injured during the landing in Normandy.
Nick and Tony, who spoke perfectly our grandparents' Pietracupa slang, consolidated Camillo's dynasty in America: the first, giving birth to four children, the second even nine.

5) Uncle Igino and Aunt Mary Sardella

I can conclude this saga of the Camillo family in America, with the memory of **Uncle Igino, my father's brother and Aunt Mary**, his wife, born in Pietracupa and married in America. From their union two daughters (Antonia and Gina) and a son (Nino) were born.

Uncle Igino left at a very young age to go to fight on the Italian front during World War I. At the end of the war he emigrated to

France and then left from the port of Marseille for the United States. He was a man of noble and kind traits. In his youth he had a very adventurous life, which led him to emigrate to the USA, the nation in which he planted roots to create a strong and cohesive family.

A group of grandchildren and great-grandchildren of Uncle Igino came to visit us last spring, and it was a wonderful meeting which allowed them to visit Italy, but especially to visit the region of origin of their Pietracupa's ancestors.

6) Uncle Umberto Di Iorio

In the years before World War II, Uncle Umberto, the brother of my grandmother, with his brother Peppino / Castellino emigrated to the USA, where he joined the family of the other two sisters, Concettina and Silvia, residents in Chicago and later in Milwaukee. Uncle Umberto soon called **his son Michele** to America. Michele later married Maria, a beautiful and nice girl from Pietracupa, and had two children, **Teresa and Michele** who now reside in Chicago.

Uncle Michele was a famous tailor, and received many awards from the world of American fashion. Uncle Umberto, with his brother Peppino / Castellino, before the outbreak of World War II, decided to return to Italy to his wife Aunt Teresa and daughters Angelina and Antonietta.

The couple had the misfortune of losing their first child. But in the following years they were cheered by the friendship of **Aunt Antonietta**, a lady full of kindness for her fellow men, and the son-in-law, **Uncle Vittorio**, a gentleman from another time, and especially by the birth of **Othello and Angelo**, their grandchildren, who have important roles in teaching and politics. The first is head teacher and entrepreneur while the second is deputy in the Italian Parliament.

I keep affectionate memories of Uncle Umberto and Aunt Teresa. Their stories about the grandparents I never met, their kindness and especially their availability in the dark years of the war, left a sign of humanity and gave meaning to what it means **to be family.**

7) Uncle Rosario Sardella and Aunt Carmela Santilli

Uncle Rosario and Aunt Carmela's story was told me in a letter by **their daughter Anita** and the text, which I translated from English, respects exactly the content of the original. I take this opportunity to say thank you to Anita not only for her collaboration, but especially for that Italian spirit she brought in Pietracupa's community and the affection and esteem that have bound me to her since the year 1953, when I met her for the first time in front of Uncle Peppino / Castellino Pietracupa house.

In the following years, our family relationship was increasingly cemented during our meetings both in Italy, and in New York, and in Florida and in her home in Stamford. Over there I had the opportunity to see again **her daughter Margherita** with her husband and their beautiful **daughters, Jessica and Rebecca**, very respectable female students as well as talented athletes and established musicians.

Anita retains all the qualities of communications manager carried out in a large American company.
During the years of her work, and through our telephone contacts and e-mails, I managed to have important news about Pietracupa's community in the USA. The other members of her family are her sons **Robert and Richard**, both married to American women, and her brother **Pat** married to Franca Durante and, finally, her sister **Mickie**, married and mother of three sons, who now resides in Arizona.
The text of Anita's letter is: *"My father was 13 when he spoke seriously with his mother Rosa Marcellina, telling her that it was his intention to leave to Sao Paulo in Brazil to go to work in the coffee plantation of his uncle Nicola. The purpose of this trip was to gain some money, necessary to pay some debts of the family. With these intentions, he embarked on a ship, and sailed for several days before arriving at the port and receiving the embrace and welcome of his uncle Nicola Saliola.*
"Uncle Nicola had a family of 5 daughters and the arrival of this nephew was a positive event. Rosario was a not very known boy in the village. He had only attended the primary school and at age 13 he left for Brazil.

"In the new country he needed to learn the local language, which was Portuguese, and had to learn very quickly, both coffee technical marketing and the most suitable places for retail.

"It was the year 1918 when all Italians who were out of the country were called home to fight on the front of World War I and be useful to their homeland. He returned to Italy to fight on the front of the Piave and, when he was released, two proposals were made him: return to the country in which he had been the last time or choose another country.

"He chose to go to the USA. This decision upset my grandmother Rosa. He had left the village at a young age to go to Brazil and then decided to start again to a country far away from Italy. My father was born in Pietracupa in 1899 and was 3 months old when his father Pasquale Saliola died; my grandmother never remarried.

"In the passenger list of the ship that brought him to America, he had been enrolled as a general worker direct to Schenectady, NY. The first days in America were very difficult - he hadn't a family, or financial assistance, or a home to live in, nor did he understand English. In any case, the owners of the guesthouse where he slept had taken to heart his problem, favoring him in some way, during his period of stay.

"My father was busy looking for work wherever it was needed. The starting salary was 50 cents a day; he then left Schenectady to go to the Bronx New York, where another employer offered him $5 a week. He was often in contact with his fellow countryman John Di Sarro who lived in Minerseville, in the State of Pennsylvania. John had found him a job in the same company where he worked, in a coal mine of that State.My father moved to Minersville, but after only 28 days of hard work thanked his friend John, saying that he preferred to die elsewhere, rather than underground in a coalmine.

"By then had passed several years since his arrival in the USA, and Dad thought it was time to find a wife and start a family, so he returned to his homeland to find a wife. It was April 1927 when Dad married Rosa Carmela Santilli who was eighteen. Dad decided to buy a small house at Pietracupa for his wife.

The American immigration law was very strict in those days, and at least two years passed before my mother was able to enter the United

States through Ellis Island, in New York. At the time there was a quota system to be observed and only a set number of people could enter the USA. My mother left for her new life in America, the rest is history. The year was 1932, when my father Rosario Sardella Saliola and my mother Carmela Santilli Saliola, decided to work together. Dad was in hospital for an accident at work in the ice factory. After the injury, he left the Bronx to come to "garden-like", a community of Mount Vernon, NY, Westchester County. The chance to move elsewhere had presented after reading an offer to rent a small grocery store that measured 25 feet by 100 feet deep. My father was a proud man, and once he prepared the shelves, he wanted to call the store with the name of the Italian province from which he came, "Campobasso".

"The project had immediately a great impact with the neighborhood, made up of people of different ethnicities, which took note that there was an Italian shop in Mount Vernon Avenue. One of the first customers of the store was a man who congratulated my father telling him that he was born in a village near Pietracupa named Torella. In the year 1933 an adjoining shop was also made available and immediately my father bought it widening the existing initial structure. In 1947, as business was booming, my father thought to initiate a new type of income, so he decided to buy a property that could accommodate seven families, including the shop which had been expanded. The name given to the new structure was "Campobasso Supermarket".

"The success of my father was phenomenal and he earned the respect of the entire local community. It was his generosity and his "know-how" that made the store popular and successful. When my brother Pat returned from the war in Korea, he joined in the management of the store, and when, later, the health of dad worsened, he became the owner. The "Campobasso Super Market" was active from 1932 until 1974, when it closed when my brother, who by then was married to Franca Durante, moved permanently to Florida, where he currently resides.
"As a child born in the USA, my parents enrolled me in a school that had included me in the group of immigrants composed of foreign students, generally boys of the neighborhood. The school was a new experience for me and I did not think too much about it until I realized

that there were two separate groups of pupils in the same class. Certainly my parents came from a small town not far from Rome, and at home they only spoke Italian dialect. But I insisted to them that they go to school to tell my teachers I was American, and only later I was included in the group of Americans.

"Life in the community of Mount Vernon was quiet, the families used to help each other, it did not matter if you were French, Italian, Jewish, German, African or American. Many dinners were shared with neighbors and knowledge of tastes of different national foods was something very special. All belonged to the same social status and so we were all on the same level. The playground was the heart of the neighborhood, and there were many talents in the games of basketball, baseball, volleyball and jump rope. Many immigrants from the neighborhood came from different countries, so, at a certain point, all foreigners were called with other names according to their country of origin; for example Italians were called greenhorns, dagos, wops; Germans were called Nazi or kike and other things.

"In 1939 World War II began *and many things worsened. Food and gasoline were goods hard to find and we were all waiting for promises of peace. In those years we saw many young people join the army and some of them never returned. It was a time to learn, to forgive, to understand what the world had to offer.*

"Things changed after the war and the country then was reborn. Restaurants, motor industry, imported foods, factories, plans for education and leisure travel, it was a prosperous period to see and live. **The young generation had prospects for a better future,** *a chance for a better education and a real career opportunity.*

"As everyone knows, life is not a hobby, it is a precious gift. We were the only lucky ones to have had the opportunity to take what was offered us, we enjoyed rewarding experiences, we savored the best that life could offer us, from people and places to passions.

"I have spent many long hours of my time to research and find information regarding my family in Italy; something I have not yet found. My father was especially my main model of life, the person who taught me the meaning of family. I am proud and grateful to be Italian-American."

Anita wanted to integrate her first letter with a subsequent one in which she wanted to tell anecdotes about **some frequent Pietracupa's visitors** at her home in Mount Vernon. *"Dear Claudio, I would send you three stories of which I have already talked about a few years ago and I send you the pictures too. The stories concern **Uncle Angelo Di Iorio (Mom's cousin), Uncle Pasquale Camillo and Uncle Giorgio Sardella**.*

*"**Uncle Angelo Di Iorio** did not live with us, but for many years visited our home, especially on Saturdays and during public or religious holidays he used to have lunch in our home. In America his fellow villagers called him the "compassatore'"; he married for the second time with a girl from Limosano and had a child named Dario. I'm not sure if I wrote the names correctly, but I'm sure the information is accurate.*

"My family came in contact with many of our countrymen. My father's house was the first point of arrival for anyone who came to the United States. It was like a filter station, and it was wonderful to meet all our fellow Pietracupa's citizens who came to the USA to start a new life in this great nation. It was 1936 and a close family friend that we children called Uncle Pasquale Camillo, made the decision to return to his home in Pietracupa in Italy. The memories of those years are useful to tell you that Uncle Pasquale was a generous man. That year it was also the time for him to return to his village of Pietracupa, and my brother and I were sorry to hear that he was leaving us. He gave as a present, a small fire engine to my brother and every time the siren of this toy sounded, my brother exclaimed, this is the greeting of Uncle Pasquale. He gave a big Hershey's chocolate to me.

*Agricultural technician

"My family consisted of my father, my mother, my brother and myself; but when Uncle Pasquale was with us, he was always welcome, because it seemed that our family was wider.

When he left, we all went to the port of New York to see him get on the Italian ship called Rex, a luxury ocean liner for the time. For the occasion we have been taken away from our parents. Suddenly a loud

215

speaker made the announcement that all visitors had to abandon ship; my brother and I were very frightened! Anyway we were taken off the ship and nothing more happened.

"The uncle returned peacefully to his beloved Pietracupa and never returned to the United States. We had a great affection for Uncle Pasquale.

"**Uncle George Sardella** was a relative of my father, Rosario Sardella Saliola, both born and educated in Pietracupa. George married aunt Concetta, who was from Pietracupa, and both represented a wonderful married couple. Immediately after their honeymoon of approximately 40 days, George announced to his wife that he had an opportunity to emigrate to the United States! Leaving, he promised he would come back after a certain period of time and in the meantime would support her with remittances.

"He was a man to be admired for his intentions. But the years passed and it seemed that George remained in America for a period of time longer than expected. Uncle George would come to visit us in Mount Vernon every Saturday. He lived in Jersey City or in other cities in New Jersey and worked at the Company of the Gas and Light of that state and was estimated and paid very well.

"We children in Mount Vernon always were anxious for a visit from Uncle George because he always brought the delicious desserts of New Jersey. He had the habit of taking the train and the subway to pay us a visit and never bought a car. I do not believe he had a driver license.

"Every time he came to visit us, the Uncle used to bring a dirty shirt so that during the time he was with us, eating food cooked at home, my mother arranged to wash his shirt, and I had the pleasure to see him going back home with a clean and ironed shirt by myself.
"Uncle George communicated regularly with **his wife Concetta**, who had remained at Pietracupa, and was the first to modernize their home in the village. He sent regularly the funds for renovation by his uncle, so it was easy for Aunt Concetta to go ahead with the remodeling.

216

"My father insisted that Uncle George have more communication with his wife and talk to her about his daily life, his financial condition, and so forth. He did so.

"Uncle George was a small handsome man, blond haired, with blue eyes and a great sense of humor. The years passed and before his retirement he thought to return to the village he had always on his mind. He prepared documents for his way back and at the appropriate time he said goodby to friends and our family. We were disappointed by his absence, but we understood that his place was with his wife Concetta. So both his visits on Saturdays and the pastries he bought in New Jersey ended.

"Uncle George was glad for his Pietracupa's house good look and all the modern equipment purchased in the village through the General Electric Company. His retirement lasted only a short period, because he got sick and died immediately. Aunt Concetta remained alone one more time."

I have read very carefully the letters sent to me from Anita, also because I have had the pleasure of meeting many of the people mentioned in her stories. Last summer, I asked **Giuseppe Camillo** about the story and the photo sent me by Anita concerning his Uncle Pasquale. With great attention, after viewing the photos, he told me that it was him and he told me a detail of uncle's wife.

He told me that she never wanted to join her husband in the USA, because she feared that the village people would have criticized her because, for a woman it was not an honorable behavior to join a man who lived alone abroad. So Uncle Pasquale returned to his country to be near his wife and help the grandchildren in their life path.

In 1965, during the **New York World's Fair** I was a guest of Aunt Carmela's family in their beautiful home at Mount Vernon, and entered their "Campobasso Market" full of customers. Seeing all those customers waiting to be served, I understood the great commitment and skill of Uncle Rosario in creating the business that promoted the products of our Italy.

In their travel to Europe in 1956, about which I will talk later, Uncle Rosario and his family had lunch with the owner of a major industry, **Mr. Buitoni**, as welcome guests and their main importers of Italian pasta which was sold in the USA.

8) Uncle Giuseppe Santilli and Uncle Donato Santilli

 The two Santilli brothers had married two sisters of the family Di Iorio, that of "Gallinella". They were **Aunt Anita and Aunt Concettina**, my grandmother's sisters. Both men left to seek their fortunes in the United States.
Uncle Donato later was joined by his wife and they settled permanently in the United States at Milwaukee. Uncle Donato and Aunt Concettina had seven children, Michele (born at Pietracupa), Rosa, Vincenzo, Carlo and Antonio (all born in the USA). The eldest son Michele studied in the USA and **graduated in medicine**, becoming an accomplished doctor, highly respected by the local community for his significance and generosity. He married a girl from Abruzzo, the city of Bussi, Natalie Silvestri and had 5 children (Dennis, Robert, Ronald, Daryl, Susie) all established professionals in medicine. I was lucky enough to meet some of these cousins, both in America and in Italy and recently, I got to take to Pietracupa the youngest of the group, the lovely and sweet Susie.

 Uncle Giuseppe, instead, was a guest in the house of his son-in- law and daughter Carmela and Rosario in 1939, and after many years of work in the USA, in 1948, embarked on the ocean liner Conte di Savoia and came back to his wife Anita and his five children who had remained at Pietracupa (Alfredo, Michele, Cesira, Angela and Olga).

Each meeting was always exciting to find that Italian spirit as distinctive and prestigious note to their role as established professionals in American society, but with that little bit of our Italian national, which adds a special value to their way of being.

9) I would like to finish my roundup on Pietracupa's community in Wisconsin and Illinois, citing **Uncle Alfonso Santilli and Aunt Silvia Di Iorio, the sister of my grandmother**. Uncle Alfonso and Aunt Silvia opened a well-known Italian food store in Milwaukee, and had three children Mary (mother of 5), Nicholas (father of one son), Vincenzo / Jimmy (the father of two daughters). Aunt Silvia often coordinated among Pietracupa's residents fundraising for the feasts of the patron saints of the village.

Immediately after the war, there were other Pietracupa people arriving in the city of Milwaukee.

I remember Guglielmi family with sons Alberto, Graziano, Giovanni. The same Michele Cacchione, my dear friend since the games at Casarino, who married, Luisa, the daughter of Giovanni Cacchione well-known journalist of a daily newspaper in Italian. And finally **Giovanni Di Sarro**, one of the inhabitants of Via Vico I ° S. Anna, moved in 1960 to this industrial city, the home of motorcycle Harley Davidson. Giovanni was a skilled tailor known in most of America. He moved from Milwaukee to Chicago, to San Francisco; then he went to Las Vegas and now he resides in Florida. But he often comes to visit the family of his sister Peppina in Italy. When I meet Giovanni, both in Italy and in the United Sates, it is always a nice chance to talk of memories and Italian songs, which he plays with great feeling.

In the east of the USA, particularly in New York and in Westfield there is a large community of Pietracupa's people. I collected the stories of some of them I consider representative of the experiences of our Pietracupa's fellow citizens and of the last and latest generation of emigrants to arrive in the United States.

10) Vincenzo and Margaret Di Iorio

Vincenzo was a cousin of my father, but there were only a few years difference in age between me and him, so we had the same taste and the same dreams of the youth of '50s and '60s. He had been orphaned at an early age and his maternal aunts took care of him in the village until after the war, when one of his maternal aunts who had previously emigrated to the USA, called him to live with her, in the town of Westfield.

Our relations were never interrupted; Vincenzo deeply loved Italy and every summer, after his arrival in the USA, he would spend his holidays with us, especially in Rome, where he would find sister Angelina's family and mine. The summers spent with him in Rome are unforgettable, the city was truly magical in those years particularly discreet and shrouded by the scent of the "Dolce Vita", immortalized by vintage movies and photos.

In one of our evening walks, sitting at **the "Gran Caffé" of Piazza Esedra**, Vincenzo met the woman of his life, **"Margaret"**, a charming American girl on vacation in Italy, born in New York, coming from Molise's family Roccapipirozzi. This meeting was an opportunity to know and see each other again in New York and get married. From this union were born two very affectionate twins, **Bianca and Mary**.

I have been several times to visit Vincenzo and his family at their home in Astoria and in 1988, during a holiday travel with my whole family in New York, we were their guests. We spent very happy days, full of loving attention from the whole family, especially Bianca and Mary. They guided us in the districts of New York to enjoy the chaotic charm of "Big Apple". Vincenzo, on that occasion, took me to visit the "Brooks Brothers" department store, where he worked and was highly respected and appreciated.

Unfortunately, shortly after our meeting, he died of an incurable disease and this was our last meeting.
I still keep the very beautiful tie from Brooks Brothers, which he gave me during that visit, like the memory of a dear relative and especially a close friend, who with his kindness, his humanity, his commitment to the work, was able to create something solid, lasting into the new world where he emigrated as a young man.

This something is his family, linked to the principles and traditions of our Italy, Bianca and Mary and the lovely granddaughter Margherita keep alive, integrating them with the modern reality of American society.

11) Giovanni Saliola

During the "Estati Pietracupesi", Giovanni, who lives in Westfield, is always present in the village with his family and the family of his brother in-law Nicola Fusaro. During our meetings in the square, he has always said that he loves Pietracupa and every year wants to be present at the celebrations of the patron saints of this village where he was born.

The daily program of his Pietracupa days begins with a morning walk towards the plain, then towards the well on the via nova, with final arrival and breakfast at the Bar of Vittorio, in Via Trento. My window overlooks the bar, so when John arrives with friends in tow, I go immediately to spend some time with them, considering this banquet of friends **"the elegant meeting in Pietracupa"** that relaxes me, too, for the funny jokes and stories about the old days. Last summer, John told me some anecdotes of his life spent in the village and later in the United States, describing with great reality Pietracupa's human stories of postwar emigrants.

"In the years immediately after the war, we were all a bit hungry due to the scarcity of food, but even so, we in the group of young Pietracupa people, were very close and had fun with little. Often we would stay in the Bar square, where there was **Pasquale Lombardi** *shoemaking and with us often* **Uncle Aldo Ferri**, *who, with his sagacious humor, his irony, guided us, made us happy and, sometimes, to soothe the pangs of hunger in our stomachs, he advised some feasible culinary initiative, as polenta and birds in skillet.*

"Uncle Aldo was a brave and worthy of respect person, although suffering from a disability in his foot, suffered when he was a service man during World War II, he was always close to us for help and advice.

"When we were boys he would build for us the reed flutes that gave us to animate our games. In the moments when hunger reached unbearable levels, we young people of Casalotto, had devised a fast, quiet and functional method to lure the roosters and hens swarming unattended along the way, then, we would hide them in a lot of old canvas and go to one of our farms to pluck and cook them on the grill. To avoid suspicion, the feathers of the cooked birds were laid underground in a pit that we made ourselves in secluded places, not to be discovered by our parents. The only critical point of this initiative was the screams of the owner of the moment, who, when he realized the lack of his chickens, used to go out to the street wishing that the pens removed to his hens had remained on the face of the unknown authors of the crime.

*"When the village became aware of my imminent departure for the United States, every morning I would meet Uncle Aldo on the road, he greeted me by first saying "Wall Street". As I was frightened by this strange greeting I wondered: "why Uncle Aldo, appoint me every morning r 'Ualle? (The rooster), he may have heard of some mischief with fowl disappearing?". Only going to the USA, I realized that Wall Street was a street of New York and that uncle wanted to greet me with an American term as a sign of good luck, but with my lack of language knowledge of the time, **American r'Uool and Molise r'Ualle were confused, and for me they meant the same thing in Pietracupa's slang.***

*"The day I left to go to the port of Naples, near the little house on the via nova, there was almost all the village to greet me and over all there were my childhood friends. While waiting for the bus, we joked a bit all to ward off the gloom of the moment. But inside me there was a great sadness at having to leave my home, my people, my fields. And when Scarano bus arrived, I hugged all my friends of many youth raids and in particular, in greeting my friend **Pasquale**, the neediest and most dear to me, I took off the new coat I was wearing and I left it to him as a souvenir, thinking that he would have need it more than me.*

*"On the ship that brought me to the USA, unlike what happened in the years of the early twentieth century travel, immediately I realized that the atmosphere of food poverty was about to end. In fact, on the boat, lunch and dinner were served on a table spread and the waiter on duty handed travelers a list with the menu of the day, for orders that everyone preferred to choose from the list. My first order was unfortunate, because I wanted to choose an exotic named dish, **the partridge**, but by miserable content. That's why in the following days I was very careful to order Italian food known to me. However, I always thought of my friends left in Italy, who had to get along every day to fill their stomach, while I thought to be lucky.*

"The new land welcomed me warmly and I was able to realize the dream of my life working in the clothing industry. I married Olga and weI put together a family, but, even appreciating America, my heart is always tied to this small town of Molise in which I was born."

12) Vittorio Carnevale.

Vittorio was one of the youngest Pietracupa inhabitant of the postwar years to emigrate with his entire family to the United States, in 1954. Last summer, sitting in front of his house in Via Trento, he told me about his experiences and life faced in varied American society.

*"My first difficulty encountered in the USA was the knowledge of English, but applying at school and being young, I immediately passed this hurdle. I started to work cooperating with the husband of my sister Lina, **Ottavio Cacchione**, in the pastry shop opened in Westfield. Later I had a further experience in the commercial transport sector.*

"My local friends, with whom I spent my free time, were mostly born or derived from Italian families. As a youth I had to be very careful what people I could attend, because it was easy to run into gangs of rowdy boys with the risk of being bogged down in very risky matters, regarding drugs, criminality and so on.

*"At some point in my life I thought it was appropriate to make a new life experience, enlisting as a soldier **in the USA Army**. After a training period at home, I was sent to **Korea**, then to **the Hawaiian Islands** and finally to **Italy**, in the military base of Verona. This opportunity allowed me to spend a short holiday at Pietracupa, I had left a long time. Here I saw Angela again, whom I married and later she joined me in America.*

"I was a close friend of the mayor of Westfield and I led him to invite Italy to twin this pretty town of New Jersey with our equally lovely Molisano village, birthplace of many residents in Westfield. I hoped this twinning might produce its cultural effects, especially among young students of the two twinned villages.

"About my childhood and youth period in Italy, I have the memories of days spent in the cellar of my father and of all that the village customers microworld would bring in those four walls, like attitudes of individuals, political and interest disputes, jokes, experiences proved very important in the rest of my life path on American soil."

13) Antonio Durante

Teresa Di Iorio, Uncle Umberto's granddaughter, who was born and lives in Chicago, last month told Anita that while paying with her credit card in a large supermarket in the city, she was told by a smiling employee, responsible for the checkout, who had read her Italian name, that her husband too was Italian and came from a small town in Molise, Pietracupa.

I replied to Anita with an e-mail telling her that I knew **Antonio** very well and as a boy I would often play with him and some of his brothers. I added that both in Rome and at Pietracupa, I meet his brother Domenico and wife Italia and that just last summer he gave me news of his brother- in-law.

Antonio left at a very young age to go to work in Belgium, in a coal mine; then he moved to Australia and later to the United States, where he married Chris and currently he is doing artisan work in this great metropolis of Illinois .

 In the Museum of "Pietracupa's people in the World" is on display an interesting photo of Antonio with the big truck by which he visits his many customers in Chicago. The best memories I have of Antonio are his solitary daring and courageous climbing he used to perform in the village to reach the summit of the "Morgia". He was the only one able to do it with consistency. These adventures were reason for fear and despair for Uncle Corradino who often used to walk in the square of Briscinia to go to church inviting him with dramatic gestures to come down from that peak.

14) Ciro Verde

 Ciro is a dear friend who lives and works in New York. He is highly respected in the village, where he bought a nice house, to come and spend his holidays with family. Last summer, during a nice musical evening in Via Nicola Portone, Ciro told me the story of his life and his links with Pietracupa.

"My father and my mother were natives of Naples and moved to New York, together with my three brothers, all born in Italy. In 1965, I was born, the only member of the family born in the USA.

"In the district "Astoria" lived several families of Greek and Italian descent, between the last ones there was the family of Giovanni and Antonietta Del Monaco who for me have been like two second parents, for the loving relationship that developed between our families. I consider the same Cesira, daughter of Giovanni and Antonietta, as a sister.

My first job was in the year 1985 as "pizza-maker" at the Bar / Restaurant Ferrara in Mulburry Street, in the district of "Little Italy". Then I continued to work always in the restaurant business and opened a restaurant in Lexington Avenue in the district of Manhattan. I married an Italian / American girl who, like me, loves Italy and particularly Pietracupa, the village where I have many friends. It is my intention, if the objective conditions will allow me, to open a small restaurant in the village, subsidiary of the other I have in New York. My project aims to boost the local economy and to enhance the food and wine products of this small village of Molise, a true jewel set in unspoiled nature."

Some years ago I went to visit Ciro's restaurant on Lexington Avenue and I must say that it is a very well known and frequented local by famous people who live in this exclusive Manhattan district street.

Belgium / Germany

15) Riziero Grande and Peppina Di Sarro

Riziero and Peppina have a house in Via Vico I ° S. Anna and my family has been united to them by affection, respect and esteem, and every important moment of our lives, both joyful and sad, has always been characterized by our respective presences and participations. But beyond this personal aspect, Riziero has often told me how were the living conditions of an Italian who emigrated to a Northern Europe industrial /mining country.

"In the immediate post-war, Italy was gripped by a deep crisis, with few job opportunities especially for us young people of the south, so I thought to emigrate to England to go to work in some building industry, the so-called kilns, very active in that country after the terrible bombing suffered during the war by German aviation.

"The work I was meant to deal with was a very congenial one, because as a boy I had worked with my father and my brothers to send forth one of the major Molise kilns that unfortunately, after the war, no longer had the demands of production as previous years.

"My English experience was brief, because the living and safety conditions at work were very bad, so I thought to return to my homeland. Immediately after the birth of my first child Manfredo, I had to leave again to look for better luck abroad and this time I decided to emigrate to Belgium. The opportunity arose because after the agreements signed by some European countries, including Italy (CECA)* (SCEC), the Italian borders were open and organized to allow the entry of Italian workers, to the signatories States of this agreement. In those years, along with me have left many young Pietracupa's people with families in tow, to go to work to Belgium or Germany.

"Life in the mine was very hard; we entered into the bowels of the earth and worked for many hours digging out the rock and cut coal. The danger of collapse or a sudden explosion caused by gas scattered in the air, were the order of the day, and every worker in the narrow excavation tunnel, always prayed that this never happened. Another sneaky and dangerous enemy was the dust that emanated during the excavation and that each miner was breathing like a light poison that in the long run causing silicosis and other cardio/circulatory pathologies.

---

* *N. of the T. CECA - Steel and Coal Economic Community. (Comunità Europea Carbone e Acciaio)*

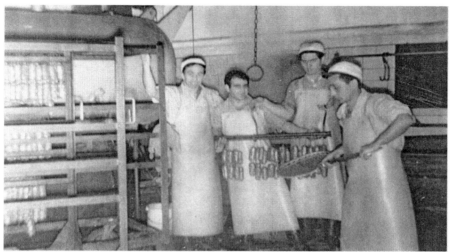

Germany – Pasquale Camillo

Belgium – Italian miners

Belgium – Pietracupa's community

Belgium – Pietracupa's migrants

Belgium – Pietracupa's community

"Miners' life followed always the same rhythm, work, family, meetings on holidays with Italian friends and relatives there; the women were busy with household chores in the house and the children attended schools in the local offices.

"During the years spent in Belgium my second son, Giovanni, was born. But I had already planned to set aside a bit of money and return to Italy, in Rome, where my brother-in-law and my brother Luigi already lived. When I had the chance I returned to Italy with the

228

whole family to go to work in the capital, the rest is part of the Italian story of my family."

16) Pasquale Camillo

Pasquale is my same age, and since I was a boy I have had with him a nice friendship. He is very frank and lively and has an ironic mind, but at the same time is very deep in thought. Despite having the same surname, we do not belong to the same line of the family, but he is an avid lover of the register family tree, that's why he often contacts people from other cities, who have our same surname.

During summer vacations we always have the opportunity to talk about our youth spent in Pietracupa and also of our lives. In particular Pasquale told me about his experiences as an emigrant in Germany and of his life in a small town of the Milanese, **Cologno Monzese**, where he has been living with his family for many years:

"My dream was to stay at Pietracupa and start a sheep meat slaughter and sale. In the early postwar years I also tried, but the proceeds and customers were scarce, even though I had put this warning in the shop – "The customers are requested not to ask for credit because the firm so fails".

"So I had to think to go abroad to try to set aside a bit of money and assess what to do in the future. I left for Germany, along with other Pietracupa people. After passing various health and administrative checks in Verona, I arrived in the German city of destination, where I started working in a large factory for meat processing.

"The local population, although in general was polite to us, was not very friendly to newcomers. This was felt especially when we walked in public places where distrust of foreigners was evident. For this we preferred to go to a few locals managed by Italian staff. The situation was the same for other workers from other countries, such as Greece, Spain and Turkey. Among us emigrants, there was a different spirit of solidarity. I had a great relationship with a family from Spain.

"After my experience abroad, I came back to Italy and I got married. So I decided to go to the north of Italy, in the wake and on advice from

other villagers who had emigrated earlier and at last I found my final arrangement. I was hired as a janitor in a large housing complex of Cologno Monzese, a town in which my son was born and where I currently reside.

"Now that I am retired, I spend my days meeting with old friends of the place, play at bowling and spend my summer vacations at Pietracupa. I remember you as a kid, I grazed sheep and you went for a walk; but I have always respected you."

The story of Pasquale is a bit as the stories told me, with different tones by **Antonio Cirese** who emigrated to Germany too and then settled near Milan, with all his family.

By Peppino and Osvaldo La Guardia, returned to Italy and properly inserted in the employment context and **their Italian sister Tonina** who lives peacefully with her family in Germany.

By now we are all included in the reality of the great European Community (EEC), which from that very first Treaty of SCEC, signed by our founding fathers of the Republic, has triggered the migration narrated above.

The hope of all of us is that the European Community will become a Confederation of States having a new constitution and a greater importance on the world stage to bring to the other international communities its wealth of cultural resources and historical experiences for peace in the world.

Argentina and Venezuela

18) Uncle Nicolino Saliola

I had the pleasure of knowing Uncle Nicolino in the '70s. He had lived and worked for many years in Argentina. Once he retired, he wanted to return to his native country to spend the last years of his life.

Uncle Nicolino was the grandfather of **Antonietta Del Monaco**, my dearest childhood friend, born in Pietracupa and lover of her country to the point that, in the 70's, she was elected President of Pietracupa's Community in Rome, to which she devoted much of her leisure time. For a short time Antonietta's family emigrated to Argentina, at the grandfather's home, with the intention to stay forever in that nation. But the cases of life wanted that the family came back to Rome and Antonietta was employed in an important Italian company.

Uncle **Nicolino**, during the years of his retirement, was an affable craftsman full of initiatives and life; he turned his basement in Via Trento, into a fully equipped workshop that allowed the dynamic uncle to spend time making the renovation of his house.

In the morning, when I went to breakfast in the Bar of Concetta, I always met Uncle Nicolino who greeted my kids saying, "Good morning muciaciti", and for his nice greeting Massimiliano and Claudia remember him as "Uncle muciacito". Still today when I walk near his cellar I remember the beautiful person he was, an emigrant of the first wave.

19) Giuseppe Brunetti

During the war years, Giuseppe always walked to Via Vico I ° S. Anna, where his family had lived for a short period of time. Giuseppe in the '50s, during the great exodus, thought to go and look for better luck in **Venezuela.** So he did, and in this South American country he has taken root, has created a family and became an important breeder on his ranch.

I have a very beautiful memory of Peppino, not only for the period of my childhood spent in Pietracupa and for the human relationship I had with his family, but especially for the kind gesture that he wanted to give to my father, **to come and say goodbye** to our Roman home, a few days before leaving.
I was a kid and I never forgot that gesture full of deep feeling and friendship for my family. I saw fleetingly Peppino, only once in Pietracupa, but I always ask for news about him to brothers Gino and Albino.
I end this chapter, noting that Pietracupa's emigration continued even with the young people born in the seventies, but the phenomenon has assumed different characteristics compared to the past. As I wrote earlier, the successive departures are related to family and socio / economic reasons of a more complex nature.

Market globalization, the use of new media, social relations evolution and the role of women in modern society, show other scenarios that historians will have the task to analyze and crystallize over the years to come, for a comprehensive examination of our very recent past and present.

But whatever happens, both the old and the new immigrants have always remained linked to the small village of Molise.

My daughter, who is part of the new generation of Pietracupa's natives attending the village, always tells me that she and even her peers, when leaving the village, seeing disappear the quiet and majestic image of Morgia from their sight, are taken by a feeling of homesickness for what they leave and already plan to go back soon.

The following poem was written about 40 years ago and expresses the feelings I felt and I still feel every time I return to the village, and I think many of the old emigrants feel, thinking about the Pietracupa of the past, full of unexpressed memories, but rooted in the depths of our souls.

Pietracupa, Images and Feelings

Four houses clinging to the gray rock beaten by wind.
The old bell that chimes nine o' clock,

The square, the races of children in the narrow streets
lit by dim lights of the evening.

The return of the farmers from the fields,
the buzz of the young, the old tavern
with players of all time.

The stories of the emigrants, the sincere embrace
of old friends, the new dress on the feast day,
the mother church, the long staircase
where we met by guys.

The quiet sweetness of the landscape around,
shooting stars on the via nova
in the night of San Lorenzo.

The deep silence in the afternoons in the countryside,
long vigils, serenades with songs of the past,
the magical concert of nature in August evenings.

Images and sensations of my country,
my people, preciously closed in my heart.

Images and sensations of real,
ancient, unchanging things, that I carry within me,
as I wander through the world.

-The Great Beauty and the American Dream

Immediately after the war, saying to a friend "Has arrived your uncle of America?" was a nice way to wish him the arrival of an unexpected fortune. For Italians of the '40s and '50s, the arrival of Uncle of America was as a kind of happy event, comparable to a big win at the football pools or the Lotto game. Of course everyone was aware that it was an auspicious joke; but the story makes very well the attraction that the Italian people, and young people in particular, had for the opulent American society, which was often represented in numerous epoch films, screened in small rooms in the suburbs. The beautiful film with Alberto Sordi (An American in Rome), even though had ironic touches to the American myth, portrayed very well what was the American dream that every Italian boy had within him: marry a rich American girl and do the nabob in USA. The America dream in those years was a kind of Eden, where everyone could find the opportunity to realize one's life at optimum levels and to find happiness.

On the other side of the ocean, however, Italy was considered the garden of Europe for the "Great Beauty" represented by its sea, its mountains, its cities of art, its museums, its beautiful medieval villages, its historical artifacts of Greek, Etruscan, Roman, Renaissance period, its inspired cuisine, by its music and by that Mediterranean warmth synonymous with hospitality and joy.

So, thousands of American and foreign tourists were planning to visit our country, also attracted by the events of the Holy Year and by the desire of many of our countrymen, emigrated overseas, to return to visit their country of origin.

During the '50s and '60s I lived both experiences and feelings related to the "Great Beauty" in Italy and the "American Dream" in the USA, which I intend to tell the reader as a kind of travelogue, for any reflections.

Following the thread of my memories, the first Pietracupa visitors arrived in Italy in 1954, to enjoy the great Italian beauty, were **Aunt Maria, accompanied by her son Alfredo**, from Chicago. Aunt Maria had married **Uncle Angelico Di Iorio** from Pietracupa, relative of Uncle Arturo, and had two sons (Giovanni and Alfredo) and five daughters (Ida, Ester, Antonietta, Jannette and Gloria), all born in America.

My father, on the occasion of their arrival in Rome, thought to rent a car and drive these relatives to visit Pietracupa, birthplace of their husband and father. Pietracupa, in those years, was the old village already described in previous chapters, with rough roads, petrol available only in Frosolone, lack of running water and bathrooms, even if the people were warm and welcoming. To overcome these drawbacks, my father thought to book two rooms in the only hotel of Frosolone.

The two guests spent two days cheered by affection and pleasantness of Pietracupa's people, as well as by the special dishes of Molise authentic cuisine.

In the following years all Aunt Marietta daughters came to visit Italy by booking the travel through American agencies. Their itinerary always included Venice, Florence, Rome, Naples and during their stay in Rome, we always had the opportunity to meet them and spend a few days with them . During these loving and pleasant meetings, it was possible to show them, away from the usual tourist routes, the scenic beauty of that little provincial, **but romantic and less chaotic Rome than today**, which was advertised and immortalized by the American cinema in several successful films, such as "Vacanze Romane."
Many other arrivals followed one another in the time, like those of the journalist Cacchione family and the timely arrival of Vincenzo Di Iorio, who every summer came to visit us in Italy.

A special memory of those years is related to the arrival of **Uncle Rosario Saliola with his wife Aunt Carmela and daughter Mickie (Michelina)** in July 1956.

That summer was unforgettable for me. Uncle's family stayed in Rome for two weeks at the Hotel Universo and since I was free from school commitments, I was a guide to my relatives during the entire period of their stay in Rome. We visited museums, archaeological sites, heard the *Aida* in the theater of Terme of Caracalla and attended variety shows with comedians and singers of national fame. **My cousin Mickie** was a beautiful girl, an American style typical beauty, very elegant and witty even when she spoke of her alleged suitors, known in her visit to the village, all in search of a young Italian / American to marry. She did not speak the Italian language and I started to venture my superficial English to make myself understood by her.

Back in the United States we kept our relationship by correspondence which was very useful to improve my language skills and also to learn about American lifestyle through her writings. Mickie got married in the USA, and had three sons. We met again in Rome in the summer of 2006, along with her sister Anita, all my welcom guests. We remembered that bright summer of '56 spent with her family in the city, we remembered our expectations of the epoch and smiling, we concluded that we were inwardly still young, thanks to our families too who have given a sense of positivity and concreteness to our lives today.

But my fondest and most unforgettable Italian memory of great beauty is related to the travel to Italy that **my cousin Toni Durante** undertook in 1963, coming from Milwaukee.

It is not easy to describe the great bond of affection that my father had with his sister Anna Maria, who as a child had been his mother after the death of my grandmother. Similarly it is not easy to make today's reader understand the thoughts and feelings that ran through my mind and in my heart in having to meet the first American cousin descended from Camillo family all residents in the USA, except my father. Upon arrival of the tourist bus coming from Florence, unbeknownst to her, all of us were waiting for her at the Hotel Napoleon in Piazza Vittorio.

While the tour group participants descended to the bus stop, my mother, through the window, recognized Toni and made her a nod. The hugs, the emotion and the outpourings of all of us, were observed by the tour members, who were the joyful crown to their countrywoman, amazed by that reception for they are unusual in the United States. But this too is the great beauty of **Italian heart and feeling**.

Toni spent two weeks of vacation with us. And by my first legendary car Fiat 600, with my father and my brother, we traveled through the streets of Rome, to the castles, Tivoli villas and especially in the south of Italy, Naples, Capri's Grotta Azzurra, Ischia, Pompei, Sorrento, Ravello, Positano, true pearls of our Italian South, immortalized by popular songs and writers from all over the world. Toni was enchanted by this Italian tour and glad for her travels in Italy.

Antonio Durante – Chicago

2014 – Jessica and Rebecca, Stamford – Granddaughters of Anita

Vittorio Carnevale – Westfield

Giovanni Saliola

Pietracupa's people at Westfield – Nicola Fusaro

238

I must say that Naples in those years was a city still suffering from the wounds of war. But even if you could see, looking around, a bit ragged air, streets, alleys, and people identified with **l'Oro di Napoli***, there was a smell of rebirth, of joy. And thinking again now, I feel a sense of sadness at seeing the piles
of garbage and everyday news related to nowadays drug and Camorra, that still feed the will of all Italians, Neapolitans the first, to fight this degradation.

Toni, in the following years, returned several times to Italy, with her brother Phil and mother, but our first encounter was memorable for all of us.

The travel of **Aunt Anna Maria** in 1971 was another opportunity to realize what an old woman who after 40 years returns to visit her native country may feel in her heart. I was not present at her arrival in the village for business reasons; but the meeting with relatives, with her friends of youth, the return in the family home, for her were moments of emotion and deep reflection, that Aunt told me in detail on her return to Rome.

In the following years, all my American cousins of the first, second and third generation belonging to the **families Camillo / Durante / Porchetta / Di Iorio / Santilli / Saliola** came to Italy to visit her great beauty, and especially to go to Pietracupa, where their ancestors were born. I can testify that often, during their stay in the village, I have seen welling a few tears of emotion in their eyes. In these tears there were all the memories of their grandfathers' stories, there were the fading images of photos of the epoch seen in family albums, there was over all the joy and the awareness **to feel, even they in some way Italians**.

Even today, many Pietracupa's community young people spread in the world come to visit us, to strengthen the bond of common belonging to tradition and teachings coming from the ancient roots of Molise. I would like to conclude the argument citing two people who weren't born in Italy, coming from far away and both in love

---

* N. of the T. **"L'Oro di Napoli"** a book published in 1947 by Giuseppe Marotta (1902-1963) a neapolitan author and reporter.

239

with the great Italian beauty: **Michael,** the husband of my dearest childhood friend **Elvira Del Monaco** and **Norma**, a very nice woman, born in Argentina from Fossalto parents.

Michael was a respected and excellent professional in the field of naval radar management, at the NATO of Bagnoli. He was born in the USA, but after having met and married Elvira, chose to remain in Italy, not only for family reasons, but mainly because he found here the great beauty and the atmosphere that fascinate every traveler who comes from far away.

Michael and Elvira have built a delightful cottage in the interior of a shady wood in Pietracupa that is an invitation to peace, to rest, at contact with nature. I have often been their guest during Pietracupa's beautiful summer evenings spent talking and arguing, along with other friends from Molise. The hours spent with them remain strokes of culture, of joy, of friendship and good taste that reinforce that spirit of Molise community that is within us.

I met **Norma** by chance, at Fossalto, while waiting for my wife in the hair salon run by **her friend Carmelina**. Norma told me that it was the first time she came to visit Italy and above all it was the first time she came to stay in the native country of her parents.

She expressed the great emotion she felt when she saw the small town of **Fossalto**, imagined in the memories of her childhood, through the stories of her parents in Argentina. Now, she has had the chance to touch the reality of the country, she felt happier, closer to these people who had received her with great joy and great participation, as if she were a daughter returned home after many years away.

Norma, during our chance meeting, told me that her vacation was over and she was about to leave the small village of Molise to return to Argentina. But she was leaving bringing in herself two things: the great beauty of the landscape and Italian people, and the certainty she would come back again to Fossalto, to savor again the smells and that air of family that she had found during her visit to the village.

The other topic of the chapter is the **"American Dream"** that every emigrant would carry within him when he left for America. I'm

240

convinced that the stories of our emigrants reported in the previous chapter can give the reader an idea of how the dream developed and after achieved for many of them.

But this time I decided to tell **the American dream of many young Italians** who, in the '60s, fascinated by that America full of color, music, quirky events, wanted to follow it to find out for themselves the charm of its experience, that media advertised with great emphasis.

In the '60s, I indeed was a young man eager to go to the USA to find out "on the road", **the modern and futurist beyond the ocean world;** and especially I had a dream to meet all my Italian / American relatives whom I only knew through the stories of my father and the photos that came to us by letter. I had been planning my travel for a long time and as soon as my work allowed, I immediately started, at the American Embassy in Via Veneto, the process for requesting a tourist visa, valid for six months.

At that time it was very difficult for a young Italian to have a visa to travel to the USA, but the statement of my company and the availability of Dr. Lalli, a friendly Embassy clerk, a native of Salcito, allowed me to obtain the visa at once.

I left from Fiumicino by a British Airways plane and after about 10 hours I came to Chicago, where I was expected by my relatives. Remembering that travel I can say that it was the first time I got on a plane and the views from the window of the city below me and especially the view of the mountain range of the Alps, were the crown of that flight dreamed since I was a boy.

But the memorable part of the trip was meeting with my uncles and my cousins at the Airport Ohare of Chicago. They were all there waiting for me, Aunt Anna Maria, Aunt Elisa, Uncle Igino, Uncle Vincenzino, Toni, Phil, Nick and even today, as I'm writing this story, I feel shivers and a great emotion in thinking back to that day of **September 1965.**

Milwaukee's Pietracupa community welcomed me with open arms and the house of Uncle Arthur and Aunt Anna Maria, where I was staying, was for days the crossroads of relatives and friends, happy to meet and greet one of their fellow countryman come from Italy.

I was a guest in turn of the families of all my cousins in their Milwaukee homes, in Round Lake and at last in the home of my cousin **Nick Camillo in Chicago and his brother Tony,** that with the army of their four plus nine children Camillo, the wives and Aunt Concettina, filled a local for the welcome lunch.

I visited Chicago, its downtown, the art museum and the City Hall where Nick was employed. But the memorable day for me was when all three American cousins, met to take me along **Lake Michigan**, to spend a day outdoors. I still have the photo from that day taken at **Balbo Dr.**, the commemorative square where the brave Italian aviator squadron, commanded by General **Italo Balbo,** glided on the sea with their seaplanes during the Atlantic Raid by Italy/America/Brazil on January 31st, amazing all the world. The mayor of Chicago, on that occasion gave to the General the key to Chicago, preserved in the Museum of Vigna di Valle Bracciano and has dedicated to him the name of that square.

During lunch on the Lake, Nick, Phil and Angelo told me about **my grandfather**, their relationship with him as children, about his tenderness and his great distinction in the way of being, and in dealing with people.

The second part of my 1965 American holiday ended in **New York**, where, with my cousin Toni we were guests of **Aunt Carmela in Mount Vernon**. That year in New York, **the World Fair** opened and the nations around the world were present there, with their stands. Moreover, in those days, **Pope Paul VI** had been invited to New York by the Secretary of the United Nations to talk about peace in the world before the General Assembly, presided over by Congressman **Amintore Fanfani**. As an Italian I was proud of all these events, especially when I saw the precious **Pietà by Michelangelo** displayed in the Vatican stand. The fair was also an opportunity to learn more about culture, technology and world industry.

On that occasion I had the opportunity to inspect some experimental technology in the motor industry and in the field of communication, especially from the USA. But I must also say that in the **Italian**

242

stand of Olivetti, in a soft and little advertised way, was shown an experimental computer that soon would invade the world, transforming it. The Olivetti Company no longer continues that ingenious innovation, but that experiment led the way for other industries that have continued on the path traced by the prestigious Italian company from Ivrea.

I came out from the World Fair listening to a little song that Walt Disney spread in the air "It's a Small World After All", which still I remember. But my stay in New York was not just a visit to the World's Fair. It was also a series of walks along **Central Park, Fifth Avenue, Rockefeller Center, Times Square, Madison Square, Broadway**, to **Little Italy**. I flew up by the Empire State Building elevator to see from the top of its tower this mythical city made of skyscrapers, lights, sounds, movement, people of different races, that make of her **the Big Apple** that includes within it all these things.

I wanted to explore the nightlife too going to see a variety show at the famous **Radio City Music Hall**. Another night I went to the famous **club "Copacabana"**; another night I went to dinner at **"Mamma Leone"**, a well known Italian restaurant All this to taste a little of American sweet life and make comparison with the Roman sweet life, which at the time was in vogue around the world thanks to Fellini.

The city tour bus too, allowed me to see some important points of the city, such as Wall Street, the Brooklyn Bridge and the Bowery with its public houses intended for drunks, who from 10 am were leaning on the walls along the street so they would not fall down.

And at last, the visit to the locations of successful films like "West Side Story" and "Fronte del porto" and the homes of famous celebrities residents in New York, was very nice. The penultimate day of my vacation I had dedicated to go to **Westfield**, home of numerous Pietracupa's community emigrated to this town in New Jersey before and after World War II. **My cousin Anita** was my guide during this visit, which lasted only one day, but was very intense for the people I got to meet and for the impressions that I got talking to many of them.

The person who Anita introduced me to first was an elderly lady of the first generation, whom I had never known. We had just entered her house when a neighbor of hers knocked on the door and in perfect Pietracupa slang asked her if she could swap **a "piece" of $10**. This familiar atmosphere took me back to the habits of Pietracupa and all day took place in this familiar atmosphere, despite being miles and miles away from the small village of Molise. On that day I visited **my cousin Linda and Benedetto**, then we went to the family of the old friend **Petrina Santilli**, to the family of **Uncle Guerrino Carnevale**, who made me visit **the famous club** which he managed and meeting point and pride of the whole Pietracupa community of Westfield. I went with him to the bakery opened by his **son in law Ottavio, by daughter Lina and her son Vittorio**, all friends of my same age and as I entertained with them there also joined us Uncle **Francesco Grande**. On his arrival, I was moved in finding a dear neighbor of Via Vico I ° S. Anna, whom I had not seen for years.

The great beauty. Aunt Marietta and Alfred Di Iorio at Pietracupa in 1954

The great beauty 1956. Visit to Aunt Antonietta – Fossalto

1956. Uncle Rosario and Angelico

**1956. Claudio and Mickie
Roman vacations**

1965. Camillo babies in Chicago

1965. Nick Camillo

1969. Milwaukee – Meeting between brothers and sisters

1965. Di Iorio family and Pasqualino Saliola

1965. The American dream

1965. Pietracupa's people at Westfield – Meeting with Claudio Camillo

1965. At Linda and Benedetto's with Anita

1988. Italian Festa at Milwaukee

When the voice of my presence spread there, Cenzino Cacchione and Giovanni Saliola came to visit me. I spoke with them for a long time talking about our present and Pietracupa's past. Everyone wanted to invite me to dinner, but there was no time and Anita had to return home. On the way back it seemed to me that we were doing the usual trip Pietracupa / Rome, instead of realizing that I was going through one of the bridges of New York, to go to Mount Vernon. That Pietracupa atmosphere had diverted me from the American reality.

Over the following years I came back other 10 times to the United States of America and two of these travels had a particular meaning outside the holiday spirit inherent in every departure abroad. I refer to the journey made in 1969, with my father and my mother, visiting my American relatives, and the journey of 1988, with my whole family.

The journey of '69 was the occasion in which my father met his brother Igino for the first time
in his life and his sisters after about 50 years. No other words are needed to give this visit the human significance it had.
I can qualify it as the transition from the heroic epoch of migration linked to great distances, to the great desertions, up to nowadays, by which, over only a day you can fly to the other side of the globeto close the gap and unite humans.

The other travel undertaken with my family **in July 1988,** was intended to make known to my young children, Massimiliano and Claudia, and my wife the other part of the family residing in the USA and to travel with them across this great country. For me it was also an opportunity to complete **my American dream** and resume my journey "on the road", started in 1965. Within a month of vacation, **we visited the eastern United States** - New York, Philadelphia, Boston, Washington, Pennsylvania and the Amish County, Buffalo and Niagara Falls, New Jersey. With a domestic flight we went to **Chicago and Milwaukee** to meet our relatives and, still by plane, we landed in **San Francisco in the West of the USA, guests of Aunt Adalgisa**. The week spent with her was wonderful both for the human aspects and for the landscape.
We visited Palo Alto and the famous Silicon Valley, the prestigious Berkeley and Stanford Universities, the Golden Gate Bridge,

Sausalito, Sonoma, Jack London Park, Napa Valley and the amazing spectacle of the city of San Francisco. There we crossed from **Fisherman's Wharf to Chinatown**, up to **Lombard Street** also taking the famous **little cable car,** clinging to the steps of this city tram like in the days after the war in Rome. Our journey continued with a rented car on the famous national Highway 101, to go to **Los Angeles and Hollywood**, then to **Disneyland, Las Vegas, the Grand Canyon, up to Arizona, to visit Monument Valley**, the land of Navajo Indians, location of all John Ford Western films.

I should write another book to tell the emotions, the feelings and meetings related to this trip to America, all this to say that **my American dream of the '50s and '60s later became reality and so we can dream,** even to have the drive and determination to achieve our dreams.

1965. World Fair in New York

The '20s and '30s. Pietracupa's men

251

CHAPTER V

THE YEARS OF ECONOMIC BOOM AND
OF PROTEST (1960/69)

-*The Events in Italy and in the World*

The sixties, are remembered as the years of the Italian economic boom, so everyone thinks that they were years of prosperity and peace. But it was not exactly like that.

Actually, all over the world, they were years full of dramatic events, such as the Cuban Crisis, the Vietnam War, the Six Day War in Egypt, marches organized by Martin Luther King in defense of the rights of blacks, the youth protests of students, and so on. Even if in Italy, the signs of economic development were tangible and obvious.

The beginning of the decade was characterized by the presence of statesmen and men of religious faith with a strong persuasive and operational personality. Among them stand out the figures of **Pope John XXIII**, Pope Paul VI, the American President John Kennedy, the Soviet Communist Party President Nikita Khruschev. Pope John XXIII was the keeper of the peace in the world, with his pleas and its policy of mediation between the USSR and the United States, managed to make a positive impact on the ideological excesses of the two nations always on the verge of a "cold war".

In 1962 he opened the **Second Vatican Council**, to make the Catholic Church closer to the needs of its faithful and the clergy, and also to open a comparison with the other monotheistic religions of the world. The encyclical "Pacem in Terris" written by Pope John in April '63 was a milestone for men and their rules on the principles that have to guide the world so that everyone can live in peace without war and destruction. The encyclical was written two months before his death, which occurred on June 21st 1963.

The successor of John XXIII was Cardinal Montini, ascended to the throne of Peter on June 21, 1963, with the name **Paul VI**. In 1964, the first time for a Pope, he visited the Holy Land. On October 4, 1965, he traveled to the USA and, as a pilgrim in America and at the

United Nations, has remained famous for his speech on world peace (*let the weapons drop from your hands*). Even his encyclical "Populorum Progressio", about the freedom of peoples and "Umanae Vitae" on the defense of life, have had a major impact worldwide (*every marriage act must remain open to the transmission of life*). During his pontificate, the liturgy of the Church was reformed, with the mass spoken in the language of the nation celebrant (1965), and reformed the Roman Curia in the year 1968.

John Kennedy, a Catholic, took up office at the White House in 1961. His presidency was characterized initially by the failed "Cuban coup" in the Bay of Pigs (1961). But subsequently he showed firmness and the ability of government to manage, as a great statesman, the issue of atomic warheads traveling with the Russian ships to Cuba. He convinced Russian President Khruschev to recall the ships of the Soviet fleet that had arrived in the Gulf of Mexico, and to return to their ports of departure. The world in those days remained in suspense, fearing the start of a third world war, with atomic weapons.

President Kennedy remained unforgettable for his speeches on the **new frontier** (*ask not what your country can do for you, but ask what you can do for your country*). Or the speech made in Germany about the Berlin Wall, in defense of Sector East Berliners' freedom (*two thousand years ago, the greatest pride was to be able to say: Civis Romanus sum, **today in the free world it is to be able to say, I am a Berliner**).

His visit to Italy, in August 1963, first in Rome and then in Naples, had great success in the midst of a cheering crowd fascinated by his way of showing and interacting with people. His last affectionate greeting to the Italians was "I will return next year". Unfortunately, six months after that visit to Italy, on November 22nd 1963, he was assassinated in Dallas in a dismal sequence of events, which are still subject to assessments and assumptions from the media. During the tenure of his successor, Lyndon Johnson (1963/1968), in August 1964, because of an exchange of fire that took place in the Gulf of Tonkin between Vietnamese vessels and a unit of the American Seventh Fleet, began the escalation of a war against the North Vietnamese that claimed thousands of victims between the two belligerents. In 1968 at the presidency of the United States was elected the Republican Richard Nixon, and it was Nixon in 1973 who declared the end of the war against North Vietnam.

In 1963 on the world stage appeared another charismatic leader, the Rev. Martin Luther King, defender of civil rights of blacks. He, on August 28th in Washington in front of 250,000 people, delivered the famous speech (*I dream that one day, in the red hills of Georgia the sons of former slaves and the sons of their former masters can sit together at the table of their brotherhood*). The Reverend was assassinated in 1968, the year in which there was also the assassination of Bobby Kennedy. But his dream has come true; the proof is that the current USA President, Barack Obama, was born of a black man and a white woman.

Nikita Khruschev, was a tough and tenacious opponent of the "American imperialists", as he called them in his speeches. But in the most critical moment of this cold war (the armed ships traveling to Cuba) he had the thoughtfulness and political sensitivity to make sensible decisions, so as to avoid the clash of war in the Gulf of Mexico. Even the decision to excommunicate the policy of **Mao Tse Tung** (1960) and then to dissociate himself from the communist nation of China, denotes the personality of a ruler convinced of the goodness of his ideas.

The raising of the Berlin Wall (1961), initiated by the Kremlin to physically divide the boundaries of the two Germanys (East and West), was another of the critical moments of political and military confrontation between the USSR and the United States. The wall became a symbol of the lost freedom of a people. For many years it was the scene of events, tragedies, of dramatic escapes over the wall which had their epilogue only in 1989 (28 years later) with the fall of the Berlin Wall and **the fall of the Republic of the United Soviet States under President Gorbachev**.

Khruschev was deposed on April 12th 1964. In 1965 a new Secretary of the Soviet Communist Party was elected: **Leonid Brezhnev** remained in power for 16 years.

The competition between the two superpowers continued in the field of space conquest too. Large sums have been invested for experiments and launches of space vectors to demonstrate the capabilities of the one or the other nation. The proof of this continuing challenge is confirmed by travel in space of Yuri Gagarin in '61, of Alan Shepard with the Mercury spacecraft in '61, of Martina Tereshova in '63, of Leonov with Voshod 2 in '65, of the American Mariner IV probe in '65, up to the Lunik 9 probe of '66, and the coupling with the Gemini 8 with Agena in '66. These experiments opened the doors to the greatest adventure in space, **man landing on the moon on July 20th 1969 by the Apollo 11, which was carrying astronauts Collins, Armstrong and Aldrin.**

The last two years of the decade, 1968/1969, were eventful in the world. Just think of the Prague Spring of 1968, inaugurated by the President of the Communist Party **Alexander Dubcek,** who tried to initiate a process of democratization of the state of Czechoslovakia. The attempt was quickly suppressed by the USSR, who sent its tanks to quell incidents and restore the previous policy, replacing Dubcek with Husak, confidential man of the Soviet apparatus.

In those frantic days of street demonstrations in Prague, the whole democratic world was moved by the sacrifice of the young student **Jan Palace,** who sacrificed his life by setting himself on fire in Wenceslas Square in Prague in defense of his ideals of freedom and democracy. Even in the USA, in 1968, a wave of protests inflamed the students of some American universities, e.g., Columbia and Berkeley, decided to demonstrate **to demand the end of the war in Vietnam**, which was claiming thousands of victims and mutilating young lives.

France, under the chairmanship of President De Gaulle, was infested by the student demonstrations of the **"French May"**. On March 28th, 1968 began the protest of students, led by Daniel Cohn-Bendit, with the occupation of the Sorbonne after fierce fighting with the police. At that point President De Gaulle, with the sentence "the party is over", decided to call new elections, which, contrary to the predictions of the experts, gave the President a most unexpected majority. But in a '69 referendum, voters exempted the old leader from any political office.

In Libya, because of a military coup, **the commander Gheddafi** took power by ousting King Idris.

Analyzing Italian events of the decade 1960/1970, it is clear that Italy had made a huge leap in the economic, industrial, cultural and arts fields that brought our nation to be considered the fifth-largest economy power (currently the tenth). Already in the year 1960, the Committee of the London newspaper, **Financial Times, had assigned to the Italian lira the Oscar of Finance**. What is obvious is that in the sixties our creative ferment, our industrial and financial machinery had produced a situation of widespread prosperity in the country, so as to let historians say that the decade of the sixties was the one of **the Italian miracle**. I will not go into the details of such a miracle, thinking of remittances and other factors of a political / economic nature, that by the year 1964 had people talking about the "economic situation". One thing is certain, the '60s in Italy, were years of prosperity and development.

From the political point of view, the scene has always been dominated by the Christian Democratic Party which, after an initial stormy and hotly contested alliance with the Italian Social Movement of the Government Tambroni (1960), resumed its cooperation with the Center parties, until getting to the alliance with the Socialist Party of Nenni, who, from the year **1963 (first government Moro)**, **gave birth to the Center-Left governments** which ruled Italy for about six years. Prominent figures of this period were the three Presidents of the Republic, **Gronchi, Segni and Saragat,** and the various Presidents of the Council such as **Fanfani, Moro, Leone, Rumor.**

Among the most important measures of governments that occurred in the '60's decade, we include: school reform (1963), the plan Gescal (a State program to build houses for workers, also 1963), the nationalization of electricity (1963), the increase in taxes (1964), the five-year plan of economic planning, decentralization.

The most important events of the decade were: the Universal Exhibition in Italy in '61 during the centenary of Italy unification, the opening of St. Bernard and Mont Blanc tunnels, the Vajont disaster, the opening of the motorway of the sun, the flood of Florence (11/04/66), the earthquake in Belice (1968), TV color (1967), the opening of the Milan Underground.

In the field of sport, the year 1960 was the year of the Olympics in Rome, with the victories of Berruti, Benvenuti and the conquest of 16 gold medals in various Olympic disciplines. In Italy, during the decade 1960, the activities in different sports of Nencini, Pietrangeli, Pamic, Mazzinghi, Adorni, Motta, Agostini, Senoner, Monti, Nones, Thoeni, Pigni, Lopopolo, Scarfiotti ignited the hearts of Italian sportsmen and the name of Italy led all over the sport world.

Even football teams, like AC Milan, Inter and Juventus, excelled in various international competitions and **Italian football team, in 1968, became Champion of Europe**.

In the field of culture, art and music, movie directors such as De Sica, Antonioni, Visconti, Risi, Monicelli, Germi, Pasolini, the Taviani brothers, Leone, Zeffirelli, gave to audiences around the world artistic movies as Il Gattopardo, Senso, il Sorpasso, il Giudizio Universale, l'Avventura, la Dolce Vita, Divorzio all'italiana, La Battaglia di Algeri, l'Armata Brancaleone, and so on. The Oscars delivered to De Sica in '64 (Ieri Oggi e Domani) and to Fellini in '65 (Otto e mezzo) are proof of their fervid imaginations and great ability of our Directors. Actors like Sophia Loren who won an Oscar for La Ciociara, Marcello Mastroianni, Gina Lollobrigida, Silvana Mangano, Claudia Cardinale, Anna Magnani, Alberto Sordi, Vittorio Gassman lent their faces to the myriad of dramatic characters, comedians, brilliant characters that delighted spectators and lovers of Italian cinema. **The same Cinecittà**, in the '60s, was called the "Hollywood on the Tiber", because many famous American directors came to Rome to shoot films such as Three Coins in the Fountain, Cleopatra, Ben Hur, The Bible.

Even the world of song in those years saw the presence of new singers who replaced the old melodic Italian, Claudio Villa, Luciano Taglioli, Nilla Pizzi, leaving room for many young singers and songwriters who are still in the business. Among this group of singers stood out: Tony Dallara, Gianni Morandi, Rita Pavone, Gino

Paoli, Bruno Lauzi, Gianni Meccia, Eduardo Vianello, Jimmy Fontana, Gigliola Cinquetti, Patty Pravo, Lucio Battisti and especially Domenico Modugno with the worldwide hit "Volare", as well as the great Mina and Adriano Celentano who accompanied the dreams of Italians in the roaring '60s.

Songs such as Sapore di Sale, Ventiquattromila baci, Azzurro, Il Cielo in Una Stanza, Pregherò, Il Mondo, Cuore Matto, Ragazzo Triste, Emozioni, C'era Un Ragazzo, are sung on TV shows and in dance clubs, not only as revival for of the older generation of '60s, but also because today's youth like them.

A special mention should be reserved for the Beatles, the famous English band who since 1962, have fascinated their listeners with their songs like Yesterday, Michelle, Yellow Submarine.

The last two years of the decade (1968/1969), were years marked by **student demonstrations** born under the incentive of the students ready to fight the state apparatus. They intended to modify the structure of a world and a state they considered obsolete, elitist, inadequate to the needs of young people of that time, and that had disappointed expectations with the proposed university reform n. 2314, presented by the government in the fall of '67.

The graffiti on the walls during the demonstrations, "we don't change but strike the bourgeois state," says a lot about the ideas that drove the young students of '68 to demonstrate in the streets and inside the University (Milan, Rome ,Venice, Padua and so forth).

The shy and submissive female Italian community too began in the 60's on its way to emancipation towards equality of rights with the male. The trials of women who wore short skirts, **the Viola case**, the Sicilian girl who refused the shotgun wedding after the abduction of her suitor, the trial of the case of the school newspaper "**La zanzara**" in Milan, are the first ferments of protest that in the following years triggered that movement of struggle towards the emancipation of women.

The decade of the '60s ended with the famous "**autunno caldo**" for the renewal of the national labor contract, which, after heated clashes between the parties, saw its conclusion only after the signing of new agreements between Confindustria and Union Trades that took place on December 21st 1969. But before this union agreement, **on December 12th, 1969**, there was the attack on **Piazza Fontana Bank of Agriculture in Milan,** which opened the season of **Terrorist Outrages ("years of lead"),** also known as **the years of the strategy of tension**.

-MEMORIES OF THE '60s

If some young curious wanted to ask a twenty year old graduate of the '60s, now aged seventy, this question: "how did you live the '60s, you young of the epoch?", certainly he would answer that they were intense years where everybody was feeling full of energy, enthusiasm, to move, to travel. Anyway, we were breathing a new air, full of positive expectations. And this is the same answer that I myself can give those who, in 1960 turned 20 and got the high school diploma in technical studies.

 In October 1956 my family had moved to Piazzale Ionio 42, in the new house that my father had bought at great sacrifice in the district of Monte Sacro. A "little Pietracupa" was also present in my building. In fact, on the ground floor of the building lived Uncle Nicola, but mostly lived **his son Antonio Di Iorio**, who had opened a tailor shop, where often would pass Pietracupa's youth of my generation along with other Roman customers. Tonino was a person of great generosity and great spirit of observation. The times I spent with him were unforgettable. The dance parties in his house, evening walks, games seen on television, the stories about the old Pietracupa people, the jokes in dialect, accompanied my youthful years until 1970, when I got married and Antonio, for the occasion, sewed my suit for the ceremony.

Tonino was very fond of his native village, to the point that he had recently requested to have the City residence in the village. Unfortunately, a few days after receiving the news of accepting his application, he suddenly left us, with great sorrow of all of us who loved him.

Returning to talk about the spirit of the '60s, I can say that, for a young graduate in technical subjects, it was easy to find a suitable job in that period in which the large and medium industries had begun to produce again according to a trend of exponential growth.

The large public or private companies in need of young technicians, addressed directly the most prestigious universities and technical institutes, such as the **Galileo Galilei of Rome**, to obtain the names of qualified persons or graduates of the last year.

Therefore, in this climate of operational availability, as soon as I graduated engineer I received many job offers from major companies such as Acea, Alitalia, the Teti and by the **Sielte / Fatme / Ericson**, a multinational leader in the field of telephony, with which **I signed my first contract of employment**.
But the labor market was always in search of dynamic young graduates. So the following year, the **Company SpA Monte Amiata** sent me a job offer better than Sielte and, as I mentioned earlier, I accepted the proposal and left for **Abbadia San Salvatore**, a charming village in the province of Siena, to work at the said mining company which ran one plant for the extraction and processing of cinnabar finalized to the **production of mercury**.

Abbadia S. Salvatore was and is a wonderful Tuscan village in the Valley of Paglia, at the foot of Mount Amiata. It's a holiday resort in both summer and winter for many mountain lovers, especially Lazio and Tuscany people, and home to many pre-season camps for First League football teams like Roma, Fiorentina and Napoli. I remember the first time I reached the village by bus from Rome, in October '62. In the streets were circulating a few people and I had a very long uphill climb to reach the headquarters of the new company. At that time the experience of living and working was begun for me - very educational for a young novice as I was.

There were two main situations I faced in those two years spent at Abbadia: **working life in the mine and the relationship with the youth of the village** during my spare time. Working in the mine was not a simple thing. Not so hard for me who was a technician and used to descend in the underground mine two or three times a week and only for a few hours, but especially for those **poor miners** who, from six in the morning until late in the evening were

260

buried in the bowels of the earth. The rooms were damp and dusty, illuminated by dim lights of acetylene lamps, and the miners used jackhammers to extract rocky granulate from the rock, load it on the wagons, arm a cage of holding and continue to engage in other excavations. The transport wagons of the granules, after reaching the hatch of the elevator, were shipped to inside factories for hot work necessary for the mercury to evaporate from the same granulate.

But behind this brief illustrative description, there was a whole world of families living by this work. There were accidents, occupational diseases for miners silicosis, their sacrifices, their dreams for a better world to offer their children. There were the Sunday walks in the main square with their simple party clothes, the sincere invitations to their homes (owned by the Company), which I would always accept with great joy, also to listen to their stories.

Like a precious family photo, as I'm writing the faces of Paul Sbrilli, Alfredo Sbrilli, the Tondi, the Santoni, Gusman, the Capecchi they called the "Grillone," pass before my eyes. They were co-workers, close friends, who, in those years, made me understand the meaning of what it means to work hard and especially what it means **the defense of the dignity of workers**, that since my youth experience has always been present in my work activities as company executive and lecturer.

I always remember **the first day I went down into the mine. Mr. Di Noi, an engineer** and my direct superior, accompanied me. After donning overalls and with an acetylene lamp, we went down with the elevator into the long meandering 200 level excavation. Walking across those silent, gloomy tunnels, I thought of **Dante Alighieri** and the description of his Inferno; and I thought then of the television drama with Alberto Lupo, "**La Cittadella**" by Cronin, the weekly television broadcast which relates the life of the miners and tragedies in mines. By chance at the precise moment I was thinking that, I heard the roar of a sudden explosion. I slumped on a huge boulder in the ground, saying in my mind, "I just cheated the day of my first visit in the mine". But looking at the calm of my companion, I realized that it was a normal phase of work and I did find courage.

The fear of every miner is **not to go back to see the stars**, once he entered into the bowels of the earth.

My relationship with the youth of the village was one of great harmony and a special availability they had to me. By my accent and my Roman jokes, I gained their affection. **Hotel Roma**, managed by Mr. Pilade and his family, was my abode in the village; the neighboring bar of Mr Trento, Pilade's brother-in-law, was the usual meeting place for many young people in the village who for two years were my pleasant companions of those days in Tuscany.

In my office also worked **Rosario Lucchesi**, a dynamic, cheerful, very intelligent person with a great vitality. Often I was a guest for dinner at his home, greeted with great affection by his wife **Juliana,** a respected teacher of Siena, and by **Vanna** their lovely daughter. They made me feel the warmth of a close friend especially in the winter months.

But during the summer, the town and the hotel were filled with vacationers, young men and women who filled my evenings with cheerful raids to Chianciano, Santa Fiora, Montepulciano, on the shelters of the Monte Amiata. **Paolo Ietta, Gianpiero, Silvio, Montesi** were my companions on those evenings "badenghe"(in Abbadia) in which I not only breathed the scent and the proximity of so many beautiful girls, but also the pleasure of many beauties of nature that Tuscany, even now, offers tourists from all over the world. Among other things, right on the famous climb of Radicofani, I had earned my driver's license, driving a flaming 600 I had bought for the occasion.

In July 1964, with some regret, I left Abbadia. Having won a national competition organized by ATAC, I returned to my city, **starting a new life path in the Roman transport company**, which I only left the day of my retirement on December 31st 2003. **The ATAC** has been for about forty years my resource, my world of work, and I have always tried to give the best of my commitment as a manager, first, and then, as a winner of a national competition.

I will not bore the reader in speaking of a transport company, which is not the subject of the book. But I just want to say that these service companies are part of the story of the city and the nation. Speaking of the efficiency of public transport in large cities such as Rome, London, Paris, New York, Moscow **is a way to evaluate the efficiency and image of the city itself.**

Rome transport Company, established at the time of Mayor Nathan, has a hundred-year historical background, made up of workers, of services rendered, cityscape, and public engagement during the war. Although some recent events have scratched its image, they are fleeting moments. Rome cannot give up its company's city mobility, representative icon of our Capital in many photos of the past and present.

Back in Rome, I re-established contact with old school friends like Paolo, Gianfranco, Vincenzo, Giorgio, who at that time were fascinated by the so-called "Roma to drink". And even I plunged myself with them in the brilliant life of evenings in nightclubs, beach holidays, travel to Spain, France, Austria, Yugoslavia, flirting, friendships, fleeting encounters. In short, **the youth of those years had the world in their arms, and it seemed that the race had never ended**.

The girls of the epoch began to open up to the opposite sex in a more communicative dialogue, although the sphere of relations was always cloaked by a certain modesty and romance - very far from the world of today's young people, which is certainly more free but circumscribed in an atmosphere of lack of communication and group socialization that creates inner loneliness, identity problems, uncertainties and hasty decisions.

This period didn't correspond anymore to my usual summer vacation in the village. The small village of my childhood was a thousand miles away from my mind. I would chase other goals, as did all my male and female friends of Pietracupa's '50s students old group I began to meet again only since the '70s, all married and with children, like me.

During the year 1965, I was invited to a party of friends where I was not anxious to go, but fate was lurking around the corner. Casually during the party I made the most important meeting of my life. **I met my wife Gabriella** and from that very day we have never been apart. My sweet Roman life was more aware and my holidays moved to **Cattolica** in Romagna, where Gabriella spent her summer holidays with her relatives who lived in the charming town of Romagna.

On April 4, 1970, we got married. The ceremony was held at the church on the Aventine Hill, near Foro Romano and was attended by many friends and relatives, including Rosario and Giuliana from Abbadia, and a large representation of Pietracupa's friends who graced us with their presence. Soon after the honeymoon in Paris, I wanted to visit Pietracupa with my wife. The village, without our knowledge, wanted to give us a wonderful Night Music, with primarily **the organ of Gregorio Durante**. Through this nice tradition they wanted to give us their best wishes and welcome us back.

One of my most important memories of the '60s, was my meeting with **Pope John XXIII.** The last year of school I won a prize for religion, banished among students in Roman schools.The award was handed to me during a ceremony at the Vatican in the presence of the Supreme Pontiff. That day the simple but touching words of the Good Pope struck me deeply, with his placid figure, and were for me an encouragement for my future life and the work I was about to face.

Another reminder of the time is that of the President of the Commission of my final exams. **General Umberto Nobile was the commander of the airship Italy,** who over twenty years earlier had crashed with his airship on the ice of the North Pole, causing a series of dramatic events related to the rescue of the survivors, admirably told in the movie " The Red Tent" with Sean Connery.

Commander Nobile, after the examinations, invited all the students of the course to a seminar in the classroom to give us some useful advice on the future we had to face. His face, excavated by the many adventures of the past, his vibrant look and especially his advice on our work lives, were very helpful in the choices I made in the years to follow. Every time I go to the Museum of Vigna di Valle and see the photos of his exploits, I always remember my old professor.

An event of the '60s which puzzled me deeply, is the death of the young Czechoslovak student **Jan Palace**, who sacrificed himself to protest against Russian tanks during the Prague Spring. I already mentioned in previous chapters about this episode. I just want to add that I have visited in Prague Jan Palace's tomb in Wenceslas Square, and I found all around me the same indifference with which the Russians of the time had accepted the death of this young man who set himself on fire, considering him a "Hippy". I do not think that this is the reason why Jan Palace killed himself; but that day, on that great square, which has now become the peaceful gathering place of young people from all over Europe, I thought that the Czechs should have had more respect for the ultimate gesture of a young student who had sacrificed for the freedom of his people.

The '60s were also the years of major infrastructure, especially in the field of national roads.
In recent years, the journey to Pietracupa was improved by the opening of the **Autostrada del Sole** and the subsequent interventions which allowed the opening of the tunnel Nunziata Lunga, the construction of the bypass isernina, the construction of the overpass on the Venafro railway, and the opening of Bifernina and Trignina. They have made it possible for motorists from Rome to improve the time and manner of the way to Molise.

Pietracupa of the sixties was changing its look. Its people started to go to Rome, Milan, Turin and to industries or mining areas of Belgium, Germany, England or Holland. We felt, from the speeches of the people, a sense of worry about leaving the old for the new. But in their eyes we could read the determination of peasant people used to hard work and to bite the bullet, who had chosen to leave the home of their ancestors to try to seize the opportunities that the new realities of urban and industrialized society could offer them.

I still remember Gervasio who was going from house to house in the village to say goodbye to his friends, as well as the goodbyes of **Riziero and Peppina**, who together with their **newborn Manfredo,** came to see us before leaving for Germany, as well as many other people leaving who embraced their grandmothers and their old aunts with tears in their eyes. All these people who in those years left the village, found their way to a better life.

But it's not easy to go with a light heart when leaving your own home and native country, where every corner, every street, every stone, every house, speak to your childhood, your happy and sad moments, as a young man of your dreams. And I realize what was going through the minds and souls of these, my fellow countrymen, when they climbed on the bus with their suitcases, their dreams and their sadness in leaving the cradle of their childhood, Pietracupa.

On July 20, 1969, a man landed **on the moon**. I do not want to highlight the great scientific achievement reached on that occasion, as I do not want to emphasize the accelerated leap that science has made in recent years and the reflections that all this progress has led and still leads to.

In that memorable moment, while Ruggero Orlando and Tito Stagno commented about the first steps of the astronauts on the moon, my mind suddenly went to the magical evenings of the summer, in Via Vico I ° S. Anna, where, along with other boys, I watched the Moon. And with our imagination we would think about a totally different world from that of the TV showed us that evening.

I want to conclude the topic of this paragraph with the memory of the many Pietracupa's and Molise girls who, in those years, began **their higher studies outside their region**, with the enormous difficulties of settling in the host cities and, especially, of meeting people outside their usual circle of acquaintances.

To remember these girls and their experiences out of the village, I want to tell **the story of Nicole**, a young Molisan girl that I met on the legendary train Roma / Campobasso in the year 1959/60.Nicole's father had emigrated to the USA and her mother lived in the village, waiting to join him in New York. She was finishing her studies at a school in Rome; for this she was a guest in the home of her aunt. Every Saturday she went to visit her mother in the family residence.

Following our first meeting we met several times after school and, during some family party, Nicole told me of her loneliness in the city.

266

She talked about her dreams and her hopes for the future, and every weekend, in the hours before the departure of her train, we met in the center of Rome for a walk waiting to get close to the Termini Station. At the end of her studies, Nicole left for America and I did not
hear from her anymore.

April 4th 1970. Claudio and Gabriella wedding

In 1987, during a vacation in China, my wife and I went to a typical Chinese restaurant on the **bay of Hong Kong**. The local was immortalized in an old American movie, "Love is a Many Splendored Thing". Coincidentally, right next to our table, sat a woman and her Italian husband, commander of a US military ship docked at the port. After a few minutes spent in pleasantries of fact, the woman told me she came from a village of Molise and had studied in Rome, at that point I recognized Nicole, the nice friend of my younger years, to whom I had devoted a poem.

We embraced with joy before our respective spouses, amazed at what had happened. I have not written to Nicole any more, but I wanted to publish in the book the early poem written for her and I dedicate it to all Molise offsite students, those of the '60s and of today, likely protagonists of some romantic story.

A ROMAN SUMMER

There was a bit of your perfume that summer in Rome,
on the old steps of Piazza di Spagna
between those Baroque lines, in the evening sunset.

There was the glint of a thousand lights, in the old Trevi
fountain,
there were our young hopes, our smiles,
there was the joy of our fleeting encounters, stolen at the time.

There was the charm of my Rome, its shadows, its smells,
its deep mysteries, the stories of the old Tiber:
stories of the Popes, stories of women and brigands.

But above all, there was our freedom, your smile,
the sweetness of our feelings, the magic of those hours
among the colors of the evening and the mists of a sunrise that
separate us with the puffs of a train that went to the South and
my hello.

CHAPTER VI

THE YEARS OF LEAD (1970/89)

-The Events in Italy and in the World

Scholars, in their analysis of two decades from 1970 to 1989, unanimously identify this period of Italian history as "the Years of Lead". By this term, they want to refer to the many deaths of statesmen, politicians, judges, professors, students, activists of political parties, trade unionists, the Red and Black Brigades, the anarchists, the fixers, workers, and innocent ordinary citizens, killed by the lead of a firearm or the lead of some bomb exploded during the so-called "strategy of tension". This tension was fueled by armed groups of militants belonging to opposing extremist political ideologies, both the right and the left, who tried to pursue a single goal: to destabilize the Italian State, for their political purposes.

Lead is the metal indeed to characterize these years full of tragedies and events not always easy to interpret from an historical and political point of view. Respecting the aim of this book, I will abstain from giving any political, social or historical opinion of these years, and I will only try to summarize all the events that characterized the so-called Years of Lead, for the reader's information.

The governments which took turns in Italy from 1970 until June 28th 1981 were all led by men of the Christian Democrats (CD). Their formations included center-left parties (Rumor, Colombo, Andreotti, Cossiga, Forlani) or only one color formation like CD (Andreotti, Moro), or formations which included the outside support of the Communist Party, the famous historic compromise, the two Andreotti's governments.

On June 28, 1981 Congressman Spadolini, after 45 years of Democrat leadership, formed the first five parties government after the war led by a liberal. The following governments, always formed by center left coalitions, were chaired by Spadolini, Fanfani, Craxi, Goria, De Mita and Andreotti. During the chairmanship of Congressman Andreotti, in Germany the Berlin Wall was torn down,

271

which marked a turning point in relations between the two major powers of the world's political and economic scenario.

In Italy, this event preceded the end of the First Republic, with the scandal of "mani pulite"* and the advent of new parties and new political figures such as Berlusconi, Bossi, Di Pietro. But we will discuss this in the next chapter.

At the end of the last two decades of the 1900s, there were three Presidents of the Republic and two Popes: Joseph Saragat, Giovanni Leone, Sandro Pertini and Francesco Cossiga; Paul VI, John Paul I and John Paul II.

The main measures resulting from the activities of governments that alternated at Palazzo Chigi in the years from 1970 to 1989, were the Financial Law for the Establishment of Regions, the Workers' Statute, the Law on Divorce and the subsequent abrogative referendum with the victory of the no's, the Reform of Family Law, the Law on Abortion, the Institution of the National Health Service, the Decree on Counterterrorism about Reduction of Sentences, the referendum **on Abortion and Public Order, the new State / Church agreement, the new Crimina**l Procedure Code.

But the events that dramatically characterized the years of lead were the attacks and violent, bloody conflicts among the Red Brigades, the Black Brigades, police, members of Loggia P2*, corrupt bankers, mafia, occult forces of the state and corrupt politicians, magistrates and executive public servants, trade unionists, emeriti Professors who were active and passive subjects of the complex events of the years 1970/89.
This was a period during which the kidnapping and killing of Congressman Aldo Moro and his escort of March 16th to April 9th 1978, were the emblem of a period full of light and shadow and great

---

* N. of the T. Mani pulite. Indicates a period of the 1990s when there were some judicial investigations of political and economic leaders. These investigations spotlight a system of bribery, extortion, illicit funds to the parties, up to the highest levels of Italian political and financial worlds called "Tangentopoli".
* N. of the T. Loggia P2. Criminal and subversive organization led by Licio Gelli.

suffering for the population, the astonished spectator of all that was happening, and that was a prelude to the authoritarian change in the young Democratic Italian Republic.

Taking a brief look at what happened, just remember the violent deaths of Feltrinelli, Calabresi, Coco, Occorsio, Bachelet, Tobagi, the General Dalla Chiesa and his wife, Pio La Torre. And still the massacre of Piazza della Loggia in Brescia, the massacre on Italicus train with 48 deaths, the massacre at Bologna train station, the massacre of train in San Benedetto Val di Sambro, the wounding of Montanelli, Bruno, the kidnapping of the magistrate Sossi, Sindona's death by poisoning. Without forgetting the processes of Curci, Moretti, Sofri, Bompressi, Pietrostefani, Fioravanti, Mambro, Fachini, Picciafuoco, Valpreda, Loockheed scandal, the scandal of Licio Gelli 's P2, the resignation of President Leone and so on which are elements sufficient to describe the complexity of all that happened during the years of lead.

In other parts of the world, the end of the Vietnam War, signed by USA President Nixon on January 27th 1973, put an end to a long-running conflict that produced thousands of dead and wounded soldiers on one and the other front. Nixon, who in April '71, with the strategy of the table tennis had opened the door to detente with China, in August '74 had to resign as President of the United States because of the Watergate scandal. Vice President G. Ford, President J. Carter, President R. Reagan, President G. Bush succeeded him.

In Europe and around the world, the figures of **Michail Gorbachev** (Secretary of the CPSU in March 1985) with his policy of **"perestroika"** and, especially, the Polish **Pope John Paul II** (Karol Wojtyla) left a strong imprint on national events of many states. Its most striking results were the democratization of the Republic of Poland, the fall of the Berlin Wall and the democratic restructuring of Soviet society.

The visits of the Pope in Poland (06/16/83), in support of the struggles carried out by the trade union **Solidarnosc** led by **Lech Walesa** (September 1980), produced their desired effect in December 1990, when Walesa was elected President of Poland.

But the great personality of the Polish Pope is not only limited to the story of his country.

During his long pontificate, he traveled to all the far corners of the earth, bringing his words of hope and redemption to Africans, Mexicans, Cubans. He spoke of peace with all the powers of the world, launched messages of peace and joy to all nations' young people. Unforgettable are his meetings with them and with their deep need to find answers speaking to their hearts. In a society of empty symbols and sterile messages, Pope Wojtyla was able to give the right answers to the young people's expectations. The day of his funeral, Rome was overrun by thousands and thousands of young people coming from all over the world, who wished to pay their last respects on earth to this great Pope.

Smiling girls

Pietracupa's beautiful young girls – the '60s

-Memories of the Years 1970/89

My memories of the years '70 / '89 are wonderful, especially regarding **my private life**. As I mentioned earlier, **on April 4th, 1970 I got married to Gabriella**, crowning our plans to have a family. In January 1972 and July 1973 were born **Massimiliano** and **Claudia,** who for us are the most beautiful gift that the good Lord could offer us. M**y brother Lino** followed in my footsteps, marrying Carmen, with whom he had two children, **Cristiano and Elisabetta,** and blessed now with the loving presence of granddaughter **Clara,** the daughter of Elisabetta and Daniele.

If someone wanted to ask this question*: Claudio, in 1970, you went from a carefree and brilliant life to a more careful and reflective one made up of responsibilities and commitments to other people. Have you ever had any regrets for the carefree life of the '60s that you had left?*

To this question immediately I would answer that, except for the love and my obligation to my wife, I have not even had the time to think about the "good old days" of the '60s. Immediately I faced a new commitment, enrolling in **University** and, 10 years after my diploma, I started again to study for a degree in Business and Economics at the University La Sapienza of Rome. Obviously, my decision was not a whim of the moment. After years of carefree youth, I felt the need to follow a path of academic studies, both to enrich myself and for practical reasons designed to be able to obtain senior positions in the company for which I worked.

The success of my plan was linked to the results of the first exam I was going to take immediately after my marriage. Fortunately, everything went forward according to my plan and in four years I achieved the desired degree in Economics and. In later years I won the position of manager.

I want to tell a funny anecdote about my determination and the efforts to achieve this goal.
During my honeymoon in France, time was approaching for my first exam, which I had been preparing for months. Therefore, my tension was so high to overcome the obstacle that, driving the car to Paris,

along the curves of Mont Blanc, **in my mind I reviewed codes and codicils, mathematical rules, economic and statistics theories** - all the subjects of the planned tests.

But beyond this detail related to my Molise determination and my stubbornness, **my honeymoon days** with Gabriella, spent in Paris and along the Loire Castles, **were unforgettable**. The crossing on the Seine by the Bateaux Mouches, the Eiffel Tower, the bohemian atmosphere of Montmartre, the show at Lidò on Champs Elysees were essential ingredients for two romantic newlyweds on their honeymoon.

On the occasion of our 10th wedding anniversary, we retraced the same route with Massimiliano and Claudia; we are thinking about doing it with the whole family again next year, for our 45th anniversary.

Returning to talk about the years spent at the University, my best memory is linked to **my Professors** of graduate courses: Professor Onida, Prof. Caffé, Prof. Cacciafesta, Prof. Luzzatto-Feggiz, Prof. Chiacchierini, Prof. Celant, Prof. Simoncelli from Salcito, Prof. D'Alessandro, Prof. Baffi, President of the Bank of Italy, Prof. Gabriele Pescatore, President of the Fund for the South and the Prof. Amintore Fanfani, President of the Council. They were all luminaries in their fields and held positions of political and economic importance. In particular, Prof. Fanfani reminded me my first trip to the USA in 1965 and the meeting with him, along with the group of Italian tourists visiting the UN building. I can proudly say that the current President of the European Bank, Prof. **Draghi** and the President of the Bank of Italy, Prof. **Visco**, graduated from my own faculty during my years of study.

I especially remember in the university atmosphere **Emilia Saliola**, **Giuseppe Santilli**, and in the final stage of their studies, **Giovanni Santilli and Gervasio Porchetta** with wife **Valeria.** All these colleagues and dear friends were Pietracupa's descendants, and our meetings in the classrooms of the University on Street Castro Laurentiano, were always moments of pleasant relaxation. After graduation, they all held important positions at the Ministry of Finance, at the Ministry of Education, at the Institute for Foreign

Trade and at the State Railways. We all were rewarded for our efforts and our success in university studies.

But the days of the '70's in Rome were **hard days.** We breathed in the air something imponderable, of evil, like a tsunami that at any moment could drown us. I remember one day, on my way to work, the traffic on the east ring road was blocked; later we were informed that, about two hundred yards from us, a shootout between police and the Red Brigades on the run had happened. Another day, through Viale Ionio, I noticed a crowd of people near a body covered by a white sheet. It was the corpse of **the magistrate Amato,** gunned down in the morning by some members of the Red Brigades. In the ATAC workshops, no workers spoke; people were afraid and no one trusted the other. **Sundays with no traffic**, to save gasoline, made even the days of celebration gloomy. When I brought Massimiliano and Claudia to the children's park, in my heart I thought, *I hope these days will pass soon and will return to the lighthearted atmosphere that characterized the '60s so that these innocent children can run through the fields without some madman beginning to shoot.*

The University too was pervaded by protest and ferment. 1968 was not far in the past, but the difference in my age compared to the younger students kept me from any involvement. I was too busy dividing my time between family, work and study and affording some space to my wife who, during my study hours, tried not to disturb me, even taking care of small children. Knowledge, for each person, is never too much and, with this motto, I continued to attend the University, as well as other studies related to my profession and to my role as a teacher. But this chapter of my life is part of another story and another context that does not matter to the reader.

The days of the Moro kidnapping were lived by all Italians as a national tragedy. Public television pounded listeners with stories of research about those kidnapped and the contents of the press releases that were sent by the Red Brigades to the newspapers. Citizens were subjected to continuous checks by patrols of police who stopped them and controlled everything.

In March 1978, during the Moro kidnapping, I wanted to spend Easter with my family in Pietracupa and to free my mind from the

278

gloomy air of Rome. But both leaving Rome and returning were full of checkpoints of police stationed along all consular roads, asking for your documents and ordering you to open the trunk - even while having two children on board.

On March 9, 1978, the reporter Bruno Vespa announced via TV the **news of Moro's death.** I was very moved listening to that news and I had a fleeting memory of the Professor **Moro** whom I met by chance some years earlier along the University avenues, while he was talking to his students. The immediate image left in my mind at that chance meeting, was that of a simple, helpful and very friendly man, beyond his capacity of governing or of his alleged political errors. And in this capacity I thought of Moro, when they announced his death: I saw in him **the father, the grandfather, the affable professor of many young students**, and as he had appeared to me in that brief encounter along the Sapienza Avenues.

As God wanted, **the night passed**, and to close the topic of the gloomy '70s, I'll describe an episode pertaining to the topic, in which I was featured later in 1995. Every day, on my way to the office, I took the Metro B, at the stop of departure in **the station of Rebibbia.** Every morning at the same time, a grizzled bearded man dressed in jeans, T-shirt, and sneakers went up and sat in front of me. I was sure I knew him, but couldn't remember on what occasion I had met him. It was usual at our meeting on the Metro, that in seeing each other we exchanged a nod. One day, reviewing some photos of the '70s, I found that the man was **the legendary Renato Curcio**, the Brigades man of the "years of lead" and so I commented to myself, *everything passes and time clears all.* Curcio, with the new law on the Red Brigades, had the chance to become part of social services and, in style Fonzie, every morning he would leave Rebibbia to go to work in the city. Anyway, personally I could feel comfortable because the darkness of the night of the '70s had become daylight for all citizens, even for Curcio.

At the end of my memories of the '70s I want to remember two characters of great moral and religious importance: **President Sandro Pertini** and **Pope Karol Woytila**, a true icon and landmark of Catholics and non-Catholics during the last years of lead.

I met **President Sandro Pertini** with the student body of my son in one of the regular appointments he reserved for Italian schoolchildren, at the Quirinale. His unmistakable pipe, his blunt demeanor and, especially, his pleasant pet phrases with the students of elementary schools, left the image of a kindly grandfather full of attention and advice for his growing grandchildren, while remaining the proud antifascist fighter during the years of these two decades.

I met **Pope Woytila** twice at two special events. The first time was for his pastoral visit to the St. Pontian parish in the district of Talenti, where I had been living since the days of my marriage. The second time, I met him at the Central District of ATAC in Via Prenestina, where, just in the Department which at the time I was directing, a stage had been set up to receive the distinguished guest, after the greeting by the mayor of Rome. Both meetings were moments of great humanity and great piety. My special memory was the first meeting because in the square outside the church were present Massimiliano and Claudia dressed in their **first communion** clothes. Pope John Paul II, with his charismatic eloquence, was able to find the right words to touch the hearts of children and adults attending the ceremony. The day of his funeral, I was there too, in St. Peter's Square, to honor the old Pope, who by his example and his words of comfort, eased many of our days during his pontificate.

I want to add another anecdote about a famous Pole, **Lec Walesa**. I had the chance to know him closely in 2003, when, no longer in public office, he would travel around the world to bear witness to his past duties as Secretary of Solidarnosh. The occasion of the meeting took place at the headquarters of the **Lazio Region**, in Via Cristoforo Colombo. There, the President in office at the time had organized a Conference on Institutional Resources of Lazio. They also invited some leaders of ATAC and, for the prestige of the program, had invited the former Polish President who on that occasion was interviewed by the director of RAI 2.

The impression I had of Walesa, beyond the typical Polish character with the big mustache that gave him a look of good-natured common citizen, was that of a simple but determined man. On that occasion, he became emotional when he remembered the days of the struggle with all the workers of Solidarnosh.

I believe he had a Union Trader heart and that he remained a Trade Unionist, even after his experience in the government was over and he was less famous compared to the glorious days of Union Trade demonstrations for the freedom of workers and the Polish people.

The years of lead ended with **the fall of the Berlin Wall**. I still remember that night of **November 9th, 1989**, when the Italian TV journalist, Lilli Gruber, with microphone in hand, sent pictures of the Wall near the area of the Bundestag. The citizens of both East and West Berlin joyfully had climbed on top of the wall and all together, with chisels, picks and various equipment, began its demolition to demonstrate that German people didn't need walls, but rather needed bridges and a common Homeland, together with a democratic government, freely chosen by the people.

There is no doubt that **Gorbachev's Perestroika** set the stage for the event. And, like a sand castle, the great Republic of the Soviet communist countries dissolved in the wind of Gorbachev's restructuring and gave rise to other autonomous states. The famous **Iron Curtain** collapsed that very day, and the cold war of past years became less hard in a context of globalization.

But it is clear that the fall of the Berlin Wall marked the end of an epoch and began a new era.

The tourist who travels to Berlin can see what is left of the wall and principle American and Russian garrisons at the point Charlie, who for over 45 years kept the two nations on the edge of an impending war. Nowadays, Berlin is a fully restored city with modern districts of daring architectural structures. Only a relic of a church bombed, near the zoo, and the old palace of the Soviet regime, near Alexander Platz, with asbestos roofs and undergoing restructuring, remain of the past.

Near the old wall only **some limited pieces** remain standing. These too are a reminder of the past as is the work of graffiti artists who drew figures and images praising freedom on the remaining facades. In souvenir shops, bags with bits of old wall for tourists to buy are still for sale. The current Ukraine crisis, the Russian intervention, and the discomfort of the USA make me think of historical courses and recurrences. I hope I am mistaken and that the thaw between the parties, started in France on the 70th anniversary of the Allied landings on June 6th 1944, has a positive outcome.

-The New Pietracupa Parish Priest, Fr. Orlando Di Tella

In the early lead years, Pietracupa had the appearance of a quiet village of Southern Italy, with a population of residents mostly made up of people employed in the public, private and agriculture sectors, and of many retirees. The great exodus to northern Italy and towards foreign countries was ending, so the number of residents had fallen drastically and we could count births on the fingers of one hand.

In this situation of obvious demographic reduction, there was another, very positive, phenomenon: the interest of Pietracupa's emigrants **to invest in the renovation of their homes in the village**. This interest was fostered both by greater disposable income than in the past and by the improved conditions and viability of national roads and, above all, by the desire to be able to stay in the home country during the summer holidays.

For these reasons, the village in the early '70s was a flourish of construction sites, open to renovate houses/cellars/stables according to the personal tastes of the owners - which sometimes clashed with the neighboring ones. However, there were no gross irregularities of the plan and the village, even today, has maintained the appearance of a pleasant village, with features dating back to medieval times.

After renovating their homes, families formed the habit of returning regularly to the village, keeping alive the sense of belonging to a community of deep values, and keeping close ties with one's native country through the ages. In this socio-economic background of the 70s/80s, the village in September 1977 had the gift of **a new parish priest, Fr. Orlando Di Tella**, who came to replace Fr. Manfredo who retired from the post of parish priest due to illness. As happened previously with Fr. Manfredo, even now I find it hard to speak with detachment about Fr. Orlando because I am bound to him by a great respect, esteem and friendship, developed over the years.

Therefore, without falling into banality, allow me to explain with facts the importance of the human and religious contribution Fr. Orlando has given and is still giving the village of Pietracupa. **It was September 1977** when, while walking along Via Trento, Uncle Corradino Delmonaco stopped and introduced me to Fr. Orlando. The first impression I had of him was positive. Don Orlando had and has an imposing physique, a face marked by an intelligent look, a sincere, honest smile and a strong voice. After this meeting, I remember that, back home, I told my wife that I had met the new parish priest, and added: *I noticed in him some physical and natural resemblance to Don Camillo, the character born from the pen of the writer Giovanni Guareschi, but in Molise version.*

In the period following that meeting, Fr. Orlando, in a short time, became the most popular and most beloved character in the village. I remember that, at the time, Mr. Angelo Gallo was mayor of the village. As there was a rumor that the Bishop of Trivento was planning to move the newcomer elsewhere, there had been a meeting of residents. So a group of local delegates wanted to go to the Bishop, to make him desist from any idea of removing the new parish priest.

His first house in the village was located near Via Trento and the **Carnevale family** took care of him for many years in a loving and family way, as, in later years, did the family of **Remo Di Sarro**.

Fr. Orlando, in his 40 years of pastoral life in the village, obtained two important results. The first one is purely religious, and was to have implemented the directives resulting from the Second Vatican Council and to have reported many village parishioners to attend church. His merits, recognized by many people were: a great charisma, his organizational and oratorical skills to simplify and make easily comprehensible to all listeners the philosophical concepts of Catholic doctrine. To all this, we must also add his attention and daily care to the problems and **difficulties of his parishioners**, especially to the sick and the young people, to whom he has always paid particular attention in guiding and helping them practically in their path of life.

The second result was to have stimulated, in the appropriate forums, and contributed to having the cultural, religious and artistic value of a small unknown Molisan village such as Pietracupa recognized so that it is now included in the group of the most characteristic villages of Italy and is discussed in magazines and books of national interest, such as those published by the Touring Club. The most obvious results of all this work are the restructuring of the wonderful crypt's Dome with the beautiful wooden crucifix of 1500 and the restructuring of the Dome itself according the rocky style of early Christianity, the renovation of the Church of San Gregorio with frescoes from 1200.

The recovery of these cultural assets is the reason that many travelers and tourists include in their tours of Molise a visit to the small picturesque rocky village. Culture is not the heritage of the individual. Culture is the world's heritage and Pietracupa, at this point, is part of the world.

In 2009, Fr. Orlando celebrated the 50-year anniversary of his priesthood. I was not present at the ceremony, but they told me that many people, who came from all parts of Molise, were present to show their affection to a priest who has always been attentive to their spiritual and human needs. This, I think, was the best way to say thanks to their parish priest, also gratified by the Curia, who elected him Monsignor. But the most beautiful presence was that of his new and old students, grateful to their professor for being an educator and a teacher who knew how to inculcate not only professional knowledge, but especially, culture for the training of students today and men for tomorrow.

During a confidential meeting recently Fr. Orlando told me the story of **his priestly vocation**. His story, which I reproduce in full, is indicative of the spirituality and deep unconscious invading those chosen to be a servant of God.

"In the land where I was born, Capracotta, my father owned a bakery located right next to our house. One evening, a friend of the family came to visit us and, in the middle of a conversation, addressing my father asked him: "what way will have to take this young man in the course of his life?" My father then began to evaluate all the activities that I could have done. Thus speaking, he suddenly asked me: "what

*do you think of my proposals?" - Without any hesitation I answered by telling him about a proposal not included in his list and I said loudly " **I want to be a priest** " and in saying these words I heard inside me **a great warmth** and a great desire to go outdoors, to run and to externalize the intense joy invading my person. I went to church and I started **ringing the bells** calling the attention of many people, including my father who had followed me into the street. After this episode, I started my training at Trivento Diocese and I never lost the joy of being useful to the Lord. In the seminary I suffered much because I missed my mother with whom I was very close. But the Lord has rewarded me with other joys, those to be helpful to him and to my neighbor."*

When during the winter, I go to Molise, in a deserted and abandoned Pietracupa, the presence of Fr. Orlando is reassuring because it means that the village is alive; the flame of our traditions is always kept lit by the Mayor, the parish priest and the other 220 people on site. In my private life, there are two moments in which I felt most deeply Fr. Orlando's humanity: during the funeral of my parents, and his presence on the occasion of my daughter's marriage, which he celebrated in the Basilica of Santa Sabina in Rome. I'll probably sound like a hopeless romantic, but that day of July 11th 2004, in the splendor of that ancient Basilica of the Roman era, in the midst of so many friends and relatives even from America, the presence of that priest, his affectionate and moving words to Andrea and Claudia, who he had seen grow up, made me feel the presence of a friend and spiritual adviser who shared the joy of a father watching his daughter start her radiant future as a woman and a mother.

285

2013. Fr. Orlando Di tella – Parish priest of Pietracupa

July 2004.Claudia and Andrea wedding in Santa Sabina's Church

July 2004. Claudia and Andrea wedding – Relatives from the USA

CLAUDIA

Her deep black, thoughtful, magical eyes, veiled in mystery.
Her rebellious hair, a bit 'ruffled, caressing the wind,
on long summer afternoons by the sea.

The rocking of her measured pace, her style 90s jeans,
her records, her sequins, her necklaces,
her concerts on Saturday evening, the dazzle
of her sincere and friendly smile,
her bad mood, her sulkiness, her torments
This is Claudia for her friends today.

For me instead she is the star of an old film full of memories.

A July 25ᵗ in the old Rome,
Among those baby kicking in the hour of sunset.

The first shoes, the first tooth, the first words,
the crazy races on the winged dragons,
in the long stories at nightfall.

The first day of school, the first snow
and the thousand stories of endless moments spent together.

Today, the old Leo of the zodiac
does not take me anymore that one child of those days,
but a very sweet woman, my daughter.

My hair is grey, my wrinkles are deeper,
but my heart is not changed
and follows you on the road of your life.
Good luck, my little one,
Take our smiles in your path.

-Pietracupa Summers (1970/89)

In previous chapters the topics of leisure and festivities honoring the patron saints of the village were discussed. On occasion of the arrival of the new parish priest and noting that residents outside the village could participate in the festivities only during the summer, it was decided to move the celebration of St. Gregory and St. Anthony to the month of August.

I wanted to include this topic in the book, because in the period characterized by protests and the lead of the terrorists, Pietracupa's people found in their village the atmosphere of tranquility necessary to remove from the mind the difficult times that the nation and the world were experiencing.

I think the summers of the '70s / 80's were the best times that Pietracupa has been able to offer to residents and vacationers. The factors that allowed the organizers to achieve this result were: 1) the generational exchange between fathers and sons, in qualitative and quantitative terms; 2) greater commitment and willingness on the part of both the local residents and of outsiders in a period with no apparent internal friction; 3) greater interest and participation by the public and local religious authorities.

I will not go into detail with tedious descriptions. But the parade of period costumes, the exhibition of old photos in Via Trento, theatrical performances and texts with non-professional actors chosen from among the people of the village, the poetry competitions for adults and for children, children's show on stage, soccer and volleyball competitions played in the renovated Campo Casarino, are the pearls of a '70s and '80s necklace which I think all those present at the time are able to remember - including the now forty-somethings who, in those evenings, although they were still young, had fun and cemented their friendships, which still endure after many years. **In the summer of 1989**, I celebrated with my Pietracupa's friends my fiftieth birthday,which I wanted to remember with a poem.

The merits of these Pietracupa summers also benefitted the three major public establishments operating in the village: **the bar of**

Rina and Vincenzo Cornacchione, the bar of Remo and Concetta and the bar of Americo Santilli.

Along Via Trento and the stairs of the Cathedral, there was all a bustle of people meeting each other, sitting at tables, attracting the locals according to age. Young people were the regular customers who frequented the bars of Rina and Vincenzo; **older people** preferred to sit in the other bars in the village. This differentiated choice was motivated by the reason that **Gianni**, his twin brothers **Michele and Fabrizio and Katy, children of Rina and Vincenzo,** were all four young students who, during the summer, were helping their parents. It is a natural fact that young people attract young people, so the three Cornacchione brothers launched initiatives and some cocktails that attracted the large group of young people, their peers.

Anyway, all three bars had great success during the '70s / '80s summers. Currently, only one bar remains open, Morgia Bar, owned by Concetta and Remo and **managed by Vittorio Di Risio**. It is frequented by young and old people of the village and also by external customers. It is the only place where people can meet, talk and socialize, especially on cold winter days.

In Rome, when a public enterprise closes its doors, it is **a loss for the whole area's community.** Seeing the bar of Rina and Americo (recently deceased) closed made us a little bit sad for the history that these enterprises represented in the community.
On this subject, I want to insert a special mention on **the bar *Italia* of Fossalto** and, especially, its unforgettable owner **Domenico Carosone**, who for many years brought fame and notoriety to this enterprise whose specialties are sweets and its incomparable ice cream.

Domenico was born in Fossalto; his mother, Italia, was from Pietracupa. Being orphaned at a young age, he immediately worked to fast forward the business of the family, turning it into a place of enjoyment for its ice cream, famous throughout the Molise region, and for home baked cakes. I especially remember the moral and humane figure of Domenico. He had for all a smile and a kind thought. Conversation with Domenico ranged over an infinite number of topics, from politics to football, the latter especially animated him if one talked about Juventus, his favorite team.

I had the opportunity to talk to him closely about his life and his plans during a trip to Brazil, organized by the CIM. Unfortunately an incurable disease has stopped his earthly race. But the bar *Italia* is still operating in the memory of a great and sensitive friend who was Domenico, always present in the memory of his fellow citizens.

During some Pietracupa summers, a particular activity was offered by the Roman group of "Singers of Molise" which, accompanied by the accordion of **Romano Quartullo**, often colored those evenings with Roman and Molise songs.

Another special memory of Pietracupa holidays is related to Easter and **the living representation of the Passion of Jesus Christ**, born during the events of Pietracupa's summers. The whole village worked hard under the guidance of the parish priest, to organize during the winter and to interpret during Holy Week this rite of Christian tradition. In the '70s on Holy Friday, the streets of the village were the backdrop to a large group of Pietracupa's actors who walked and animated the fourteen stations of the cross with the intensity of their Catholic devotion. There are no words to describe the importance of this representation with respect to the public.

There were performances full of religious significance and of great visual effect. I remember the sorrowful interpretation of Christ made during the Easter rites by **Antonio Durante** who, under an unexpected snowstorm, proceeded barefoot down the street. When he came near the three crosses in via Garibaldi, he was tied half-naked to the Central Cross and his suffering face, his arms and his body stretched out, gave the real picture of a dying Christ who had taken upon his shoulders the salvation of all men on earth.

In recent years, there has been some revival by the current generation of young people born in the village. They, in collaboration with public and religious local authorities, are giving a new impetus to summer events. In fact they propose some initiatives both cultural and of food and wine, with the famous day of "**Addò z 'magna e z'veve**", ("**where you can eat and drink**"), during which the alleys and old cellars of the village have resumed life with dancing, singing, ancient sounds and appetizing foods prepared according to traditional Pietracupa recipes.

In one hot summer of the '70s, at Pietracupa was inaugurated an area with a votive statue of Padre Pio. That night all the villagers were present to venerate this saint, famous all over the world. **Domenico Meale** told me a story about **Padre Pio** that seems miraculous. Domenico and his wife for many years have taken care of the flowers in the area where there was a statue of the saint. Unfortunately, last winter, he entered the intensive care unit of the hospital of Campobasso because of health complications that were difficult to heal.
Domenico told me that an unknown man, at night, entered his hospital room and told him to stand up. The next day the same man came again to his room, this time together with Padre Pio, who had his face smeared with a grey substance. The saint said to his companion: *"there is still time to get to other people;, my face is dirty and I must wash it."*

The morning after this vision, Domenico recovered from his serious illness and the doctors, amazed, released him a few days later. Back in the village with his wife, he immediately went to the statue of the saint, which, while he was in the hospital, had been smeared by bird droppings. Domenico and his wife thanked Padre Pio for his miraculous intervention and proceeded to clean the statue and to continue their task of pious faithful by keeping the area tidy and full of flowers.

Pietracupa's summer in the '70s

Pietracupa's summer in the '70s

Pietracupa's summer in the '70s – Wedding clothes

Pietracupa's summer in the '70s – Women's clothes

Pietracupa's summer in the '70s – Women's football team

Bachelor – married team-   **Pietracupa's summer in the '70s**

FIFTY YEARS

And I'm fifty, lived, recited on the big stage of life,
Among the joys, sorrows, happiness, sadness, in a various world,
full of surprises.

Years passed quickly, between flashes of wars and scents of peace,
in a flurry of people, events, hopes and disappointments.
With the memories of my childhood, of my youth, with my songs,
my affections, my dreams, my belief, my mistakes, my good things.

And I'm fifty, with what I have given and received,
with the achievements and my regret,
with my white hair, with my deep wrinkles,
but still with the desire to love, to fight, to believe in the good things
in which I believed, and with my experience to offer these young
peopleon their way in the tortuous paths of life.

CHAPTER VII

THE YEARS OF CRISIS AND THE NEW TWENTY-FIRST CENTURY (1990/2014)

-*The Events in Italy and in the World*

The events of these past 24 years of history are so recent that it is very difficult to be able to tell them to make a neutral judgment without being influenced by emotional or personal factors that might upset the historical view of the events themselves. Only the passage of time can help to metabolize the emotional nature of the present.

With this premise and taking up the thread of the previous chapter, interrupted in 1989, world events that have characterized the historical period from 1990 up to the present day, can be so resumed:

1990 - the division of the USSR into various autonomous and independent states;
1991/2000 - the division of the Yugoslav Federation after the death of Tito; the fratricidal wars between Kosovo, Serbia, Croatia;
9/11/2001 - Islamic terrorists attacks on the twin towers and the American Pentagon;
2011 - the death of Osama Bin Laden;
11/2001 - the war in Afghanistan, with the Italian presence;
03/2003 - the war in Iraq, with the Italian presence; and
12/2006 - the hanging of Saddam Ussein;
the Israeli / Palestinian fight and Jewish wall;
10/2011 - the Libyan crisis and the killing of Gaddafi, with the Italian presence;
02/2011 – the Egyptian crisis and the fall of Mubarak;
03/2011 - the crisis in Syria;
2014 - the Russian / Czeczen crisis in Ukraine;
2014 - the crisis in Venezuela against Maduro;
2014 - the crisis in Turkey against Erdogan (2014).

The most prominent figures appearing on the world stage were: the three Presidents of the United States of America, **Bill Clinton**, **George W. Bush** (December 2000), **Barak Obama** (January 2009); the three Popes of the Catholic Church, **John Paul II**, who died in

298

May 2005, **Benedict XVI** (living) and **Francesco** (elected Pope in March 2013).

In Italy, four presidents of the Republic were elected: Cm. Francesco Cossiga (1985), Cm. Luigi Scalfaro (1992), Cm. Azeglio Ciampi (1999), Cm. Giorgio Napolitano (2006 and 2013). In Russia, were elected in succession three Presidents: M. Gorbachev, Boris Yeltsin (1989-2000), Wladimir Putin elected in 2000 and still the President in office.

Ukraine, in 2014, was hit by a worrisome civil war, with uncertain outcome, between Czeczen secessionist pro-Russia vs. Ukrainian nationalists favorable to the alliance with the countries of the European Community and the United States.

New emerging countries such as China, Brazil, India, and Russia ("BRIC") have had active participation in the economic field with the advent of new means of mass communication and the subsequent globalization of world markets, which influenced the stability and fluctuation of world economies.

In this context, countries like the United States and some members of the European Economic Community, including Italy, have had to adjust quickly to new market developments, with the difficulties of adaptation and the effects on the population still unresolved.

In the environmental field, the problems related to water and air pollution, waste disposal, protection of soil, etc. have been topics of debate in many International Conferences, none of which found unanimous agreement among the world countries, but which have highlighted the need to continue research and cooperation to ensure the continuity of human race.

To all of that, one must add **the disasters caused by typhoons, tsunamis, earthquakes, landslides**, which have claimed thousands and thousands of victims all over the world. We are referring to the Indian Ocean tsunami of 2004, Hurricane Katrina that destroyed the city of New Orleans in 2005, the earthquake of 2009 in L'Aquila, the tsunami in the Pacific in 2009, Typhoon Ketsana in the Philippines in 2009, the earthquake with the nuclear disaster in Japan in 2011, the disaster in the Cinque Terre in Liguria with landslides and floods in 2011, the earthquake in Emilia-Romagna and Lombardy-Veneto of 2012, the earthquake in Chile in 2014 (which also showed the close relationship between the disasters and the neglect/carelessness of man). The practical example is the so-called land of fires in Campania.

 Italian politics in recent years (1990/2014), has experienced three different seasons. The season started after the Tangentopoli scandal (1992) with the fall of the old political apparatus (Craxi, Forlani, Andreotti, and so on), and the end of the First Republic, with the investigations and convictions of "mani pulite" . The season after Tangentopoli with governments led by Andreotti (1991), Amato (June '92), Ciampi (April '93), Berlusconi (May '94), Dini (1995), Prodi (1996), D'Alema (1998), Amato (April 2000), yet Berlusconi (June 2001), and the political season began in 1992 and ended on November 2011 called **"the season of the Second Republic"** or **"twenty years of Berlusconi."**

 In this period new political aggregations like Forza Italia, the Lega, the Ulivo (Margherita, Democratic Party), the National Right were born, which designed a new set of parties for Right, Center and Left deployment. The guidance of the government since 1994 and especially from June 2001 until November 2011, has been assigned to Silvio Berlusconi, leader of Forza Italia (Popolo delle Libertà). Berlusconi has ruled with an aggregation of Right and Center Forces, except for a brief appearance of the Prodi government in 2006-2008.

The character of Berlusconi was strongly opposed by Milan magistrates who involved him in various investigations, which led the Premier to say that many magistrates were politicized in favor of the communist left. This great battle that characterized the years of Berlusconi ended in 2013, with the condemnation of the Premier to 4 years in prison for tax fraud against the Italian State.

 The season of the so-called **third republic**, which we are experiencing now, just started with the fall of the Berlusconi government in **November 2011**. After a failed attempt by the Secretary of the Democratic Party (DP), Mr. **Bersani**, followed

Mario Monti broad alliances government, then the government of **Enrico Letta** (April 2013) and, currently, the Government of **Matteo Renzi** (February 2014), Secretary of the DP, backed by Alfano New center-right and a pact agreed to with Forza Italia, on Institutional Reforms and the Election Law. The parties remained more or less the same, hit a bit equally by old issues of a new "**Tangentopoli**" (Forza Italia, Democratic Party, IDV, Lega Lombarda, and so on).

On the wave of discontent towards these parties, we have had to register the birth of a third political party **M5S** (5 Star Movement). It is led by a showman, Beppe Grillo, who, in the last election campaign, had a significant and unexpected consent of voters, and which is also pursuing an apparently far-left, anti-European policy targeted to the abandonment of the Euro (introduced in Italy on January 1st 2002).

An important role in the formation of these governments has been that of **the President of the Republic, Giorgio Napolitano**, an attentive guardian of the founding principles of the Constitution.
The program of the government Renzi contains very important goals to be achieved: the revision of public spending; the end of bicameralism with the abolition of the Senate; the revision of the labor law; rationalization of taxes; the abolition of the provinces; Industry incentives; the reform of the Electoral Act. These objectives are matters of debate and are currently awaiting approval by the Parliament and the Senate, in a context of majorities equally distributed between Deputies and Senators belonging to the DP, Forza Italia, and the M5S, often in opposition to each other.

The intention of the current President of the Council is that of wishing to proceed as a "steamroller" in the implementation of his program in view of the fact that the percentage of unemployed stood at 13% and 40% of young people between 18 and 25 years have not yet found a job.

The current Premier also turns his gaze to Europe, not only to reduce the National deficit according to December 9th 1991 Maastricht agreements, but also to re-launch, worldwide, Europe's role in implementing a more flexible financial policy towards the Member

States, targeted also to let Italy resume the role of Country leader, which sets it as one of the top 10 world powers. The same reduction in consumption and the stagnation of industrial production is a clear sign of a creeping crisis that created new poor, especially among middle-class citizens, as current customers of **charitable Institution Canteen** show.

Also in the **area of migration**, the new Italian government is working to raise awareness of all European countries to consider the problem of migrants from African nations at war, who arrive by the thousands in Italy, with all the problems of rescue, reception, assistance and integration of refugees. The small and Apennine village of Pietracupa had to face the reality of acceptance of **some political refugees from Somalia**, with understandable problems that these events bring with them.

Finally, the long standing problem of **mafia infiltration** present in some State apparatus, is another of the issues that the Italian government and the Italians all have to face. The massacres of Capaci and Via D'Amelio in 1992 with death of Judges Falcone and Borsellino; the attacks on San Giovanni Church in Rome and the Uffizi Museum in Florence; the deaths of Fr. Diana, Fr. Puglisi, the killing of 10 black immigrants in Castelvolturno, institutionalized trafficking of drugs in the Neapolitan district of Scampia, the kickback for the Expo 2015 in Milan, the scandal of Venice's Mose have all been events that have to make us think, and for which the government will need to act firmly for its credibility, and especially for the security and development of the Nation.

The recent European elections of Sunday, 05/25/2014, have expressed a confidence in the current government in office, with about 42% of voter preferences. The Italians, however, are experiencing hard times with **rising unemployment and difficulties of going on day by day;** they are waiting for serious measures to resolve this creeping crisis.

-Memories of the Years 1990/2014

My first memory of this historical period is that of the fratricidal war in the 1990s that began in neighboring Yugoslavia, between Serbia /

Montenegro and Bosnia / Herzegovina militias, and later between Croatian / Bosnian and Bosniaks / Muslims in Bosnia / Herzegovina.

In the year 1966, I visited this region. Then it was a part of the Socialist Federal Republic of Yugoslavia, during the regime of President Tito. I was fascinated by the beauty of its landscapes and especially by **Mostar, its beautiful city of art**. In this city, I spent a few very nice and serene days. In the evenings, with the group of my Italian friends, I would always go to the center of the old town, and we would sit in a quaint coffee shop near the wonderful Old Bridge (Stari most) of 1500, on the banks of Narida river.

This river connected the area of Bosnian Muslims, to the Bosnian Croats one and, right near the bridge we would meet with other young people of both ethnicities. All together, happily and fraternally we would spend the evening talking about music, sports, plans for the future.

After the fall of the Tito regime, the wars of secession of individual federal states began. From the 1990s until the 2000s they have set fire to the Yugoslav territory, with ethnic cleansing and genocide, for which contingents of UN peacekeeping forces, including Italy, had to intervene to put an end to all acts of war.

In November 1993, when Italian TV announced **the destruction of the Mostar Bridge**, I remembered those young people of the '60s, full of hopes and dreams similar to the dreams of our young Italians. I thought instantly that, perhaps during the civil war, they had abandoned their goals of peace and had shouldered their guns, armed against each other to kill and subdue the losers. **This thought** has greatly saddened me, and taken by an impulse of anger, I tried to mitigate my sorrow by dedicating a poem to those friends I had met in that summer of peace spent in Mostar.

Then the old bridge was rebuilt, even with the aid of the UN, which declared the town of Mostar a world heritage site, to be protected and safeguarded.

Another dramatic memory is that regarding **the terrorist attack of September 2001**, which destroyed the twin towers of the World

Trade Center, hit by two planes in flight, hijacked over the city of New York by Islamic terrorists. That day I was in the office of my company, in via Prenestina 45, when some employees came to my office asking me to turn on the TV because something serious was going on in New York City. On the TV monitor appeared the images of **two towers torn** by the impact of the planes and a large tail of smoke and flames coming out from the upper floors. We followed the dramatic events moment by moment until the final fall of the towers, which were liquefied by the strong heat of the fire. They were terrifying images, dramatized by the people who were thrown from the top of the two skyscrapers as their last hope of salvation. All around there was a chorus of shouts and people on the run, fleeing from the hell of flames and smoke, accompanied by the deafening sirens of first responders who rushed immediately to the scene to rescue people.

I do not intend to tell what happened in the days following September 11th during which the American people and the whole world was holding its breath, wondering what was happening. I remember that I immediately tried to get in touch with my relatives living in New York, but the phone lines were overloaded. After several attempts, I managed to communicate with them, and except for the fear and sorrow for what happened, they told me that everything was ok.

An indelible image has remained in the eyes of all those who watched on live TV the chronicle of those days of terror. It was the image of the families of the people trapped in the towers, who had gone to the attack zone to post on the gate of the nearby small Lutheran church, photos and messages for news of their loved ones.

In September 2013, while visiting New York, I asked my cousins Mary and Bianca Di Iorio, to accompany me to visit **"Ground Zero"**, now cleared of debris and occupied by the work on the construction of a museum in memory of the attack victims. At that time I wanted to visit the small Lutheran church. Inside we saw all the photos and messages of that September 11th, which changed the fate of the world and sealed the fate of men, women, fathers, mothers, children, ordinary citizens, innocently killed in this horrible tragedy.

On **May 15, 2014, President Obama** inaugurated the new museum area designed by architects Arad and Walker. It includes two pools built on the area previously occupied by the destroyed towers, with all the names of the 2,983 people who died, written on plates of bronze. The museum nearby contains within it the two steel tridents of the North Tower, with the relics of that terrible September 11, 2001.

The whole area is surrounded by five new skyscrapers, including the Freedom Tower which gave new life to the new "World Trade Center". The presence of important companies such as **Armani and Eataly**, inside the towers, means that life has taken its course again, even in the memory of past tragedies.

In these years of tragedies, we must not forget **the genocide of over 800 thousand ethnic "Tutsi"**, brutally killed in Rwanda in 1994, by the ethnic population "Hutu". The beautiful film Hotel Rwanda manages to document the reason for so many atrocities perpetrated by the Hutu towards their brothers, and especially manages to explain the reason why the United Nations has remained so indifferent and "deaf" as well as uninterested in the course of that tragedy.

The earthquake of April 6th, 2009 in L'Aquila with 309 victims who died under the rubble of their homes, is another piece of news that has hit us Italians hard. **This very beautiful city of Abruzzo**, is particularly dear to me, not only because of its ties of culture and history with the Region of Molise, but also, and above all, because for many years I did my work as a teacher at the local State University. So the reader can understand my reaction when I heard about the earthquake in the city. Immediately I tried to get news of the many friends and colleagues residing there; the answer that they all gave me was always the same: "We have saved our lives and the lives of our families, but all of our homes have been destroyed."

The fate, then, of those poor students of the University, dead under the rubble of the home university, hurt me even more, thinking about those young people, their families, their projects vanished under a heap of stones. Among the victims of the earthquake, the three hundred and ninth one was a little girl who was to be born that very

April 6th 2009; she died in the womb because of the earthquake. Her grandmother, with great dignity and great Christian participation, attended the candlelight vigil that was held this year along the city streets to remember those killed, five years after the tragedy.

L'Aquila earthquake reminds us also of another serious tragedy caused by the 2003 earthquake, which hit Molise and in particular the village of **San Giuliano di Puglia**, where **19 innocent children with their teacher died** under the rubble of their school. That event, through the media, has been seen around the world, and has moved whole nations to unite spiritually and materially to the sorrow of the citizens of San Giuliano.

The new World Trade Center, inaugurated on May 15th 2014 by President Obama

Vacation in Dubai

Vacation at North Cape

Finally, one cannot forget the barbaric bombing of Nazi matrix, which **took place in Oslo and the nearby island of Utoya on July 22, 2011** by the right-wing extremist Anders Behring Breivik, who killed **77 people** and injured **96 more**. The day after the attack **I was on a visit to Oslo** with my wife and I remember the **dignified sorrow of Norwegians** in the central square of the city, completely full of flowers and votive lamps. At a few steps from the square there was the headquarters of the Nobel Peace Prize, the symbol of the spirit of that democratic and pacifist nation. The silence I felt was like a **scream**, the scream of the famous **painting by Munch** displayed in the nearby National Museum, which was at that time the sorrow of a people struck in its deepest feelings.

These last 25 years are not only remembered for the sad events, but there were also moments of social, of joy, of evolving economic, political, cultural and sporting activities, which marked the end of the 20th century and the beginning of the 2Ist.

Taking a quick rundown on the latest events, we can recall the visit of John Paul II to Cuba in 1998, the peace agreement between Catholics and Protestants in Belfast in 1998, the beatification of Padre Pio in 1999, the birth of Europe with the 25 European nations in 2004, the signing of the new European Constitution in 2004, the victory of the film "*La vita é bella*" "Life is Beautiful" with the Oscar in 1999, the victory of Italy in the World Championship in 2006, the victory of the film "*La grande Bellezza*" "Great Beauty" with the Oscar in 2014.

Wanting to make a balance of these years, referring to my own experience, I can say that I am living and I lived years full of changes and surprises in a nation that we often criticize, but we love anyway. My memories are sad, happy, trivial, deep - memories that belong to the subtle way in which each of us has chosen to live. I can say that I have set my life **on the family, on work**, on sincere friendship, loyalty, understanding towards others - values that my parents handed down to me. I'm not perfect and I am convinced I made many mistakes and have hurt other people, but without malice - but that is a part of human nature.

Over the past 25 years I can count among my less pleasing memories **the deaths of my father and my mother,** which occurred in 2001 and 2003. We cannot express what passes in the soul of a man when a parent fails. I just want to say that my parents, on the day of their journey to heaven, left us with a smile on their lips. And with that smile, I think, they wanted to say: *Thank you for your affection, we go to heaven happy with what we did and for the lessons we have left to you.*

Many other people have left me to go to heaven, friends, relatives, colleagues, neighbors. It is a spinning wheel, and the deep meaning of this wheel is to be found in the very essence of life, its values, in our religious or lay beliefs.

But wanting to do a personal assessment of these 25 years, I can say that they were years cheered by so many important events. **My 25 years of marriage anniversary, with my children to act as witnesses, the degrees of Maximilian and Claudia, the marriage of my daughter and the birth of my wonderful grandchildren, Alessandro and Julia**, all with the loving presence and commitment of **my wife Gabriella, the central focus of my entire family**.

There has always been **my brother Lino and his family** near us, in a relationship of deep affection that made me understand the true meaning of the expression **"being brothers"**. I applaud his efforts and his achievements in the field of research at the European Space Agency, where he worked, and that has brought success to the skills of many Italian technicians.

In public, I was lucky to meet many simple people, some important, some less important, politicians, government officials, church, poor, rich, lay, Catholics, Protestants, sincere, fake, gloomy, happy people, and especially **many students** who enriched me with their energy, their spontaneity and their involvement in their studies, which leaves me with much hope for the future of our Nation.

Even my **work effort** was important; I can say that I have worked with great concentration, **but I also had fun;** and that's the beauty of the work, the pleasure of discovering every day something new to do and invent.

And finally the World, **our wonderful world**, made up of people, countries, races, costumes, breathtaking views.

This was **the only cultural diversion** in which we participated, **my wife and I**: the silence of the African deserts, the magic of the midnight sun at the North Cape, the greatness of the Egyptian pyramids, the Taj Mahal and the Ganges in India, the Forbidden

City in Beijing, the secrets of Machu Picchu in Peru, the Maya civilization in Mexico, Nepal with Himalayas and Buddhist monasteries, Malaysia, Thailand, the Caribbean, the Blessing Christ in Rio de Janeiro, the neighborhood of Boca in Argentina, Niagara Falls and Iguassu ones, the Australian coast and the Bay of Sydney, places of our Christianity in Palestine, the Nabataean city of Petra, Dubai with the swirling and tallest skyscraper of the world, the European cities with their epoch charm, great museums with their content of art, and small villages like **Pietracupa.**

All these are the gifts that God has willed to reserve to men, making us say **"what a wonderful world".** It is this wonderful world that we have to enjoy and save from neglect, hatred, war, hunger and social inequality.

The Wind of East

A chill wind blowing in Eastern Europe,
a wind of war, death, destruction.
The friend kills his friend, brother kills his brother, there is no rule,
there is no peace, old, children, women, a pile of bodies lying lifeless.

What happens, what is this madness, why do people kill,
why do people die, why do people rape?

For God, for a piece of land, for a racial hatred?

But perhaps God is not the God of all,
for whites, for blacks, for Christians, for Muslims?

And the land, the green land of the East, is not so great
as to contain its children she generated?

And hate, this terrible hate, which takes the man in crazy times
Why does it exist?

I see flashes of fire away from my house in the border
that looks toward the east, and I do not know what to do.

I would like to get out, I would like to talk, I too would like to write
something,
I would like to shake the indifference surrounding this tragedy,
but I just have to pray and turn to you, my God.

Stop the sharp blade of this death that destroys and dries up
everything.

Give back peace among my brothers so lonely and so desperate.

Let shine the sun in those ancient cities of the East,
so bright, in my memories of a serene summer of many years ago.

-Pietracupa: A Holiday Village, Present and Future

In previous chapters, Pietracupa's social, infrastructural evolution and that of its community were described over the years from 1940 up to the present, and the historical reasons behind this evolution were explained. By the title given to this paragraph I want to explain to the reader why I consider today's Pietracupa a place that has the features and the vocation of a holiday village.

To support this imaginative thesis, I took the liberty of drawing, below, a hypothetical descriptive brochure, in the style adopted by the tour operators in the tourism sector, when they want to encourage and entice their customers to spend their holidays in places they outlined.

Pietracupa is a charming village of Molise, with 223 inhabitants, of which about 30 are young people aged between 15 and 25 years.

It is governed by a mayor and there is a city council with headquarters in Via of Casaleno. The population has the opportunity to take advantage of a garrison of pharmacy, a post office, a doctor, a parish priest, two churches, a crypt, an industrial furnace (Flo. Car-Florio / Carosone), a grocery store, a bar, a tobacco shop and newsstand, three museum sites, a hair salon, a field equipped for soccer and tennis, two bowling greens, a town hall for events and receptions, a hotel-like communal structure for summer or winter vacations, a small area with children's games, and a former hotel designed by Mr. Michele Camillo and currently used as a home for 25 elderly residents (Punta Paradiso).Nearby there are agricultural settlements, that you can visit, with adjoining houses for the production and processing of agricultural and dairy products, poultry and pigs.

The town is twinned with the City of Westfield, New Jersey (USA), and is renowned for having healthy air, certified by a public facility and validated by the many long-lived elders present in the village and several centenarians celebrated in recent years (Uncle Angelo Camillo, Uncle Michele Guglielmi, Uncle Vincenzo Ciavarro, Aunt Giovanna Guglielmi, Aunt Lucia Guglielmi, Aunt Amalia Porchetta, Aunt Gemma Santilli). The neighboring towns have all the characteristics of the medieval village with the presence of historical artifacts dating to Sannita and Roman epoch; particularly important are the sites Sepino and Pietrabbondante. The nearby Trivento is home to a Catholic seminary and its Church and Crypt are located on an ancient Roman temple of Fortuna. The regional capital, Campobasso, is a charming town about 25 km away from the village. It has an important hospital, specializing in various branches of medicine, as well as of a University with various orders of studies.

The sea is about 60 km away (San SalvoTermoli / Tremiti), and the mountain (Campitello Matese and Capracotta) equipped with ski run slopes, is also about 60 km from the village. All these places are easily accessible now by smooth flowing roads. The period of greatest influx is during the month of August, when Pietracupa's people living in Italy and abroad are in the village to spend a holiday enjoying the many cultural, culinary and religious activities of Pietracupa's summer.

With this postcard presentation anyone can safely say that Pietracupa could be considered a well-equipped **"holiday village"**, as one sees so many filming in Italy and abroad, or even might resemble a vacation place for rich foreign tourists, like those living in Tuscan farmhouses in Val d'Orcia or in Val di Chiana. It lacks only one lender to activate the village and a promoter of events.

But this is only my imagination and, wanting to keep our feet on the ground, it is good to describe the reality of the present. In the village, older people can live better or worse with the pensions paid by the state. The problem is for young people who have difficulty finding a job and survive by doing odd jobs that are offered from time to time. Many of them, as was done in the past, have in mind to leave the native village and go elsewhere to seek better fortune, thus starting the final exodus of residents. This is the big problem that must be addressed and resolved.

Obviously I do not have the magic recipe to tell what to do, because I do not know the local reality; however, I applaud the research initiatives and outreach to public and private companies that mayors and the council, followed one another over time, are trying to do, together with even the current parish priest. But I think that we should not wait for manna from heaven. We must take steps to ensure that resources - landscape, museum, tourism, organic farming, combined with other fields of work in the area of elderly care, catering services, property maintenance, production and marketing of local products, clean energy - may be potential areas to be examined to form, schedule, and impress work activities suitable to the potential of the area, and necessary to allow our young people to stay in the village, guiding them also to specific training courses.

Often, when I am discussing the problems of young people, both related to the present and to the near future, I always say that I am optimistic. I think that we Italians are able to restart the production engine and industrial development, and make sure to give our young people the opportunities of living and working as we have had in the years of economic boom.

This is not just a wish or a simple poetic "I would like" as I have summarized in the poem written for my grandchildren. But it is also an invitation for young people to "grasp the time flying away" to build a future of work, of values, of solidarity, commitment and respect for others, ever questioning our past, to grasp some ideas of creativity.

The past and the present of the family

I Would Like

I would like to stop time to fix still the sparkle of your eyes,
the whiteness of your smile, the joy of your child's world
that brighten my days with you.

I would still run in the enchanted woods of our games, along
with Minnie and Mickey Mouse, do a thousand battles with the
pirates away,
find the magic sword of Merlin and leaving with King Arthur and his
knights.

I would like, I would like, I would like; but time is running out,
it is a moment, a flash in the sky,
a flash of light, and you run, my little one, grab the fleeting time,
seize on the essence of its frantic race, with your innocence, your
joy of living, your values, your memories as a child.

The future – Our babies

The future – a glance in the past

CONCLUSION

-The Past and the Values of Life

My journey in the past and present of Pietracupa's community ends with this chapter. I go to Pietracupa to store the symbolic cardboard suitcase of my father in the attic of the house where I got it last summer, to face this long journey, also through the memories of my seventy-five years of life that I'm celebrating this year.

I just started to walk along Via Garibaldi and I pause a moment to observe the wonderful view of Pietracupa bathed by the warm sun of April. Then I look towards the houses around me and I remember all the people who have driven this stretch of road in the '50s. But the memory is only a momentary illusion; the road is empty and everything is silent as if it were a village completely abandoned. I reflect for a moment on this feeling of abandonment and say to myself: this silence is only apparent, because in the world there are thousands of Pietracupa's people, who have inside their hearts this small village of Molise. So the village is alive, as well as those traditions, those teachings and values that the peasant society of that time expressed.

I continue my downhill walk and meet Nicola, Maria and Diego; I see from afar Rina who nods to me. I greet all these people and I go to the bar of Via Trento. Sitting inside the room there are six or seven young people who are celebrating the victory of Pietracupa's football team. I sit in the middle of them and toast for the important football result obtained. All these young people, together with the other inhabitants of the village, and symbolically united to the many Pietracupa's people around the world, testify that Pietracupa is not an abandoned town and cannot die. I am sure that within not many years, some of them will begin a journey like mine (although certainly not with a cardboard suitcase) to tell the continuation of this never-ending story. They will have within them the same love for Pietracupa I have had during this long journey in time that I conclude today, in this dear village of Molise.

By now the sun has set and a pale moon of spring appears in the sky. I leave the bar and watch the beauty of creation and this is poetry. I take my leave of my readers too with the last poem in the book.

It Is Poetry

-It's poetry, the geranium which refines your balcony,
blossoming between the gray rows of huge buildings,
which obscure the horizon.-It's poetry, the grayness of winter,
the scent of spring, the colors of summer,
the autumn wind that sweeps the yellowed leaves
-.It is poetry, hope that guide our youth,
the innocence of their smiles, their songs, their anxieties, their
fears.-It's poetry, the embrace of a friend, his solidarity,
his understanding, his closeness in the dark hours.
-It's poetry, the whiteness of the old,the trembling of their hands,
the uncertain gait of my parents,the desire to embrace them, to help
them.-It's poetry, the sweetness of my wife, her serene gaze,
the deep affection that emanates, the security she gives me.
-It's poetry, the smile of my son, his steadfastness, his moral
strength,his joy, his sensitivity.-It is poetry, my old village in Molise,
its history, its people,The haggard faces of its peasants, my memories
of the past.
It's poetry, when I turn my eyes to the infinite and look for a reason
of my life, of my time, of my anxieties and I find you, my Lord.

APPENDIX:

Pietracupa Tells by Franco Valente (Art Historian)

 I usually spend summer touring around the villages of Molise to tell their story and their monuments in the squares. I met Claudio Camillo after one of these stories in a summer evening of 2013 at Pietracupa and I am honored that this friendship was born. When he decided to give the prints memories of his cardboard suitcase, he asked me to make a small contribution that somehow remembered that very special evening spent on the steps of the church of St. Antonio Abate. An evening that is part of Pietracupa's recent diary. This seemed to me a good opportunity to remind Roberto Pietracupa, a character whom we would not know almost anything if he had not left mark of his ground way on the lintel of a damaged portal being in S. Gregorio's church back.

A small trace of Pietracupa's history is found in the catalogue of the Barons from which we learn that the feud had been given in concession to Berardo from Bagnoli and his brothers Roberto and Tustaino: Berardus de Balneola fratribus cum suis et Robberto Tustaiano tenent Bagnolum quod est sicut dixit Berardus feudum ij militum, et Petram Cupam Castelluccium et quod est feudum ij militum et cum augmento obtulerunt milites et octo servientes x. Iste tenet de predicto Berardo et fratribus suis.

 The Catalogus Baronum, although report in an absolutely essential data for every feud, is now the only tool that allows us to understand the importance and, perhaps, also the size of the feud with its conomic capacity in the first decades soon after the half of the twelfth century. As we know, the original sheets of the catalogue have been lost during World War II, but we know the text through the transcription by Evelyn Jamison who published it in 1972 after reviewing the previous editions by Carlo Borrelli, Carmine Fimiani and Giuseppe Del Re.

 The catalog of the Barons is nothing else that the register made draw after 1150 by the Norman King Ruggero II (1130-1154) for a general draft necessary to form a large royal army supported by all free men living aside their social status and their feudal relationship.

The number of milites that the three lords of Pietracupa and Castelluccio had to provide the Norman army, of course, was in proportion to the importance of the feud and was specifically stated in the royal grant. Therefore, although the news looks gaunt, it is sufficient to create a not thriving situation of the economy of the village. Nevertheless, in substance, it was similar to most other feuds listed. We know well that Bagnoli along with Pietracupa and Castelluccio feuds, being the holder obliged to supply a soldier armed for every twenty ounces of gold income, had the value corresponding to eight milites, that is to say 160 gold ounces.

We only know that Roberto Bagnoli, one of three brothers feudal Lords, on May 1185 signed in Boiano, in the presence of Count Ruggiero of Molise, the minutes of a process between William Abbot of S. Sofia of Benevento, and Ruggiero Bozzardi, sir of Campolieto (E. Jamison, Molise and Marsyas, App., Doc. 5).

The archive documents are particularly stingy of news about Pietracupa and we don't know anything of what happened during the subsequent Swabian and Angevin power. Add to this that even those few stones that are present in architectural contexts heavily processed in time, are difficult to read.

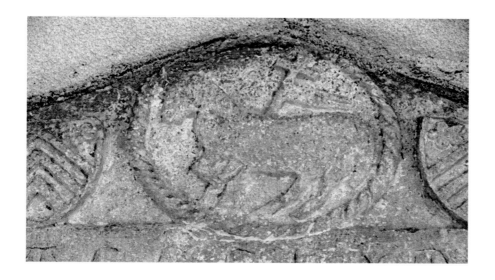

Among them there is a small portal that is on the back of the church of St. Gregory. Mrs Aurora Delmonaco has dealt about it in her book "Those of dark stone", published in 1989, but left unresolved the emblem issue repeated twice on the side of a Crucifer lamb. It is a document certainly important for the history of Pietracupa, first of all to the fact that the inscription which still survives, although heavily damaged, is useful to take a certain date to the artifact. On the Lintel, which probably originally was in another part of this church or another church, we read, on two lines:
+ ADMCCCLX MAGIST.
RICCARD. SYMONI. ME. FECIT
The meaning is clear: in the year of the Lord 1360 Maestro Riccardo of Simone made me.
At a side survive some not so much understandable letters :
RI TR (?). I
TR. C. G.
TR, as shown by the dash superimposed should be a shortening for TEMPORE. So it had to mean that the work was done at the time of a certain "CG". It is difficult to assume what the higher acrostic means (RI TR (?). I). The only clue could be the name of the epoch feudal Lord, imaging that R. refers to our Roberto of Pietracupa.

Only the date helps us because we know something of this character just by a parchment cited by Aurora Delmonaco and which is kept in the State Archives of Naples in the Fund of Caracciolo of Torchiarolo. It 's a bull in which the bishop in 1361 grants Giannotto Coppola from Naples the title of abbot of St. Alexander on presentation of Roberto of Pietracupa. May therefore the two letters that are on the right main epigraph refer at the time of Giannotto Coppola? It is difficult to imagine that the stonemason, adding the other letters the following year, has made a singular error by reversing the C with G, before putting first the family name and then the abbot birthname. In which case you should read TEMPORE COPPOLA GIANNOTTI. But it is highly unlikely.

Instead it is not farfetched the idea that the coat of arms showily dominating the epigraph, belongs precisely to Roberto of Pietracupa. You get there by exclusion. No matter how hard I did, it was not possible for me to trace this blazon among countless coats of arms of the Kingdom of Naples. The represented family has three chevrons accompanied by two rosettes in the head. We don't know very much about Roberto of Pietracupa by the aforementioned appointment bull of abbot Giannotti. From it we know that in 1360 he was far from his land, but obviously in the same year he returned if it is true that he participated in the signing of that act. The date and the presence of a coat of arms with no religious signs have to be placed in relation between them and lead to the conclusion that the church of which the portal belonged was built at the expense of the feudal lord of the epoch. And that the author of the work has been the master Riccardo of Simone. We actually don't know what Church is it. Surely the portal is not to be referred to the church inside the village and that today, defined in the modern era "crypt", is subjected to the one dedicated to St. Nicola. About their church, people have very fantasized, much attributing unprovable relationships with warrior monks who would have gathered inside it. The things are more easily. The so-called "crypt" was nothing more than a rock church probably dedicated to the Savior.

Witness is the ancient portal which contains the ashlar of a portal generically dating back to the Angevin and that because of the collapse of part of the cliff, was changed in a window for the inability to access there from the outside. On the ashlar survives the image in relief of a Pantocrator Christ of which disappeared the head and the judging hand. While one can still read SALVATOR well. We do not

324

know in what epoch the collapse took place, but probably is to be due to the disastrous earthquake of 1456 that wreaked havoc across the region. On the other hand the architectural character of the upper church of St. Anthony suggests that in the eighteenth century an earlier church of two centuries before has been transformed.

Early 20h Pietracupa migrant

(Studio Paolo Scarano – Trivento/Campobasso)

ACKNOWLEDGEMENTS:

-I thank my family for their patience and for their loving suggestions that allowed me to write this book.
- I thank my brother Ezekiel for providing me accurate information about the various episodes of the postwar and for coordinating all the relations with Pietracupa's community in the United States.
- I thank Anita Fasanelli for the precious cooperation she offered me, especially for her tales of life lived in the United States, and Susy Santilli for photos.
-I thank Toni and Cheryl Durante for news regarding Pietracupa's community in Chicago and Milwaukee and Cheryl for editing the second version of this journey.
- I thank the friends of the "Salon of Pietracupa" Giovanni Saliola, Dino Di Iorio, Antonio Di Iorio, Domenico Meale, Giuseppe Camillo, Pasquale Camillo, Enzo Cirese and Mario Saliola who, during our morning breakfasts at the bar "La Morgia", told me some interesting stories of the past, which were included in the book.
-I thank Letizia Di Sarro, for providing me the news preserved in the municipal Archives with diligent punctuality.
 I thank Andrea Guglielmi, Andrea Florio and Ezdra Fazioli, for the information about Pietracupa's young people and the football team.
-I thank Antonio Santilli, Michele Vanga, Mario Di Iorio (Pietracupa's great old people), and Gino Brunetti, for historical memories of the village.
- I thank all Pietracupa's community in Italy and abroad for their affectionate collaboration.
- I thank the Mayor of Pietracupa, Mr.Camillo Santilli, for his sensitivity and interest in this initiative, addressed to yesterday and today Pietracupa's people.
- Last but not the least, I thank Fr. Orlando Di Tella, Pietracupa's parish priest, who, with his advice and suggestions, spurred me to continue the compilation of this book, intended as an act of love to Pietracupa's community.

On August 26th 2014 Fr Orlando di Tella died; during the year 2015 it was the time of Uncle Mario di Iorio and Domenico Durante; on Easter Monday 2015 died Michele Santilli; and on March 18th 2015 in the USA Antonietta Durante (Toni) left us.

I remember them with love.

Finito di stampare nel mese di Giugno 2015
per conto di Youcanprint *Self - Publishing*

Lightning Source UK Ltd.
Milton Keynes UK
UKOW02f0138190815

257150UK00003B/274/P